BLOOD WHISPERS

John Gordon Sinclair was born in Glasgow, Scotland. He moved to London in the early Eighties and now lives in Surrey with his wife, Shauna, and their two children. John's first film won him a BAFTA nomination for Most Promising Newcomer to a Leading Film Role. His first outing in London's West End won him an Olivier award for Best Actor.

Seventy Times Seven, his first novel, was published in 2012 and was described by Barry Norman as 'a remarkable first novel' and as 'an impressive debut . . . Fast and bloody . . .' by *The Times*.

Praise for John Gordon Sinclair:

'Impressive . . . Sinclair scores top marks for the exceptionally vivid dialogue.' *The Times*

'Superb characterisation, pounding narrative and a story that twists and turns like a dervish . . . a stunning journey of nerve wrenching adrenalin. Just a superlative thriller.' Ken Bruen

'Both the beautifully convoluted plot and the main characters are so fresh and original that they come at you from left field. As a thriller writer myself I'm deeply envious.' Barry Norman

also by John Gordon Sinclair

SEVENTY TIMES SEVEN

Blood Whispers

JOHN GORDON SINCLAIR

FABER & FABER

First published in 2014
by Faber & Faber Limited
Bloomsbury House
74–77 Great Russell Street
London WC1B 3DA
This paperback edition first published in 2015

Typeset by Faber & Faber Ltd
Printed and bound by CPI Group (UK) Ltd, Croydon CR0 4YY

Extract from Hermann Hesse's *Demian: The Story of Emil Sinclair's Youth* reproduced with kind permission of Writers House LLC on behalf of the Estate of Hermann Hesse

The right of John Gordon Sinclair to be identified as author of this work has been asserted in accordance with Section 77 of the Copyright, Designs and Patents Act 1988

A CIP record for this book
is available from the British Library

ISBN 978-0-571-28391-0

For Shauna, Eva and Anna.

'I have been and still am a seeker, but I have ceased to question the stars and books; I have begun to listen to the teaching my blood whispers to me.'

Hermann Hesse

One

'Have you ever woken in the middle of the night and reached out for someone who isn't there?'

The guy didn't have to think too hard before shaking his head and saying, 'I can't say I have.'

'It's not something you'd forget . . . the feeling.'

'What sort of feeling?'

'Longing, regret . . . isolation, I don't know. It's an emptiness, like your soul is missing something.'

'Are you alone when this happens?'

'Usually, but not always; it's got nothing to do with loneliness or being on my own.'

'What do you think your soul is missing?'

Keira Lynch shrugged. 'I don't know?'

'Is it the "dream" that wakes you up or the "longing" feeling you've just described?'

'The dream exists on its own, it's separate: they're not connected . . . they happen at different times.'

'So it's not the dream – the girl screaming – that wakes you?'

'It can, but that's not what I'm talking about. I'm asking if the emptiness, the "reaching out" thing, is something you've come across before, that's all.' Keira felt exposed, vulnerable, like the guy hadn't been listening. 'And in the dream, it's not a girl screaming, it's a young woman, there's a difference,' she corrected him. 'I know what you're thinking, but you're wrong.'

'What am I thinking?'

'It's me screaming . . . my younger "self", making the sounds . . . but it's not me.' Keira's teeth set against each other. 'They're not a product of my imagination, they're a recollection – the memory of something that happened – an actual event.'

'The screams?'

Keira nodded her head. 'A young woman howling and shrieking like an animal being slaughtered: much worse and far more sickening than could simply be described as a scream.'

'In your dream do you know who this young woman is?'

'In real life I know who this woman was . . .'

He waited for her to continue, but could see she was reluctant and changed the subject.

'Is it connected to the thing with your wrists?'

Keira glanced down and saw that her hands were crossed and her wrists were pressed firmly together.

'I suppose . . . yes.'

'Do you rub them together like that often?'

'Only when I'm stressed.'

'Are you stressed now?'

'Yes.'

'Do you want to stop?'

'No.'

'How does rubbing your wrists help with your stress, d'you think?'

'It reminds me not to take life for granted.'

'Why would you take life for granted?'

'I don't . . . I rub my wrists together and it reminds me not to.'

'Okay, why that particular action?'

'It helps me remember: no matter what situation I'm in,

nothing could be worse than this . . .' Keira held out her upturned palms to reveal two, thin scars, one across each wrist just above the line of her cuffs. 'Sometimes I wish the scars would disappear; sometimes I'm glad they're there. They remind me that life is precious, and trying to make it shorter than it is already is a dumb thing to do . . . I'm lucky that I *can* remind myself.'

'Do you want to tell me how you got the scars?'

'No. Not right now . . . I will . . . but not right now.'

'Okay, sorry . . . let's rewind.'

The psychiatrist looked down at his notes. 'You were going to tell me what you remember about the house.'

'Every detail . . . even what it smelled like. A two-up-two-down tomb. It was damp, musty, stale; like it had been abandoned, left empty for a long time, the doors and windows never opened. Like the air inside had been there for ever.'

'Where did it happen, where was the house?'

'Where it happened isn't relevant.'

'I'm just trying to get a picture . . .'

Keira cut in on him, 'It doesn't matter *where* it happened. What matters is that it happened.'

He shrugged and continued, 'Had he assaulted you?'

'No . . .' She thought for a second, then added, 'Do you mean physically or sexually?'

'Sexually.'

'No. My hands were tied behind my back and my mouth was taped – except when they were feeding me. I guess you'd call that assault.'

'Who are they?'

'There were two others.'

'How long were you held for?'

'The room was in total darkness the whole time I was there – the windows boarded over – so I had no way of knowing. I found out later it was three days.'

'How old were you?'

'I can't tell you that.'

'Why not?'

'Too specific.'

'Roughly how old?'

'Less than ten.'

This revelation stopped him.

He sat, slowly shaking his head from side to side, his eyebrows raised. 'You must have been very frightened,' he said eventually.

'That's one thing I don't remember . . . how I felt at the time. I know what I feel about it now, but when I think back it's like watching a movie with the sound turned down. I can describe everything I saw, or smelled even, but not what was going through my mind. I feel somehow detached from my younger self, as though she were someone else.'

'Like it happened to someone else?'

'No.' Keira was adamant. 'I know it happened to me, but I have no recollection of what I was feeling . . . emotionally.'

'What do you feel about it now?'

'Guilt . . . mostly.'

'Why would you feel guilty about being kidnapped and held against your will?'

'I don't. I feel guilty about what happened . . .' She paused once more, choosing her words carefully. '. . . How the situation was resolved.'

'How was the situation resolved?'

Again she took her time before answering.

'The way most problems were solved in those days . . . with a gun.'

'The situation was resolved with a gun?'

'That's what I'm saying.'

'Who had the gun?'

'I did.'

'Where did you get it from?'

'My dad . . . though I didn't know that at the time.'

A look of confusion flashed across his face. 'Didn't know that he'd given you a gun?'

'Didn't know that he was my dad. I'm still not sure. And he didn't *give* me the gun . . . I took it from him.'

He was staring back at her, like he wasn't sure where to take it next.

'Why would you not know he was your own father?'

'He wasn't around when I was growing up. I had an uncle who was always over at our house. For whatever reason, I just assumed that *he* was my dad: that he and my mother had split up when I was born, or some shit like that, and it was easier for my mum not to say anything. Then one day his older brother – who everyone assumed was dead – showed up out of the blue and it seemed to make more sense that it was him. I'm still not sure if that's the case. But it seems the most likely scenario. We've never discussed it. I can't say for sure, but I don't think he even knew I was his daughter. It sounds complicated, but complicated is my normal.'

The psychiatrist wrote something in his pad, but didn't comment. Instead he asked another question.

'Who is "we"?'

'My mum . . . and my gran.'

'Why d'you think they didn't discuss it with you?'

Keira shrugged. 'Who knows! Too painful, maybe? I really don't know.'

'So what happened with the gun? Can you tell me?'

'I went back into the house, along the hallway.'

'Back?'

'My dad and I had managed to escape.'

'Why didn't your dad go back inside?'

'He couldn't. He was injured. He'd been shot in the leg. He could barely stand.'

The guy nodded for her to continue.

'There was a fight at the top of the stairs . . . on the landing, between my uncle and the main guy.'

'Did you know him: the main guy?'

'Not at the time, but I overheard my dad and uncle talking about it afterwards . . . I heard his name then, but that's something else I need to keep to myself.'

'You said there were three men altogether: what were the other two doing at this point?'

'Nothing . . . they were already dead.'

'So this guy was attacking your uncle?'

'Yeah. He was screaming and howling, his arms flailing around, punching out. There was blood everywhere.'

'Were you trying to get the gun to your uncle?'

'I said a moment ago that I don't remember what I was feeling at the time. That's true, but I do know what I was thinking. From the moment I had the gun in my hand I knew what I was going to do. There was never any doubt. If I'm being honest, I don't think I've been as certain of anything in my life since.' Keira stopped talking and stared at the floor.

After a while the psychiatrist said, 'Are you okay?'

Keira nodded, but didn't speak.

'D'you want to leave it there?'

This time Keira nodded her head and said, 'I don't think I can say the words out loud. If I keep them inside I can almost pretend to myself that it never happened.'

'Have you ever discussed this with anyone else?'

'No. There were only four of us – including myself – who knew what happened that night.'

'What about the other three?'

'They're dead. There's maybe a fifth,' continued Keira, 'a priest . . . but I'm not sure how much he knows.'

'Maybe we should leave it there for now.'

'I've tried everything else: drink, drugs, suicide. The only thing I haven't tried is talking about it. But now that I'm sitting here, and it's real . . . I don't think I can.'

'It's okay . . . another time.'

'This thing is hollowing me out. It's time for me to take control of it. I need a different perspective.'

'Do you think that by talking it through you'll achieve solace or redemption? How do you see it changing your life?'

'I see it filling the emptiness.'

Two

Tonight her name was Lisa.

Kaltrina Dervishi had read the tag in a magazine and even though she couldn't pronounce it properly, liked the way it looked written down: a scrawled, looping signature, across the chest of some minor celebrity.

The red silk dress she was wearing was on loan – shared amongst the other girls whenever they had a date – as were the bootlace-strap heels that showed off her arched, stocking-clad feet and long shapely legs. The dress was backless and had a plunging neckline that revealed the cup of her bare breasts every time she leant forward. The man she'd just had dinner with started the evening trying to avoid looking at her cleavage, but as the night had worn on and the alcohol had started to loosen him up she'd caught him – plenty of times – sneaking a glance. He'd also started leaning on her name every time he said it: letting her know he was smart enough to realize it wasn't her real name, but doing it in a really dumb way. All he had done was piss her off.

'What would you say if I invited you back to my room for a nightcap?' asked the fat guy who'd told her his name was Nicolas, sliding his large, sweaty hand along the bench-seat and on to her thigh.

'Only nightcap?' she'd replied in a thick Balkan accent. 'Why not we fuck?'

The Radisson Blu standard guest room overlooking the River Clyde looked much like any other hotel bedroom. It had everything necessary for a comfortable stay except a feather pillow. Kaltrina could sleep on a slab of concrete if she had a feather pillow; but even the most luxurious pocket-sprung mattress could be ruined by the foam and polyester versions available in most hotels these days. It was the first thing she checked if her work involved an 'overnight'.

Kaltrina came out of the tiny bathroom to find Fat Guy had turned off all the lights and closed the curtains. He was either trying to set the mood or he didn't want 'Lisa' to see what shit shape he was in. Kaltrina figured she wouldn't win any prizes for guessing which of the two it was.

There was a bottle of champagne open on the table next to the mirror with two glasses sitting alongside.

Fat Guy had removed his jacket and tie and was standing at the foot of the bed looking awkward. 'How long have we got?'

'The driver, he wait in lobby for me till finished. You do good business with Mister Abazi, I do good business with you . . . as long for as you like.'

'Wee glass of champers?' he said in a cod Scottish accent that made her want to slap him.

'I'm not sure what you say,' she said, messing with him.

'Champagne, would you like a glass?'

'Oh, I not allowed to drink.'

'Don't worry about that. I can square things on that front. If you want a glass you should have one.'

'Okay, make it a double!'

'Treat the whore, she'll give you more.' Fat Guy had a grin on his face that made her want to punch him on the mouth this time. Instead she strolled alluringly towards him and planted her full lips on to his mouth, kissing him passionately while fumbling to undo his belt.

'Maybe I'll order another bottle.'

Kaltrina unzipped his trousers and – hooking her thumbs between the top of his underpants and his flesh – slipped them down over his buttocks revealing his rock-hard erection.

'Someone pleased to see me,' she said, breaking free from the kiss. 'You're a big guy, I gonna be sore.'

It was a line she threw at all her johns. In reality the guy was below average, but it always put a smile on the assholes' faces. Fat Guy was no different.

She took hold of his cock with one hand and steered him backwards on to a chair in the corner of the room.

'You like I'm in charge?' she asked, giving him the full fuck-me smile.

'I like.'

'Put your hands behind back, you not need them for now.'

Fat Guy did as he was told, then let her tie his hands together using the belt from his trousers.

'Where you from? You have nice accent.'

'A little place called Silver Spring, near Washington . . . You?'

'Me . . . from nowhere.'

'From heaven, I'd say.'

'You say nice thing. You're cute!' replied Kaltrina, keeping up the bullshit.

'Man, you've got everything pointing in the right direction,' he said as she moved round to stand in front of him. He watched as she put a hand up under the front of her dress, then, wiggling her hips from side to side in a slow provocative movement, pulled her lacy pants down till they dropped to the floor and she could step neatly out of them. Fat Guy didn't say much, but he was obviously enjoying the show. Still standing, she straddled his legs, making sure she pushed her cleavage into his face as she delicately placed her pants on top of his head then pulled them down over his eyes like a blindfold.

She leant down – letting her long, brown hair brush against his face – and whispered in his right ear, 'I'm to fuck you good,' her hot breathy voice sending a shiver of anticipation over his naked body.

This time Fat Guy replied with a long, low moan of appreciation.

'Mister Abazi want to say thank you,' whispered Kaltrina as she knelt between Fat Guy's legs and – pursing her lips – gently blew a jet of warm air across the top of his penis.

She reached over and picked his tie off the bed, then used it to secure his right ankle to the leg of the chair. Taking her thin leather belt from round her waist, she tied his other ankle. 'You like kinky?'

'Whatever you're selling, babe.'

She lifted the edge of the pants up a little from his eyes to let him watch her taking off her stockings. She sat on the edge of the bed and slipped off her shoes, then slowly rolled each stocking in turn down the length of her leg, taking care to let him get a good view of her bare crotch. At just over twenty years of age she knew all the tricks: all the right things to say. 'You making me so wet baby,' was just another example.

'You let me gag you with my stockings?'

'What's the difference?' asked Fat Guy, trying to keep his voice low and in the mood.

'You nice and quiet, I'm nice and gentle ... take my time. You are making lots of noise, I'm to get rough: could be all over before you know what's happened.' Kaltrina gave a slight shrug of her shoulders, 'Up to you.'

'Why don't you come and sit yourself right here and we can discuss it?'

She raised her eyes to the ceiling, playing it cute like she was thinking about it, then said, 'Okay, move your ass forward on the chair and spread your legs, cowboy.'

She sat on the edge of the bed and slipped her shoes back on then stood up. Fat Guy edged forward and opened his legs so that his balls were hanging over the front edge of the chair.

Taking a small step back, Kaltrina swung her right leg up as hard as she could, catching him between the legs with the full force of the blow. He let out an agonized yelp and tried to stand up, but in the same movement Kaltrina swept the champagne bottle off the table next to him and slammed it hard into the side of his face.

The force of the blow knocked him sideways on to the floor. The end of the bed broke his fall as he glanced off it, screaming, 'Fucking whore.'

He was writhing around, his ankles still tethered to the chair, desperately trying to free his hands from behind his back.

'Keep it down, you noisy son-of-a-bitch,' said Kaltrina, raising the bottle high in the air and slamming it down on the back of his head again, 'Next time you see Abazi,' and again, 'tell him I quit,' and again. Each sickening thud punctuated by a loud agonized grunt until eventually Fat Guy stopped moving and the room fell silent again.

He was lying face down on the floor with blood seeping from a mess of hair and gore on the back of his skull.

Kaltrina was breathing heavily and her hands were shaking.

Fat Guy's trousers were gathered in a twisted bundle round his ankles. Kaltrina picked her way through the folds and pulled his wallet from one of the pockets. His credit cards were of no use to her. Moving quickly, she removed all the cash – almost two hundred pounds – then tossed the wallet across the room.

She grabbed his coat from the wardrobe and pulled it over her shoulders, then, stepping gingerly over his body, she headed over to the telephone sitting on the bedside table.

It took a few moments for someone to pick up. She didn't want the guy to die.

Fat Guy started to groan.

Finally, a voice at the other end said, 'Reception.'

'Please can you send someone. My husband he is taking very ill. Please, you send someone straight away.'

Kaltrina replaced the receiver and made her way back over to the door.

'Hey Fat Guy,' she said over her shoulder as she left the room, 'you really fucked now.'

Three

Valbona Dervishi grabbed the overhead handle to steady herself as the Durrës bound bus pitched her forward and juddered to a halt on the outskirts of Dushk. The automatic doors hissed open and Valbona turned and nodded her appreciation to the driver before stepping off.

She had a part-time job as a cleaner at the Bar Piazza in the centre of Fier, a small town thirty-five kilometres south of Dushk in western Albania. She made the same round trip every day of the week except Sunday. It took her almost as long to travel to and from Fier as it did to do the work itself, but it was regular money at a time when there were few jobs around. The first scheduled bus was at six in the morning and she was usually on her way back by about ten. Today, however, was market day, so Valbona had spent a few hours browsing the colourful but sparse stalls, and caught a later bus: returning home with the week's ration of fresh fruit and vegetables, which she carried in two bulging carrier bags looped awkwardly over her left arm.

The sun was high in the warm cloudless sky and insects buzzed in haphazard flight patterns around the scattering of wild flowers growing along the dusty track that led away from the main road, up towards her cottage.

The small plot of land surrounding the cottage sat two kilometres or so into the foothills that encircled the village.

An impoverished life had left its mark on Valbona's once

handsome features; she looked much older than her fifty-five years. A dark nest of unkempt hair fell around her shoulders in a dry lifeless weave: her weather-beaten skin, which was creased in deep lines along her forehead and around her eyes, had baked into a permanent frown. The light blue flower-print dress she wore was faded and frayed and hung loosely from her bony shoulders. Her eyes, which appeared closed, were set against the harsh rays bouncing up from the bleached, arid landscape of her surroundings.

The wide path was edged by a chest-height, drystone wall to her left that stretched in a long arc for its entire length and climbed gently into the craggy hillside. After just a few hundred metres Valbona started to notice something different in the way the loose stones lay on the ground – at first almost impercept-ible, but as she walked on further she could quite clearly make out a set of tyre tracks impressed into the thin layer of dust cov-ering the surface of the heavily compacted soil. She stopped for a second and followed the line of the tracks with her gaze until they disappeared from view round the gradual curve in the road. It struck her in that moment that in all the years she had lived there she had never once seen a car, nor any other vehicle for that matter, on this stretch of road. There were three other small cottages similar to hers dotted along the hillside, with Valbona's being the furthest away, but none of her neighbours owned a car. As she made her way past each of their houses in turn it be-came obvious to her that whoever had driven along this way had most likely come to visit her. Moreover, as there was clearly only one set of tracks, and the road was a dead end, the probability was that they were still there.

A look of anxiety crossed her face and she set off again at a quicker pace; every instinct in her body screaming at her that this had something to do with her daughter Kaltrina.

Fifty metres from her house she saw a white Mercedes parked outside the breach in the wall that marked the entrance to her small garden. A man was leaning casually against the driver's door smoking a cigarette. From the short-sleeved black shirt and dark sunglasses he was wearing it was obvious to her that he was a member of the Clan. When he spotted her approaching he pushed himself off the vehicle and stood watching her dispassionately as he finished off his smoke.

He waited until she was just a few metres away before he spoke.

'You're late.'

Valbona didn't respond.

The small area of overgrown grass in front of the house was littered with the flaked and rusting skeletons of obsolete farm equipment. Aware that he was following just a few paces behind, Valbona continued on up to the front door, her heart pounding in her chest. The door opened directly into a small kitchen, with an opening on the left leading to a cramped living area and another door on the right that led to a narrow corridor with a bedroom on either side. An insufficient, wooden-shuttered window at the far end kept the corridor in almost total darkness.

Her husband Edon was sitting at the kitchen table with another man directly opposite. Edon stared up at her with heavy, doleful eyes that struggled to focus. The top half of his cream shirt had deep, red stains spattered down the front and across the shoulders. There was significant swelling around the left-hand side of his face. A steady flow of blood glistened as it dribbled from the side of his mouth where his lip had split open.

They all turned as if they had been waiting for her.

Valbona placed her shopping bags on the worktop by the sink and started to unpack the fruit and vegetables.

She didn't know what else to do.

'You want us to wait until you've finished putting everything away?' said the man at the table. 'Why don't you leave that for a minute and come and sit down, Valbona? We've been here for two hours already.'

Valbona glanced at Edon and saw the look of fear on her husband's battered face. He gestured with a small nod of his head for her to come and sit beside him. As she drew in her chair she felt Edon take her hand under the table and squeeze. It was only then that she noticed a third person, sitting on the arm of their tattered sofa in the far corner of the room, their features partially obscured by shade. The figure was dressed differently from the others in a smart black tailored suit with black shirt and tie and fine-leather, dark brown brogues, hair neatly combed in a side parting, hollow eyes staring straight ahead as if entranced, seemingly unaware of the other people in the room.

It was Engjell E Zeze: the Watcher.

Valbona tried to swallow, but her mouth was suddenly dry.

Engjell was a contract killer. With an uncanny ability to avoid capture, the Watcher was rumoured to inhabit the spirit world: a fallen angel whose only purpose on earth was to destroy life. The number of people murdered varied wildly from village to village, with some estimates running into the thousands, but whatever the number, the Watcher had become a very wealthy individual from the business of death.

The man opposite Valbona had his hands resting on the table, spinning a mobile phone on its diagonal with a nonchalant flick of his finger. 'Where's Kaltrina?' he said without shifting his gaze from the phone.

She looked at Edon and shrugged.

'You don't know?'

'She has been gone over two years now,' replied Valbona in a quiet, controlled voice. 'We don't hear from her . . .'

'At all?'

'No.'

'When was the last time?'

'A few years ago,' replied Edon, cutting in. 'I already told you.'

The guy looked up at Edon like he was going to hit him again. 'I wasn't asking you, I was asking your wife, so shut up.'

'She was in Scotland,' said Valbona quickly. 'Said she had a job in a café and was going to stay there for a while.'

'Did she say where?'

Valbona shook her head. 'I don't know! In Glasgow. Near a university, I think. With Kaltrina you take what you're given. And she doesn't give that much. That was all she said. She was just ringing to tell us she was okay.'

'You haven't heard from her in the last few weeks?'

'No,' answered Valbona shaking her head. 'Has something happened to her?'

He ignored her question and from the breast pocket of his shirt pulled a small piece of folded notepaper. He tossed the scrap of paper across the table to her and said, 'Read this out.'

'What is it?'

Again he ignored her.

Then he lifted the phone and pointed at her, nodding for her to start.

Valbona let go of Edon's hand and lifted the piece of paper

from the table. She could feel the man staring back at her impatiently, but took her time to unfold the note and scan what was written on it. The effect the words had on her was immediate. Her face flushed hot and her hand started to tremble as she struggled to hold back the tears that burned at the corners of her eyes, but she was determined not to give them the satisfaction of seeing any weakness.

The man could see her hesitating and frowned. 'Just say the words.'

'Why...' Valbona started to say, but he slammed his fist down hard on the table, making both her and Edon jump. 'Because I'm fucking telling you to! Just read the note.'

Valbona stared back at him defiantly and started to read; her voice dull and monosyllabic.

'*Stop çfarë jeni duke bërë, Kaltrina. Nëse ju nuk e bëni... ata do të vrasin babait tuaj. Pastaj – në qoftë se ju ende vazhdojnë të tregoni gënjeshtra – Ata do të më vrasë.*'

Valbona turned to Edon, but he refused to meet her gaze. Edon knew exactly what his wife was thinking, but didn't dare acknowledge her in any way for fear the other men would read her mind. But she still added the words, '*Ai është në rregull!*'

'Shut up, that bit's done.' The man flicked the phone on to pause and stood up. 'Okay, that's the "Before", now we do the "After".' With that, he stepped away from the table.

Engjell E Zeze suddenly emerged from the shadows with an arm outstretched pointing a gun towards Edon.

'Wait, I got to press RECORD,' said the man, holding up the phone.

The next instant there was a loud crack and Edon's head snapped back at the neck, the force of the bullet's impact tipping both him and the chair back against the kitchen wall. Valbona touched her hand to her face and wiped spatters of her husband's blood from her cheek, then stared up at the Watcher in disbelief. The gun was trained on her now.

Valbona's last thought was not of her daughter, Kaltrina, but for the child. She hoped that wherever Edon had hidden the boy he would be safe until the men had gone.

The air exploded again and Valbona felt a sharp, scorching sensation tearing through her chest. There was another loud crack, which threw her off to the side, where she lay dying on her dead husband's lap.

The man stopped recording and held the phone up in front of Engjell.

'You want to see?'

*

It was well after dark before the small hand appeared at the edge of the thin piece of cotton fabric hung across the front of the kitchen sink and pulled it to one side. It had taken the young boy over three hours to pluck up enough courage to crawl out from underneath. He would have stayed there longer, but his throat was dry and his stomach ached with hunger. The quiet drone of cicadas, carried by the warm evening air, drifted in through the door left open by the departing Clan members.

As the boy stood in the middle of the room and stared with large brown eyes at the bodies of Valbona and Edon, he felt something cold creeping in and around the sides of his bare feet.

Ermir looked down and wiggled his toes, watching intently as the dark red pool of liquid, covering most of the kitchen floor, slowly surrounded him.

A sudden spasm from one of the bodies startled the five-year-old.

With his heart pounding in his chest he whispered, 'Wake up please, Grandma, I'm hungry!'

Four

Kaltrina used almost the last of her money to pay for coffee and a sandwich, then sat for a while scanning faces for any signs of Abazi's men. When she'd eaten half the sandwich she folded the rest neatly into a napkin and placed it in her jacket pocket for later.

Even at 5.30 a.m. Glasgow International airport was busy.

Today she was called Teresa McVeigh; at least that was the name on the passport she was using to try to leave the country. Her name had changed so often she wondered whether she would turn if someone used her real one. She mouthed the words in silence to remind herself of who she really was, and who she wanted to be again, 'Kaltrina Dervishi'.

Satisfied that no one was paying any attention to her, Kaltrina drained her coffee and headed through to departures.

There were four ticket desks all showing the same destination.

Having scanned the faces of the check-in staff and picked the friendliest looking, Kaltrina joined a long queue leading up to an Asian woman who sat, smiling and chatting distractedly as she checked passengers' passports and tickets: a soft touch.

Kaltrina tried not to look conspicuous as she glanced around the check-in area, but she was nervous. Armed police officers were patrolling the large cathedral-like hall, but didn't appear to be looking for anything or anyone in particular: a reassuring presence for travellers rather than any threat to her. However, the machine guns and black military-style uniforms still left her feeling apprehensive.

The ticket she was holding read Malaga, Spain. It had cost her virtually everything she had: the money she'd taken off the fat guy in the hotel plus the small amount she'd set aside from overcharging clients. She'd hidden this money from Abazi, but it was a dangerous game. None of the girls were allowed to keep any of their earnings. It was supposed to be a fifty–fifty split, their share to be set aside and given to them when they returned home or retired, but no one survived long enough to actually get their money.

Abazi's men would turn over their rooms every few weeks, searching for cash or drugs. All of them had their passports confiscated. The line was, 'You can leave anytime you like: the grave's already dug.'

When they first started working all the new girls were shown photographs of a corpse covered in cuts and bruises and warned that if they tried to cheat Abazi or leave without permission, this is what would happen to them.

Just a few weeks earlier his men had come in the middle of the night to do a random search. After they had ransacked Kaltrina's room and discovered nothing they'd gone into her friend Tulla's room across the hall and had found a small amount of money and heroin. Kaltrina had lain awake and listened as Tulla pleaded with the men. Her punishment had been savage and seemed to go on for hours until suddenly it all stopped and the house returned to silence.

After a while, when she was sure the men had left, Kaltrina had sneaked out of her room and knocked on Tulla's door. There was no answer. She'd tried the handle but the door was locked.

Back in her bedroom, she'd sat on the end of her bed rocking backwards and forwards until the first light of dawn seeped through a crack in the curtains. Wondering how she would ever escape.

Later in the morning, when she went to check on her friend again, she noticed the dark streaks of blood running the length of the hallway. In that moment she realized two things: she would never see Tulla again and it was time to get out.

Abazi had his favourites: some, simply because they made more money than the others and some – like Kaltrina – who were beautiful as well as being good earners.

Occasionally she would be taken out to dinner. If the client was involved in a business deal, she would be included as part of the bargain: the sweetener. She could eat whatever she wanted, but she wasn't allowed to drink alcohol: Abazi didn't like loose talk. If the guy was interested he would take her back to his hotel and screw her. Abazi's men were always waiting outside the room or in the lobby of the hotel to take her back to the house. Sometimes they'd drive her over to Abazi's place afterwards and he'd fuck her too. Either way, the evening would always end with Kaltrina crying herself to sleep.

She always knew in advance when something was going to happen. A dress would arrive, with shoes and jewellery. She would be expected to look sexy: low tops and high heels. If it was a business dinner, she had some stock questions to ask to get the guy talking. She would flirt with him: do lots of bending forward to let him see her cleavage, then sit back and listen to the asshole bleating on in a language she barely understood, while stroking his balls under the table.

Her father used to tell her it wasn't how far a person had

risen that made them great, but how far they had fallen. For over two years now her life had been skinning its knees along the bottom of existence. The time had come to stand up and fight her way back to the top. When she got to Spain she'd have no money and nowhere to live, but anything would be better than the life she was leaving behind. Hopefully – if things worked out – she'd send for her son: spend her days looking after him and loving him the way she'd always dreamed of.

Kaltrina lifted a small compact from her handbag and checked her face in the mirror. The long hair was gone: in its place, a short spiky cut that she had dyed blonde to match the woman's photograph in the stolen passport. Unfortunately there was no way of matching their ages or their wildly differing facial features. Make-up could only do so much; after that it was down to luck.

She turned the mirror slightly to check the two cops standing by the main entrance. They seemed relaxed: chatting idly to one another.

As she neared the front of the line she could feel the adrenaline kicking in. Her skin felt clammy and her hands were trembling. Nothing fitted her properly; everything she was wearing was stolen. Even the shoes were too small, making every step uncomfortable: all this was adding up to a sudden lack of confidence. If there was any hesitation or a suspicious glance from the woman behind the counter she would have to turn and run, leaving behind her only hope of escape.

The woman nodded for her to come forward.

'Where are you travelling to?'

'Malaga.'

'Any bags to check-in?'

'No.'

'Passport and booking reference please.'

Kaltrina handed over the documents then quickly placed her trembling hands down by her side out of view.

'You should have checked in online, saved yourself standing in that big queue,' said the check-in clerk, handing back the passport. She had barely glanced at it.

'Flight is good on time?'

The woman checked her monitor. 'Everything running to schedule today! Have a nice flight.'

'Thank you,' replied Kaltrina, unable to keep the look of relief from her face as she turned and headed for the escalators.

She wouldn't be able to relax fully until she was sitting aboard the plane, but the first big hurdle had been crossed: for the moment everything was going okay.

*

The departure area had brightly lit shops that appeared to sell nothing but perfume, alcohol and cigarettes. Even if she'd had the money Kaltrina wouldn't have been tempted to buy anything. It was a reminder of the world she inhabited but couldn't afford to participate in.

She checked the departures board. Her gate number wasn't up yet. She rummaged in her pockets for some loose change and counted out enough to buy a regular coffee. As she made her way along the concourse towards the coffee shop she was suddenly aware of someone watching her. Twenty metres ahead a man was crouched forward on a chair with his hands clasped together between his legs, staring at her. Kaltrina stopped dead.

She glanced over her shoulder in the hope that there was someone behind her he was looking at, but when she turned back he gave her a thin smile and held her gaze.

She had a sick feeling in her stomach as she realized she recognized him.

Edi Leka – one of Abazi's men – there was no mistaking that skinny hangdog face.

He'd picked her up from the house a few times and driven her to and from jobs.

The only way he'd be allowed into departures was if he had a ticket to fly, but there was no way Leka could have known where she was heading.

Even if he wasn't boarding her flight, all he had to do was follow her to the gate and he'd find out.

When she arrived in Spain one of Abazi's 'friends' would be waiting for her with the grave already dug.

Kaltrina turned and started back the way she had just come.

She glanced over her shoulder and saw that Leka was on his feet now, moving towards her.

Suddenly she sprinted forward, then took a left and headed up a long ramp into one of the lounges. She ran straight through the large, open seating area towards a bar at the far end, beyond which were signs for the toilets.

Kaltrina had no idea where she was going.

The short corridor leading to the toilets was a dead-end, forcing her to double back. She could see Edi Leka strolling casually through the seating area heading straight for her, taking his time, both of them aware that there was nowhere for her to go.

She emerged from the corridor and took a seat at the bar, acting like that's where they'd arranged to meet.

Edi knew there was nothing he could do to her in front of all these people. His instructions were – if he found the girl – to simply have a quiet word with her, offer her a deal, tell her anything to get her out of the airport. Once she was in the car he would shoot her in the base of the spine to incapacitate her, then slit her throat and let her bleed to death.

It was the same for anyone who had betrayed the Clan.

It looked like this job might be easier than he'd imagined.

Kaltrina nodded to the barman. By the time he'd made his way from serving at the other end of the bar, Edi Leka was standing next to her.

'I'm not sure we've got time for a drink.'

'Sure we do,' replied Kaltrina giving him the big eyes and cute smile. 'We got plenty of time.'

'What'll it be?' asked the barman.

'You have Sauvignon Blanc?'

'Three kinds: French, Australian and South African.'

'Which is most expensive?'

'The South African.'

'That, please! Do you want anything?' she continued, turning to Edi.

He shook his head. 'I'm driving.'

'Small, medium or large of the Sauvignon?'

'Bottle and two glasses, please, in case my friend Happy Edi decide he join me.'

Edi Leka pulled up a stool and sat down next to Kaltrina while the barman opened the wine and fetched the glasses.

'So what's on offer? I know how much Abazi likes to do a deal,' said Kaltrina.

'Mister Abazi is concerned for your safety. You're his favourite girl and he wants you to come back. I've been authorized to offer you whatever you want . . . within reason. He just wants to talk to you: negotiate a way forward. If you're still not happy your passport and the money you've earned will be returned to you and Mister Abazi will drive you back to the airport himself.'

'Is that what happened to Tulla?'

The question momentarily ambushed Edi, caught him off guard. Kaltrina could tell from his reaction that he knew exactly what she was talking about.

Edi shrugged his shoulders and gave a lame reply. 'I never heard of anyone by that name.'

The barman arrived with the bottle of wine and glasses and placed them on the bar in front of Kaltrina. 'Would you like me to pour?'

She shook her head.

'Thirty-eight pounds fifty, please.'

Kaltrina turned to Edi and, playing it straight, said, 'Thirty-eight pounds fifty, please. Mister Abazi can take it off the money he owes me.'

Leka shot her a look, before fumbling around in his jeans pocket and slapping a couple of twenties on the bar-top.

Kaltrina took her time pouring the wine: filling the glass right to the brim, careful not to let it spill over. She then lifted the glass to her lips and took a long slow draught: draining half of it in one go.

'Okay, Edi, I think I know what I would like.' She placed her glass back on the counter and refilled it. 'Twenty thousand euros wired over to my mother and father's bank account, along with the money I'm owed. I also want my passport back and to be given my own flat to work from so that I'm free to come and go as I please. Does that sound "within reason" to you?'

Edi Leka stared back at the girl wondering what fantasy world she lived in. There wasn't the remotest chance that Abazi would agree to any of this and he couldn't believe that she was so naive as to think he might. Edi was already tired of the little charade: sitting there like she was the one holding all the cards. If they weren't in a crowded airport he would slap her down with his bare knuckles and teach the bitch a lesson. As it was, he simply nodded and said, 'Yeah, that sounds within reason.'

'So how we gonna make that happen, Edi? A money transfer could take two or three days to clear and I'm going nowhere until the money's in the account. So what do we do? Sit here and wait?'

'Mister Abazi said you can have whatever you want. You're gonna have to take my word for it that the money will be transferred. You know him, If he says he's going to do something . . . that's it. It gets done.'

Kaltrina sat staring at her glass.

'Get him on the phone, then,' she said, after deliberately making him wait. 'So far all you've given me is *your* word, which counts for shit. Get Abazi on the phone and let me hear him saying it. If he does then I'll come with you.'

Edi could feel the muscles in the back of his neck tensing up. He was starting to lose his patience with the girl. Mister Abazi wouldn't appreciate the call, but if that was all it was going to take to get her skinny arse off the stool and out of the airport it would be worth it. Abazi might promise her the money, and if he did, would make a show of transferring it to her parents' account, but by that point it would be too late.

Edi pulled a mobile phone from his pocket and punched

in a number. He waited a few seconds then spoke. 'Sir, I'm with the girl. She's ready to come with me, but she wants to talk to you first.'

As Kaltrina reached out to take the phone from Edi her elbow knocked the almost full glass off the counter and sent it tumbling to the floor, where it smashed into three or four large fragments. Most of the wine had tipped on to her lap and she could feel it soaking through the thin fabric of her trousers and running down her legs.

Edi Leka's instinctive reaction was to bend down and pick up the pieces. As he did so Kaltrina grabbed the wine bottle from the counter and brought it down in a wide sweeping arc on to the back of his head. She grabbed the other glass and smashed it against the counter, then thrust its jagged edge as hard as she could towards the side of Edi's neck. Edi dropped the phone to the ground and grabbed hold of her wrist just in time to stop the razor-sharp point from puncturing his throat.

The first blow to the head had knocked him to his knees.

As he struggled to his feet Kaltrina raised the bottle and struck him again. Edi Leka's legs buckled and he dropped back to the floor, unconscious.

The commotion had already attracted a lot of attention.

Two police officers at the far end of the lounge were sprinting toward Kaltrina, shouting at her to put the bottle down.

Kaltrina smacked Edi Leka across the head one more time, then carefully placed the bottle back on the counter. She bent down, scooped the mobile phone off the floor and started toward the cops, talking as she walked.

'This is for my friend Tulla, you son-of-a-bitch. All I wanted was to go home, Abazi, now . . . I'm going to destroy you.'

With that she dropped the phone to the ground and raised her hands above her head in surrender.

'My name is Kaltrina Dervishi and I travel with false passport,' she said as the two cops grabbed hold of her.

Five

Jay-Go's pace quickened as he reached the top end of Hope Street. He swaggered from side to side as he moseyed his way past the other pedestrians with his hands tucked inside his jacket pockets and a single-skin roll-up hanging loosely from his top lip: giving the stare to anyone who unintentionally caught his eye. His skin was pale and haggard – messed up by years of doing class A.

A crooked boxer-nose, fashioned on the streets rather than in the ring, was flattened against his long, scrawny face, which was topped-off by a No. 1 all-over buzz cut. There was a hole in the nylon lining of the right-hand jacket pocket, big enough for him to put his fist through and grip the mottled handle of the gun he had tucked into the top of his well-worn Wrangler jeans. He'd been walking at a steady pace for nearly two hours now and despite the cool breeze had worked up a sweat that made his T-shirt cling to his back and the Walther PPK feel clammy and uncomfortable to the touch.

His heart was beating hard, dragging the mixture of cigarette smoke and cool air into his lungs like burning brier.

No worries, thought Jay-Go. *Nearly there.*

*

Keira Lynch cleared a space amongst the clutch of legal documents spread out on the table in front of her and placed her half-empty glass of Irn Bru in the centre. The Pot Still bar was stocked with more than three hundred types of whisky, some of which ranked in her all-time top ten, but even though it was after hours she was still working, so soft-and-fizzy was the limit. She was sitting at one of the tables on the raised section of platform that took up half the entire back area of the cosy bar. The ceiling above had ornate cornicing dating back to the period when the building was first erected some time in the early 1800s and there were comfortable, green leather, button-backed rows of bench seating running around the walls of the upstairs section, with a similar version in red leather on the ground level below.

Keira suddenly became aware of a presence next to the table and looked up.

'Ye awright, Miss?'

'Jay-Go. Didn't have the Pot Still down as one of your locals. The Centaur closed for refurbishment?'

'Aye, you're good.' Jay-Go smiled back at her. 'When Ah discovered the joys of classy-class A, Ah lost my appetite for the bevvy. Ah hivnae set foot in the Centaur for about ten year. Great pub, but the last time Ah wis in there it wis after hours.'

'A lock in?'

'Robbing the place. Ah'd offer to get ye a drink, but it'd break the terms of my parole.'

'I think buying alcohol for your lawyer would be seen as a pardonable offence rather than a breach of your parole conditions, but why don't you sit down and I'll get you one.'

'Don't want to end up back inside,' replied Jay-Go. 'No alcohol must pass these lips.'

'If you promise not to tell anyone, I will too.'

Jay-Go pulled a chair out from under the table and sat facing her.

'If you think it'll stand up in court, I'll have a vodka and Coke.'

'Have you ever heard of an Ardbeg 1974?'

'Can ye snort it?'

'Practically. They do an Ardbeg '75 here, which is as near as damn it. If you're going back inside for breach then you might as well enjoy a decent whisky. Ardbeg'll give you something nice to think about when you're dreaming of your next score from behind bars.'

'Aye, you're good. Fire up one of those fur me.'

Keira made her way to the bar and ordered a large '75 and another can of Irn Bru. The whole time she was aware of Jay-Go's eyes following her.

When she got back to the table he had picked up a few of her documents and was scanning through them, feigning interest as he browsed.

Keira placed the drinks down on the table and lowered herself back into her seat.

'Anything interesting?' she asked, prising the sheets of paper from his hand and slipping them back into her small leather work-satchel.

'Naw! Ah cannae read. Ah was looking to see if there were any pictures. You not joining me?'

'I don't drink when I'm at work.'

'Ye want some gear?'

'I don't do that either, not any more.'

'Man, that's grim. How d'ye get yer kicks? Sex?' Jay-Go downed the Ardbeg in one gulp and sat staring at her, like he might be interested in a liaison. 'Man, a bit of make-up and you'd be a looker. You've got that Lois Lane vibe goin' on. Pure stealth, you know what I'm saying? Second-glance stunner.'

Keira ignored the remarks and changed the subject. 'How did you get here?'

'Grabbed a cab, Miss, cost me nearly twenty quid. Any chance you could spot me a refund and some cash for the journey back?'

Keira knew Jay-Go and his type all too well. She'd represented him and hundreds like him, over the years in court, against crimes and misdemeanours ranging in severity from possession, and loitering with intent all the way up to murder and rape.

Jay-Go was always working the angles, pushing for a quick fix and instant gratification, but he was at the bottom end of the social structure where the pickings were mostly the leftovers from society's plate. If his effort and cunning could be employed more fruitfully Jay-Go would be a multimillionaire. He was as good a liar and a cheat as any of them.

Keira tried again. 'Did you get the bus?'

Jay-Go stared back at her like he was going to take her on, then changed his mind. 'Na! I walked it. Where would I get the money to splash on a luxury trip in the back of a cab?'

'You walked all the way from Easterhouse?'

'Aye. "Ah'd walk a million miles" an' all that. But listen, I can see that you're busy so I'm no' gonnae keep ye back.' Jay-Go stopped abruptly, as though he'd had second thoughts over whatever he was about to say next. He suddenly seemed nervous and started looking distractedly around the bar. Keira repeated his name three times before his focus came back round to her.

'Jay-Go, are you all right?'

'Aye fine. Ye got any smokes on ye?'

'What were you going to say?'

'Let's go outside for a smoke an' I'll tell you.'

'Why can't you tell me in here?'

'Nae reason; I'm just dying for a fag.'

Keira lifted a soft pack of Virginia Plain with two roll-ups ready-made and a Zippo from her handbag, then nodded towards the entrance. 'Okay, let's go.'

*

The traffic on Hope Street was building up as the town-centre office workers spilled on to the streets and started to make their way home.

Keira lit the two expertly rolled single skinners and handed one to Jay-Go.

'Man! I thought you'd be smoking one eh' them posh brands like Mayfair, or those French fags that smell of shite.'

'Gauloises is French for shite.'

'Is it?' asked Jay-Go, thinking he'd guessed correctly.

Keira gave him a look.

'Aye, well, they'll be the ones.'

'I prefer to roll my own: I smoke less and enjoy it more. When did you get out?' Keira drew down a lungful of smoke.

'Last week.'

'And how's business?'

Jay-Go flicked her a look. 'It's shite, by the way, because Ah wis busted, naebody'll sell me stock, and even if they did the punters think the cops are still watching me so they're blanking me too.

And the bawbags that moved in on my area of the scheme when I was sent down, they think I'm aiming to chisel my way back in again so they've put a marker on me: fuckin' Serbians. When the Poles moved in it was fine, 'cause they'd deal with anyone. They recognized there wis enough for everybody, but the fuckin' Serbs are mad. They're all ex militia, man! Too aggressive, ye know what Ah mean? It's getting pure lawless up there. It's a self-limiting business, anyway . . . I know that. How many junkies d'you know over thirty-five? I *am* planning to start up again, but just till I get the one big score, then I'm fuckin' off out of it. Off to New York on a cruise liner, pure *Titanic* fashion, know what I mean? Gonnae do rehab over there. There are more junkies in the States than the population of Belgium, so they know what they're on about; clinics are better quality. Got a cousin in Dublin's a fuckin' riot: take him along for the craic, and the crack . . . if he's got any.' Jay-Go half smiled to himself, thinking it was a good line. 'But that's no' the point,' he continued. 'When the economy is on the downturn, recreational drug use is on the up. There's plenty business out there for us all to have a share. But now I have to watch ma back the whole time, man: carry a shooter, just in case, you know what I'm saying?'

'Don't tell me things like that, Jay-Go,' said Keira coolly. 'Chances are your parole officer will be writing to me to sign-off on all the papers, which I won't be able to do if I know you're walking around with a gun in your pocket selling drugs.'

'You asked the fuckin' question, Miss,' he retorted.

'I know I did, but I didn't mean it literally, I meant how are things in general?'

'Aye, well, in general, things are pure Gauloises . . . So there you are.'

The two stood in silence for a few minutes, watching the passers-by and finishing off their smokes.

Eventually, Keira said, 'Is that it?'

'Is that what?'

'Well, I'm presuming that since you spent the best part of two hours walking from Easterhouse to find me, there must be something more than just a confession and moaning about the Serbian mafia.'

'Aye, well that's right.' Jay-Go was suddenly serious. 'A bit of info for you. And the only reason I'm telling you, is because you're a stand-up bitch and I know you'll not land me in the shit over it.'

'Should I take that as a compliment?'

'Fuckin' right you should. This is serious and I'm only gonna say it once, then I'm off. No questions, right? I'm no' a grass and I never have been, but this is payback time.'

'I don't know why you're saying that, Jay-Go. You don't owe me anything.'

'You're not like all those other monkeys you work with. You looked out for me, so now I'm looking out for you. I've got your back, Miss, that's how the Jay-Go works, but no questions, all right?'

Jay-Go was staring at her now, his expression intense, waiting for her response.

'I'm not quite sure what I'm agreeing to, but if that's what you want, then fine – no questions.'

'The girl—' started Jay-Go, but Keira interrupted him.

'What girl?'

'No questions!' snapped Jay-Go. 'Just listen.'

Keira nodded, but she suddenly had a bad feeling; an uneasy

sense of foreboding that made her want to tell him to stop whatever he was about to say.

'There is only one girl,' he continued, 'and you know exactly who I'm talking about, so don't say another word, just let me finish. She's cursed. You've got to stop any dealings with her 'cause there's gonna be no survivors: pure bad news. You need to protect yourself from her. It's all shit, Miss, and the word in the Bar-L is the bogey man's coming.'

'You're not making any sense, Jay-Go,' said Keira, holding up her hand to stop him from protesting, 'and I'm not asking a question, I just don't understand what you're telling me.'

'The whore! The one that got lifted at the airport – they've ordered a hit on her.'

With that Jay-Go turned on his heel and started up the road.

For a moment Keira could do little more than stare after him. How could he know about the girl? How could he know that she had been appointed to represent her; no announcement had been made, official or otherwise. It was supposed to be a closely guarded secret. How could he possibly know? The Bar-L – Barlinnie – was Scotland's largest prison, but who in there could have found out? Keira called after Jay-Go just as he rounded the corner on to West Regent Street. She ran after him calling his name, but when she reached the corner just a few seconds later, Jay-Go was gone.

Six

Keira sheltered inside the porch to the entrance of the Prosecutor's office in Blythswood Square. She was leaning against one of the pale Georgian support pillars, finishing off the last of her roll-up. The square of cream sandstone buildings overlooked a public garden that in Victorian times would have been filled with bedding plants and well-tended perennials, but over the years and – more recently – with successive cuts in local council spending the garden had been neglected and left to manage itself. When it was first built, the plot had been enclosed by metal railings, but the shortage of steel for bomb making during the Second World War led to their removal and left the small green area feeling exposed and ill defined. Keira could see the irony in the metal once used to protect an area of beauty in the centre of a town being cut down and fashioned into something whose sole purpose was to destroy similar places in a different country.

It had started raining and there was a cool, blustery breeze whipping over the top of the hill on which the square was located, just a few minutes' walk from Glasgow's city centre. Keira was killing time till her 10 a.m. appointment. It was still only 9.50 and she was already on her third cigarette: if she kept smoking at this rate she'd be all out of tobacco before lunch.

Keira was habitually early for appointments. It was a trait she found irritating in herself, but she couldn't help it. This morning, however, it had worked to her advantage: given her some more time to think.

The conversation with Jay-Go the night before had been un-settling. She was trying to figure out whose best interests would be served by making this knowledge public, but so far she had drawn a blank.

Then there was the death threat against Kaltrina. Jay-Go couldn't possibly have known the importance of this girl's co-operation in the case that was being built against Fisnik Abazi, but someone did; and that someone had passed the informa-tion on to Jay-Go in the knowledge that it would find its way back to her. It was this train of thought that had kept Keira up for most of the night. As soon as she was back from visiting her grandmother in Dumfries she would track Jay-Go down and find out who he'd been hanging out with. In the meantime she would have to be even more careful. If nothing else, it had made Keira more determined than ever that no more harm would come to the girl.

A voice behind her made her jump.

'Your office have just called and asked if you could get in touch. Sounded serious.'

Advocate Depute Patrick Sellar appeared over her shoulder. He was a short wiry man in his mid fifties, with a ratty face and a ghoulish complexion. Long strands of greying hair were swept across his balding pate and there was a faint odour of decay if he stood too close. He gave Keira the creeps. She'd come across him in court a few times, so she was aware that – despite ap-pearances – he was sharp to the touch, and liked nothing better than a good scrap. If you took him on, your defence was likely to bleed to death through a thousand tiny, painful incisions.

The slimeball was not to be underestimated.

'Lost your mobile?'

'No.'

'Battery dead?'

'Brain tumours.'

Sellar made a face. 'The frequency they transmit microwaves at isn't in the same bandwidth as the ones that cause cancer.'

Arsehole! thought Keira.

'So you don't use one.'

'I do. I just don't let them use me. I'm not quite as reliant on one as everybody else seems to be. If anything, I find life a little more tolerable without them.'

He still wasn't convinced.

'What about emergencies?'

'Depends what you define as an emergency.'

'Do you want to use mine?'

'I'll head straight back there at the end of our meeting, but thank you. And thanks for seeing me today instead of tomorrow. I'm sorry to muck you about,' she said, following him through the small lobby.

'Not at all. Your secretary gave the impression you were jetting off somewhere. Business or pleasure?'

'Neither. A family matter. And not exactly "jetting off": driving to Dumfries.'

As they reached the stairs, Sellar announced, 'There is a lift, but it's only two storeys. I prefer to walk,' as though his was the only opinion that mattered. He indicated for Keira to go first.

Keira walked up the red-carpeted stairs ahead of him, conscious of his eyes on her backside.

Nether of them spoke again until they were inside his office.

'You were probably surprised I agreed to see you at all,' said

Sellar as he eased himself into the large swivel chair behind his glass-topped desk, 'given that I'm not known for doing deals.'

'It did cross my mind,' replied Keira taking her place on the other side of the desk.

'I keep hearing good things about you. Wanted to see for myself how you operate. Would it be fair to say you're a promising up-and-comer?'

'I've never really assessed my career, or the path it's taking. I just do what I do.' She uncrossed her legs, then noticed Sellar gazing at them and crossed them back again.

'Modest, too: I like that. And a looker: always an advantage. I can see why you attract a lot of business.'

Keira let the 'looker' comment pass for the moment. She was soberly dressed in a light-grey shapeless wool suit and not wearing any make-up, but was well aware of Sellar's reputation for being a lech.

'Do you want something to drink?'

'No thank you.'

'The Albanian girl is an interesting case. What's your pitch?'

Now that the pleasantries were out of the way, Sellar was straight into it. Keira responded likewise.

'I want the charges against her dropped before it goes to court.'

'On what grounds?'

'On the grounds that both she and I feel as though she's being blackmailed into appearing as a witness against Fisnik Abazi.'

'So? If we drop the charges she's free to go, and if she's free to go she'll disappear. If she disappears a major component for the case against a major criminal disappears also.'

'So you *are* blackmailing her.'

'I wouldn't put it quite so strongly as that: more like using whatever leverage we have as effectively as possible. You look mildly surprised, but that's the way it plays.'

Keira was more than mildly surprised. She had been expecting him to argue the opposite, but he appeared to be confirming what she believed.

Sellar continued, 'She was working as a prostitute. There's CCTV footage of her stealing from a shop. She broke into a house and stole money, a passport and various items of clothing. She was caught red-handed trying to leave the country using said passport, having attacked a man at the bar. He was lucky to survive. Prostitution, assault, theft, burglary, et cetera, et cetera: we didn't trump up any of these charges, they're real.'

'Abazi hasn't even been arrested yet. She could be stuck in jail for months before anything happens on that front; I don't think prison is where this young woman ought to be.'

'I haven't met a defence lawyer yet who doesn't think their client should be walking the streets rather than serving their sentence.'

'She hasn't been convicted of anything yet; she's not serving a sentence.'

Sellar ignored the interruption and kept talking. 'Abazi is under twenty-four-hour-a-day surveillance. When all the pieces are in place they'll move in and make an arrest. I'm led to believe that is imminent. The girl is too important to the prosecution's case to simply let her walk away. It was she who suggested giving evidence against him in the first place. It's in everyone's best interest to press on with charging her. There has been talk of deporting her, but if she co-operates with the

Abazi case then I'm sure there will be some room for manoeuvre on that front. That's as much as you could hope for at
this point, Keira. But it's obviously all speculation on my part.
These things are not within my powers to gift . . . yet.' He then
added, 'I've been given the nod that I may be prosecuting the
Abazi case, but nothing in writing.'

'Kaltrina Dervishi has given me her word that she will appear as a witness, she wants this guy put away just as much as
everyone else, but pursuing the case against her is much less
likely to make her co-operate. It'll make her back away from
that position at a hundred miles an hour. And threatening her
with deportation will only reinforce her unwillingness.'

'Just to correct you on one point,' replied Sellar. 'No one is
threatening anything. I merely mentioned deportation because
there's been some background chatter on the subject.'

Sellar thought he was being smart: letting the fact that there
may have been a discussion over deporting the girl linger for a
moment in an effort to ramp up the pressure.

Keira was happy to play along.

'If they deport her she will be murdered.'

Sellar was shaking his head. 'We have no cause to believe the
girl's life is in any danger. Abazi's a bad bastard, no one's deny-
ing it, but there has been no indication that anything like that
would happen at all.'

'I've received information from a reliable source that there is
already a contract out on her.'

Keira paused for a moment to let that one sink in.

'Then I'm confused. Why would you want her out on the
streets if you believe her life to be in danger? If she's locked up,
she's contained and out of harm's way.'

'I didn't say I wanted her out on the streets, I said I wanted the charges dropped. I also think that rather than being stuck in jail, she should be put in the witness protection programme. Then everyone gets what they want. You get your witness and I get some degree of safety for my client.'

'I take your point, but it's an expensive process and at this moment in time I'm not entirely sure it's necessary.' Sellar let out a snort. 'As it stands she's the accused, not a witness. And we can't put her in the programme until Abazi is under arrest. Technically there is no case against him, therefore no such thing as witnesses.'

Sellar was being an arse. He could just as easily have agreed that the witness protection programme was a good way forward, and – given Abazi's reputation for violence – probably necessary, but instead, he was choosing to play the power game.

Sellar noticed Keira start to rub her wrists together. It was a small subconscious gesture, but one that made him smile inwardly. Over the years he'd made a habit of researching anyone who might have any bearing on the outcome of a case he was involved in. Judges, fellow solicitors, the accused; it didn't really matter to him. Something always turned up that gave him a slight advantage over them. It was usually a small and seemingly inconsequential fact, or story, but even just a few hours spent panning the Internet would usually produce a golden nugget. And here, once again, his rigour was paying off right before his eyes. The one little nugget he had found out about Keira Lynch from a casual conversation with her boss, John McKay, was that she rubbed her wrists together when she was on the back foot, unsure of her ground or nervous about something. That one small involuntary action gave her away. He wanted to ask her if she ever played poker; maybe challenge her to a game and then sit back and smile benevolently as she marvelled at how well he could read her. But that would just be toying with the poor girl.

'One other thing I should mention.' He paused as if he was still deciding whether it was a good idea to continue, then started shaking his head as if, despite his reservations, he simply had to.

It was all an act, and not a very good one; nowhere near as good as Keira's. She had already decided that no matter what he said she would make no response.

'There is a small additional complication with regards to the case for deportation.' This would give Miss Lynch something else to worry about on her way back to the office, thought Sellar as he delivered the body blow. 'They're looking at the possibility of citing Part II Section 15(3) of the 1971 Immigration Act as one of the grounds.'

Sellar turned his hands to the ceiling and gave a little shrug of his shoulders as if to say 'I'm sorry'.

He watched her closely for a response, but she wasn't giving anything away. After a few seconds he said, 'I'll write it down for you so that you can look it up when you get back to your office.'

Keira sat for a moment weighing her options. She had all the ammunition she needed to blast Sellar into the air and keep him bouncing around like a tin can in a cowboy movie. But that would almost be too easy. The professional option was to thank him for his time, then walk out and tear him apart in court. But she was going to do that anyway.

Stillness descended over her as she sat quietly collecting her thoughts. Her wrist rubbing routine had worked again: the feint before the sucker punch. She knew now what the Advocate Depute was thinking in relation to her case – in fact she had gotten far more than she had bargained for. She also knew exactly what Part II Section 15(3) of the 1971 Immigration Act contained: it meant an appeal against deportation would not be granted on the grounds that Kaltrina Dervishi was considered a threat to national security. How that – in any way – related to the girl was something she would investigate later, but for the time being she wasn't going to give Sellar the satisfaction of entering into a conversation about it. Keira let him think he'd rattled her for a few seconds longer, waiting until the silence in the room had gone beyond awkward before making any kind of response.

Sellar was squirming around in his chair, obviously feeling the strain.

Keira had made a decision. She'd take him apart now *and* in court.

Her tone was calm and measured.

'Kaltrina Dervishi didn't come to Great Britain on a holiday visa and decide to stay after it had expired so that she could become a prostitute and a thief. Yes, she did all these things that you are accusing her of, but let's get some context here. She was effectively trafficked to this country. She thought she was coming over to a better life, but it was all a con. She was allowed one phone call home to say she'd arrived safely, then her passport was taken and she was forced to work in the sex trade. She has been raped several times: not just by Abazi, but also by a number of the men who work under him. She's also been beaten and tortured by these same men. She did break into someone's home to steal some clothes, but only because her own were covered in blood. She did steal food from a shop, but only because she had so little money or means to support herself that she could do nothing else to prevent herself dying of starvation, and yes she did try and leave the country using a false passport, but given the level of abuse and exploitation she had suffered, wouldn't you have done the same? A point to note: she effectively handed herself in, and the reason she handed herself in was because one of Abazi's men was waiting for her in departures: he's the one she assaulted in order to get herself arrested. In anyone's book, Abazi's actions represent far more than just a threat. She strongly believed that Abazi's man had orders to kill her. Without special protection she is a sitting target.'

Patrick Sellar made a gesture like he was going to interrupt, but Keira held up her hand and waved her finger at him. 'Uh, Uh! You've played your cards, now it's my turn. If you think I'm going to let another man, particularly one whose task it is to uphold the law, try to exploit or abuse my client by blackmailing her into appearing as a witness, and if you think you have even the remotest chance of a jury convicting this girl of any of these charges, then I'll be very happy to stand against you in court. One other question before I leave,' continued Keira as she stood up and gathered herself together. 'Do you have my CV on your desk?'

Sellar looked back at her as though a grenade had gone off in his stomach and was about to explode out the top of his head. 'I'm not sure I understand the question.'

'I'm not interested in your summation of how you think my career is panning out. I'm not here looking for a job; I'm here *doing* my job.' Keira stood to deliver the head shot. 'If you're using looks as a measure of someone's ability to perform a task, you would have to mark yourself down as a "fail".'

She headed for the exit, but she wasn't finished. At the door she grabbed the handle and turned. 'I win cases because I'm good at what I do, not because I look good when I'm doing it.'

Seven

The offices of McKay and Co. Solicitors occupied all three floors and basement of Elmore House in Royal Crescent, just off the lower end of Sauchiehall Street on the western edge of Glasgow city centre. The terrace of whitewashed Victorian buildings had survived the bombs of the Second World War unscathed, and – although attractive to look at – appeared at odds with the modern office blocks surrounding them. There were three police cars sitting outside with a number of officers milling around the entrance. Keira recognized her boss, John McKay, from behind, talking to one of the officers. McKay was a media bunny. He loved the limelight. He wasn't that great a lawyer, but he knew how to sell. Early on in his career he'd been involved in some high-profile cases and had made the most of the publicity generated to start his own practice. The Armani suit was from a few seasons ago and the swept-back hair was grey and cut in a style that in no period of hairdressing had ever been fashionable. He wore a gold Rolex, drove a Porsche and named his dog Maggie in homage to the former Tory leader.

He turned as she approached.

'You getting busted for possession again?'

'Aye, right. We've got a crime scene, but no crime!'

'How does that work?'

McKay shrugged, 'Beats me. Where's your phone, we've been trying to get a hold of you all morning?'

'I left it on my desk, on the charger,' answered Keira lamely. 'Needed charging. Why? What's going on?'

'Did you swing by the office earlier this morning on your way to the meeting with Sellar?'

'Why are you asking?'

'The alarm was activated at about five a.m. Looks like we've been burgled.'

'So why were you trying to get hold of me?'

'They opened the inner doors using your pass key.'

That wasn't the answer she was expecting.

'Was anything taken?' she asked as she rummaged in the over-the-shoulder rucksack that passed as her handbag.

'Not that we can see. Nothing obvious. Everyone has checked their computers, but nothing seems to have been tampered with ... More to the point, all the computers are still there. Curious. D'you think you might have misplaced the key card?'

Keira opened the purse she had just lifted from her bag and pulled out a blank rectangle of plastic with a brown magnetic strip on one side. 'This is it,' she said, handing it over. 'Could just be a fault in the system.'

John McKay shook his head. 'The surveillance system shows quite clearly a figure entering the building.'

'Shit, really? What were they after?'

'No idea! Have you been known to sleep walk?'

'Did it look like me?'

'Face was covered. And we're fairly certain it was a male. You're in the clear.'

'Whose rooms were they in?'

'We don't know. The disc was erased.'

'So how d'you know they got in?'

'The camera at the entrance door is on a different system. It backs up to my computer rather than the DVD. That's the only reason we know someone definitely entered. They must have erased the disc thinking it covered all the cameras. You're the last to check in. Let's go have a look round your desk, see if anything's been taken.'

They climbed the stairs to the third floor and entered Keira's office: one of four rooms that led off a small square landing.

The building was a converted Victorian family residence with high ceilings and ornate plaster cornicing. The cornicing had been painted over so many times it looked like melted sugar-icing. Her office was in the attic space, with two large dormer windows looking out over a small crescent garden to the new-builds across the street. The room was filled with natural light and had a bright, airy feel. Keira threw her coat on to a peg on the back of the door and headed over to her desk. Everything was just as she had left it the night before.

'Looks fine.'

She sat behind the desk and pulled open each drawer one at a time.

'Yours the only desk without a computer?' asked the police officer. 'Or has it been stolen?'

'I write everything longhand or dictate it and my secretary types it up. If I need a computer, I use his. Some people see it as quaint, some as a pain in the arse. Truth is, I'm not a very good typist. I can do things a lot faster with a pen.'

'So, nothing out of place?' asked the officer.

'Not that I can see.'

Keira followed John McKay's eyeline and saw that he was staring at the phone on her desk, unplugged: the charger nowhere close by. She was sure she'd left it on charge, but quite often the cleaner would pull it from the wall to hoover so that wasn't too unusual.

'You'd know better than most,' said the police officer to McKay. 'If no crime's been committed, there's no criminal. Someone entered your building using one of your employees' security passes and didn't steal anything, didn't spray the walls with graffiti or have a shit on your carpet. The bastards even reset the alarm as they were leaving. Even the headline writer at the *Daily Record* would be struggling to get anything out of that scenario. Obviously it's not always apparent straight away, so if anything does come up, let us know. It could be they were disturbed and had to leave or – the only other option I can think of – they may have left a listening device or bug or whatever. You know, it might be an idea to get one of those firms in to scan the place, but I'm clutching at straws. I only mention it because of the type of work you do and the type of people you have to deal with. I wouldn't put it past some of them . . . It's a weird one!'

The phone on Keira's desk started ringing just as John was following the cop back towards the door. 'Okay, well, thanks for your help, officer, we'll let you know if anything—'

'Wait!' said Keira suddenly.

The two men turned back to face her.

'It's not mine . . . the phone!'

'You sure?'

'It's the same model, but it's not my phone . . . not my ring-tone.'

Keira looked up at the cop. 'No caller ID. Should I answer it?'

'Why not,' the officer made his way back to the desk. 'D'you mind if I listen in?'

Keira lifted the phone to her ear, angling it so that the policeman could hear the conversation, then waited before saying anything.

A dull, guttural voice at the other end said six words, then hung up.

'Open the video, Keira. Press play.'

Keira slowly placed the phone back on the desk. John McKay was staring at her expectantly.

'Anyone we know?'

Keira shook her head. 'No idea.'

*

Parked on the opposite side of the street from the small, green crescent garden outside Keira's office sat a white Ford Transit van. The driver cut his call, then dialled another number. He didn't have to wait long for someone to answer. 'She's got it,' he said as he casually flicked a cigarette from a soft-pack and pressed the lighter button.

The phone was a standard BlackBerry modified with military grade voice encryption. Speaking in his native language meant most people in this country who weren't Kosovan couldn't understand him anyway, but even the most sophisticated monitoring equipment couldn't listen in either.

'What did she say?'

'She didn't say anything, I didn't give her a chance.'

'Get back here and pick up the Merc.'

'What time's E Zeze's flight landing?'

'Sometime early evening: could be sooner, could be later: it's down to the Americans.'

'When d'you want me to go?'

'Now.'

'Why don't I drive up in this? I put my foot down, this thing could fly me there.'

'Stop trying to think for yourself, Besnik. Get your fat ass over here and pick up the Merc.'

'Okay, see you in half an hour.'

Besnik replaced the mobile in its charging cradle and turned the engine. The Duratec six-litre V12 shoe-horned in under the bonnet was taken from an Aston Martin and sounded like a peal of thunder as the van pulled away from the kerb and roared up the road.

Besnik took a long drag on his cigarette and smiled. Even if the cops across the street gave chase, they'd never catch him.

Eight

'Horsefly to EGEC, Horsefly to EGEC, looks like we are gonna make it in time for a pinkie.'

'Horsefly, this is Spec War Detachment One, broadcasting live from EGEC: We got you, Marine. You got a civilian crate at thirty thousand, west and three miles out, apart from that the sky is yours and the runway is clear. Throttle back and set her down anytime you like. How long you visiting for?'

'Just long enough to top off and grab a beer. Got a black-shoe to drop off, too. Ain't spoke a word since he boarded and – perversely – is wearing brown shoes.'

The air traffic control officer in military fatigues continued, 'Say your state, Marine.'

'State one plus one-zero to splash, so more than good, but if I don't get a beer I might ditch her anyway and swim to the nearest bar. Got a transatlantic ahead of us we're feeling oh-so warm and fuzzy about.'

'I hear you, Horsefly. We'll stick a few in the freezer: get them nice and chilled.' The officer was operating from a secret command-and-control bunker in Machrihanish on the west coast of Scotland: International Civil Aviation Organization airport code EGEC. The facility was located inside a little used domestic airfield that was also home to a detachment of US Navy Seals. He checked the location of the small white blip on his screen then pressed the talk-button again. 'What's the view like on this fine and pleasant evening? I got you just over Stornoway.'

'Man, I don't care what it's called, got no goo for as far as the eye can see to the west and maybe three lumps of *cumulus mediocris* overland to the east – it's beautiful. I'm thinking to emigrate here it looks so fine. There's even a goddamn beach.'

There was a brief silence followed by a short crackle of static then the pilot spoke again. 'EGEC, this is Horsefly, we got three down and locked, get the bottle opener on standby.'

*

Besnik Osmani left the outskirts of Campbeltown just as the sun was setting. Rose-coloured rays grazed the underbelly of three huge white clouds cruising gently above the two-mile-long runway of Campbeltown airport, Machrihanish.

Besnik pulled off the single-track road running alongside the perimeter security fence of the tiny airport and came to a halt in the car park adjacent to the domestic terminal building. His was the only vehicle there. The building was the same length as two average-sized terraced houses joined together and appeared to be deserted. All the window shutters were closed and the storm doors covering the entrance were padlocked. Besnik wondered for a moment if he'd come to the wrong part of the airport, but the instructions had been very specific, although there'd been no mention of the place being shut.

The journey from Glasgow had taken nearly five hours, past Loch Lomond heading north to Inveraray, then doubling back south past Lochgilphead on the Kintyre peninsula. The spectacular scenery he'd driven through reminded Besnik of a greener rendering of the area in Albania where he'd been born. With proper road markings, finished hedgerows and lochs full of expensive looking boats marking the only differences between the two.

Besnik was hungry and needed the toilet. He got out of the car and stretched away the stiffness, then strolled across to the end of the terminal building and pissed against the wall.

A few hundred metres to his left was the conning tower and at the far end of the runway he could see three large grass-covered bunkers.

The only signs of life were a few seagulls gliding silently overhead.

He checked his watch. Despite the heavy traffic coming out of Glasgow he had still managed to get there ahead of schedule, but if he'd known that the airstrip was in the middle of nowhere and too small to include anything like a restaurant or café he'd have stopped off on the way and picked up some food. He didn't have enough time now to drive back to Campbeltown village.

It was then that he became aware of the noise: a low rumble at first, in the distance, but all the time gaining in volume and intensity. The shutters on the terminal building started to rattle and shake as if the whole building was about to crumble to the ground.

A few seconds later a military transport plane roared overhead, flying so low that Besnik's instinct was to duck. The plane sped on towards the mountains, banked to the left and started to climb up through the clouds – momentarily disappearing from view – until eventually it turned full circle and dropped back towards the far end of the runway. A few minutes later there was a loud screeching noise as the huge rubber tyres of the C130 skidded and smoked along the tarmac and eventually taxied to a halt just yards from the bunkers.

Besnik wandered back to his car, climbed in and twisted the key in the ignition. He turned down the volume of the up-tempo folk song blasting out of the sound system, wound open the window and lit a cigarette. He was careful to hold the cigarette outside the car and made sure he exhaled out of the window too.

The sun had now disappeared behind the distant hills and the burnt-orange sky was beginning to fade.

He flicked the half-finished stub on to the nearby grass bank and wound the window back up. Moments later someone opened the boot of the car and threw something heavy inside. Before Besnik could get out to open the passenger door they'd climbed into the back seat.

There was no exchange of pleasantries. Besnik stuck the shift into drive and pulled out of the car park. A couple of miles along the road he was thinking about his stomach again.

'You mind if I stop and grab something to eat?' he said, glancing at his passenger in the rear-view mirror. The question got no response. Besnik checked the road was clear then turned and looked over his shoulder figuring maybe Engjell E Zeze was wearing headphones or something.

He tried again.

'If it's okay with you I'm thinking I'll stop and get something to eat?'

'Do you like to do things you're not supposed to?'

'Do what?' replied Besnik, trying to figure out what E Zeze meant.

'Were you told you shouldn't speak to me?'

'Sure.'

'So what are you doing now?'

'I'm speaking to you,' said Besnik, trying not to give E Zeze too much attitude, but not afraid to take on the little fuck.

'Even though you were specifically told not to?'

'Well, I figured that meant shit like, "How was your flight?" and "How long you on vacation for?" That sort of bullshit. I didn't think it meant not speak to you at all.'

'What if it did?'

Besnik checked E Zeze out in the mirror again. The guy was small, probably weighed less than seventy kilos. Sitting there with neatly combed hair wearing a suit, wiry and lean. He couldn't put his finger on it, but there was something about him that gave Besnik the creeps. If E Zeze did start getting smart he would stop the car and give the freak a slap. Besnik decided to ramp it up a little. 'If it did mean that I shouldn't have said a word to you, then we got ourselves a problem, 'cause I just have. Now, I don't really need to ask your permission to stop and grab something to eat, I was just being polite. But in order to be polite I have to open my mouth and speak, unless you know another way of doing it.'

E Zeze didn't answer.

'You got something up with your voice?'

'No.'

'You sure? You sound to me like you've had your balls cut off, you know what I'm saying? Like you iron your sheets and listen to musicals: all soft and quiet. That why you don't want to talk . . . 'Cause you sound like Michael Jackson?'

E Zeze turned and stared out of the window for a moment

deep in thought, then said, 'Did they tell you not to smoke in the car?'

Besnik smiled to himself. 'I didn't smoke in the car, the cigarette was outside the whole time.'

'That's not what I asked. I asked if they told you not to.'

'They told me not to, so I didn't.' He let a little edge creep into his tone.

'You like Greta Tafa?' asked E Zeze, referring to the folk music that was playing quietly through the car's speakers.

'I like her, but not the music so much. Why? You don't like to have music playing either? I didn't get a note about that.' Messing with E Zeze now. 'She's pretty hot. Do you think she's pretty hot?'

'Yes.'

'You sure? I figure maybe you'd prefer her husband.'

'Is our destination programmed into the satnav?'

'Yes,' replied Besnik, after giving it just enough time to let the little shit know he was the one breaking the rules now by doing all the talking. 'But only the city, not the actual address: that I keep in my head in case we get stopped by the cops; so we don't give them any idea as to where we're headed.'

'What are you going to eat?'

Besnik screwed up his forehead. 'What?'

'When you stop for food, what are you going to get?'

Besnik shook his head slightly. 'Why? You hungry now?'

'Depends on what you were thinking of.'

'So now 'cause *you're* hungry it's okay to have a conversation.'

E Zeze didn't look too happy at that one, but Besnik didn't care. 'I don't think you get to choose round here. You just have to go with what you can find that's open and be prepared to eat something that's been fried.'

Besnik checked the mirror again. E Zeze had zoned out.

Neither of them spoke again until Besnik pulled up – almost an hour later – outside a chip shop in the small coastal town of Tarbert.

'Why are you stopping?'

''Cause I got my foot on the brake . . . and I need some food!'

Besnik turned off the ignition. He didn't ask E Zeze if he wanted anything, figuring if he did, he would make him ask. He had the door open and was halfway out of the car when E Zeze mumbled something.

'What d'you say?' asked Besnik, ducking his head back inside.

'Would you mind leaving the music on? Tafa is a particular favourite of mine.'

Besnik shot E Zeze a look. 'Sure,' then leant in and stuck the keys back in the ignition.

As he walked away he glanced over his shoulder and caught Engjell E Zeze's unpleasant little face peering at him through the rear window. E Zeze gave a twisted half-smile which made Besnik want to walk over to the car and punch the little fucker unconscious. It was the only way he could see himself getting through the rest of the journey back to Glasgow.

There was a short line of people waiting to be served inside the chip shop.

'Fish'll be a few minutes, do you want me to put one in for you?' asked the girl serving behind the counter as Besnik joined the back of the queue.

'Yes, is okay.' He had been in Scotland for just over three years now and although his spoken English wasn't good he could still understand most of what was being said.

He pulled out a pack of Marlborough and his Zippo, and lit a cigarette.

'Not allowed to smoke on the premises. If you want to stand outside I'll tap the window when your fish is ready . . . okay?'

'Ah, yes, is okay.' Besnik headed outside.

The sky overhead was black and clear. The fish-and-chip shop overlooked the natural harbour – one of only a few in the whole of Scotland. Besnik leant with his back against the large pane of glass and looked out across the water to the lights twinkling on the far shore. He took a long drag on his cigarette then exhaled with a deep sigh. This was the sort of place he could imagine bringing up a family: well away from all the shit that was going on in Glasgow, far enough away from Albania not to be recognized. He looked along the road to where he'd parked the black Mercedes in a pool of light cast down from an overhead street lamp. The top of the little creep's head was only just visible above the headrest. Besnik couldn't make out whether he was reading or sleeping, but E Zeze's head was tipped forward slightly.

A rap at the window made him turn.

The girl inside nodded to him that his fish was ready.

Besnik flicked the rest of his cigarette along the pavement and ducked back inside the shop.

The fried fish was sitting on a sheet of greaseproof paper waiting to be wrapped.

'Salt and vinegar?' asked the girl as she shovelled on a pile of chips.

'A lot, please.'

The girl used both hands to pour on the salt and vinegar simultaneously, then expertly wrapped the food into a neat little bundle.

'Six pounds fifty, please.'

Besnik handed over the money, then, after waiting a few moments for his change, exited the shop.

He had only travelled a few metres along the pavement when he stopped dead and swore under his breath.

The space where the car had been was empty.

The Mercedes was gone.

Nine

At 2.30 a.m. Edi Leka noticed a missed call from Besnik Osmani's phone. When he returned it, Engjell E Zeze answered.

'I need your address.'

'Where is Besnik?'

'Let me speak with Mister Abazi.'

'Mister Abazi is sleeping. I've to wake him up when you get here.'

'So, give me your address.'

'Put Besnik on.'

'Besnik is not here. What is your address?'

Edi wasn't sure what to do. They were expecting the Watcher's arrival, but this was a variation from the plan. Reluctantly, he told E Zeze the address, then added, 'When you get to the front gates stay in the car and don't speak, or wind down the window. We're being watched. When the gates open drive straight ahead into the garage and wait for someone to come and get you. Don't get out of the car. Just turn off the engine and wait. Do you understand?'

'I'll be there shortly.'

Edi took a long draw on his cigarette and wondered what the hell had happened to Besnik.

Twenty minutes later the black Mercedes appeared on the large computer screen he was monitoring. Several other images of different areas of the house were displayed in boxes that came to life whenever any motion or heat source or sound was detected. The car had just drawn up at the wrought-iron gates leading to a small inner courtyard in front of Fisnik Abazi's house, triggering the camera and setting off a small alarm that beeped every couple of seconds until it was attended to.

The headlamps flashed and Edi pressed the gate release.

*

Fisnik Abazi and Engjell E Zeze greeted each other with a firm handshake and a head-over-the-shoulder embrace. Both wore blank expressions, so it was difficult to tell if they were pleased to see each other. Even though he wasn't in the Clan, Abazi had used Engjell's services on several occasions back home. The guy was prim and prissy, everything had to be neat and tidy, but he was a pro who never screwed up and always did what he said he would do.

'Engjell, my friend, I would say it's good to see you, but I know when you arrive – and I mean no disrespect by saying this – it's Death that's carrying your luggage.'

Engjell nodded slightly, but that was all.

Fisnik pointed to one of the two large sofas facing each other adjacent to the fireplace and gestured for Engjell to sit down.

They were in a large triple-aspect lounge where everything, including the furniture, looked new and there was a lingering smell of fresh paint. Fisnik saw Engjell checking it out and answered the question before it was asked. 'We've just done the place up ... one of many. We don't actually live here, we move from property to property, keep the authorities guessing. We're making so much money over here, but we need to take it to the laundry. Property is still the best way: high-end only, though. No point scrabbling around with the poor folk when you don't have to. Where you got your money stashed? You must have a few million lek invested in your pension by now.'

Engjell smiled enigmatically, but still remained silent.

Abazi was wearing dark jeans with black leather Converse All Stars and a black fitted T-shirt. A gold-plated tag showing a wolf baring its teeth hung around his neck as a reminder of his days in the Frenkies: the Serbian special forces. Apart from being unshaven, everything looked clean and sharp: he was in good shape. His bare arms were lean and well defined with a tattoo of the same snarling wolf as his tag showing just beneath the sleeve of his right arm. His cheekbones were set high on his face and there was a thin scar running along the side of his left temple where a bullet had once grazed his skull. An inch further to the right and his life would have been over. It allowed him to use his favourite line when anyone asked how he'd got it: 'I was an inch from eternity, but didn't like the view, so I turned and came back.'

'What happened to Besnik?' asked Abazi, crossing to sit on the sofa opposite.

'Who's Besnik?'

'Your driver.'

Engjell thought for a moment. 'He talked to me.'

'He "talked" to you ... so what?'

'I asked for a driver that would keep his mouth shut. Besnik just kept talking.'

'So what did you do, put a bullet through his head and dump the body on the side of the road?'

Engjell wondered if Abazi was asking a serious question and

answered as if he was, 'There was a moment when I considered doing that.'

'Where is he now?'

'I have no idea.'

'You don't know what happened to him?'

'I do know what happened to him, but I don't know where he is now.'

'Jesus Christ, Engjell, it's three o'clock in the morning, help me out here. What the fuck happened to Besnik?'

Engjell E Zeze gave Abazi a curious look, as if he couldn't see why he was getting upset. 'He pulled over for some food and left the key in the ignition, so I took the car.'

'And left him behind?'

'I told you, he was talking . . . and the car smelled of cigarettes. I asked for someone who wouldn't speak and didn't smoke. I got a talking chimney. I figure if I don't get him out of the car, I will end up killing him and that I don't do unless someone is paying me.'

Abazi shook his head – which Engjell didn't like either.

Accepting that he wasn't going to get any further, Abazi changed the subject.

'Are you travelling light?'

Engjell knew he was referring to the holdall full of heroin the uniformed Marine had handed to him as he'd left the plane.

'It's in the boot of the car.'

'D'you need anything else?'

'Have you found the whore?'

'Not yet, but they've just appointed her a lawyer, so any minute now. I'll give you the lawyer's home address before you leave.'

'You can tell me now.'

'I'll write it down for you in a minute.'

'I don't want you to write it down. If you tell me now, I'll remember.'

Abazi shrugged, 'Okay. Her name is Keira Lynch. She lives at 490 Glasgow Harbour Terrace, in flat 70.'

'And her date of birth?'

'Her what?'

'Date of birth,' repeated Engjell. 'Do you know her date of birth?'

'Why? You want to send her a birthday card?'

Engjell wasn't enjoying Abazi's tone so decided to take him on. 'What d'you mean?'

'I told you her address, and now you want her date of birth?'

'Yes . . . her date of birth. But why would I send the lawyer a birthday card? I don't know her.'

Abazi was starting to get exasperated. 'Shit, you are one tricky little fucker, Engjell. It's just a joke, you know: I'm not trying to mess with you.'

'Why am *I* a "tricky fucker", because *you* decided to use an inappropriate tone with me when I ask for a date of birth. It's you who is being tricky.'

Abazi could see where this was going. If it was anyone other than E Zeze he would drag them down to the garage and shoot them in the mouth. 'I didn't mean to use an inappropriate tone, I just want to supply you with whatever gear you need for the job and let you get on with it.'

Engjell still wasn't happy, but was prepared to let it drop for the moment.

'I need some GSM pinhole cameras and as many GSM

microphones as you are happy to lose, but I want quad band so I can monitor it from a phone when I'm out and about. I don't want to have to sit staring at a computer all day. I'll also need a tres-eight or a nine-mil with a suppressor, but there is no hurry for that. I can wait until we find the girl.'

'You can take it all with you tonight. Got a nice Beretta, could be the one, and all the surveillance shit you could ever wish for.'

'Doesn't matter if the nine is clean or dirty, so long as it works. In fact I prefer if it's been used already: the dirtier the better. A gun like that is a get-out-of-jail-free card: makes it difficult for the cops to tell who fired what, where and when . . . I'm thirsty.'

Abazi stared back at him for a second. 'What?'

'I'm thirsty. You have anything to drink?'

'Sure.' Abazi got up from the sofa. 'What d'you want?'

'Tea.'

'Tea? I think we got any kind you like so long as it's English breakfast.'

'No mint?'

'No, we got no mint. You planning to be here long enough for it to get made, then cool down enough for you to drink it?' He didn't wait for a reply. 'Much as I'm enjoying your company, I got things to do, Engjell, like get some more sleep. How 'bout I get you some water?'

Engjell nodded. 'Water will be fine.'

Abazi opened the door leading to the hallway.

'Andrej, go get my guest a glass of water. And bring up a Beretta 92f with a snap-on Hush Puppy and a box of shells. Then go get as many GSM cameras and mics as we've got.'

71

A young guy with his hands clamped behind his back like he was on guard duty replied 'Yes, Sir,' and headed off down the hallway.

'A few things you should know,' said Abazi as he came back into the room. 'My backers think I should take a holiday until you've finished the job, but to me that's a fucked-up way of thinking and here's why. I am under surveillance. A lot of badly dressed guys hanging around on street corners get their headsets on every time we pick up a phone: couple of our cars have had fast deploy GPS trackers clamped to the underside; so we know we're being watched and we know they're serious. If they are watching my every move and I'm scratching my balls in a bar somewhere when the whore is silenced, they're going to know straight away it wasn't me. Funny how these guys think they are the only ones with access to high-end surveillance shit though. From the outside it looks like it's just the cops, but we have intel that it goes higher up the chain than that: security services. We also got a campfire under our asses from the local dealers unhappy with the way we're running things: a lot of them going out of business, because we can undercut them every time. The assholes are trying to make trouble for us, passing on info to the cops if they see one of our dealers, but we've got eyes and ears in all the main players' houses – make sure it doesn't get out of hand. We are not just one step ahead of them, we're standing at the finish line waiting to start the next race. The whore could give us a fucking headache so we want her killed quick and clean, then you can clear the country fast as you like. When we're done here Edi Leka will take you to one of our shops, but you got to get in the back of a van with all the groceries. We got a delivery business too. He's wearing a bandage beret and sporting a couple of black eyes

72

where the whore smacked him across the head with a bottle and tried to stick a glass in his neck. Don't mention it to him 'cause he gets upset and I don't want to lose another driver. Once you're in the shop, just walk out front and order a cab to wherever you want to go. You booked into a hotel?'

'For the first few nights.'

'I'll get you a mobile's got the latest triple-layer encryption so it's safe to call us if you need anything else. The only other people got your number are the CIA. You're playing with the big boys now, Engjell. I'll contact you when we find where they're keeping the little bitch.'

'You don't need to. I'll find her.'

'It's up to you,' said Abazi with a shrug of the shoulders. 'Where is Besnik's phone?'

'I left it in the car.'

'And don't hit anyone else but the whore, okay?'

'I understand.'

'We're juggling enough sticks of dynamite without adding any more. Anything else you need, you got to tell me now, 'cause after today, I'm hoping we won't be seeing each other anytime soon.'

'Just a glass of water, and the lawyer's date of birth.'

Ten

Janica Ahmeti sat in the waiting area of the remand centre of HMP Cornton Vale, cradling a polystyrene cup full of a lukewarm, brown liquid that could have been tea or coffee, but didn't taste like either. The women-only prison was situated on the outskirts of historical Stirling, 'Scotland's oldest town and newest city'.

Through the plate-glass partition that separated the waiting area from the rest of the remand wing she could see Kaltrina Dervishi's lawyer standing by a pay phone, with an unlit hand-rolled cigarette dangling from her lips and the receiver clamped between her shoulder and ear while she rummaged in her bag for what Janica presumed would be a lighter. Restrictions in the remand wing were considerably more lax than the rest of the complex and inmates wandered freely up and down the central corridor ignoring the no smoking signs stuck to every wall. It struck Janica that Keira Lynch was the type of person who ignored most signs telling her what to do. She had an easy, laid-back confidence that people responded to: a coolness that wasn't manufactured. When they'd first been introduced Janica had found herself blushing as they shook hands. Throughout the course of the day she'd tried to analyse her reaction, but finally had to admit she found Keira oddly attractive. If she was wearing make-up it didn't show: Keira didn't need it. Her Celtic-ginger hair was naturally wavy: cut in a short, fifties style, with a straight fringe that looked like she'd done it herself. The hair suited her oval-shaped face and gamine features. The colour was in sharp contrast to the pale skin and impenetrable blackness of her eyes, which showed little emotion. Her flat expression gave no clues as to what she might be thinking, which Janica also found curiously attractive. She left the impression that she was concealing something, a secret 'darker than the devil's shadow', as her grandfather used to say.

Janica closed her eyes and tried not to think about the meeting they'd just had with Kaltrina Dervishi. The girl's descriptions of sexual abuse and mental cruelty at the hands of Fisnik Abazi and his men had been difficult. It was the calm, ordinariness of the delivery that made her words all the more chilling.

A tap on her shoulder made her jump.

Janica opened her eyes and looked up.

Her face flushed again.

Keira was standing next to her. 'Did nobody warn you about the tea?'

'Is that what it is? I've been trying to work it out.'

'D'you mind if we take this outside?' asked Keira, referring to the cigarette in her mouth. 'I can hardly breathe in here.'

'Only if I can have one too.'

'Tired?'

'Trying to forget,' replied Janica, getting to her feet.

'I know what you mean: it's harrowing shit.'

'I hear a lot of bad things in this line of work that I'd rather not have to listen to, but the girl has barely any English. She needs someone to tell her story, even one so terrible.'

Keira nodded over at a prison officer who pressed a buzzer to let them into a small holding area, where they were searched before being allowed to exit through a heavily reinforced metal door that opened on to a small car park in front of the low-rise prison building.

The air outside smelled fresh and clean and Keira took a few deep breaths before lighting up.

'If you moved up here you'd be in big demand, Janica: one of a kind.'

'You have a hard time finding Albanian interpreters in Stirling?'

'I've had a hard time finding an Albanian interpreter in Scotland. There's no such thing: never mind one with all the relevant clearances.'

Janica raised her eyebrows, 'Not in the whole of Scotland? Maybe I should move up, although not to Stirling. It is full of ghosts, I think. I keep having the feeling someone is watching me. This place gives me the creeps.' Janica raised her eyebrows and gave a slight shrug. 'I'm crazy, no?'

'No, I know what you mean. Where are you staying?'

Janica looked puzzled, 'Staying?'

'Yeah, sorry it's the British way of asking where you're lodging. Have they put you up in a hotel?'

'Ah, yes, in the centre of Stirling. You?'

'No, I have to get a train back to Glasgow.'

'Sounds far.'

'About an hour: not too bad. You'll find out for yourself tomorrow. I wondered if you could translate a video we've received. Aimed at the girl. We're pretty sure it's some kind of threat, but we need to know what they're saying before we show it to her. Would that be okay?'

'Sure.'

'Say . . . midday? I'll call you first thing to confirm.'

'Sure.'

'I'm going to walk to the station. We could talk on the way, or if you'd rather we could share a cab?'

'No, let's walk . . . give the ghosts something to think about. You want to go for a drink?' Janica felt the warmth rush to her face again.

'Sorry, I can't miss my train. Another time.'

The two women set off along a narrow footpath that bordered their side of the road. Opposite was a rough grass verge that gave way to the open countryside beyond.

After a few hundred yards walking along the unlit footpath they came to the edge of an estate full of grey council houses and the welcome glow of street lamps.

'Is Glasgow where you're from?' asked Janica, making small talk.

'I wasn't born there, but it's where I grew up.'

Janica nodded. 'I too am one of the displaced: forced to leave my country by Milošević when I was just a teenager. When I look at Miss Dervishi my eyes sting. She has the look of the forsaken that I once had.'

'Do you ever think of going back?'

'All the time, but the Serbian troops destroyed our passports and papers so we would have no way of proving where we are from. The ones that do go back are called liars and cheats then chased away or . . .' she hesitated, 'or worse.'

Keira flicked her cigarette into the air and watched as it hit the pavement in a flurry of orange sparks then tumbled off into the gutter.

'Why d'you only smoke half the cigarette?'

'It makes me think I'm smoking less.'

'It works?'

'No!'

'I don't like being a smoker,' said Janica filling in the silence that followed. 'I don't like the hold it has over me. When I can't smoke I want one, and when I do smoke I don't enjoy it because I know it's screwing up my health. There's also something perverse about being made to stand outside in the fresh air when you want to fill your lungs with smoke.'

Keira didn't reply.

'No matter what I do, I can't stop.'

'You're thinking about it too much.'

Janica nodded in agreement. 'I do think about it too much, you're right; at least twenty times a day. That's one hundred and forty negative thoughts per week, times fifty-two over the year; what's that add up to?'

'A headache, you'll make yourself ill. You're probably doing yourself more harm worrying about the cigarettes you haven't smoked, than if you'd just smoked the damn things in the first place.'

'Probably.' Janica smiled.

'So what did you want to ask me?'

Janica glanced over her shoulder. Despite the street being deserted she lowered her voice and checked that no one was in earshot. 'She has lots of problems, the girl?'

'Yeah, quite a few. You're in a unique but unfortunate position, Janica. Obviously you hear everything that is being said, but I can't really talk about the case with you . . . you understand that?'

'Of course, I understand, but it is not the case I wish to speak of.'

'Okay.'

'Fisnik Abazi sounds like a . . .'

'An arsehole.'

'I was going to say "piece of work", but arsehole is good too.'

'I would also be careful about mentioning that name out loud,' Keira said seriously. 'You never know who might be listening.'

'Please, you have no worries with me. I come from Kosovo, I know of such men there and what they are capable of. I know when to keep my mouth shut. This is why I need to speak. I think maybe he is a member of the Clan. If you are agreeable, this I will ask the girl tomorrow.'

'The Clan?'

'They are heavy into the drug trade, prostitution also: mostly ex-members of the Serbian army, so they are fighting lots of battles under Milošević, and very violent. You must hope that they have not come to Scotland.'

'Are they a gang?'

'More an organization.'

'Like the Mafia?'

'Sure, but worse, much more ruthless,' answered Janica with a frown. 'For them a human life is nothing, but they are fiercely loyal to each other. They will never give evidence against another member. This is why I am scared for the girl.'

Keira already knew the answer to the next question, but asked anyway. 'Why are you scared?'

'If Abazi is a member of the Clan – and she is saying things about him, or against him – they will not let her live.'

There was no drama in Janica's voice.

'I am sorry to say these things, but I believe the girl is in danger, there is a bad feeling around her, don't you think?'

Keira stared straight ahead. She didn't want to acknowledge it to Janica or to herself, but she had the same sense of foreboding when it came to Kaltrina.

'I'm not going to let anything happen to her,' replied Keira, even though she wasn't sure she believed it herself.

Eleven

The lone figure of Engjell E Zeze stood at the window of the hotel room on the fourteenth floor looking out over the twinkling city nightscape. The hotel soared some twenty storeys into the darkness and looked like a cubist version of an art-deco building. The faint background rumble from the lanes of traffic speeding along the M8 motorway below was temporarily drowned out by the sound of a kettle coming to the boil on the bedside table. Spread out on the bed, covering most of the duvet, was a collection of pinhole cameras and a tangle of cables with miniature microphones attached, and various boxes of different-sized batteries. Engjell had just finished sorting through the mess of surveillance equipment Abazi had provided and was taking a break before putting it all back into a holdall ready for later.

The kettle clicked off in the corner of the room.

Engjell moved over and sat on the edge of the bed to examine a small dish containing an assortment of teas and coffees, then swore in Albanian before picking up the phone and dialling zero for reception.

'Good evening, how can I help?'

'I can order some tea?'

'There is a kettle in your room, sir, but if you'd rather, we can make you a pot and bring it up.'

'You have mint tea?'

81

'Of course, I'll just get someone to look in the kitchen and then call you back. If we do have any, would you like me to order you a pot?'

This was why Engjell hated conversing with people. They didn't think about what they were saying before they spoke. 'I didn't ring to check your stock levels. Yes; if you've got any send me up a pot.'

'If we don't, would chamomile or green tea do?'

'Is that what I asked for?'

'No, sir.'

'Did I ring and say I want chamomile or green tea?'

'No, sir.'

'Then why would either of them do? If I wanted chamomile I would have asked for chamomile. If I'd wanted green tea I would have asked for green tea. I asked for fucking mint tea, because that's what I want . . . Mint tea. What is your name?'

'My name is Paul, sir.'

'Thank you Paul . . . I'll see you later.'

*

Engjell stood in front of the bathroom mirror and after applying a thin line of spirit-gum to the relevant areas, lifted a false moustache and beard from the shelf below it and carefully pressed the two pieces into place.

He checked the mirror again before returning to the bedroom.

The loaded Beretta was sitting on the bed next to a medium-sized Bladen tweed holdall containing one change of clothes and all of the recently sorted surveillance equipment.

Pulling the clothes from the bag, Engjell tossed them on to the bed before flipping the Beretta's safety on and pushing it into the side pocket of the holdall. After one final check in the bedroom mirror, he hoisted the bag up and left the room.

*

A short taxi ride later the small hunched figure of Engjell E Zeze was walking along a narrow pathway that ran along the front of a row of modern apartment blocks. The newly built development was sandwiched between Castlebank Street and Glasgow Harbour Terrace on the north bank of the River Clyde. Keira Lynch's block was at the far end. There were no shops or bars nearby, which gave the whole area an eerie, deserted feel. In the time it took to find the entrance to her building only one car had driven past on the main road.

Engjell checked the burnished steel call-panel at the side of the large framed-glass entrance and pressed number 68. A few seconds later a voice crackled from the small speaker, 'Hello.'

'I've got some urgent documents for Keira Lynch, but she isn't answering. Would you mind buzzing me through so I can stick them through her door?'

'Sure. What's the name?'

Engjell played it dumb. 'Keira Lynch.'

'Yeah, I meant what's your name.'

'It's Paul, I work beside her at McKay and Co.'

'Okay. You know where you're going?'

'Yeah.'

The glass double-door suddenly parted and Engjell was in. Head down to avoid the camera in the corner of the small atrium, he headed straight for the fire door leading to the stairs.

Pushing the door firmly closed, Engjell took out a small bullet-shaped object. The dull-black gadget had a microswitch at one end and a compact circular lens at the other. When he switched it on it projected a thin red laser beam that ended in a tiny dot on the wall. Quickly peeling off the protective layer of film from an adhesive strip running down one side of the small cylindrical device, Engjell stuck it to the frame above the door, ensuring that the red dot was pointing at the floor. A code punched into the mobile phone that Abazi had given him activated the SIM card built into the sensor above the door: a second later it beeped twice. The message ALARM ACTIVATED flashed up on the screen of the phone.

Engjell opened the door just enough to break the beam of light and watched the screen start flashing red while the phone vibrated silently in his hand.

Engjell then climbed the stairs to the seventh floor. There was a camera on each of the landings and another at the far end of the long concrete corridor leading to the lawyer's flat.

With no security guard on duty in the atrium, the chances of the cameras being monitored were small. They were most likely recording to a central hard drive and accessed only if there was an incident like a break-in or a robbery.

Halfway along the corridor Engjell stopped outside the lift and pressed the call button. As the lift made its way up the muffled sound of a television and the dull thumping bass-beat from an unrecognizable song could be heard reverberating along the hallway.

When the lift arrived and the door opened Engjell held it

with one foot and leant over to insert a small skeleton key in-to the slot marked MAINTENANCE. With a single turn, the lift was disabled.

Standing outside Keira's front door, Engjell punched a num-ber into his phone and waited. After a few seconds a muted ringtone could be heard from somewhere inside the apartment. Engjell put an ear against the door and listened. There were no sounds of any movement inside the apartment. After four rings Keira's answering machine clicked on and he hung up. Engjell pressed the doorbell and waited for a few moments in case she was screening her calls, but there was no response.

Producing a thin piece of plastic that measured double the size of a credit card, Engjell slid it behind the door jamb in line with the lock and leant against the door to apply some pressure. A few seconds later the door sprung open.

The apartment was in darkness.

Most alarms were programmed to sound within thirty seconds of being activated.

The clock was ticking.

To the left, opposite the front door, was a row of cupboards with louvred doors. Experience told him that this would be the most likely location for an alarm: close to the main entrance, but concealed from view.

Sure enough, the cupboard nearest the end wall housed the control panel.

Engjell used a small atomizer full of clear liquid to spray a fine mist over the keypad, then waved a key ring that had an ultraviolet light source over the area. The spray adhered to the natural secretions of sweat left behind by contact with skin and the UV revealed the thin swirling lines of Keira's finger prints.

Engjell's watch read ten seconds left.

Three of the keys glowed Day-Glo blue.

Keira's birthday was the third of April nineteen eighty-four. The keys numbered three, eight and four were glowing bright blue in the darkness along with the key marked ARM.

Five seconds.

Engjell reached out to press the numbers, then stopped, gloved hand hovering over the keypad. The alarm had not made any warning noise when the front door had been opened: none of the usual beeping sounds associated with the count-down to its activation.

Time up.

Nothing happened.

The lawyer must have forgotten to set it.

Engjell closed the cupboard door, then moved down the hallway and into the lounge.

For him, this was the most exiting moment: standing in the darkened room of a stranger's house, the nervous anticipation of exploring a person's life in its unguarded state. Like the party guest who has arrived too early, before everything is ready. You get to see things as they really are.

Engjell drew the curtains closed and switched on the over-head light. It was time to get to work.

*

Keira paid the taxi driver, then stood for a moment and watched as it drove off, waiting for the street to return to silence. A thin mist had started to form in the cooling autumnal air, giving a hazy definition to the pools of light surrounding the street lamps dotted along the walkway that led to her block of flats. She considered having one more cigarette before going indoors, but she was tired and wanted to get to sleep straight away. The nicotine would probably keep her awake, so she decided not to.

As she set off, Keira looked up towards her small balcony on the seventh floor and frowned. There was a dim glow emanating from behind the drawn curtains. She wondered if the cleaners might have left the light on by mistake, then remembered that they weren't due for another few days.

She counted the floors again: it was definitely her flat.

Keira started moving towards the building without taking her eyes off the window.

Suddenly she stopped.

A shadow passed in front of the curtains.

Someone was in there.

Keira rushed inside the building and stood for a few moments hitting the side of her fist against the call button. When the lift failed to arrive, she turned and headed through into the stairwell taking the stairs two at a time.

When she reached her landing she pulled a small can of pepper spray from her purse and made her way along the corridor until she was standing outside her front door. Pepper spray was illegal, but so was breaking and entering.

Sliding her key into the lock, Keira opened the door as quietly as possible and slipped cautiously into the darkened hallway of her apartment. Her heart was pounding in her chest as she pushed the door gently shut behind her. She stood for a moment listening, her ears straining for any sounds that didn't match the familiar creaks and groans of the flat.

The door to the living room was open, but the light had

been switched off. There was a faint odour of sweat and cheap aftershave: a musky scent that didn't belong.

As she moved into the lounge Keira felt a sudden surge of adrenaline. The curtains were now open.

Light from outside lined the edges of every object and piece of furniture in the room with a pale orange glow.

She slowly scanned the room, but there was no sign of movement.

Suddenly the sound of the telephone ringing cut through the silence and made her flinch. 'Holy shit,' she muttered under her breath.

Keira didn't move, but stood waiting for the answering machine to click in.

'Hey, Keira, it's David. Just checking you got home okay. If you're not too late getting in, call me back, otherwise I'll see you in the morning.' Her assistant's voice rattled loudly against the stillness. She stepped towards the kitchen worktop and snatched the phone out of its cradle. 'Hey!'

'You're there!'

'Are you nearby?'

'I'm at home. Are you okay?'

'I'm fine, but I think someone's been in my flat,' she whispered, unaware of the figure moving through the shadows in the hallway behind her.

'I can hardly hear you. Is everything all right?'

'I think I've been burgled.'

'No shit! Do you want me to come over?'

'No, but will you stay on the line while I have a look round?'

'First the office and now your apartment . . . Shit. Have they taken anything?'

'I don't know, I've only just come in.'

'Jesus. Keira, hang up and call the cops . . .'

'No, just stay on the phone.'

Keira flicked the lights on and looked around the lounge. Everything was exactly how she'd left it. Suddenly she felt a cold draught of air as the lounge door swung open and slammed hard against the wall.

David heard her gasp. 'Jesus, Keira, what's going on . . . Keira?'

Keira couldn't speak. The front door that she'd closed just minutes earlier was now wide open.

'If I don't call you back in sixty seconds, call the police.'

Keira didn't wait for a response. She hung up then threw the telephone on to the sofa and ran to the front door. The fire door at the far end of the corridor was also wide open, filling the hallway with the sound of wind howling around in the stairwell beyond. Keira sprinted past the lift, on into the stairwell and down the stairs. She was soon on the ground floor. The glass sliding doors at the main entrance were drawing closed as she squeezed between them and emerged into the cool night air, panting for breath.

She stood for a moment peering into the shadows, but the street was deserted.

Twelve

Keira sat upright and swung her bare feet off the sofa. The telephone was ringing on the coffee table next to her. Half awake, she quickly scanned the room to reassure herself that she was on her own before lifting the receiver.

She didn't want to admit it, but the day's events had definitely rattled her.

Keira glanced at her wristwatch.

It was just after midnight.

'Hey?' Her voice sounded hoarse.

'Did I wake you? I'm sorry!'

'No, it's all right, Ma. I'd nodded off on the sofa; you're doing me a favour. Is everything okay? I'm sorry, I meant to call earlier. It's all going off at work. I had to go through to Stirling and, well, it's just the usual . . . shit . . . really.'

'Don't worry. What were you doing in Stirling?'

'Cornton Vale; I've got a client on remand there . . . How's Gran?' she asked quickly, changing the subject.

'Not great, I'm afraid.' There was a short silence before her mother carried on. 'I don't think they expect her to last long . . . I was struggling to make out what the doctor was saying; he was speaking so fast, but the official line is, she's "very poorly".'

Keira sighed heavily. 'Have they taken her in?'

'Sure, they wanted to, but she insisted on staying at home.'

'You can hardly blame her.'

'She keeps asking for you. Every time someone walks into the room she says your name, then shakes her head when she realizes it's not you.'

'Stop it, Ma,' said Keira, rubbing her hand along the frown on her forehead.

'I'm not trying to make you feel bad, I'm just telling you how it is. I know you've a lot going on, I'm not trying to make things harder for you, I'm just saying. And I can handle everything down here, you know that, it's fine.'

Keira stood up and started pacing round the room.

'There's something she wants to tell you,' continued her mother.

'Like what?'

'I've no idea; she won't say – not to me, anyway. I don't know if it's the drugs they're giving her or what, but she's repeating it, over and over. Mumbling to herself, you know.'

'Repeating what?'

'Your name.'

'I'll leave work early and drive down tomorrow. I've already booked the afternoon off.'

'No, listen, that's not why I was calling,' insisted her mother. 'It was just to tell you what was happening and make sure you were okay. It's unlike you, not to call.'

'I know, sorry! It's been a bit of a day, and then I fell asleep on the sofa. You've saved me from a sore neck and an imprinted face that says flock cushions. Drugs or no drugs, if Gran says there's something she wants to tell me then there's something she wants to tell me. I want to see her, too.'

'I'm not going to lie to you, Keira; I don't know how long she'll last.'

Keira stood frozen for a moment. It may just have been her

imagination, but she was sure she'd picked up the scent of the guy's aftershave lingering in the air: just a trace, but enough to give her a kick of adrenaline.

'Are you still there?'

'Yes,' she answered distractedly.

'Are you sure you're okay? You don't sound like yourself.'

'I'm fine . . . It's just . . . When I got home from work tonight I think I disturbed a burglar or something . . . someone in the apartment.'

'Dear God, Keira, are you serious? Why didn't you say?'

'I'm saying now.'

'Did you call the police?'

'I did, but there was nothing taken, so there's not much they can do. They came round, and were very nice, but as I say – what could they do?'

'Was he inside?'

'I'm pretty sure he was still inside the apartment when I got home. I could see the light on from the street when I got out of the taxi.'

'Jesus, Keira, that's awful!'

'I ran up the stairs, but when I got here the light was off and the flat appeared to be empty. I thought it was my mind playing tricks on me, but I keep catching a smell of the guy's aftershave . . . it's weird. Unless, of course, your mind can play tricks on your nose . . . I suppose that's a possibility.'

'Why don't you call David and ask him to come over and stay? I don't think you should be in there on your own.'

'I spoke to him, and he offered, but if there *was* a burglar, I doubt they'll be coming back. I'll be fine. David's not really the guard-dog type. He'd scream louder than me. He can stop a person dead in their tracks with a bitchy comment, but I'm not sure that would work on your average criminal. I'll see you tomorrow, okay? Tell Gran I'll be really pissed off if she dies before I get there.'

'Don't joke, Keira, she may well.'

'I'm not joking.'

*

Engjell E Zeze was lying on the bed in the hotel room, staring at the screen on his laptop. The image was split into four sections, each section covering a different area of Keira Lynch's apartment. The surveillance cameras had the facility to zoom in and out but they couldn't pan or tilt, and therefore offered only one perspective. The picture quality, however, was surprisingly clear. Stifling a yawn, Engjell tapped one of the images, which expanded to fill the screen: Keira in her bathroom, starting to undress.

There were a few things about her that didn't stack up. She was an attractive woman, but there were no signs of a husband or boyfriend or lover. She was slim, but could do with a bit of toning; the muscles on her arms and legs lacked definition. Her body shape could take anything, although she chose to dress down. Her face reminded Engjell of a photograph that had appeared in *Life* magazine; a young Sophia Loren lying on her front in a field with her legs bent up behind her. The lawyer's hair had the same messy look and style, even though it was the wrong colour and she lacked both the make-up and the glamour. Her flat had also felt surprisingly empty. Aside from boxes filled with files and papers relating to work scattered everywhere, there were few possessions: no ornaments or personal mementos. Her walls were bare, except for one framed photograph of David Bowie taken in 1979 and signed by the photographer, Mick Rock. If there were a fire, or she had to leave in a hurry, Keira Lynch could grab the photograph, leave the apartment and no one would know she'd ever lived there. It lacked an identity.

She'd spent an hour chatting to the cops, answering their questions matter-of-factly, playing it cool. Showing no outward signs that she'd been fazed by the fact that someone had broken in. She'd even refused her assistant's offer to come and stay the night.

Suddenly Keira appeared on screen, stripped down to her bra and pants, standing in the middle of the room. But it wasn't the sight of her near-naked body that caught Engjell's attention. She'd dipped her fingers in a tub on the side of the sink then gently smoothed it over her wrists before pressing them together, then rubbing them in small circles against each other, over and over again. Next she slowly swept her arms out to the side, her hands trailing in a balletic movement as she arched the small of her back and made the shape of a cross. It was surprisingly graceful, as though she was moving in slow motion. Finally, she let her head drop forward, until her chin was almost touching her chest.

It looked to Engjell as if she had stopped breathing.

She stood motionless in this pose for almost half an hour before slowly lowering her arms, raising her head and exiting the bathroom.

Engjell sighed heavily. '*Ju jeni një kurvë çuditshëm.* Man, in any language, you are one weird bitch.'

A few seconds later Keira reappeared wearing a T-shirt and

stood by the sink to brush her teeth.

Engjell clicked the small RECORD icon in the top right of the screen and put the laptop on the bedside cabinet: tiredness was kicking in. There was something thrilling about observing people in their unguarded state. Even the mundane held a fascination. But every now and then, in private, when they thought no one was looking, a person would do something extraordinary, just as Keira Lynch had. Standing almost naked, in total silence as though she had been crucified. Engjell E Zeze, the Watcher, wanted to call the lawyer and freak her out; tell her, 'I've been watching you . . .' Ask her, 'What have you done to your wrists?' and 'Who is crucifying you?' Leave her in no doubt she'd been observed, then hang up. Sit back and watch her panic.

Engjell stared distractedly out of the window.

It felt good knowing that at any time the lawyer could be destroyed. No guns, no weapons, just words! 'I've been watching you.'

Engjell pulled the computer closer again, tapped at the keyboard and waited for the search engine to come up with the results. 'Cornton Vale women's prison, Stirling.'

It shouldn't be this easy.

Thirteen

'Can you make out what they are saying? The sound's not great.'

'Of course.'

'It's pretty obvious from the state of the guy to her left – who we presume to be Kaltrina's father – that they're not sitting there having a cosy about the weather,' said David, screwing his face into a frown. 'Whatever they did to him, these guys weren't messing around: what a state!'

Keira turned her face to Janica Ahmeti. 'We need to know what the mother is saying.'

'The girl has seen this?' asked Janica.

'Not yet. She's being transported from Stirling to the police headquarters in Pitt Street; we'll meet her there in about an hour. D'you need to watch it again?'

'No, I got it.' Janica then repeated the message back. First in Albanian: '*Stop çfarë jeni duke bërë, Kaltrina. Nëse ju nuk e bëni... ata do të vrasin babait tuaj. Pastaj – në qoftë se ju ende vazhdojnë të tregoni gënjeshtra – Ata do të më vrasë.*' – then in English – 'Stop what you are doing, Kaltrina. If you don't they will kill your father. If you still continue to tell the lies – they will also kill me.' 'The next bit sounds like, "*Ai është në rregull*" – "He's okay", but it could be just, "*Be* okay". There's a noise on the first consonant. It's either, "*Ai është në rregull*" or "*Te jetë në rregull*", I'm not sure.'

Janica and Keira were standing around David's computer, watching a grainy, blown-up version of the video that had been recorded on the phone left on Keira's desk.

Even with the windows fully open and a fan blowing in the corner the office was too warm. The fan only circulated the hot air to other parts of the room.

Keira pushed back from the desk and headed over to stand in front of it.

'What are you thinking?' asked David.

'It's going to thunder,' replied Keira distractedly.

David looked to Janica, then back at Keira. 'You still got the heebies about last night? Forget it, nothing was stolen.'

'What happened?' asked Janica.

'Nothing.'

'I'd say it was a pretty big "something",' continued David. 'Some freak broke into her apartment and sprayed eau de BO everywhere, then left without so much as one stolen object. He was still in the apartment when she got home.'

'My God! Did you see who it was?'

'No. I'm not even sure it happened. It was a long day yesterday . . . I was tired . . .'

'What did he spray?'

'He didn't spray anything. Not only does David's mouth run away with him sometimes, but he's prone to exaggeration.'

'You said this morning that you could still catch the guy's scent.'

'I didn't say he'd sprayed anything.'

'Could have been a cat burglar,' said David with a grin wider than the lame gag warranted.

But Keira wasn't in the mood. 'Copy the video and send it

over to Patrick Sellar's office. Recorded delivery so that he can't deny having received it. Then make another copy and take it there yourself as back-up.'

David got up from behind his desk and headed for the door. He was used to Keira covering all the angles. If she wanted Sellar to have a copy of the tape then there had to be a good reason.

'Sure. I'll sort that out.'

After David had left the room Janica looked over at Keira. 'He is studying to be a lawyer?'

'He probably has a better grasp of the law, and – more importantly – how to apply it, than anyone in this practice, but he'd rather spend his time ordering at the bar than studying for it.'

*

David drew the back of his hand across his brow and stared off down the length of the stuffy, windowless corridor. 'Dark blue carpet tiles with khaki walls: whoever came up with that combo should be put away.'

He was sitting between Keira and Janica outside an interview room at Strathclyde Police HQ in the centre of town, waiting for Kaltrina Dervishi to arrive. Keira was struggling with how best to help the girl. She'd tried asking for the charges to be dropped and for the girl to be taken into a witness protection programme, but Sellar wasn't playing the game. It was increasingly likely that Kaltrina would have to face the son-of-a-bitch in court. In order to help the girl fully, Keira needed to know everything. There could be no secrets: no surprises when she got to court.

Up to this point her client had been communicative, but

Keira got the impression she was holding something back.

She was also concerned that the video recording was likely to have its intended effect on Kaltrina and make her stop talking to them.

*

Today Kaltrina Dervishi was being herself. The lawyer had played a big role in making her feel comfortable in her own skin. She treated her like a human being, didn't patronize her and listened to what she had to say without judging her. Kaltrina felt safe when Keira was around and regretted not being able to speak enough English to talk to her without the translator, whom she didn't trust. She would be more open if it was just the two of them. Kaltrina could judge someone's character within seconds of meeting them – in her line of business it was essential – and something about Janica Ahmeti made her feel uneasy. Kaltrina noticed how the interpreter behaved around Keira: almost as though she was nervous of her. She was fairly certain that Janica found the lawyer attractive, so it could simply be that.

Kaltrina stood, extending her cuffed hands towards Keira as she entered the room. 'They think maybe I attack you. I don't know.'

Keira put her arm round the girl in an affectionate embrace. 'How are you, Kaltrina? Is it my imagination, or has your face filled out a little since I saw you yesterday?'

The girl smiled as Janica translated the words into Albanian. Then replied in broken English, 'I eating everything they are give me in prison, but nothing is without chips. You ask for glass of water . . . it is glass of water and chips. This is why . . .'

99

she didn't finish the sentence, but blew her cheeks out to illustrate her point.

The room was small and stuffy with a table in the middle, four chairs and nothing else. Everyone took a seat while the escorting prison officer stood by the door, watching over them.

'What is trouble you today?' asked Kaltrina.

'What d'you mean?' replied Keira.

'You have *shqetësoj* on face. I can see.'

'Worry, distress,' translated Janica.

'Something is not good?'

'You're very perceptive, Kaltrina. I've brought a recording I need you to watch, but I'm concerned it's going to upset you. I'd rather not have to show it to you, but I have no option.'

'My whole life is upset.' Kaltrina shrugged. 'One more thing will make not a difference.'

On Keira's cue, David reached into his shoulder bag and pulled out a tablet computer, which he laid on the table in front of her, then without further prompting pressed PLAY.

Kaltrina's expression remained flat as she watched the video of her mother and father. It was less than a minute long, but by the end, as she lifted her gaze back to Keira there were tears running down her cheeks.

The room was silent.

It was several minutes before Kaltrina said in a quiet voice, 'I weep not for them.'

Sitting there with no make-up, she looked small and vulnerable: too young to have to deal with this sort of pressure. Keira wanted to push the table aside and pull the girl to her in a tight embrace, take the pain on herself.

Kaltrina spoke again, this time in Albanian, pointing at her stomach and gesturing with her hands. While she was talking, Keira turned to Janica for a translation, but she just sat there, almost as though she was avoiding Keira's stare. When Kaltrina had finished, Janica looked down at the shorthand notes she had made on her pad, but remained silent.

Keira was about to ask what had been said when Kaltrina spoke: 'They say on video, I am liar, to make doubt in your head. But I tell only truth.'

'I know that, Kaltrina, but these people have threatened your family. If you decide you don't want to say anything else in case they carry out the threat, I'd understand. It'd make my life more difficult, but I'd understand. We need to come up with a way of moving forward that keeps everyone safe.'

'There is no safety for my parents. They are already dead. You are not understanding the Clan, Keira. They make video for scare me, but will have killed my parents anyway.'

At this point Janica interrupted with a question. '*A njerëzit thonë, "Ai është në rregull" ose "të jetë në rregull"?*'

Keira was about to tell Janica not to ask questions without running them by her first when Kaltrina answered in English, 'It sound like "Be okay".'

'Not "*He's* okay"?' asked Janica.

'I think no. I think my mother say, "Be okay," said Kaltrina, shrugging her shoulders. Then turning to Keira she continued, 'Now I wish speak with you only.'

Keira didn't ask why. She gestured to David and Janica to leave the room, then asked the prison officer if he would mind waiting outside also. He didn't look too happy, but agreed.

Kaltrina waited for everyone to leave before leaning forward.

'You are only person I trust, Keira,' she said in a whisper.

'Good. I want you to trust me. I'm sorry I had to show you the video. It doesn't make me feel good: I feel like you've been through enough. I really hope you're wrong about your mum and dad.'

'I am not wrong.'

The quiet, resigned tone in Kaltrina's voice and the resolute acceptance of her situation reminded Keira of herself when she was younger.

This was the reason she liked the girl. From the moment they met they had been connected. Underneath was in turmoil, but the surface was flat calm.

'I'll do my best for you, you know that.'

'I know. This is why I tell only you. It must be secret. You must make promise.'

'I promise.'

'I will tell everything I know. But I need something at first.'

'You need me to do something first?'

'Yes. Last thing my mother do is send me message.' Kaltrina's eyes started to fill as she continued to speak, but no tears broke. 'She is brave one. She say, "He's okay".'

'"*He's* okay," not "*Be* okay"?'

'I tell Janica lie, because I not trusting her. "He's okay," my mother say. You must find him and make him safe. Then I tell you everything. But Clan must never know or they kill him too. Is secret and you promise?'

'It is a secret and I do promise, but who is "he"? Who is your mother talking about?'

'His name is Ermir. He is my son.'

Fourteen

An hour into the journey south, past Dalmellington and on toward Dumfries, the rain started. The old BMW 3 Series was being buffeted from side to side by the wind. Torrents of water battered off the windscreen, making it almost impossible to see the road ahead.

The travel time would have been a lot shorter if she'd taken the motorway route down to Scaur, but it was a much less interesting drive.

The sky had turned black and muted peals of thunder rolled across the scree-covered hilltops in the distance. The narrow road twisted and wended its way along the outskirts of the Galloway Forest Park. Even under normal driving conditions it was a test of Keira's motoring skills. If her grandmother wasn't so unwell, she'd turn back and try again tomorrow, or at least pull in and let the storm pass, but she was already behind schedule. She didn't want this to be the one time in her life she arrived late for an appointment.

The mobile phone sitting on the passenger seat started to buzz. Keira frowned and picked it up.

'Hello.'

'Keira?'

'Yes.'

'I wasn't expecting you to pick up.'

'Is everything all right, Janica?'

'Yes, sure. Is this bad time?'

'I'm driving; can I call you back in about an hour?'

'Okay.'

Keira could hear a hint of disappointment in Janica's voice.

'Sorry, it's like a scene from the Genesis flood narrative here. It's raining so hard I should be in a boat.'

'I've stayed on in Glasgow and was just wondering what you were up to. D'you want to meet up later for a drink?'

'I can't, Janica, I'm heading out of town. Maybe one night next week.'

'Of course: you mentioned earlier. Sorry, I forget.'

'It's no bother. I've got a situation going on with my grandmother, so I'm heading down to see her. I'd better get off the phone before I hit something. Talk to you later.'

Keira hung up and tossed the phone back on to the seat.

The CD player was stuck on 'Wild Eyed Boy from Freecloud'. It was the only track that jumped on her Bowie compilation. She pressed SKIP to jump to the end of the track then turned the volume up ready for 'What in the World'.

As she stared out at the rain pounding against the windscreen she tried to shake loose the thought that her grandmother's life was about to end. Keira couldn't bear to let the idea form fully in her head.

The three women had moved to Scotland from Northern Ireland when Keira was just eight years old.

Cut off from friends and family, her mother and grandmother had struggled to bring Keira up by themselves. Her grandmother in particular had helped her through the debilitating bouts of depression she'd suffered as a teenager. She could talk to the scared young girl who for so many years lacked the confidence to play – or make friends – with people her own age. Keira wasn't naturally bookish: it was circumstance that turned her into an avid reader. And once the information was in, she never forgot. She got on well with her mother, but she didn't have quite the same insight as her gran into who Keira really was.

Her grandmother was also the only person in the world who had ever made Keira laugh to the point where she couldn't breathe. It was for her that Keira had gone to university. It was for her that Keira had tried to stop dwelling on the events of the past and start moving forward. It was for her that Keira had studied long into the night to pass her law exams.

If it rained twice as hard, Keira would still keep going, rather than risk letting her grandmother down.

She had been so focused on keeping the car on the road that she'd failed to notice the black Land Rover Evoque that had been following her since she left Glasgow. At first she was only aware of the diffracted glare of headlamps in the rear window. Now – each time she checked – the car seemed to have moved a little closer, closing the gap between them until eventually it was sitting right on her tail. There was no reason for her to presume she was being followed, but the events of the last few days had made her more wary.

The A713 between Ayr and Castle Douglas had a single carriageway in either direction, with very few turn-offs or places to overtake. It was reasonable to assume that because of the weather and the narrow road someone on their way home from work could be behind her for quite some time, but Keira had a feeling that this was not what was happening here. She checked her mirror, hoping to catch a glimpse of the driver, but the rain hitting the windscreen and the diffused blaze of the headlamps made it impossible.

Suddenly a loud horn sounded in front of Keira causing her to veer sharply to the left. A huge low-loader hauling lengths of concrete ducting sped past in the opposite direction, the sound of the horn fading, along with the truck, into the swirls of spray left in its wake.

As she swerved out of the truck's path the rear end of the BMW slid out to the right, then whipped suddenly back to the left as she tried to straighten up. For the next twenty yards she fought to keep the car under control, swerving from side to side as it slipped and skidded on the waterlogged surface of the road, but each twist of the steering wheel seemed only to make matters worse.

Keira glanced quickly into her mirror and saw that the black car, instead of backing off or slowing down, had moved even closer, manoeuvring into position ready to shunt her off the road.

'Back off, you son-of-a-bitch,' muttered Keira as she slammed her foot on the accelerator and yanked the steering wheel to the right to try to bring the car under control. The rear end of the BMW swerved again, this time sliding sideways in a drift for several feet and spraying a sheet of water high into the air before slamming hard into the drystone wall running along the edge of the road. Keira heard the nearside tail-end crunch against stone as it clipped the large granite boulders. She slammed on the brakes and skidded to a halt, stalling the engine.

She had been holding her breath: her heart pounding in her chest, her lungs screaming for air.

When she checked the mirror, the car behind was gone.

The road ahead appeared to be empty. As far as she could remember, there were no side-roads on this stretch: nowhere for the Evoque to go.

'Jesus! What the hell is going on?'

Keira was suddenly aware of how tightly she had been gripping the steering wheel. She took a deep breath and tried to relax her shoulders, then reached across, blindly fumbling through her handbag which was lying open on the passenger seat. She pulled out a soft pouch of tobacco containing three ready-rolled cigarettes and depressed the car's cigarette lighter.

She slipped the car into neutral and turned the key in the ignition. After wheezing and spitting the starter motor eventually caught and the engine came to life again. That's when she noticed the low-fuel light had come on.

Keira reckoned she was somewhere between Carsfad Loch and Earlstoun Loch. St John's Town of Dalry was just a few miles up ahead and she was certain there was a small petrol station somewhere on the right.

She would stop there. It would also give her a chance to check how much damage had been done to the car.

When the cigarette lighter popped she touched it to the end of one of the roll-ups. The cigarette had been wrapped too tightly to draw on properly and it took her several small puffs before she could get a satisfying lungful. The last few bars of 'What in the World' faded to silence as she breathed a long smoke-filled sigh.

*

A few miles further on the rain started to ease. As she rounded a bend at the end of Earlstoun Loch she spotted the small filling station up ahead. She flipped the indicator paddle to turn right, then tensed. Sitting in the forecourt beside one of only two pumps was the black Land Rover. Keira hesitated: Scaur was only another thirty miles or so, but the BMW's petrol gauge was notoriously unreliable. It could take her all the way there or it might run out within the next mile and leave her stranded in the middle of nowhere.

She had no choice but to pull in.

Keira drew up behind the Land Rover and sat for a few moments before getting out. A quick glance as she lifted the nozzle of the pump and placed it in the filler cap told her that the Evoque was empty. She peered through the window of the small shop, but – apart from the guy serving behind the counter – it appeared to be empty too.

Keira decided not to fill the tank to the top. Instead, she put in more than enough to get her to Scaur, then went inside to pay.

A small overhead bell chimed as she pushed through the door and into the shop.

'Fine weather,' said the guy behind the counter with a half-smile as Keira handed him her card. 'Got my trunks on underneath, in case I need to swim home.'

Keira tried to smile back, but she wanted to pay and get out of there as fast as possible.

'Where'd the guy in the Land Rover go?'

The man behind the counter looked confused. 'Using the toilet, but it's not a man, it's a woman.'

'A woman?' It was Keira's turn to look confused. 'Really?'

'Aye. On her way to Castle Douglas, thought she was lost for a minute, so popped in here to use the toilet and get some directions.' He handed Keira back her card.

'Where you heading yourself?'

'Scaur.'

'Scaur! There's not many people call it that these days. Are you a local?'

'No,' replied Keira as she made her way to the exit. 'I'm trying to keep it a secret from the rest of the world, so I call it by its old name.'

'Aye, good on ye! Don't want the likes of Trump spoiling this part of the coastline as well. Safe home!'

Keira climbed back into her car and fired the engine. She briefly considered waiting to see what the woman in the toilet looked like – maybe even give her a mouthful about driving up people's arses – but instead she slipped the BMW into gear and drove off.

She lit the second of her three roll-ups and realized she'd forgotten to check how much damage the drystone wall had done.

Fifteen

CIA Officer Tommy Aquino eased his pale blue Cadillac over the junction and turned right on to Dolley Madison Boulevard to join a queue of lunchtime traffic heading into McLean; he was late for the 12.30 p.m. meeting and hungry. A few miles further on, the car swung left into Old Dominion Road and immediately pulled into the lot of J. Gilbert's Wood-fired Steaks & Seafood, where he parked up and quickly made his way through the rows of customers' cars into the restaurant. The steakhouse was full of suits, most of whom were office workers from the surrounding area. A few other officers from Langley sometimes used the restaurant as an informal place to meet away from prying ears, but mostly they came here because service was brisk and the steak was excellent. You could be in and out in an hour having had a decent lunch and some fresh air. Aquino also liked the mood music: trad jazz played at a volume that meant you could still have a conversation without having to raise your voice to be heard above the more usual, soulless muzak.

He scanned the large open-plan dining area and saw Gregg Moran gesturing to him from a table in the far corner near the window.

He made his way over and pulled up a chair.

'You're late!' said Moran brusquely, holding out his hand for a perfunctory handshake. Aquino knew it was all a front with

Moran. Underneath the sullen exterior, the guy was just like everyone else. He took the job seriously, but he liked a laugh as well. Today, however, Tommy knew the conversation was going to be a tough one. 'Sorry, by the time I'd tidied your bedroom and helped your wife get her underwear back on, I realized I was running behind.'

'Screw you, Aquino,' replied Moran without smiling. 'You know how I know you're bullshitting? 'Cause Dorothy doesn't do sex any more.'

'She doesn't do sex with you, you mean. She's set her sights a little higher, that's all.'

'I ordered you the filet mignon, blue, with the salad on a different plate, but I didn't know what you'd want to drink.'

'Coke.'

'Don't tell *me*, asshole, tell the waiter.'

Tommy Aquino and Gregg Moran had gone through spy school together. They'd been recruited at the same time, albeit from two different colleges. They had completed their trade-craft on the same day and been friends as well as work associates ever since. They'd opted for the CIA's Special Activities Division and had worked closely on a number of operations, but both of them knew that the situation they were currently involved in had the potential to not only wreck their careers, but also land them in prison.

'What you having?' Tommy asked Moran.

'Same, but well-done with a Diet Coke.'

'You'd have to drink gallons of that shit to make any difference to the size of your ass,' said Tommy, riding him a bit more. 'Might as well go full-fat and at least enjoy the taste. The sweeteners in that stuff can give you migraines, too, I heard.'

'My whole life's a headache; a can of soda ain't gonna make any goddamn difference... Okay, so where we at?' he asked, starting the meeting for real.

'The girl's lawyer is trying to get her into a witness protection programme, but the head attorney guy isn't convinced she needs it. The lawyer still hasn't persuaded him that the girl's life is in danger. Which in a way is good for us.'

'Will she persuade him?' interrupted Moran.

'Probably. Especially now that the Serb has made a home movie for the girl that puts the threat beyond reasonable doubt, but I'll tell you about that in a minute.'

'Then what?'

'If she goes into the programme, she'll be out of our reach.'

'Do we know where she is yet?'

'Finally, yeah. A women's lock-up in a place called Stirling. It's the only goddamn women's jail in the whole of Scotland. At first we thought they'd be hiding her someplace much more secure, but they either don't know what they've got or they're profoundly incompetent.'

'What's the Serb's state of play?'

'He's still on the street, working away like he's invincible. Doesn't seem too worried about the girl. Having said that, he's not so dumb as to think there isn't a problem, especially since Edwin Kade got busted. I think he's more concerned about that.'

Even though both men were not referring to Fisnik Abazi by name they were making no effort to disguise their conversation. They both knew well enough that people only started listening when you behaved like you had something to hide.

'The problem is,' continued Aquino, 'the Serb's trafficking activities have already brought him to the attention of the security services over there; he is now under surveillance, and Edwin Kade has given them a direct link to us, so we have to ask ourselves if we should back out until things calm down or get out altogether.'

Gregg Moran was shaking his head. 'We'd have to take the Serb out. If he's arrested he won't go down quietly, and we can't afford to have him shouting his mouth off, which – knowing the son-of-a-bitch – is exactly what he'll do. If we take him down we'll have to do it ourselves, no one around him will touch him: clan loyalty and all that bullshit. And if we do give him the ultimate fuck-off tablet, we're left with an even bigger headache: trying to find someone as well connected in the Balkans. For the moment the Serb has to stay. But let's look into the logistics of sending him on holiday. Who's running the surveillance on him over there?'

'Local. It's being done by the cops, but the security services are looking over their shoulders, fairly low grade.'

'So our biggest problem is the hooker. If we get rid of her, everything just might return to normal.'

'And getting Edwin Kade the hell out of there.'

'Why doesn't he just jump on a goddamn plane?'

'His head is mashed up pretty bad: can't fly. If they make the link, he may be asked to give evidence against the hooker.'

'Jesus Christ!'

'The Serb reckons he should be able to deal with the hooker issue easily if we can get her back out on the street. He's already made contact with her parents back home. This is what I was going to tell you. Got them on camera telling her to keep her mouth shut. He figures when she sees it she'll be too scared to say anything. He has someone in place now, so I figure the hooker's covered . . . it'd still be better if we could get her released.'

'Trouble is, we don't know how much the she's said already.'

Aquino nodded in agreement.

'What'd Abazi do, threaten to kill the parents if she talks?'

'In the first video.'

'How many videos did he make?'

'Two.'

'So in the first he threatens the parents, and in the second . . . ?' Moran let the question hang for a moment.

'Who knows, but you can make an educated guess. He's only sent the first video so far, but the point is he's already made the second, which of course the girl doesn't know. My guess is, either way, the parents didn't come out of it too well.'

Moran shook his head. He didn't need to watch it to imagine the scenario. He took a slug of Diet Coke, then said, 'He's a nasty son-of-a-bitch, no doubt about it.'

'He's holding the second video in reserve, in case the first one doesn't have the desired effect. Although I'm still not sure that killing the parents is gonna motivate her to stay quiet, but he's the one making the play.'

Moran let out a thin whistle between his lips.

The waiter arrived holding the side orders of salad and a couple of plates on which sat two perfectly cooked steaks. 'Can I get you guys anything else?'

Aquino answered. 'Yeah, can I have a Coke; the full-fat version?'

'Sure.'

With that, the waiter left.

Moran picked up where they had left off. 'Okay, so this situation may not be as bad as we first thought. I'll put in a call to London and tell them we may have an interest in Abazi and the hooker. I'll also ask what they can do about the charges against her. If they're dropped then she's free to go and we can leave the rest to Abazi.'

'If we call London we're going to alert them to our involvement and that could land us in the shit,' said Aquino, cutting into the steak and taking a mouthful. 'Especially if the girl ends up staring at the sky with six feet of dirt in her eyes . . . damn this steak is good! So far they haven't connected the girl to Kade . . . but they will.'

The waiter was back at the table with the Coke. 'Anything else I can get you, gentlemen?'

'We're good,' replied Moran. He waited until the waiter had gone before starting again. 'Leave London to me. Because of Kade, they already know there's something going on. The next question, however, is the one that's gonna knock a few pounds off your gut: gonna ruin your appetite every time it pops into your head.' Moran finished chewing, then swallowed a large mouthful of Diet Coke to wash down the beef before continuing. 'The lawyer: what do we have on her? If something happens to the girl, the lawyer's going to start sniffing round like a TSA dog snuffling at a bag of explosives on the carousel.'

'So far we've drawn a blank: no dirt,' Aquino said. 'She's quite highly regarded, not only by her contemporaries, but also by the criminal fraternity: a lot of the big players want her to represent them. The establishment see her as a bit of a pain in the ass: she's a scrapper, a troublemaker even. Seems dedicated to her work. Followed the usual career path: did a postgrad legal practice course for a year after getting her law degree, then a two-year training contract before fully qualifying. Even took a job as a legal secretary in her holidays from college to "broaden her knowledge".'

'What's her field? Criminal?'

'Criminal law and human rights, but the human rights thing is more of a sideline. Things that stick out: suffered severe bouts of depression as a teenager. Sees a shrink on a regular basis. Doesn't use her cell much, and it's not exactly what you'd describe as a smart phone . . . it's a basic model, so no info to be gleaned from it. Doesn't email at all and she does all her shopping in a goddamn shop!'

Moran's forehead creased. 'What the hell? She doesn't have a cell phone or use email?'

'She does have a cell, she just never seems to use it. And she sometimes uses email in her office, but she always logs on using someone else's computer.'

'Social networking sites? Facebook, Twitter, any of that shit?'

'She still posts things in a mailbox.'

'Jesus Christ! You gonna tell me next she sends the important stuff by frickin pigeon.'

Aquino laughed.

'So she's hiding something,' said Moran matter-of-factly. 'Possibility a significant event when she was a child that would link in with the depression and the shrink?'

'We're still working on it, but to date she's proving to be something of an enigma: nothing on her before the age of eight. Like she popped up out of nowhere.'

'Okay, well, we need to pop open that particular *matryoshka* and see what's inside. We need something we can use to discredit her if she starts making too big a noise. In fact . . .' Moran took another slug of Diet Coke then stared Aquino straight in the eye.

'What?'

'It might be no bad thing if she got caught in the crossfire when they take the hooker down, you understand what I'm saying?'

Aquino looked uncomfortable. 'Well, I don't think we should go there right now, Gregg. It won't be long before something turns up that we can use on her: contain her if she starts messing our game.'

Moran shrugged his shoulders slightly. 'Fair enough, but I would still get word back to Abazi: let him know that no one this end would be that upset if she got hit. So far nothing has shown up on the police computers. We're right inside the lead investigator's laptop and nothing is showing. Whatever the girl has told the lawyer hasn't been passed on yet. If we act quickly enough we could stop the spread.'

'I disagree, Gregg.' Aquino's voice was steady and calm. 'If the lawyer gets taken down there are going to be a whole lot more dogs sniffing round the shit pile. I think the word to the Serb should be the opposite: avoid any other casualties at all costs.'

Moran nodded a few times then said, 'Yeah . . . maybe you're right. Anyone else we should keep an eye on? What about the interpreter? We got any concerns there?'

'None.'

'You having dessert?'

'Shit, it's no wonder your ass is getting so big, Moran. You haven't even finished your main course and you're already thinking dessert.'

'You got to plan ahead, Tommy. Only way you're going to prevent yourself from becoming a star on the wall.'

Sixteen

It was just after teatime when Keira turned off the A710 and drove the final few miles down into Scaur. The village's only road ran alongside the Urr estuary and was bordered on the landward side by a thin row of white fishermen's cottages behind which rose the dark green wooded slopes of Mark Hill. There was one pub halfway along and a small village shop at the far end that sold a few essential food items and an odd mixture of randomly selected keepsakes. Jubilee Path rose steeply from the shop at a right angle and was barely wide enough to fit a car. The house her mother and grandmother lived in was near the end of this path and had a view that stretched all the way from the start of the River Urr at one end, along the full length of the tidal estuary, to the wide, open Solway Firth at the other.

The BMW climbed the steep gravel path and came to a halt at the side of the house facing out towards the estuary. Keira killed the engine and stepped out into the rain, which had eased to a drizzle, then stood for a few moments taking in the view. The air was filled with a complex aroma of rich pine from the surrounding forest and salted sea air carried in over the Irish Sea, along the Solway and up from the sandbanks below.

The light was already beginning to fade.

In the distance small patches of blush-red sky had started to appear through the breaks in the cloud, throwing rays of fading sunlight on to the sea below. The sound of rainwater could be heard seeping through the moss and into the soil beneath her feet.

There was a rustling noise in the large laurel bushes over to her right. As Keira turned, the sound immediately stopped.

She caught a glimpse of something moving: a black shiny object glinting in the darkness.

Something, or someone, was watching her.

Keira stood frozen, peering into the tangle of branches for several minutes, waiting for whatever it was to move again.

The metallic clank of a bolt being unfastened behind made her turn sharply. As her mother appeared at the back door a large black crow battered through the knit of laurel stems with a flurry of beating wings and rose shrieking into the night sky.

'You coming in?'

'Just getting some fresh air.'

'Did I give you a fright?'

'I thought there was someone hiding in the bushes.' Keira made her way across the loose gravel path towards the light of the porch. 'You scared the bejesus out of me.'

Inside, the windows of the kitchen were covered in condensation from the pots simmering on the stove.

'Hungry?' asked her mother as she closed the door and gave her a hug.

'Starving.'

Keira's mother was in her mid fifties, but looked much younger. She had a beautiful face with few wrinkles, and kept herself toned and fit. Keira had gone through a phase of trying to encourage her to go on dates, but after several failed attempts to find a partner her mother had taken her aside and told her she'd 'met, loved and lost the only man who ever mattered' to her and she really wasn't interested in dating: after that Keira stopped trying.

'Where's Gran?'

'Up in bed, or at least she was. I heard her moving about a minute ago, probably trying to get herself dressed. She hates for you to see her like this.'

Keira frowned. 'Jesus, as if I care how she looks. I care how she is.'

'D'you want to have a quick bite first?'

'No, smells great, but I'll go up and see what her craic is, then eat later.'

Keira made her way upstairs on to the short landing and knocked on the door of her grandmother's bedroom.

'Come away in,' croaked a voice in a broad Newry accent.

She stepped into the room and closed the door gently behind her.

For a brief moment the sight of her grandmother's withered frame made Keira blench. She was standing in front of the wardrobe mirror fiddling to close the buttons on her cardigan. Her gaunt face was stretched with pale, yellowed skin, through which it was almost possible to make out the solid mass of chalked bone underneath. Her hands and wrists were thin and frail as though the muscle underneath had dissolved, leaving only the skeletal outline behind.

'Ye never seen a corpse before?' said her grandmother as she shuffled over to an armchair by the window and gently lowered herself into it. 'You've a face on ye like a Lurgan spade.'

'A talking corpse: there's something. Stop playing for the sympathy vote.'

Her grandmother nodded her head as if she approved, but

said, 'Less of your cheek.'

'What are you doing out of bed? You're not supposed to be up.'

'Says who?'

'The entire medical profession.'

'What do they know!'

'Everything that you don't.'

'I'm trying to keep in shape.'

Keira raised an eyebrow.

'Did you see the Morrigan out there?'

'It's just a crow.'

'I heard it screaming at you. Been sitting there for the last three or four days waiting for me. It knows my soul is about to go back on the market and it's got first call.'

'You're not turning into one of those cranks that believes in all that shite, Gran, c'mon.'

'Aye, well, we'll see soon enough. Haven't I always told you this place is magic. Sure, it's the only place you ever get a good night's sleep. That's because you're safe, protected: you're watched over here. When we first arrived in Glasgow, all those years ago, you used to wake up screaming in the middle of the night so often it got to the point you were scared to go to sleep at all. That stopped when we moved here. Why d'you think that was?'

'Therapy.'

'Yer arse. It was nothing to do with therapy. You know fine well there's something about this place so let's just leave it there. Anyway, I have a question. When you get to heaven, d'you think you arrive in the state you shuffled off in?' Every few words her grandmother spoke were punctuated with shallow gasps for air. 'It'd be hellish . . . if you had to spend the rest of eternity . . . looking like this. Sure if heaven's all it's craic'd up to be why don't we all just kill ourselves anyway?'

'You seem fairly convinced that's where you're heading.'

Her grandmother smiled then took the next few minutes gathering her strength in order to continue. 'I want your abiding memory of me to be the woman you grew up with ... not this clattering bag of bones in front of you now ... It's bloody awful. If I had my way you'd be ... talking ... to me ... from the other side of the door.'

Keira didn't patronize her by telling her she looked fine. Their relationship through the years had been based on honesty and now was not the time to renege on that pact.

'The woman I grew up with wouldn't have given a damn what she looked like.'

'Aye, true enough.'

Her grandmother's face suddenly creased and her eyes closed tight as another agonizing spasm took hold.

'Are you okay? D'you want me to get you anything?'

Without opening her eyes or lifting her head her grandmother raised her forefinger and waved it gently from side to side. 'I'm fine,' she whispered. 'When I've said what I have to say, I'll take my medication, just give me a moment.'

'What d'you mean, "take your medication"? Why haven't you taken it already?'

The old woman tapped the side of her skull with her finger. 'You can't string a bloody sentence together when you're on it. When I leave I still want to be able to read the exit sign.'

A moment later she had recovered enough to continue. 'You look terrible, darling. Tired. You working too hard?' She lifted her head and stared straight at Keira.

'I'm fine.'

'Good.'

'Is that what you wanted to say?'

'It's coming now, just give me a second ... I spoke with Father Anthony, a few weeks ago – he's moved to somewhere in the Glens of Antrim – but he's agreed to come back and take the Mass.'

'What Mass?'

'I know you're not going to like this,' continued her gran, 'but I want to be cremated and my ashes spread over the boys' graves back in Newry. I want the service to be held in the cathedral.'

Keira stood in silence for a few moments, aware that her gran was waiting for her response.

'You don't know what you're asking...'

Her grandmother held up a hand to stop her. 'Well now, that's where you're wrong darlin'. I know exactly what I'm asking. You don't want to go back because that's where your demons are, but I want you to go and confront them. It's time to smite those bastards into the ground and take your life back before it's too late. You're a beautiful young woman, walking round with a weight on your shoulders that's crushing you into the ground: it's destroying your life. It's time to stop. The priest has something to give you; something that'll help.'

'Help with what?'

'Come on, now, it's me you're talking to. You've never breathed a word about it, but I know you want to find out about your father too. Who he was, what he was like, what happened. It's all waiting for you. It's time.'

'Jesus, Gran!'

'I know it's a lot to ask, but there's a lot to gain.'

Keira was shaking her head. 'I'd do anything for you, Gran,

you know that, but I'm not sure I'm up to it. Really, I just don't know if I can go back there.'

'Well, I do know . . . and I know you won't let me down. That's not to say you shouldn't be careful over there. You may not have set foot in the place for over twenty years, but there are still people in Northern Ireland hold grudges over what happened between Finn McCool and Gol Mac Morna and that was in the third century. No announcements in the papers or anything like that. I want a quiet affair. One other thing,' she continued. 'I'd like a piper: someone playing the uillean. Let Father Anthony choose the music: he has a good ear.'

'You're breaking my heart here, Gran,' said Keira, her eyes starting to burn. 'Is this why you wanted to see me? To make your funeral arrangements?'

'It's not about me, darling, it's about you, I want to give you the key to unlocking your past.'

'I'm not sure it's a door I'm ready to go through just yet.'

'I know that, but you need to. And when you're standing on the other side you can slam it shut behind you and get on with your life.'

There were so many things that Keira wanted to say to her, but mostly she wanted to be strong for her grandmother and if she tried to speak now she knew that she would lose it.

'Come here now and take my hand,' said her grandmother, as if she were reading her mind.

Keira moved to kneel on the floor in front of her chair and clasped the old woman's bony fingers between the palms of her hands.

Her grandmother responded with a gentle squeeze. 'When you know something in here,' she said, banging her fist in the middle of her chest, 'it doesn't need to be spoken. Never once trouble yourself that I didn't know what you thought of me, or I didn't realize we had a special relationship. But if I'm to get through the long silence, I need to know that you're happy . . . That's why you have to go back. Father Anthony's your starting point. Don't think you're doing it for me because I've asked you to: you're doing it for yourself. I know a lot more about what happened that night all those years ago than I've ever let on, and the time has come to put it right.' The old woman was staring at Keira with tears in her eyes. 'I know I'm asking a lot of you, but I need to go home and I want you to take me there. When the time is right I want to be with my sons up at St Mary's. Sure, Monkshill has a better view over the city, but it's always blowing a bloody gale or raining up there.'

The two women sat staring at each other, holding each other's gaze. Suddenly Keira said, '"Smite!" Really?'

Her grandmother caught it straight away. Her head tipped back as she started to laugh, her thin shoulders shuddering helplessly as she tried to control the sudden outburst and catch her breath.

Eventually Keira joined in, until they were both rocking back and forth with tears running down their cheeks.

*

The figure hiding in the bushes broke cover and started back down the steep path leading to the black Land Rover Evoque, which was parked near the water's edge. There was nothing more to see. All the necessary information about the lawyer was now known: where she lived, where she worked, where her family home was. Most of it would be irrelevant – back-up information should it ever be needed – but thoroughness was essential: even the smallest details could prove useful. The trip had been worthwhile.

Keira Lynch was the one person with access to the target: the more that was known about her, the less chance there would be of making a mistake.

From the roof of the house, the crow watched as the figure climbed into the black car and slammed the door.

Moments later a cloud of smoke billowed from the rear tyres as it screeched off along the front and disappeared into the darkness at the far end of Scaur.

*

Keira was woken by a strange tapping noise from outside that sounded as if someone was throwing small stones against the window. Her bedroom was in total darkness except for a small pencil-slit of moonlight flaring between the curtains and fanning out across the floor. As she turned to look at the time on the bedside clock, she noticed her grandmother standing at the foot of the bed.

She should have been alarmed, but instead she felt strangely calm, almost as if she had been expecting her.

'Are you all right, Gran? What's wrong?'

'Nothing's wrong, I've come to say goodbye.'

Suddenly a large crow appeared silhouetted against the curtains, flapping its wings and squawking loudly, its beak tapping noisily at the pane of glass.

'Don't go over there,' whispered Keira, the sense of panic

rising in her voice as her grandmother started towards the window. 'Don't go over there,' she repeated, but her grandmother wasn't listening.

Just as she reached the window she turned and looked back at Keira. 'It's time. You take care now, my darling, and remember,' she said banging her fist against her chest, 'when you know it in here ...'

Keira opened her eyes and lay for a few moments staring up at the ceiling, the strange dream lingering in her consciousness. The shadow cast by the Morrigan may have been a figment of her imagination, but she was aware that something was different.

She pulled on a robe and made her way next door to her grandmother's bedroom, but there was no reason to hurry; she already knew what she'd find when she got there.

Seventeen

Father Anthony looked up from the pages of the Bible laid out in front of him on the pulpit and surveyed the congregation as he drew the early evening Mass to a close.

He'd overfilled the censer again. The Three Kings Pontifical incense evoked memories of his days in the Vatican, but tonight it hung in the air in thin choking wisps, aggravating his asthma.

He'd been aware of the young woman sitting in the pew near the back of the church since she'd entered, ten minutes after the service had started. She was modestly dressed in a light blue tailored suit that fitted neatly around the waist. It was a style more in keeping with a professional from Belfast or Dublin, rather than someone living in the small rural parish that he ministered to these days: definitely not a local. She was in her late twenties and throughout the entire service had never once taken her eyes off him, staring with a cool intensity that – whether it was intended to or not – was making him feel self-conscious. What was more disturbing about the young woman's presence, however, was not her rapt attention, but that somewhere in the back of his mind he was convinced he knew her.

He glanced once more at the handwritten note – smuggled on to the lectern before the sermon had started – then answered the question written on it. 'Yes, for anyone interested, I *will* be taking confession after this evening's Mass. The Mass is ended. Go in peace to love and serve the Lord.'

The congregation responded, 'Thanks be to God,' then rose as one and started to shuffle along between the pews as they made their way outside.

The priest stepped down from the altar and exchanged pleasantries with a few of the older members of the parish before heading over to the corner of the church to the confession box. The dark brown mahogany frame was a replica modelled on a seventeenth-century confessional housed in the Vatican and had intricate carvings on the columns at each end and a wider spiral column in the centre that separated two thick red velvet curtains. Father Anthony pushed aside one of the curtains and took his seat inside the cramped cubicle, taking care to draw the drape firmly closed behind him. He then slid a set of bi-fold doors into place so that he was completely cut off from the noise of exiting parishioners and sat for a moment enjoying the silence. A small bluebell-shaped shade in rose-frosted glass glowed dimly on the wall above his head, providing just enough light to pick out the ornately patterned brass grille that divided the cubicles and obscured the confessor from view. Seconds later he heard the door of the adjacent booth being locked into place and someone shuffling on to the narrow wooden bench. A long silence followed.

'The usual opening line is "Bless me, Father, for I have sinned",' said Father Anthony.

'I stopped believing a long time ago and haven't been to church since. I'd feel like a hypocrite, asking for a blessing,' a woman's voice replied.

'In order to have stopped believing you must – at one time – have believed; that'll do for now. Why do you want to take confession?'

'I've something to confess.'

'Fair enough. How long has it been since you were in a church?'

'Twenty years.'

Her whispered tones made it difficult to tell for sure, but she didn't sound Irish, as he had expected. The lilt was more Scottish than anything, although he was convinced he could pick out certain words that still had an undertone of Newry in their vowel sounds.

'Twenty years!' whispered the priest, grimacing. 'Well, before you launch into anything too elaborate, can I just remind you that I have a dinner engagement planned for this evening.' He heard a slight snort but couldn't decide if it was through a smile or to hold back a tear. 'And while I have your ear,' continued the priest, 'I presume it was you that left the note on the pulpit?'

'It was,' came the faint reply.

'You didn't sign it.'

'I thought the whole idea of confession was that the priest wouldn't know who he was talking to.'

'Indeed, that's true. And believe me, to my mind the seal of the confessional is inviolable: I'm with Father Francis Douglas on that one. I wouldn't expect you to have heard of him, but during the Second World War he was tortured to death by the Japanese because he refused to divulge information he had received in confession about the Filipino guerrillas. It is an extraordinary sacrament, but I lived through the seventies and eighties over here when the security forces were secreting listening devices in churches frequented by well-known republicans. Ever since then I've never been a big fan of the thing. Also . . . I think I recognize you. If you are who I think you are then it might be more conducive to meet somewhere we can have a proper conversation, don't you think?'

'I thought you could only hear confession in a confessional?'

'For someone who hasn't stepped inside one of these things for the best part of your life you seem to know a lot about it. You're quite correct. The Code of Canon Law does say that, but it also adds "except for just reason", and the fact that I'm on the verge of an asthma attack and can't breathe for the smell of frankincense is just reason enough. Also, if – as you state – you are a non-believer, we're wasting our time. That, in concert with the fact that you are known to me, seals the deal. How many others are waiting outside?' he asked, searching his pockets for a scrap of paper.

'Four.'

'The one night you're in line for an early finish and you have a festival of sinners in your church. Would you have a pen on you? I'll give you my home address.'

'I know where you live.'

Father Anthony raised an eyebrow and flicked a sideways glance in the direction of the brass screen.

'It's quite a walk.'

'I have a hire car.'

'Well, aside from absolving the wrongdoers of Waterfoot, I have a few things to finish off, but I could meet you there in an hour or so. Would eight-thirty be too late?'

'What about your dinner engagement?'

'A ruse to stop those that haven't been to confession for a while from blathering on; pay no heed. If you get to the big houses on the left you've gone too far.'

*

Keira drove along Glen Road for a few miles inland from the beach at Waterfoot, then pulled left on to the soft verge outside a solitary, grey, pebble-dashed house that looked like a child's drawing with two windows upstairs and two downstairs, both set on either side of a moulded plastic door in a style too elaborate for the rest of the building.

It had been over twenty years since Keira had last set eyes on the priest. Seeing him today in the church had brought back a lot of unwelcome memories and emotions.

She lifted the rusted scrolled-metal latch on the garden gate. Any misgivings or thoughts of turning back were cancelled by the rusted hinges squeaking loudly as she pushed through. She had no choice now but to make her way across the concrete slabs and press the doorbell. If the priest hadn't already heard her car drawing up, he definitely would have heard the gate.

Suddenly the front door opened and a warm, subdued glow filled the darkness in front of her.

'Come away in.' Father Anthony stood to one side with his arm outstretched into the narrow hallway in a welcoming gesture. 'Who needs a guard dog when you have a creaky gate?'

Keira squeezed past him.

'Straight ahead, the kitchen's on your left at the end,' he added as he closed the door and followed behind her. 'Can I get you anything to drink? I have a bottle of altar wine, stolen from the church: gives it a certain piquancy that makes it almost palatable.'

'Palatable altar wine; is there such a thing?'

'I take charge of ordering it myself. It's a Mont La Salle from the Napa Valley. Really quite good! As a result I have some of the most devout parishioners in Northern Ireland.'

'That'd be grand.'

The kitchen was sparsely equipped, with none of the usual modern gadgets in evidence, but it still felt cosy and inviting. Father Anthony had lit a couple of large altar candles and placed them on the window ledge, aside from which the only other illumination was from a small reading lamp sitting at the edge of a drop-leaf Formica table pressed hard against the wall, which had a chair on either side and two place settings. There was a pile of dirty dishes on a stainless-steel sink unit waiting to be washed and a cream stand-alone gas cooker with a pot bubbling away on one of its rings.

Keira realized in that moment that she hadn't eaten anything all day.

'Can I get you something to eat?' asked the priest, reading her mind.

'Only if you have enough.'

'Sure there's plenty! I make a huge load of the stuff on a Monday night and that does me for the rest of the week, but don't look so worried, I made this lot fresh this morning. Take a seat and I'll get you sorted. Help yourself to the wine.'

She sat at the table and poured two large glasses of red from the bottle.

'I presume as you know where I live you would also have my telephone number?'

The priest had his back turned. She couldn't read the expression on his face. 'I didn't think it would be the right thing to do . . . talk to you over the phone. I felt I should do it in person.'

'I hope you don't mind me saying,' continued Father Anthony, 'but you look so much like your mother I can hardly believe it. It threw me when I saw you at first, like jumping back in time. Quite striking!'

'Thank you,' she answered, aware that he was paying her a compliment.

'How is she? Did she ever remarry?'

'She's grand. Still has no end of admirers that she plays off against one another to amuse herself, but she's never really settled with anyone. Doesn't seem that interested.'

Father Anthony spooned out two bowls of stew and placed them on the table, then picked up his glass and swallowed a large mouthful of wine before sitting down.

He watched her staring vacantly at the bowl, but not eating.

After a few moments he spoke again.

'Well, nice as it is to see you, I have an awful feeling that you haven't flown all this way to share my company, nor my cooking, nor for that matter my wine. No offence but – if I'm being honest – my heart sank a little when I realized it was yourself.'

Keira placed her wine glass on the table and tried to reply, but nothing came.

'I'm assuming that your presence here can mean only one thing,' continued the priest, 'so let me just ask you this. When did it happen?'

'She died a few days ago.'

Father Anthony dropped his gaze to the floor. 'Ah, dear! Well I'm truly sorry to hear that. I've spoken to your grandmother at intervals over the years – more so recently, since she was diagnosed – but I hadn't heard from her in a few weeks. I did start to wonder. She mentioned that you had changed your name when you moved away. What do you call yourself now?'

'Keira . . . Lynch.'

'Nice. I like it. Would it bother you if I stuck with the name I know you by, otherwise I'll end up getting confused?'

Keira shook her head. 'I don't have a problem with that.'

'Okay, Niamh McGuire it is, then. I presume you're over to make arrangements for the funeral?'

Keira nodded. 'She asked if you would consider doing a Mass in Newry ... at the cathedral. She wants to be buried with her sons. Although she put it in an odd way.'

'Odd? Why odd?'

'She said that, when the time was right, she wanted her ashes scattered over her sons' graves. It seemed like an odd thing to say.'

'Well, I presume she was meaning after she was dead. Anyway, I had spoken to her about St Patrick's and I gave her my word I would make that possible. I'll have to discuss it with Father Doyle, who runs the cathedral now, but I can't see that it should be a problem. The boys' graves are up at St Mary's, is that right?'

'Yes ... I know it's been a long time and things have moved on, but I'm still not sure it's the right thing to do ... go back. There are still a lot of ... unresolved issues. I'd appreciate it if it was kept as quiet as possible.'

'I understand your reluctance and I'll certainly try. There's no one will hear it from my lips, and I'll pass that message on to Father Doyle. I should say, however, that your grandmother was a very popular woman. A lot of the mothers in Newry around the time of the Troubles had been through similar experiences and Kathleen was always there for them. I'm sure there would be a number of them would want to pay their respects. It'll be hard to keep it a secret, but I'll try my best.'

'She also wanted a piper: the uillean. She asked if you'd mind choosing the music.'

'Certainly. And I know the very thing. Have you ever heard of "Róisín Dubh"?'

Keira shook her head. 'No.'

'It means Dark Rose. "*A Róisín ná bíodh brón ort fé'r éirigh dhuit.*" "Little Rose, be not sad for all that hath behapped thee."'

'You're going to set me off, Father.'

'I'm sorry. I'm not trying to upset you. Let's just say it's a beautiful piece of music that will fit the occasion very well and we'll leave it there.'

Father Anthony took another drink from his glass.

'She mentioned you had something for me . . . but didn't say what it was.'

'Indeed. I have it safe, a small package, not much to it. Your grandmother entrusted it to me twenty years ago, bound and taped to within an inch of its life. Her instructions were to keep it safe until she passed away, then give it on to you. All very mysterious! There's a box of knives as well: don't ask me where they came from . . .'

'Knives? What sort of knives?'

'I'll get them as soon as we've eaten and you can see for yourself, or if you'd rather I'll fetch it now?'

'No, that's fine, let's eat.'

Keira still hadn't touched her bowl of food.

She was abstractedly rubbing her wrists together in small circular movements.

'What sort of knives?' she asked again.

'Throwing knives, if I remember. I haven't looked at them for a very long time, but I believe they belonged to your uncle Danny.'

She was suddenly eight years old again, standing in the small back garden of her terraced house in Ballinlare Gardens, Newry, her uncle Danny showing her the box containing a set of intricately tooled throwing knives. He'd taught her how to use them, how to hold the blade, tip pointing at the ground. He trained her to raise her arm, then bring it forward in a straight line with as much force as possible, and at the last moment flick her wrist and release. But strength wasn't the main factor. It was as much to do with the timing of the release as the energy behind it whether the blade would stick point first, but Keira had mastered it quickly.

'I remember them.'

For a moment the two of them sat in silence, both aware that there was another subject still to be discussed. Father Anthony studied her as he ate a few more mouthfuls of stew. Her grandmother's passing was not the only thing on the troubled young woman's mind; she hadn't gone through the whole rigmarole of getting him into the confessional just to tell him that. Such information could easily have been delivered over the phone. There had to be some other reason, something that made her want to talk in private.

'How do you feel about going back to the cathedral? I don't suppose you've set foot in it since the last time we met?' he said, giving her an opening.

Keira didn't reply.

'In this line of work there's very little that I haven't seen or heard. From murderers, rapists and robbers to births, deaths and marriages, I've done the lot. I've become something of an expert on the human condition. I'm telling you this to reassure you that whatever is on your mind will be taken to the grave, along with many other divulgences I've heard over the years.'

'Thank you,' replied Keira, aware that she was about to reveal something she had kept bottled up inside her for more than twenty years. 'You are the only person alive who knows what really happened. I don't think my grandmother realized what she was asking me to do by making me go back there. She doesn't know what really went on. She thinks it's what I saw that caused all my problems, but she was wrong. It's what I *did*.'

Father Anthony sat watching her in silence.

'I know what Uncle Danny told you that night,' she continued. 'I overheard you talking at the cathedral. But he was lying. He didn't kill Owen O'Brien. He told you that to protect the real killer.' Keira paused just long enough to catch her breath.

'Now, now that's enough, Niamh,' interrupted Father Anthony. He knew from experience the courage it took for some people to get to this point, and that his place was to sit quietly and listen, but he couldn't let her continue. 'I want you to stop now, okay, and listen to me.'

But Keira didn't want to stop. She had to get the words out, like some form of exorcism. 'I killed him,' she continued. 'I pulled the trigger . . .'

Father Anthony reached forward and grabbed hold of her hands. 'That's enough now, Niamh! I want you to stop! You may have heard some of the conversation that night, but you didn't hear all of it. Your uncle Danny told me that you saved his life. If you hadn't been there O'Brien would have murdered him. Now, for the moment let's just accept that what you're telling me is the truth, that you did pull the trigger. You did it to save another person's life and that, for me, negates the burden of guilt you've been carrying on your shoulders for all these years. I preach Christian values of tolerance and forgiveness every week from the pulpit, but I'm not so naive as to think that every mad bastard in the world would respond to a few kind words by laying down their weapons in surrender. Owen O'Brien was a psychopath ... he was a dangerous man, who would have killed you in a heartbeat. Yours wasn't an act of aggression: it was a defensive response to one, and therein lies the distinction between a criminal act and a good deed for me. There's no one deserves to die, but there are those who deserve to live. I want you to leave Keira Lynch here and look back on today as the first step to making Niamh McGuire's life all that it should be, d'you understand?'

She nodded.

'Your uncle Danny told me that he killed O'Brien and that – as far as I'm concerned – is still the truth ... You saved a man's life and protected your own. Niamh McGuire has nothing to be ashamed of and nothing to repent.'

Eighteen

The bright light burning overhead hurt her eyes and must have been left on overnight. Keira raised herself on to her elbows. The clothes she'd been wearing the previous night were scattered over a chair in the corner of the room. On top of the pile sat the well-wrapped package alongside the slim wooden case containing the throwing knives. She vaguely remembered stripping naked and climbing into bed, but for a brief moment she had no idea where she was.

On the bedside table stood a half-full bottle of water. Keira grabbed it and drained most of it in one gulp. She climbed out of bed and moved over to the window, where she stood gazing at the view: the green slopes of the Glens of Antrim rising away to the summit of Lurigethan Mountain. Trees and bushes, scattered randomly along the hillside, bent and swayed in the strong offshore wind that whipped across the top of them, adding even more drama to an already impressive scene. Dark grey clouds tumbled across the early morning sky and long vertical smudges of rain could be seen in the distance.

She had stayed on drinking with Father Anthony until getting in the car and driving back to Belfast was no longer an option. They had settled on the following Thursday as the day of her grandmother's funeral. That would give Keira and her mother enough time to make the necessary arrangements to have the body transported back to Newry.

After helping the priest to down two more bottles of red and a quantity of brandy, Keira had finally had enough; she was exhausted and gratefully accepted Father Anthony's offer of a bed for the night.

Keira stood naked at the window, trying to assess the impact of the previous evening on her initial fears about seeing the priest again. There was still a vague sense of unease, but she believed now – for the first time in over twenty years – that there might be a way forward. That in itself was a new thing. Saying the words out loud to another human being had made a difference. Her grandmother had been right: Father Anthony was a good starting point; already, the crippling burden of guilt she had felt for most of her life had somehow lessened, but it was only the first step. There was still a long way to go.

There was a loud rap at the bedroom door.

Keira turned her head too sharply, which made the room start to spin.

'Are you awake, Niamh?' came Father Anthony's muffled voice.

'I am.' Keira held on to the window ledge to steady herself. 'Just give me a second.'

She made her way over to the bundle of clothes, picked her trousers from the pile and started to dress.

'There's a phone call for you downstairs.'

'A call?'

No one knew where she was.

'The fella says it's urgent.'

'Did he give his name?'

'David, from your office. Will I ask him to phone back?'

Keira pulled her blouse on and started buttoning it up. 'No, I'm just coming. Would you mind telling him to hold on? I'll be right there.'

'I will.'

Keira slid her bare feet into her shoes and followed on a few moments later. The phone was in the hall downstairs, the receiver off the hook.

'Jesus, what's going on? How did you track me down here?'

David sounded tense. 'I called your mobile.'

'I don't have my mobile with me. I think I left it at my mum's.'

'Exactly! When are you heading back?'

'Sometime this morning, why?'

'I'm sorry to disturb you. Your mum told me about your gran . . . so I know this is not the best time . . .'

'Thanks, David, don't worry about it. What's the problem?'

'They're releasing Kaltrina.'

'What d'you mean?'

'She's free to go.'

'Free to go? What the hell are you talking about? When was this decided?'

'Who knows. I got a call on my mobile to contact Patrick Sellar's office as soon as possible. I was told to let you know.'

'When did you get the call?'

'About an hour ago.'

'He called you on a Sunday morning and told you they were releasing the girl?'

'Not him, his secretary. She'd gone in specially, to sort out the paperwork.'

'Did she say why? Are they dropping the charges? What is that little prick up to?'

'Who knows.'

'What were her exact words?'

'That's about it. Given the circumstances, they're not willing to press on with the charges and Kaltrina would be released sometime later this morning once all the paperwork was sorted. She said Sellar will be in the office first thing tomorrow morning if you need to talk to him in person.'

'"Given the circumstances"? What the hell is she on about? He knows Kaltrina's life is in danger. Did you deliver the recording to his office?'

'Yes.'

'To him: did you deliver it personally to Patrick Sellar?'

'Not in person, but I . . .'

'I told you to deliver it to him personally, David, no one else. Jesus!'

'What difference does it make? I gave it to his secretary and told her to make sure it was put on his desk . . . marked urgent.'

'He can still say he didn't receive it! For Chrissake, David! That recording proves Kaltrina Dervishi's life is in danger. If he hasn't seen it, then nothing for him has changed. Where the hell is she supposed to go? "Given the circumstances"? Given the circumstances, she should be going into the witness protection programme and be spirited away until Abazi's arrested and put on trial . . . What does he mean "Given the circumstances"?'

'This is the reason you need to keep your mobile phone with you, Keira. It's making everyone's life, including your own, too bloody difficult. It's an aid to communication, that's all . . .'

Keira was standing staring at the wall in a daze; no longer listening. She hadn't seen this one coming. Suddenly she was aware of a silence on the other end of the line, then David asked, 'Are you still there?'

'Yes.'

'What d'you want me to do?'

'Where are you?'

'I'm heading over to my mum's for Sunday lunch . . . or at least I was.'

'Call his secretary back. Tell her I need to talk to Sellar today and get a contact number: don't let her fob you off. It's essential that I talk to the slimy little prick as soon as possible.'

'Will I couch it in those terms?'

'Then go to the office and pick up my spare keys for the flat. They're in one of the drawers on the right-hand side of my desk. If you're there in the next twenty minutes or so, call me back on this number; otherwise I'll call you on your mobile when I get to the airport.'

'My phone's got hardly any battery left.'

'There'll be a charger in the office. Janica Ahmeti's mobile number is scribbled on one of the bits of paper lying on top of my desk.'

'Will I take a cab?'

'Yes, and ask the driver to wait outside the office, then take you to the train station.'

Keira heard David sigh. 'You want me to go to Stirling and get her?'

'Yes. I'll call Cornton Vale and tell them Kaltrina's not to be released until you arrive. Try to get a hold of Janica and ask her to meet you there too.'

'Should I wait for her?'

'The main thing is to keep Kaltrina safe. If Janica is not there by the time you're ready to leave with her, don't wait.'

'Then what?'

'Take Kaltrina back through to Glasgow; go to my flat. I'll

head straight there from the airport. But don't go on public transport, David. Order a car.'

'From Stirling? Jesus! That'll be expensive!'

'I'll sort it out later, don't worry. Make sure you get dropped right outside the apartment block. When you get into the flat, lock the door and don't open it to anyone. If I need to call you I'll let the phone ring three times then hang up and call you back, otherwise don't pick up. Okay?'

'Aye, whatever you say.'

Keira hung up, rang directory enquiries for Cornton Vale's number and jotted it down on a pad that lay beside the phone. Then she quickly dialled another number, shuffling around impatiently until eventually she heard a click followed by a message.

'Gary? If you're listening can you pick up?' She waited a few moments to give him a chance to get to the phone, but nothing happened so she left a message. 'Can you meet me at my flat around teatime tonight? There's a client of mine, a girl – I want you to arrest her.'

Nineteen

The whole world seemed to be moving in slow motion – the drivers on the road from Waterfoot to Belfast International airport, the car-rental clerk, the check-in staff, the passengers boarding the plane – even the painkillers she'd swallowed a couple of hours earlier were taking their time kicking in.

Keira was on her third double-shot espresso and starting to get the jitters. She had put in a call to Cornton Vale and told them that under no circumstances were they to release Kaltrina Dervishi until her assistant arrived to escort her. Even there, the operator seemed to take for ever to write the message down. The prison operated a 'reduced service' at the weekend and she got the impression that the girl at the other end of the line was either a part-timer or an inmate.

After a call to her mother – to let her know about the funeral arrangements and tell her she'd drive down to Scaur as soon as she'd figured out what to do with Kaltrina Dervishi – she tried to get hold of the Advocate Depute, but so far had only managed to get Sellar's answering service.

At the back of her mind she knew the son-of-a-bitch was avoiding her calls. She'd also tried to check in with David, but his phone kept diverting to voicemail.

There was nothing much she could do now until she got to Glasgow, but there was something else nagging at the back of her mind that she couldn't coax into anything resembling a clear thought: when it did hit her, it was too late; the aeroplane had already left the runway. Keira immediately reached up and pressed the overhead call button. She unbuckled her seatbelt and was halfway down the aisle when the announcement came over the speaker system that the captain had not yet extinguished the seatbelt sign and would the passenger please return to her seat.

A female member of the cabin crew was already heading towards her.

'I'm afraid you have to go back to your seat, Madam.'

'I need to get a message to someone. It's very important.'

'There's nothing you can do about that right now; you have to return to your seat.'

'Please. I need the captain to get a message to the police in Glasgow.'

The stewardess was blocking the aisle, preventing Keira from going any further. She'd also taken hold of her arm. 'I really need you sit down, Madam, then once the seatbelt sign . . .'

But Keira was talking over her.

'Are you listening to what I'm saying? I need to get a message to the police. It's an emergency.'

'I understand, but—'

'You don't fucking understand!' snapped Keira, losing her cool. 'I'm a lawyer and someone I represent could – at this very minute – be in danger. Please can you let me speak to the captain, or get a message to him to contact the police.'

'I will just as soon as I can, but I have to insist you sit down. The cockpit is locked during take-off and landing, so there's nothing I can do until the seatbelt signs go off. Then I'll talk to him, but you have to sit down . . . please.'

Keira knew she had no choice. If she started screaming and shouting at the stewardess, they'd put her down as a 'crazy' and there would be no way they'd let her talk to anyone. All she could do for the moment was return to her seat and wait.

The passenger in the seat next to her, a guy wearing a business suit, kept his head buried in his newspaper as Keira squeezed in beside him, unaware that it was because of him she'd sounded the alarm in the first place.

He'd boarded before her and had taken his seat near the back of the aircraft. As soon as Keira had stepped on the plane she could smell it: someone wearing too much aftershave. As she approached her seat her heart sank when she realized that she would be sitting next to him. That's what triggered the memory of the stale, musky odour left behind after the break-in at her apartment. It suddenly struck her that it was the last place David should be taking Kaltrina.

There were a few possible explanations as to why nothing had been taken. Either the intruder was leaving something behind – bugging devices or surveillance cameras – or he was sending a message to Keira that he knew where she lived: letting her know that she was being watched. Either way, Kaltrina would not be safe there. Keira was annoyed with herself for getting drunk the night before. The subsequent hangover had affected her thinking.

She had to get a message to David.

The illuminated seatbelt sign finally went out.

Keira was on her feet again, heading for the stewardesses before they'd finished unclipping their belts in the jump seats at the front of the aircraft. She took a card from her purse as she approached and handed it to the girl she had spoken to a few minutes earlier.

'I really am a lawyer, and I need to get in touch with the police in Glasgow. I'm sorry I swore, but it's very important. Could you please ask the pilot, or whoever it is you ask, how I go about that?'

The stewardess stared back at Keira for a few seconds, considering what to do.

'Please. It could literally be a matter of life or death.'

'Wait here,' said the young woman as she turned and knocked on the bulkhead door. A few seconds later it opened and she disappeared inside.

When she re-emerged she handed Keira back her card. 'The captain says he's sorry, but there is nothing he can do. It's against the rules.'

Keira made to protest, but the girl gestured with her hand. 'Let me finish. He also said if you took your mobile to the toilet at the rear of the aircraft and made a call, there would be very little anyone could do, but that didn't come from him. If there are any repercussions he'll deny ever having said it.'

'I don't have a phone on me.'

The stewardess stared back at her as if to say, *Are you kidding me?* then gave a slight shrug. 'I'm sorry, then, there's nothing else I can do. The plane doesn't have a Pico cell anyway: you'd be lucky to get a signal.' Keira nodded like she knew what a Pico cell was and said, 'Thank you,' before turning and heading back to her seat.

The guy in the business suit said something as Keira sat down, which she didn't quite catch. 'Excuse me?'

'I said are you okay?'

'Not really, no.'

'If you don't mind me saying—'

'Actually, I do mind,' she interrupted. 'Usually when sentences start like that, I do mind. It's like, "No offence, but..." Same thing! Straight away you know someone is going to say something offensive...'

'I was going to say, you look like you could use a helping hand.'

Keira turned and looked at the guy properly. He had a large round face and laugh-lines at the side of his eyes from smiling too much. Everything about him said 'friendly', even his soft Dublin accent had warmth in it. She suddenly felt guilty. 'I apologize. I've got a bitch of a hangover that's making me a bit cranky. My day started off shit and has been going downhill ever since.'

'Would you like to borrow my phone?'

'Do you know what a Pico cell is?'

'It's like a signal booster for mobile phones on aeroplanes to help them communicate with the ground.'

'The air hostess said the plane doesn't have one, so it probably won't work.'

'It's worth a try. You might get lucky and pick up a ground signal. They just tell you that because they haven't figured out a way of monetizing its usage. It's perfectly safe to use mobile phones on a plane, they just don't know how to charge for it, so they let you think it's dangerous.'

'What, are you an engineer or something?'

'A priest.'

'You're kidding!'

'Unfortunately not!'

'You're not in uniform.'

'Wearing the kit outside of the church is considered a bit too dangerous these days. It marks us out as a target. The Vatican has relaxed the rules a little to take that into account.'

'I don't suppose you know Father Anthony in Waterfoot?'

'Sure, I know him very well. One of the few priests with that added quality lacking in many of the others . . . spirituality. If you cut him down the middle his blood would run clear . . . or the colours of the Tricolour, probably both. I'd bet my life savings he's the reason for your hangover.'

'He was the one pouring, but I was the one drinking.'

The priest handed her his phone. 'Go make your call and we'll have a proper chat when you're through.'

Keira made her way along the aisle and locked herself in one of the small toilets at the rear of the aircraft.

The first number she tried was her friend, DSI Gary Hammond's, but the phone just beeped a few times then made a continuous tone before the words 'no signal' appeared on the screen. Keira waited a few seconds then pressed redial. The same thing happened. As she stood staring at the phone wondering what to do next the word 'searching' appeared in the top left-hand corner followed by three small bars. She quickly dialled David's number and pressed the green call symbol: a few seconds later she heard his ringtone, followed by the voicemail message.

She was tense and hurried: aware the signal could drop out at any moment. 'David, don't go to the flat. Call Detective Superintendent Hammond straight away and arrange to meet him somewhere else, but don't go to the flat, okay? They know where I live. They've been in there. Don't take Kaltrina to the flat.'

Keira hung up and dialled 999. The phone at the other end started to ring before it beeped a few times and the words 'no signal' appeared again.

'Come on!' shouted Keira.

The stewardess was knocking at the door.

'Are you okay in there?'

'Fine, thank you.'

Keira pressed the redial button, but it was no good.

The signal was gone.

There was nothing else for her to do but sit it out and try again as soon as the plane landed. That wouldn't be for another hour.

By then Kaltrina Dervishi could be dead.

Twenty

Keira wondered if she was the only person taking the situation seriously. She'd expected to see a few police officers milling around, or at least a patrol-car waiting, when she arrived outside her block of flats, but the street was empty except for a few parked cars and an old guy out walking his dog.

She paid the taxi driver then quickly made her way across the grass island to the glass entrance door.

She climbed the stairs and hurried along the corridor towards the front door of her flat, the cold, concrete walls amplifying the smallest sounds and sending strange, hollow echoes reverberating up and down its empty length.

She was out of breath.

The small flight bag looped awkwardly over her left shoulder kept falling in front of her as she fished around in her handbag for a set of keys. Even though most people were shut up indoors getting ready for the week ahead, the building seemed quieter than usual.

Eventually Keira found the key, twisted it in the lock and bumped the door open with her backside.

The door at the end of the short hallway leading into the kitchen was wide open and she could see David standing at the sink. He turned as he heard her come into the hall.

'You made it.'

'Didn't you get my message?' she asked, dropping her bags

on the floor.

'Mobile's been dead for most of the day. Couldn't find a charger at the office, but it's fine, everything went okay.'

'I tried you here as well as soon as I landed.' She took a few paces forward until she stood framed in the doorway of the kitchen.

'Really? The phone hasn't rung once.'

Kaltrina Dervishi, who had been sitting with her feet up on the sofa watching television, stood and acknowledged Keira with a slight nod of the head. 'Thank you, Keira, for everything,' she said, lifting her shoulders in an awkward little shrug. 'I am confused what happen.'

'You're not the only one.'

'Are you okay?' David had picked up on Keira's distracted stare. 'You're standing there like you've got a toffee stuck up your arse and you've forgotten how to chew.'

'We can't stay here. We need to go.'

'Now?'

'Straight away; it's not safe.'

'I was just making Kaltrina something to eat. Wee bird hasn't eaten for a few hours. At least, I think that's what she said: she was miming in an Albanian accent.'

Keira was still preoccupied trying to figure out why everything felt so wrong. 'What about Janica Ahmeti? Did you get a hold of her?'

'I left her a message, but she didn't show.'

'Have you heard from her?'

'No.'

'No sign of the police or Gary Hammond?' continued Keira, talking over him. 'I expected them to be here.'

'The police have been and gone, left about an hour ago, but

no sign of your pal Hammond. They asked if you would give them a call. Didn't seem too fussed, but they want to have a chat. The implication being that they're getting a wee bit concerned you're losing your grip on reality. Are you not going to introduce us?'

Keira stared back at him, like she hadn't quite caught what he'd said. 'Sorry, say that again.'

'I said, are you not going to introduce us?'

Suddenly Kaltrina Dervishi screamed and lunged toward Keira, her face twisted with rage.

Keira recoiled instinctively, taking a step backwards and raising her arms in front of her chest to protect herself from the attack.

That's when she became aware of a movement behind her, and realized that Kaltrina was not screaming at her, but the figure of a man standing in the hallway. Keira didn't have to look round to know who it was. The musky odour of stale aftershave had already given the intruder's identity away. Her instinctive reaction was to spin round and lash out, but as she started her turn a sharp hollow blast punched through the air and knocked her violently to the floor. It felt as though a truck had hit her from behind. Winded and struggling against the sudden pain, she tried to sit up, but a sharp, poker-hot sensation coursed in a straight line from her pelvis to her ribcage making even the smallest movement almost impossible.

There was another hissing thud, followed in rapid succession by two others as three more shots found their targets. Out of the corner of her eye Keira saw David's head suddenly snap backwards at the neck and drop grotesquely to one side as the first bullet tore through his neck. She watched transfixed as –

in the same instant – his body lurched violently to one side and slumped to the floor with blood spurting in thin jets from two holes that had appeared in the upper half of his chest.

Keira could feel the vomit rising in her throat and had to battle hard to stop herself from throwing up. She could hear a soft, lowing groan and realized it was coming from somewhere deep within her own chest. She tried to focus her gaze, but the room was swimming around her, with images pulsing in and out of focus and a strange, rhythmic pounding in her eardrums.

Kaltrina was screaming at the gunman in Albanian as she launched herself through the air punching and kicking.

The speed and ferocity of the attack momentarily took the gunman off guard. He stepped back and raised his arm to parry her blows, but Kaltrina had connected. Her fingers dug into his face and made him cry out as she ripped at his flesh with her nails: drawing deep lines of red down the side of his cheek. The attacker lashed out with the stock of his pistol, striking her heavily several times on the back of the head as he tried to shake her off. He twisted the gun round and dug it into her rib-cage ready to loose off a shot, but Kaltrina raised her elbow in a sharp upward movement and knocked the weapon spinning from his grasp. The dull metal Beretta slid along the floor and came to rest close to Keira. She stared at it for several seconds before slowly reaching out her hand towards it. The effort sent shock waves of pain stabbing at every nerve in her body.

She heard herself groaning again.

Her fingers wrapped slowly round the knurled grip and her index finger slipped inside the trigger guard.

The gun felt impossibly heavy, but she managed to lift it off the ground and point it towards the doorway. The gunman had a large clump of Kaltrina's hair in his fist and was holding her head down as she struggled desperately to throw some punches and break his hold. As they pulled each other around in a grotesquely awkward dance Keira could feel her strength beginning to fade. All she had to do was squeeze the trigger. Suddenly Kaltrina was standing in the way, blocking the shot. Keira's mind was starting to lose focus: random thoughts crowding in on her. When she was fifteen she had tried to take her own life by slashing her wrists. It was more a cry for help than a serious suicide attempt: there was never any real danger. The situation she was in now, however, was very real. She recognized this violence and knew there could be only one outcome. Memories of what had happened to her when she was eight years old – how she had watched her uncle in the same struggle for life that Kaltrina was in now – flashed through her mind. She saw herself standing on a stairwell pointing a gun at the man attacking her uncle and knew that when she pulled the trigger she would be ending not only that man's life but her own as well. The memory had haunted her ever since, yet here she was, about to leave this world, and her final act would be to take another human being's life.

Keira heard a voice calling from another room, but couldn't make out the words. It sounded like her grandmother, but that wasn't possible.

The gunman stood side-on with his back against the wall, clutching something in his hand that glinted in the darkened hallway. He was holding Kaltrina Dervishi's dazed and battered body up by the hair as her arms swung limply by her waist and her legs kicked out lamely in front of her, in a pathetic attempt to break free from him. She was exhausted, all her energy spent, every part of her clothing dripping with blood.

Keira struggled desperately to keep her eyes open and managed to raise the Beretta one last time. She followed the line of sight down her arm and along the barrel of the gun straight to where the attacker stood, his right hand covered in blood, stabbing Kaltrina Dervishi repeatedly in the stomach.

All she had to do was squeeze the trigger.

Suddenly the gun started to shake uncontrollably, as though it had taken on a life of its own. Keira's grip slackened, her arm fell heavily to the floor and she knew she had lost the fight.

She opened her eyes again and saw the attacker drop Kaltrina Dervishi's lifeless body to the floor.

There was a presence nearby.

A figure in the gloom, standing over her, slowly raising his arms out to his side, making the shape of a cross.

Another bullet slammed into her shoulder and knocked her face down on to the hard wooden floor.

In the darkness that followed there were brief, disjointed moments of awareness: noises that seemed to echo around in the dim shadows. Keira heard raised voices, but couldn't make out what they were saying. She heard more gunshots, but for some reason they sounded louder than before. Someone was speaking her name . . . a voice she recognized, but couldn't place. Keira tried to respond, but the floor suddenly disappeared beneath her and she felt as though she was falling headlong into a silent void.

Twenty-one

Officer Tommy Aquino sat with his elbow on the desk, resting his chin in his left hand and stared at a playback of the live RSS feed from BBC Scotland's newsroom in the United Kingdom.

An attractive redhead was reading the headlines. 'There are unconfirmed reports of three fatal shootings in the Thornwood area of Glasgow early on Sunday evening. The victims, thought to be a lawyer, a legal secretary and a young woman – believed to be a client – were discovered in the lawyer's apartment at around eight o'clock yesterday evening. We'll have more on that story later in the programme.'

Aquino pulled the stem microphone attached to the headset he was wearing closer to his mouth and spoke.

'You watching this?'

'The Dervishi girl didn't last too long out in the big, bad world. Five hours then Bam! That must be a world record, no?'

'You coming down?'

'I'll meet you at the coffee station in two.'

'See you there,' replied Aquino, pulling the headset off and slamming it hard on the desk.

*

Gregg Moran made his way down the long glass corridor of the CIA's Langley headquarters wiping beads of sweat from his forehead with the sleeve of his shirt. He reached Tommy Aquino – who was waiting for him with a paper cup full of steaming black coffee.

'Drug deal gone wrong. Simple as that,' said Moran with his usual offhand tone that was beginning to piss Aquino off. 'Only there's no goddamn mention of drugs. What the hell is that all about?'

'Jesus Christ, Gregg! We told the son-of-a-bitch: only the girl dies.'

'Let's take it one problem at a time. There's no frickin mention of what should have been a significant drug find in the apartment. You think they haven't found it yet, or d'you think the shit was never there?'

'I was told the end of last week it was in place, or it was definitely going to be in place. I have no idea what the hell happened, but I'll find out.'

'We've got to feed the drug scenario into the mix: get the signal-to-noise ratio working in our favour by creating plenty of static. It was only ever a back-up plan if the lawyer started screwing us about, but she's dead now anyway, so she's got nothing to bitch about if her reputation gets trashed. It could still be useful, though. It'd buy us some time, but where the fuck is it? With her discredited – whether people believe the drugs rap or not – anything else that shows up in the meantime in relation to Abazi can be dismissed as rumour and speculation too. We got anyone on the ground over there, apart from that useless piece of shit Kade?'

'No,' replied Aquino, shrugging his shoulders. 'I already told you.'

'There needs to be some merchandise found at the crime

scene to back up the scenario that the lawyer was dirty. You think that's gonna be possible after the fact?'

'Truthfully, I don't see what the hell difference it's going to make now.'

'Without the drugs it's a straightforward homicide with one possible explanation. With the drugs it opens up all sorts of possibilities as to who and why: confuses the investigation.'

Aquino gave Moran a look. 'I don't need a fucking lecture on how it works, Moran. What I'm saying is, it's too late: the lawyer is dead, we don't need the leverage, and to try and plant it in there now just to muddy the waters would be crazy. I told you already, my information was that it had already happened. As soon as I speak to Abazi, I'll find out what the hell is going on. But let's forget about that now. Whether the drugs are there or not is minor league. We have a much bigger problem to deal with. We need to have a serious look at the possibility of replacing Abazi.'

'Jesus!' exclaimed Moran, sipping at his coffee. 'Really?'

'Every fuck-up in history has had a starting point, a moment of crisis where the wrong decision is made, that's followed very quickly by the resolution point where the undertakers stand with open coffins waiting for the guys that didn't realize they were fucking up. Our starting point was Kade getting a crack on the skull and the girl getting picked up trying to leave the goddamn country: our crisis point is right now. We've got to make sure we don't make the wrong decision.'

'If – as you say – this is the touchpaper lit, let's not wait around to get our asses blown off. If it's time to move on, let's do it. Let's clean up and get the hell out of there. If it's just a blip, then we need to have someone ready to step in and take over from Abazi, but even as I'm saying this out loud, I don't believe it's the way forward. My assessment is that the Serbian is no more. Hell, we could take the asshole down in a second: we've got a whole detachment of Navy Seals scratching their butts just up the road on the west coast of Scotland. But tempting as that scenario is, we have to play it smart. He spots one cloud of the storm coming his way and we're all catching a cold in the rain, y'know what I'm saying?'

'I think we should keep our direct involvement to a minimum . . .' replied Aquino. 'How about we wait and see who reacts first? Word on the wire is that Abazi has few friends anyway. A lot of the local, well-established drug gangs are none too happy about being constantly undercut: can't figure out where the hell he gets his supply. All they know is they're being forced out of the market. But none of them can get near him: he works with a very small unit, three or four guys at the most, and they don't take any shit. Maybe we could drop one or two of his competitors a line: give them some intel on where he's at. If a narco war breaks out and he gets hit, no one's going to look deeper than what's floating on the surface. That way our involvement is barely noticeable.'

Moran was shaking his head. 'We gotta move fast. Drive this situation in the direction we want it to go. We may be on a bus with a bomb strapped to the exhaust, but we're still in charge of the GPS. A narco war is fine, but we have no control over the outcome. Let's put some measures in place that are going to guarantee the Serbian's future is a short one.'

A female in her early twenties was striding along the corridor towards them holding a brown file full of papers. She beamed Aquino a smile as she approached. 'This just in. I've got the scoop on the lawyer you're interested in.'

'Too late, Gonzalez,' interrupted Moran. 'She's getting

measured up for a wooden sleeping bag, as we speak.'

'She's dead? Are you bullshitting me?'

Aquino shook his head.

'Shit! I just hit the jackpot.'

'What'd you get?'

'Got up early this morning, too . . . should have stayed in bed.'

'What'd you get?' repeated Aquino.

'Her grandma just died . . .'

'Hold the front page!'

'Hold your dick Moran, or next time you need a favour I'll ask my supervisor if putting the CIA central computer to this sort of use without an Operations Title or authorization is strictly legal. Maybe tell them who it was that requested the info as well.'

'So, what did you get?' asked Aquino for the third time.

'Grandmother, mother and daughter were all living under an assumed name.'

'Okay. How'd you find that out?'

'Granny's death certificate. She wanted to be cremated back in Ireland, but the name on the certificate doesn't match the one she's been using in Scotland. Lynch is not the family name. Mother and daughter changed it legally, Granny never bothered. When we followed that on we found out the lawyer has a major paramilitary connection through her father: Granny's son.'

Aquino raised an eyebrow. 'Shit! You just never know the minute, do you?'

'How strong a connection?' asked Moran, suddenly showing an interest in what Gonzalez was saying.

'At one stage the father was in line for the top job in the Irish Republican Army: his brother – her uncle – was a god-damn hit man and, although not a card-carrying member of the IRA, that's where most of his work came from. Curiously, her online presence is almost zero, but by a happy coincidence MI5 have a lot of intel on her, all to do with her work as a lawyer. She was quite outspoken and regarded as a troublemaker – anti-establishment. They keep a "soft" eye on her. There's been a shift in the law over there – or they're trying to shift it – so that, effectively, instead of the state having to prove a person committed a crime, the person has to prove they didn't: something to do with agreeing admissible evidence and disclosure, I don't know the ins and outs, but she was fighting it all the way: got a "first in, last-out" work ethic. A lot of the Establishment don't like her; shame she's dead. I even did some character profiling. I liked her.'

'I told you she had something going on,' said Moran. 'All that therapy bullshit when she was younger! "Events" don't get much more "significant" than having two terrorists in the family.'

'D'you still need this,' asked Gonzalez, holding up the file, 'or did I give up my lie-in for nothing?'

'Sorry. We've only just heard the news ourselves.'

'You want me to shred it?'

'I'll hang on to it, but thanks.'

'Yeah! I'll give you one,' chipped in Moran.

'The expression is, "I owe you one."'

'I know.'

Gonzalez thrust the file into Aquino's hand and set off down the corridor shaking her head. 'You're such a loser, Moron.'

'That's Moran!'

'I know,' she shouted over her shoulder as she disappeared round the bend.

Moran waited until she was out of earshot. 'Goddamn it,

if we'd known this earlier we wouldn't have wasted our time setting the lawyer bitch up for a drugs rap. This is frickin dynamite!'

'Was frickin dynamite,' replied Aquino.

'You screwing Gonzalez, you sneaky son-of-a-bitch?'

'She's screwing me.'

Twenty-two

As he folded the thin square of foil it crossed his mind that he might be making a big mistake, but he was the test pilot and the lure of hitting the big 'float' was too hard to resist. Jay-Go had been clean for a couple of weeks now, but with all the shit that had happened in the last few days, he needed to relax and forget, even if it was only for a short while.

The quality of heroin he was used to slamming was at the lower end of the purity scale, forty, fifty per cent if he was lucky. This bag was straight off the plane, uncut; if he shot the sort of bang he was used to, he'd end up on a slab with some socially retarded ghoul doing a dodgy make-up job on him. He had to be careful.

This was considered an experiment: see how far he could fly on a lower dose. If it was as clean as he hoped, he'd have a good hit and still live to tell the tale. Then, the plan was to market the powder as Daz.

On the upside, he'd finally made the big score: he only had to sell half of it and he'd still make nearly twenty-five grand; maybe more if he cut it with some caffeine and dropped the price.

It was all profit, too. No overheads, no down-the-line dealers taking their cut, no worries as far as he could see. If he got rid of the whole lot he could buy his own boat and sail to New York, New York, so good they named it twice. From there it was a quick flight to LA and straight into rehab. Screw Glasgow, screw Abazi and his crew of shithead-sister-shaggers; Jay-Go was going straight.

Easterhouse, Glasgow, so shit they named it once.

Jay-Go's mind was in a tailspin; Miss Lynch was dead and that was wrong. He was supposed to be looking out for her. He'd given her the Jay-Go promise, then screwed the deal. Another person to add to the list of people he'd let down over the years.

The lawyer had always done her best for him. Once, when it looked like he was heading to the Bar-L for anything between four and a half to sixteen for dealing and illegal possession of a firearm – she'd pulled something out of the hat at the last minute and saved his skinny hole. He'd gone down for a year, done six months and been released on probation – which involved having to check into a clinic every day for testing – but that was still a result.

'Ah told ye the bogey-man was comin', Miss. Ye should have fuckin' listened,' said Jay-Go out loud to the empty room. 'Who's looking out for you now, Miss? Jesus and his posse of guardian angels? And, who's looking out for me now, eh?'

First thing he had to do was test the gear: make sure it wasn't a bag of baking powder. Then hit the streets and offload as much as he could as quickly as possible.

After that, he'd get his bony arse out of town.

There had been nothing on the news about her funeral: where or when. Jay-Go wasn't ever down for a pall-bearers' job, but if he could find out where it was going to be held, or where she was going to be buried, he'd maybe slip by and pay his last respects before he left.

Something else was bothering him. Should he offload the

gear locally, or take it out of town? It would be a lot safer to head over to Ireland with it and open up for business there, but Jay-Go didn't even have enough money to get to the ferry, let alone buy a ticket for the crossing.

He'd have to sell some of it first. But as soon as it hit the street the chase would start. Whoever owned it would know exactly where it had come from and track him down. Jay-Go's hunch was that caballo this pure could only have come from one source – if it was true, he'd have Abazi on his arse, and that mad fuck didn't operate a buy-back scheme, he went straight for the kill.

He glanced around at the bare peeling walls. The floor of the living room was covered in filth. A one-bedroomed pigsty paid for by the state. Most of the time he didn't notice the amount of crap everywhere, but today was different. Today there was the possibility to do something about it and that was giving him ideas. The benefit money he received every week was supposed to go towards its upkeep: heating, cleaning and maintenance, but by the time he'd bought enough cigarettes, beer and blow to get him through, there was barely enough left for food.

All that was about to change.

It was Jay-Go time.

He squeezed some lemon juice over the small pile of pale brown powder sitting on the foil, to make it dissolve properly, then boiled it up over his lighter. As the paste liquefied he quickly sucked it into the syringe standing ready on the coffee table before dipping it into a cup of iced water to cool it down.

Jay-Go strapped his arm to raise a vein, then eased the needle under the skin and gently squeezed the syringe until it was empty.

Even now, after years of doing this, it still surprised him how instantaneous the urge to throw up was. As soon as the tar hit his bloodstream he wanted to vomit. The sensation didn't last long, but it was always unpleasant.

He swallowed hard a few times and tried not to retch.

Just a few more seconds!

He started counting down in his head: preparing himself.

'Ten, nine, eight . . .'

He only got as far as seven.

It was in this initial stage of euphoria that the idea struck him.

Small-time thinking getting in the way of the big ideas! No point scrabbling around with the poor folk selling the odd bag here and there: go for the big score man. Sell it all in one hit!

A thin smile of contentment spread across his face and his eyelids started to droop. 'Man, this powder will wash your brain whiter than white,' he said as his head dipped forward and his mind floated upwards on a warm thermal until it reached the jet stream.

*

'Puff?'

'Who's this?'

'Jay-Go.'

'Awright Jay-Go, when did ye get out?'

'Few weeks ago . . . on probation.'

'What's up?'

'Fancy a beer?'

'They'd have you straight back in the Bar-L without yer arse ever touching the ground, pal; you can't associate with me, I'm a known criminal.'

'I don't want to associate with you; I want to buy you a beer. You still working for the Holy Man?'

'The odd job here and there, but I don't discuss business over the telephone, dude; too risky these days.'

'Any chance you could set up a meet with him?'

'With you?' Puff replied, a bit too quickly for Jay-Go's liking. 'I don't think so, Jay-Go. You're just out of the jail, bag man. You'll have the Funnies checking your every move. Nobody's gonnae give you any gear to sell in a million years. I can tell you now the Holy Man won't touch you.'

'I'm not buying. I'm selling.'

'Aye right! You're charged up, dude . . . I can tell by your voice. Call me when you're around the turn.'

'Wait, Puff! I've had a wee bang, that's all. Just testing the gear to make sure it's a runner. But I'm fine. Ah know what I'm saying, Ah know what I'm doin'. I've got something to sell, but it isnae just that. The hit on Miss Lynch: I might know something about it. She was the Holy Man's brief, he'll want to know too.'

'So tell me and I'll pass it on.'

For a brief moment it crossed Jay-Go's mind that maybe the Holy Man wasn't the best choice of players to sell to. All of his crew – especially Puff – had a hair trigger when it came to throwing a punch. It could make negotiations difficult, but the guy had some money behind him and was less likely to screw him over.

'C'mon Puff, put in a call. It's not just the lawyer thing. I've got a big score for him. If I end up taking it elsewhere and the Holy Man finds out he could have had first bid on some smack that's Janice Joplin-pure . . .' Jay-Go didn't finish the sentence. Puff didn't need reminding of the Holy Man's tendency towards violence. 'C'mon, *I* know I'm a fuck-up, but *you* know I'm straight up. Put in a call.'

There was a brief silence then, 'I'll think about it.'

The line went dead.

Jay-Go went to the fridge to get himself a can of beer. He popped a couple of Dihydrocodeine from a blister pack he had in his pocket and swallowed them down with a few swigs of lager. The withdrawal had started already. His head was hurting and he was getting the shivers.

There was no doubt in his mind that Puff would call back and he wanted to be ready. He retrieved a spoon from the kitchen drawer and tipped a few grams of heroin into a clear plastic bag to take with him, then put a small amount on the end of the spoon and had a quick snort: one up each nostril.

The jangles were just beginning to settle when his phone rang.

'You know St Benedict's on Westerhouse Road? If you wait in the bus stop outside, someone'll pick you up about half-eight.'

'That's right across the road from the polis station. I could meet in the car park at McDonald's just along a bit on the other side.'

'Aye, that's a good idea, and when you're still standing there waiting at one o'clock in the morning you'll know it's because you're a fuckin' dickhead. Just meet me where I told you, awright!'

*

Two hours later Jay-Go was standing in the bus shelter trying his best to shield himself from the rain sweeping along

Westerhouse Road in great torrents. The wind was gusting through the shelter as though it wasn't even there. With no money for the bus fare, Jay-Go had walked the mile or so from his flat and his clothes were soaked through. As he stood shivering in the darkness a small white car pulled up.

Without winding down the window Puff signalled from the passenger seat for Jay-Go to jump in the back.

'Unseasonably cold weather we're having. You not got a jacket, bag man?' asked Puff when Jay-Go was on board and they were safely under way. 'It's wild out there.'

'It was summertime when I left the flat,' answered Jay-Go, referring to the fact that Puff was late.

'Aye, sorry about that. Had to stop and pick something up along the way. D'you think the amount of fags you've smoked over your lifetime has affected the climate? It was roasting last week.'

'Where we goin'?'

'Off to the lab, via the dump. I take it you brought along something for us to have a look at?'

Jay-Go reached into the front and handed Puff the small plastic bag full of dull brown powder.

'Man, that's a fat bag. Where'd you get the money to buy this?'

'If the Holy Man likes it he can buy it off me.'

'If it checks out we'll take you up to see the man himself. How much have you got altogether?'

'I'll discuss that with the Holy Man, don't you worry yourself.'

'You carrying any armoury, dude?'

'A 007.'

'You can hang on to it for the moment, but if we go see him

you'll have to hand it over.'

'Aye, no worries.' Jay-Go slipped the PPK out from his belt and placed it by his side on the back seat.

Jay-Go thought he heard Puff mumble something under his breath. 'What?'

Puff looked over his shoulder at him. 'What d'you mean, "what"?'

'I thought you said something.'

'You're hearing things, dude, I never said a thing.'

Puff turned to the young black guy who was driving the car. 'You mumbling in your sleep, Frica?'

'I never opened my mouth.'

'When we at the dump?' asked Puff.

'Another ten minutes.'

'Fuck sake!' said Puff, shaking his head. 'Better pull over. It's gonnae drive me mad.'

Frica turned off the main road into a quieter street and drove along until he could find somewhere to park.

Jay-Go lifted the PPK off the seat again and held it down between his legs, hidden from view. 'What's going on, boys?'

As Frica pulled into the kerb Puff opened the passenger door and jumped out.

'I'll just be a minute,' he said, leaning back inside and picking something up from the footwell.

Jay-Go's grip on the PPK tightened as he watched Puff move round the back of the car and open the boot. The mumbling noise was suddenly louder, more urgent. Through the gap between the boot lid and the bottom of the rear window Jay-Go saw a hammer slamming repeatedly into whatever was on the floor of the boot. Each blow matched with the dull, sickening thud of metal hitting flesh. Puff continued to rain down blows until the pathetic sound of muffled screams had finally stopped, then he slammed the lid closed and climbed back into the car, wet through from the rain and dripping with blood that had spattered up his arms and over his jacket.

He was breathing hard. 'Put your foot down, Frica, and let's get to the dump.'

No one said anything else for the rest of the journey.

Twenty-three

'Anything goes down, toot the horn and meet us round the back, Frica, awright?'

'Aye, no bother.' Frica slipped the car into neutral and switched off the engine. Puff and Jay-Go left him sitting in the car and headed across Dumbarton Road to the Lios Mor.

Puff led the way as the two men pushed through the panelled door into the pub and threaded past the bar to an area at the back, nestling in the gloom. Four men were sitting round a table filled with empty beer glasses in one of the high-backed leather-lined booths that edged the red and gold damask papered walls.

A meeting was in progress.

More men loitered close to the table with drinks in their hands, their only purpose to shield the table from view. Keeping one eye on the meeting and the other on anyone entering the busy bar, they stood and watched in silence.

Puff nodded to one of the guys. 'Awright, Happyslap?'

'In good shape, wee man, in good shape! On ye go. The Holy Man said you were comin'. Is the junkie with you?'

Puff turned to Jay-Go. 'Aye, he's with me. The Holy Man knows.'

Happyslap flattened his hand against Jay-Go's chest. 'Ye carrying anything, horse-head?'

Any other time Jay-Go would have pulled the guy up for calling him a junkie to his face, but as he was a guest at the party, it would be considered out of order to cause any aggravation.

'Got a 007,' he replied, trying to think of a comeback.

'Need to take that from you, Mister Bond.'

Jay-Go stared back him. He realized he was still a bit too wasted to think of anything better to say than, 'No problem.' He should have added 'Miss Moneypenny', but the moment had passed.

A guy in his late forties – who was already starting to lose his hair and looked more like an accountant than one of Glasgow's most notorious criminals – was doing most of the talking as they approached the table. This was Jim McMaster known to everyone as the Holy Man. Jay-Go had heard a lot about him over the years, but never met him in person. He was a devout churchgoer. Whenever he or one of his team committed a murder he'd say prayers for the deceased, take confession, then leave a generous donation in the collection plate as he left the church – usually in tears.

Jay-Go recognized two of the others at the table. He was surprised to see Nick-Nick Carter from the South Side and Big Paul, leader of the Govan team, sitting there. Both of them were heavyweights and not the sort to keep company with their main business rival. *Something must be up*, thought Jay-Go. The other guy sitting to the Holy Man's left looked out of place. His skinny, hangdog face had a fresh scar that ran from the corner of his mouth to just under his left ear and his eyes flicked around the room nervously.

Puff and Jay-Go waited near the table until the Holy Man stopped talking, then Puff leant over. 'Excuse me, this is the guy Ah wis telling you about, Holy Man. This is Jay-Go.'

'How did ye get on with yer wee errand?'

'All sorted, Holy Man. Dropped him off at the dump.'

Holy Man took a few moments to look Jay-Go up and down, then said, 'This better be a good one, son, 'cause you look like a waster to me. I'm having a small funeral gathering at present. Go and get yourself a pinkie sling at the bar and raise a glass to the deceased. Happyslap will give you a shout when I'm ready.'

*

'Who's "the deceased"?' asked Jay-Go as he and Puff made their way back to the bar.

'The guy in the boot of the car. Holy Man didn't like the colour of his jumper.'

'Seriously?'

'Wise up, Jay-Go, for fucksake . . . The Holy Man's colour blind.'

'You takin the piss, Puff?'

'He owed the Holy Man some money, but was reluctant to hand it over.'

'What the fuck is a pinkie sling?'

'It's a test.'

'A test?'

'Like an initiation . . . it's a drink. All the white spirits: gin, rum, vodka, white wine, then you get to choose either Coke or orange juice as the mixer. If I was you I'd go for the orange juice.'

'Ah prefer Coke. But is there something in the Coke? Is it spiked or something?'

'Naw, it's just Coke.'

'Does it taste better with the orange juice?'

'Naw, it's just that with the orange juice – when you're drinking it – you don't have to look at the finger floating around.'

Jay-Go was at the bar on his own, waiting for the barman to finish mixing his cocktail. The barman made a big show of pouring the spirits into a shaker, then tipped the contents into a highball glass full of ice.

'Ye want Coke or jaffa?'

Jay-Go peered over at the glass to make sure that nothing else had been slipped in.

'Coke.'

'Ye sure?'

'Positive.'

Instead of placing the glass down in front of him as Jay-Go had expected, the barman disappeared through a door into the back room taking the cocktail with him. He reappeared a few minutes later and set the drink on a coaster before sliding it toward him.

'Pinkie sling . . . and Coke.'

Happyslap appeared over his shoulder.

'Where's Puff?'

'Went for a piss,' replied Jay-Go without taking his eyes off the finger, suspended in clear brown liquid, near the bottom of the glass.

'Holy Man will see you now, horse-head. Bring your drink.'

Nick-Nick Carter, Big Paul and the guy with the scar were making their way towards the exit as Jay-Go shuffled past them. Jay-Go's paranoia was kicking in. He was sure the fidgety guy with the scar was eyeballing him. Jay-Go nodded to him as they crossed paths. 'If you're after a ten-by-eight, I'm fresh out, wee man,' he said, returning the stare.

The guy looked away.

*

The Holy Man stared down at his clasped hands.

Jay-Go was only just beginning to level out. The tremors had stopped and his skin had lost the clammy feel. He was still twitching, but not as badly as before. He sat opposite the Holy Man and placed his drink gently on the table so as not to disturb him.

'Just the two of us, then?' said Jay-Go when the silence had got too much to bear.

The Holy Man didn't reply. Either he hadn't heard or he was ignoring the comment.

Jay-Go picked up his glass and was about to take a large mouthful when he remembered the finger. He rattled the ice around and placed the cocktail back on the table. The Holy Man raised his eyes and stared straight at him.

Without saying a word the Holy Man suddenly leant forward and slapped Jay-Go hard across the face.

'Jesus!'

Jay-Go didn't react in time to pull away and caught the full force of the blow.

The skin on his cheek was red and stinging and there were tears rolling down his face.

'Don't ever come to see me pissed or jacked-up. Don't ever show up to meet me after you've taken whatever shit it is you've been taking. I don't deal with junkies, drunks or dropouts and you look like all fuckin' three rolled into one.'

'You told me to go to the bar and get a drink,' Jay-Go whined, before his brain had a chance to hit the off button.

The Holy Man was giving him the stare.

'Is that lip?'

Jay-Go shook his head.

'Are you sitting there giving me fucking lip?'

'No, Holy Man.'

'I told you to go get a drink, and raise a glass to the dead. You were jacked-up when you arrived and now you're sitting in my pub giving off to me.'

'Really, Holy Man, I'm not. I apologize. I'm really no'. I just want to put a bit of business your way. That's all.'

'You're a liability. You're a threat. Arseholes like you'll do and say anything to get your next bag of scrag and I don't like that. I don't like people like you in the vicinity. And now you're giving me lip. Fuck me! Let's hear what you have to say. If I like it you're safe, if I don't then I'll cut off every one of your fingers and use them in my special cocktails . . . in the meantime, here's what you have to do. Pick up that glass and take a drink. You don't have to finish it, but the finger has to touch your lips. If it does, we'll talk. If it doesn't, or you don't want to drink . . . you can fuck off. Now that you know the terms and conditions, do you still want to play? Or d'you want to give off to me again and we'll take it from there?'

Jay-Go stared at the drink. The finger looked pale through the glass and had dark twists of blood seeping from the severed end. Suddenly he reached out, grabbed the highball glass and lifted it to his lips. As he tipped the cocktail and started to drink the finger flipped round and bobbed to the surface. The mixture of alcohol and Coke wasn't unpleasant, but it couldn't disguise the metallic, coppery taste of fresh blood. Jay-Go resisted the urge to retch. He knew this was a test, but a 'pass' was no good to him, he needed a distinction.

As the raw end of the finger brushed against his lips, Jay-Go opened his mouth, sucked the finger between his teeth on to his tongue and started to chew. It took him several minutes of grinding and crunching before it was even possible to swallow it, but eventually he opened his mouth and pushed his tongue out to show that the finger had been consumed.

'What's your pitch, horse-head?' smiled the Holy Man. He eased back into the leather padding and took his hands off the table. 'I'm told you know something about my deceased lawyer. Let's start with business first, then you can tell me what you know. I was about to order something to eat. Fancy some scampi and fries?'

Jay-Go shook his head. 'I'm full up.'

'Puff tells me you've got something to sell?'

Jay-Go nodded.

'How much?'

'Half a kilo.'

'First thing I want to know is this: why don't you want to sell it all?'

'All?' replied Jay-Go like a bad actor.

'The Holy Man knows everything that's going on. The wee skinny Serb that was sitting to my left a minute ago.'

'The guy with the scar and the face like a pair of dog's balls?'

'Aye, that's the one.' For the second time since he'd arrived at the table Jay-Go caught a smile on the Holy Man's face.

'He's my new best friend. Works for a guy called Fisnik Abazi who has just become public enemy number one. The hooker probably deserved everything she got, but don't hit the lawyer ... my goddamn lawyer. Dog-baw's name is Edi Leka: one of Abazi's drivers and general janitors: our man in the know. Claims he's disgruntled with his present employer and looking for a way out, which in the fullness of time we will provide for him. He's been telling me that Abazi is missing a kilo of uncut *heroina* and, understandably, wants it back. Then suddenly you, Mister Cellophane himself, shows up and offers me half a kilo of something sounding very similar to what Mister Abazi has misplaced, and I'm sitting wondering why are you not offering me the whole bag: where's the other half-kilo? Either you're in negotiations with someone else, or there's someone else involved, in which case, I'm out. *Or* you're keeping some back for your own private consumption. Who knows? Could be some *other* fucked-up idea you've got going, I don't really care. If it did once belong to Mister Abazi, then I am definitely interested, but either you sell it all to me or there's nothing to talk about. Before we start negotiations, why don't you tell me where you got it and how much you want for it? Bearing in mind that I could just take you out the back, tie you to a chair and beat the shite out of you until you tell me where the stuff is. Who's going to give a shit if you go for a swim in the River Clyde wearing a pair of concrete Speedos. You know what I'm saying?'

Jay-Go looked to the door at the front of the bar and wondered how far he would get if he made a run for it. Even if he reached the exit, from that moment on he would have to keep running.

Jay-Go had no choice now but to face it out with the Holy Man.

'I do have the whole kilo, but I'm only prepared to sell you half right at this moment in time. There's no one else I'm talking to, no one else involved, and if the sale goes through I promise to sell you the other half. I want thirty first time round and twenty, second. I know its value on the street, so I think that's fair.'

The Holy Man sat silently mulling things over for a few moments, then said, 'I'm going to tell you a wee story. The information I'm getting is that when the ambulances showed up at my lawyer's flat, one of them sped off straight away with a stretcher in the back. The other two ambulances stuck around until the body bags came out. But my sources tell me that only two body bags appeared. Three victims, two body bags: you don't need to be a genius to work that one out. Edi Leka told us the name of the guy that carried out the hit. An Albanian called Engjell E Zeze, but they call him the Watcher. Leka was supposed to take him back to the airport afterwards, but the rumour is that somebody survived. The Watcher is sticking around. If it's the hooker, he's got to finish the job, but it could be Keira Lynch. In which case I think he'll still go back in. Not because Abazi wants her dead, but as a matter of professional pride. Either way, if there is a survivor, they're not gonnae last long. Where is this all leading? War has been declared. Abazi and the Watcher are top of my most wanted list. I'm forming a coalition and we're about to go into battle.' The Holy Man leant over and lifted Jay-Go's glass off the table. 'Here, you may want to finish off the dregs, before I deliver the bad news.'

Jay-Go lifted the glass and drained it to the bottom.

'You may be sitting there wondering why is the Holy Man telling me this wee story?'

Jay-Go nodded.

'Our first line of attack is the silence of money. That's our main weapon.'

Jay-Go didn't know why, but he nodded again. He had no idea what the Holy Man was talking about, but he wanted to give the impression that, not only was he following the train of thought, but he might have some ideas of his own to throw into the mix.

The Holy Man was still talking, '... drop our street prices below anything that Abazi is offering. Even if we have to give the shit away for free we are going to put an end to his business. It'll only work if all the big players are on board, but so far we seem to have a cross-party agreement. And because of that, the value of your property has just halved. So I'm offering you fifteen for the first instalment and ten for the second. If you accept, we'll shake hands now and you can give me your bank details. If you decline, you run the risk of Abazi finding out that you have his smack and all the grief that goes with that scenario. You won't last a minute out there.'

Jay-Go was starting to sweat again. His hands were trembling worse than ever and his brain was pounding on the inside of his skull. Fifteen thousand was far less than the heroin was worth, but Jay-Go had never had so much money in his entire life and the Holy Man was right: once it was off his hands the pressure was off as far as Abazi was concerned. If he'd known that's who it belonged to he would have left the shit where he'd found it, but it was too late now.

The Holy Man was speaking again.

'Don't take too long to think it over, wee man. As far as I can see your jacket's on a wobbly nail. It's less than you were hoping for, but once I shake your hand, you know I'm not going to fuck you over. It's a cast-iron deal. Think of the money you're losing as your contribution to the war effort.'

Jay-Go was battling with the cocktail for control of his eyelids and so far the pinkie sling was winning. He needed something else to drink, and some class A to straighten him out.

Suddenly he reached his right hand across the table and after a cursory shake the deal was done. 'Puff tells me you brought a large sample with you, so we'll keep that and you can go party with a few quid in your back pocket.' The Holy Man shouted over to Happyslap, who was standing nearby.

'Big man, get Jay-Go a thousand from petty cash as a gesture of goodwill, and order me a scampi and fries, would you?' He was talking to Jay-Go again. 'D'you want to know whose finger it was?'

Jay-Go shook his head.

'You should have had it with the orange juice. That way you don't have to look at it. Now . . . tell me what you know about the hit on Keira Lynch.'

'I was there when it happened.'

Twenty-four

'Armed guard! Seriously?' Keira's mother was walking along the clinical-blue corridor towards a firearms officer with an MP5 sub-machine gun clamped across his chest, who was standing sentry at the entrance to the acute trauma ward.

'A precaution, Mrs Lynch,' answered Detective Superintendent Gary Hammond as he walked alongside her. His broad face and angular jawline looked like they had been chiselled out of Scottish granite and set in the only expression left on the shelf. His colleagues at work called him Happy Hammond and had a tote running to see who would be the first to make him crack a smile. The pot for the year was running at over two hundred pounds, with no signs yet of a winner.

'At some point they're going to find out that she's still alive,' he continued, 'and when that happens they may well try again.'

'Who are "they"?'

'Don't really know for sure. We have a pretty good idea who's behind it all, but we don't know who pulled the trigger. Until we get a better picture of who exactly we're dealing with it's safer if people think Keira's dead. Makes the bad guys behave differently, too . . .' Gary tailed off as they approached the ward.

The firearms officer stood to one side and held the door open for them.

*

Keira opened her eyes and stared vacantly at her mother as she crossed to her bedside. Gary Hammond closed the door gently and came in to stand behind. Keira tried to say hello, but her breathing was laboured and difficult, making it impossible to draw enough breath to manage even the faintest whisper. She was heavily sedated, but could still hear what was being said, although she struggled to make sense of the words. Despite the tubes in her nose she was also aware of the smells in the room. Every so often clean, disinfected scents wafted around her when the nurses changed her dressings or cleaned the entry and exit wounds where the bullets had ripped through her chest, shoulder and abdomen. Her eyes were leaden and slow: each time she opened them either Gary or her mum, or both, appeared to have shifted their position to a different part of the room until finally she opened them again and Gary Hammond had disappeared altogether, leaving just her mother sitting in a chair next to her bed.

There was a question she needed to ask: something important. But even though her senses were starting to return, her mind was still playing catch-up, as though part of the healing process was to keep her wits locked down until she was in better shape physically. No matter how hard she tried, the question wouldn't come to her. The more she concentrated on it the deeper it sank into the pool of random thoughts and disconnected images that fogged her mind.

'You keep slipping in and out of consciousness, sweetheart; are you okay? Are you in a lot of pain?' Her mother was trying to keep the look of concern from her face.

It took a few moments for her brain to untangle the words before she managed a slight movement of her lips to whisper,

'I'm fine.'

There was a burning sensation in her side and a similar pain near the top of her left lung.

The next time she opened her eyes her mother had shifted position again: sitting halfway along the bed now, holding her hand.

Three hours had passed. 'I have to go home now, darling, and get a change of clothes, but I'll only be gone a little while then I'll come straight back, okay? You're doing good.'

Keira wanted her to stay.

She heard a thin, distant voice say, 'Wait! I need to ask you something,' but when she opened her eyes the room was empty and she wondered if she had spoken the words out loud or just imagined saying them.

*

It was light outside when Keira next came to. Her mother turned from the window when she heard the movement behind her.

'Good morning.'

Keira's difficulty in breathing had eased slightly and the fog seemed to have lifted a little: enough for her to be able to respond this time.

'Morning?' she whispered. 'I'm not sure about good.'

She wanted to sit up, but no other part of her body was responding to the signals. 'Am I paralysed?' she asked weakly.

Her mother shook her head. 'No. But it was close.'

'What happened?' Keira suddenly winced as a sharp stabbing pain shot through her chest, causing every muscle in her body to tense.

'Are you okay?' Her mother moved to the side of the bed.

Keira nodded slowly, and felt her body relax as the spasm gradually subsided.

'What happened?' she repeated.

'That's what everyone's waiting to ask you. Gary Hammond's been here every day hoping to talk to you.'

'Every day? How long have I been in here?'

'They brought you in on Sunday night.'

'What day is it now?'

'Friday.'

The end of the week: that was significant, but she couldn't think why. The question was nagging at her again, but still skulking somewhere in the morphine-swamped shadows.

'You were in a medically induced coma for three of those days,' continued her mother. 'One of the bullets grazed your spine. They were keeping you immobile until they knew for certain there was no permanent damage.'

'Sounds like my kind of party. Do they know for certain now?'

'You're going to be fine.'

There was a knock and Gary Hammond's large, square face appeared round the edge of the door. 'Mind if I join you?'

Keira tried to sit up again, but the stabbing pains in her chest made her give up immediately.

'Rescued this from the evidence room.'

Gary placed Keira's flight bag by her bed. 'Nurses told me you seemed very keen to have it . . . kept asking for it.'

The box of throwing knives Father Anthony had given her was in the flight case. She remembered having to check it in at Belfast International, which had meant a further delay when she arrived at Glasgow airport, but she had no recollection of asking any of the nurses for it. She'd put the knives inside the case and kept the slim package with her on the plane. Inside was an old jotter and some loose photographs. The pictures were mostly of her grandmother as a young woman, standing behind two young boys or resting them on her knee; posed, but natural and unaffected. One was a wedding photograph, a rare image of the grandfather she'd never met. There were also a few faded colour photographs of the boys as teenagers with feathered haircuts and three-button high-waisted trousers, wearing platform shoes and tight Simon shirts. She had recognized her uncle Danny straight away, but it was the photograph of Sean, his brother, that had made the biggest impact. She recalled the burst of adrenaline when she'd realized the striking resemblance between herself and the man she believed to be her father. They had similar shaped faces and shared the same cool intensity of stare behind the same black eyes. She'd briefly flicked through the jotter, but had been too distracted to pay it the attention it deserved.

'You're looking a bit better today,' said Gary Hammond, breaking into her thoughts. 'Getting some colour back in your cheeks.'

'Is the colour brown?' mumbled Keira.

'Brown?'

'I feel like shit.'

If Keira had known about the tote she could have staked her claim on the two hundred-pound prize. DSI Hammond's lips cracked a thin smile. It was over quickly, but it would still have counted.

As she looked over at Gary a coldness spread over her like a cloud passing in front of the sun. For some reason his presence troubled her. She remembered something. She had left a message for him to meet her at the apartment. 'You weren't there,' she said in a slow whisper.

It wasn't an accusation, but a statement of fact.

'I was delayed. I did get there, but too late, I'm sorry.'

'You saved my life.'

Keira caught the look on his face.

'They told me . . .' started Keira, every few words punctuated with a short gasp for air, '. . . a doctor said . . . if the ambulance hadn't been called when it was, I wouldn't have made it.' She closed her eyes and paused for a second until the burning sensation at the top of her chest subsided enough for her to continue. 'My "golden hour" was down to the last few seconds.'

Hammond looked surprised.

'I didn't phone the ambulance.'

'Who did, then?' For a brief moment there was a glimmer of hope in her eyes. 'Was it David?'

Gary didn't need to say anything. Keira could tell from the expression on his face what his response was going to be. 'Did the girl survive? Kaltrina, where is she?'

He gave a slight shake of his head. His normal self-assuredness left him momentarily and he found himself staring at the floor. 'The only person who made it out alive was you . . . The call for an ambulance did come from your apartment, but we've got no idea who made it . . . It wasn't me.'

Keira was no longer listening.

She could feel the burn at the back of her eyes. She wanted to cry, but her feelings were numb. Kaltrina Dervishi was dead. David, her pal and work colleague, was dead too. But there was something else: another question. It involved her mother and Thursday and something else . . . nothing to do with Gary

Hammond or Kaltrina Dervishi or David . . . then suddenly it reached the surface.

'Her funeral,' she managed to say as she gasped for air.

'They have to finish the girl's autopsy first,' began Hammond.

'No!' Keira was shaking her head.

She could see her mother's ashen face staring back at her. 'The funeral?' she repeated.

'David was buried yesterday.'

'No!' Keira's voice was hoarse.

Her mother knew exactly what Keira was asking, but couldn't bring herself to tell her: not just yet. 'Don't be worrying yourself about that now.'

'Ma?' said Keira, pleading with her.

In a voice so low it was almost impossible to hear, her mother eventually replied, 'I didn't know what to do.'

'No . . . Ma, please tell me I didn't miss it . . . please.'

'I'm sorry, Keira . . .'

'In Newry?'

'In Scaur: Roucan Loch cemetery.'

'It's not what she wanted.' Keira's tone was flat as she repeated, 'It's not what she wanted.'

'I didn't know what to do, Keira.'

'Who was there?'

'Please, darling,' answered her mother. 'Get yourself better, then we'll have this conversation.'

'Who was there, Ma?'

'Father Anthony flew over; I didn't want anyone else, it didn't seem right. When you're better he's going to hold a memorial service back in Northern Ireland.'

Keira's back suddenly arched in the air. The pain in her side was intense. But her throat and lungs were so constricted that when she tried to scream no sound came.

She reached out in desperation toward her mother.

*

Keira was standing in her kitchen again. She heard the hiss of air behind, felt the impact of the bullets forcing her to the floor. Her chest was aching and her lungs burned as though she was breathing in a huge ball of fire.

In the confusion, just as the room started to fade from view, she could hear someone screaming, 'Help her, she needs help.'

Keira thrust into the darkness, her arms outstretched, reaching for something, or someone who wasn't there. In the silence that followed she could hear the faint echo of uillean pipes.

*

Keira woke up drenched in sweat. She had no idea where she was or how long she had been asleep. She tried to sit up, but stopped when she heard a voice from somewhere near the end of the bed, 'Just you stay where you are.'

'Ma?'

'Your mum's gone home. She'll be back in the morning, but you need to rest.'

Keira lifted her head off the pillow and saw a nurse replacing a clipboard on a hook at the bottom of the bed.

'I've given you something to help you sleep, but no more visitors for another few days. Too much excitement. It's not good for you.'

'My grandmother's funeral,' said Keira as she started to drift off. 'I've missed it.'

'Don't worry about that just now. It was nearly your own a few days ago.'

Twenty-five

'Are you ready to talk?'

'I'm ready to scream.'

'How you feeling?'

'Like I've been shot.'

'If it's any consolation, we're pretty sure you weren't the target. Word from the steamie is Abazi's brought in a hired hand to do his dirty work. But the picture's still a wee bit blurry: complicated, you know?'

'I told Patrick Sellar before all this happened that they were going to hit Kaltrina Dervishi. I know I wasn't the target.'

'Who told you?'

'I heard a rumour.'

Keira was propped up in bed with a sheet pulled up to her chin. She was still hooked up to various machines via tubes and cables, but the fact that she was sitting up at all showed she was on the mend. The medical team must have thought so too, because DSI Hammond had finally been allowed back in to ask her some questions.

'Why did Patrick Sellar release Kaltrina from custody?'

Gary shrugged his shoulders, 'Who knows?' then said, 'He made a statement a few days after the shooting saying that, based on a conversation he'd had with you, jail didn't seem like the right place for the girl.'

'I did say that, it's true, but I sent him the tape of her parents being threatened. He knew she was at risk.'

'He mentioned that.'

'He mentioned he'd watched the tape?'

'Yes.'

'So what the hell was he thinking, letting her out? When her life was under threat.'

'He said he didn't receive the tape until after the event and in any case it was the parents' lives that were being threatened, not the girl's.'

'Jesus Christ!' exclaimed Keira, shaking her head.

The Advocate Depute Patrick Sellar was just one of the many lines that didn't run straight by Keira's way of thinking, but until she had more information, she'd let it go for the moment.

'Kaltrina knew something that Abazi didn't want out in the open and that's why they wanted her dead.'

'Do you know what that something is? Did she tell you anything we should know?'

'No. She'd only just started to open up, to trust me, but . . . I never, at any time, got the impression she was carrying some great secret around. Obviously, she must have known about Abazi's criminal activities and that in itself would have been enough to get her killed, but there has to be more to it.'

'Did she see the video?'

Keira nodded.

'How did she react?'

'She was upset, but it was a strangely benign reaction. She reckoned the Clan would have killed the parents afterwards anyway.'

'It could have had something to do with the child?'

Keira wondered how Gary could possibly have known about

the boy. It was supposed to be a secret. 'Who told you about that?'

'It's in the autopsy report. Two murder charges and the death of an unborn child,' he continued.

'Jesus! Kaltrina was pregnant?'

'That's what I'm saying. Could be why she decided to run now. Not a year ago . . . or two years ago. You know what I'm saying?'

'The interpreter.'

'What about him?'

'It's a she.'

'Okay, so what about *her*?'

'If Kaltrina was pregnant, why did Janica Ahmeti not mention it?'

'Who's Janica Ahmeti?'

'The interpreter!'

'Maybe she didn't tell her.'

'I think she did. And I'm pretty sure I was there when it happened. Kaltrina was gesturing to her, having an argument in Albanian, and she kept pointing to her stomach. I think that's what she was telling her, and if it was, why didn't Janica mention that to me?'

'Maybe she just didn't get round to it. With everything else going on it probably didn't seem so important.'

'It's not for her to decide what's important and what's not. She has, or should have, no knowledge of what the case is about. It's her job to translate everything, however trivial. She has no editorial power. But it's not just that. David left her a message on the Sunday when all the shit was happening, but she didn't show. I still haven't heard from her.'

'She probably thinks you're dead.'

Keira suddenly winced.

'You okay?'

'An occasional spasm . . . can take your breath away.'

'So, d'you think being pregnant made Kaltrina try to get out?'

'Could be a few things. She'd heard one of her friends take a beating in the room across from hers. The next morning the friend had disappeared. Kaltrina didn't want to end up in the same situation. I didn't know anything about her being pregnant. Christ! As if the situation isn't tragic enough.'

'Maybe Kaltrina saw who killed her pal.'

'I don't think that's it. Patrick Sellar made a comment that makes me think there's something else going on. He was talking about having the girl deported: throwing the big guns at me before I'd even opened my mouth. Mentioned citing Part II Section 15(3) of the 1971 Immigration Act as grounds: "A person shall not be entitled to appeal against a decision to make a deportation order against him or her if the ground of the decision was that his or her deportation is conducive to the public good as being in the interests of national security or of the relations between the United Kingdom and any other country or for other reasons of a political nature."'

'You know all that shit off by heart?'

Keira flattened her legs to reveal some sheets of A4 on her lap.

'I was reading it before you came in.'

'Are you supposed to be working? You're sick: you are entitled to put your feet up and read a book.'

'I'm not sick . . . I'm damaged. He didn't shoot me in the brain.'

'So, what does all that baloney actually mean?'

'It means that I'd have had no chance of fighting her deportation. No grounds for appeal, no matter what they decided to do with her: but why? The girl was a twenty-year-old prostitute. She was wily, but she didn't have the wherewithal to pose a threat to this or any other country's national security: which makes me think that whatever Abazi is up to *does* pose a threat, or is at least linked in some way to one.'

'Do you remember the story in the papers about the guy they found unconscious in the Radisson?'

'Vaguely.'

'Obviously into some weird practices! They found him tied to a chair with his trousers at his ankles and a lump of mince where the back of his head used to be.'

'He survived though, yeah?'

'Yeah, he got quite a belt, but it was largely superficial. He didn't want to press charges, which immediately gets the small hairs doing a tango. There's footage of him entering and leaving the room with a girl.'

'Kaltrina Dervishi?'

'Looks like it. Did she mention anything about that?'

'No. D'you think it's related to what happened?'

'He's CIA.'

'How do you know?'

'The cops that responded to the call found his ID when they were checking the room: simple as that. Edwin Kade, Central Intelligence Agency. Looks far too big to be a field officer.'

'Big?'

'Fat. Not what you'd expect. We've been trying to piece together what happened, but Kade's not interested. Wants to book a flight back home as soon as possible. We've taken his passport for the time being until we can establish if there's any connection to Abazi, but the only reason he's stayed this long is to let the wound heal enough for him to be able to fly. You wouldn't think those guys would leave their ID lying around.'

'Or let themselves be tied to a chair . . . Unless Edwin Kade felt he was safe.'

'What d'you mean?'

'If Kade knew Kaltrina was one of Abazi's girls. If Abazi and the CIA had something going on, then he'd have no reason to hide the fact that he was an agent.'

'It's a possibility.'

'What's in the bag?' She nodded towards the plastic carrier bag Hammond was holding. 'If it's chocolates and a get-well-soon card, you're too late. I'll be getting out later today or sometime tomorrow morning.'

'That's not what the doctors are telling me.'

'It's what I'm telling the doctors.'

'Don't think you're going anywhere until they say it's okay.'

'I'm fine.'

'"Fine" is no good; you need to be one hundred per cent. It's not just about how well you're feeling. When Abazi finds out you're still alive I think he'll come after you. He doesn't know what the girl has told you, so, potentially, you're still a threat. We need to have a serious think about how we are going to handle this.'

'You think I should stay locked up in here?'

'You're not locked up anywhere. The door doesn't even have a key. But I don't think you should be in any hurry to leave. You know first hand what they're capable of. At least in here you have some level of protection.'

He held the bag towards her. 'Here, you might as well have it. It's a box of chocolates and a get-well card, from me and the team. I don't think you're going anywhere.'

'Thank you.'

Gary Hammond looked slightly awkward. 'Is there anything else you want to tell me?'

'About what?'

'The heroin trade.'

'Bit random! Here's some chocolates, tell me everything you know about the heroin trade.'

'Any idea how a quantity of it ended up in your apartment?'

She was aware Gary was watching her: looking for a reaction.

'What sort of quantity?'

'Not enough to get you on dealing charges, but enough to get you on the sheet as a user.'

'I've no idea. What's your take on it?'

'Not sure yet, but I thought I'd let you know. There might be some awkward questions coming your way.'

'Thanks. Were you hoping for more of a reaction?'

'Not really.'

He was just at the door, about to leave. 'Something else I forgot to mention. We have more than one suspect for the shooting. Abazi's hired hand and someone known to you.'

'Known to me?'

'Jason Gormley.'

Keira didn't respond.

'Shit, I never know how to read you. I thought you'd be more surprised. His prints are all over the apartment, along with two sets of bullet casings: looks like two separate shooters. We're fairly positive that Gormley was one of them.'

'My recollection of the gunman's face is pretty mangled, but one thing I do know for sure: the guy who shot me wasn't Jay-Go.'

Twenty-six

The tap at the basin in the far corner was running: someone filling a glass. The noise of wastewater sloshing around then gurgling into the trap sounded abstract and distant, like it was happening somewhere else.

Keira had lost all sense of time passing. The silence that followed could have lasted a second, a minute or an hour: she had no way of knowing. The only thing she was certain of was that the person was still in the room, moving towards her bed.

There was another tapping noise, or clicking... footsteps, maybe.

The pills she'd been given to help her sleep made her head feel heavy and her gaze unfocused, but the medication hadn't dimmed her hearing.

She needed to know what time it was.

All she had to do was raise her head from the pillow and look at the digital read-out on the clock by the bedside table, but physically that didn't feel like it was an option.

It wasn't unusual for the nurses to check on her throughout the night.

Keira could feel herself starting to drift back to sleep.

Suddenly a shadow passed over her face: a presence close by.

A rush of adrenaline kick-started her brain into action. There was a figure standing over her. She'd caught a faint whiff of alcohol and knew instinctively that whoever it was posed a threat. Suddenly a hand clamped down over her mouth: the rough, calloused skin stinking of cigarette smoke.

Her eyes were wide open now, her screams muffled as she struggled to break free from the intruder's grip.

Then the voice came, speaking to her in urgent whispers. The same voice she'd heard in her apartment just before she'd lost consciousness.

'Miss, it's only me. Don't scream, awright? It's only me, Miss!'

Immediately the hand was removed Keira's body went limp and her head dropped back on to the pillow.

Jay-Go was standing to the side of her bed, looking just as frightened as she was.

'For Chrissake, Jay-Go, you scared the fucking life out of me! What the hell are you doing here?'

'Keep it down, Miss, keep it down.'

'How the hell did you get in here?'

'The cop is giving it big snoresvilles out there. Walked straight past him.'

'Jesus!'

'I'd have a word with his superior and get the clown defrocked. That's bang out of order. Sorry for the hand clamp, by the way; I thought you might scream.'

'Too bloody right I'd scream! I still might! A gentle nudge would have done the trick.'

'Good to see you've still got some fight in you. A bit of good news for a change. I'm glad it was you.'

'What are you talking about?' Keira slowly pulled herself up to a sitting position.

Jay-Go was wearing a white lab coat.

'What the hell are you doing here? I'm supposed to be dead.'

'The word's out that's a lot of bollocks . . . Rumour is some-body survived. That's what I'm saying . . . I'm glad it was you. Naebody knows for sure if it wis you or the girl that copped it. Here, Ah brought you this.'

Jay-Go lifted a bottle of Irn Bru and a bunch of petrol-station flowers from the chair next to the door and handed them to her. 'Couldnae find Lucozade anywhere; I don't know if they still make it.'

It may have been the relentless boredom of lying in a hospital bed for days on end, but Keira surprised herself by being pleased to see him.

'You look awright for someone that copped three bullets.'

Keira shot him a look. 'How do you know how many times I was shot?'

Jay-Go hesitated just long enough before answering for Keira to figure whatever he said next would be a lie.

'Must have heard it on the news.'

'I don't think they reported that fact on the news.'

'Whose diary?' asked Jay-Go, trying to change the subject by referring to the tatty brown notebook on the bedside table.

'How long have you been in here?'

'Long enough to have a wee glance.'

'It's private.'

'It's interesting. And I cannae read, remember.'

'D'you think I've just met you? You can read as well as the next . . .' she paused, searching for the word.

'Junkie! Is that what you were gonnae say? I'm a man o' means these days . . . Is it your boyfriend's diary? Thought you were still a virgin?'

Keira let that one pass.

'My dad's.'

'Fuck me! Yer da! Looked to me like he was riding point for a couple of dope dealers in the States.' Jay-Go's voice was getting higher and higher with incredulity. 'That's your da?'

'So I believe.'

'Respect, Miss! All new high on the respect front.'

'How d'you know they were dope dealers?'

'It's all in there! All them figures: working out his cut for keeping the edge.'

Jay-Go caught her look. He shook his head and sucked air between his teeth. 'You need to do some time in the pokey, Miss; get up to speed with the lingo your clients use. You're looking at me like I'm talking Martian: the edge. It's like sauvegarder, you know, protect, look out for. A couple of days in jail and you'd have it down.' He shook his head again, as though he couldn't believe she didn't know this. 'You represent some major miscreants and you probably don't even know what they're saying half the time. Or is that just an act? Are you secretly from a major crime family and you know all the parlance?'

'"Sauvegarder", "parlance" – have you been studying French in jail?'

'My mum was French.'

'Really!'

'Was she fuck,' replied Jay-Go. 'Total psych! The nearest my ma came to France was drinking three bottles of claret every night before her tea.'

Jay-Go was toying with her now, trying to be a smartarse, but Keira had already had enough and wanted to get back to sleep. 'Why are you here, Jay-Go?'

'I'm heading off. Wanted to say ta-ta and check that the

rumours of your passing had been greatly exaggerated.'

'Enjoy the trip.'

'"Enjoy the trip"! Fuck me. I travel all this way to say cheerio and all Ah get is "Enjoy the trip"? I havnae even told you where I'm going yet.'

'You can send me a postcard.'

'The States, California! Going to pay Betty Ford a visit. Sort myself out: break the cycle. When you heading over? We could meet up. Is Niagara close to California?'

Keira looked at him coolly. 'Who said anything about going to Niagara?'

'There's a ticket in the back of the diary,' replied Jay-Go. 'Did your da send it over so you could go visit him?'

'My dad's dead. That ticket's twenty years old.'

'So who sent it?'

'No one sent it. It was his ticket. I think he was planning to live there.'

'But?'

'He was murdered, along with his brother. Scuppered his travel plans.'

'Heavy doors! Who did it?'

She gave him a look that let him know he'd gone far enough.

'Jay-Go, I like you, but only up to a point, and I passed that point about two seconds after I realized it was you in the room and not one of the nursing staff. None of this is any of your business.'

'I don't even know who my da is. Pissed off when I was born. My ma never even told me his name: still don't know. Every guy I pass in the street I think, "Wonder if that's him?" Mental! Does your brain in. At least you knew yours.'

Keira could easily have contradicted him, told him that she never knew her father, but that would have kept the conversation going and all she wanted to hear Jay-Go say now was 'goodbye'.

'That's why we get on, Miss: lots in common,' he continued. 'We should hook up: "a marriage made in prison"! What meds are you on, by the way? Got the jangles coming on bad here. You got anything I could borrow?'

She could see that Jay-Go was starting to sweat.

'They give me Dihydrocodeine, but I don't take it: blurs the thinking too much.'

Jay-Go snorted. 'That's the fuckin' point, Miss. Where is it?'

She could see him eyeing the small white paper pot with last night's pills still in it and realized why he'd filled a cup at the sink. 'Is that water for me?' she asked.

He knew straight away she was on to him.

'If I hadn't stirred, would you have swallowed those pills, even though you had no idea what they were?'

'You're in a hospital, they're hardly likely to give you shit that's gonnae make you more sick.'

'I suppose if I closed my eyes and they disappeared, I could always say I didn't know where they went . . . I may have swallowed them myself.'

Jay-Go gave her a look, then said, 'Aye, you could give that one a try.'

Keira closed her eyes. When she opened them again the small paper cup was empty, and Jay-Go was finishing off the rest of his water.

'D'you think if I closed my eyes again, maybe you could disappear too?'

'Aye, very good!' Jay-Go was nodding his head. 'You get the big picture. Man, you are too cool! Standing at the North Pole in a fuckin' T-shirt cool. You know the right thing to do, Miss. You know which way to look and when to cross. That's why Nick-Nick Carter and Big Paul and Holy Man are on the warpath.'

'What are you talking about, Jay-Go?'

'A few things you should know. I told you they were gonnae hit the girl, didn't Ah?'

'Who told you?'

'No questions, Miss, remember?'

'D'you know who the shooter was?'

'Listen up. You know what I said was right. So if I tell you there was a big, bad, bag of smack left in your apartment, you'll know I'm not making it up. They were probably trying to set you up, Miss.'

'Who was?'

'Abazi and the Watcher, the guy that carried out the hit.'

'Is that his name?'

'His nickname. His real name is Eggys Eezee or some shit like that.'

'Why would they try to set me up?'

'How the hell should I know, but it was there on your kitchen table; a full kilo of top-grade caballo. Maybe they were trying to blur the picture.'

'Blur the picture?'

'Aye, you know, make it look like you're dirty to throw people off the scent of what's really going on.'

'How d'you know all this, Jay-Go?'

'Ah don't know anything, I'm making this shit up.'

'How d'you know I was shot three times? How did you know which hospital I was in?'

'There's only one hospital in Glasgow that specializes in gunshots. Where else are they gonnae take you?'

'The police are working to trace the caller who phoned in the shootings; was it you?'

'If the Holy Man shakes your hand is he likely to screw you over?'

'They recovered bullets from two different guns. Theory is that someone tried to shoot the killer, does that sound about right?'

'What you asking me for?'

'Can you just answer the question?'

'You answer mine first. Is the Holy Man the type of guy that'll fuck you about?'

'No. If he's given you his word, then that's it: even if it means him taking a hit. What did you shake hands over?'

'Holy Man wants me to report back if I find anything,' replied Jay-Go, avoiding her question. 'Is it okay to tell him I've seen you're alive?'

'When did you hook up with him? I thought you were a lone gun?'

'It's a one-off. Doing a deal: some business.'

Keira interrupted. 'You're trying to sell the Holy Man the kilo of heroin you took from my apartment?'

Jay-Go shrugged. 'Man, way off.'

'Was it you who phoned for the ambulance?'

'Ah wis nowhere near your apartment.'

'How much did he offer you?'

'Eh?'

'For the heroin.'

'Ah don't know what you're fuckin' talking about, Miss . . . What heroin?'

'How much?'

'Fifteen.'

'For a kilo!'

'For half, then ten for the other half. I asked for fifty for the whole lot, which is still half of what it's worth, by the way, but there's a war on and they're using "the silence of money" as their main weapon. Whatever the fuck that means.'

'You're talking in riddles, Jay-Go. Just listen to me for a second. I want you to go back to him and tell him you've changed your mind, you want sixty.'

Jay-Go was staring at her. 'Are you still bombed on general anaesthetic? He'd stick my arse on my head like a fuckin' beanie.'

'Ask for sixty, settle at forty.'

'Are you negotiating a deal for me, Miss?'

'I'm speaking my thoughts out loud and you happen to be in the same room. He won't be happy, but you can tell him he owes me and I'm calling it in. Tell him I'm alive and I'm okay.'

'How does he owe you?'

Keira didn't have time to answer. Suddenly the door opened and the officer who was supposed to be on guard duty was in the room. 'Everything all right?'

'Everything's fine, pal,' answered Jay-Go, giving off way too much attitude for someone passing himself off as a doctor.

The cop looked over at Keira. 'You all right, Miss Lynch?'

'I'm grand, thank you.'

'I was just sorting out her meds,' said Jay-Go, winking over at her. Then to the cop: 'I could get you some amphetamines if you think that would help. Maybe give you something to stop the snoring too.'

The cop didn't have a response.

'Plenty of rest, you,' said Jay-Go to Keira as he headed for the door. 'Take that trip,' he continued, 'but don't wait too long. Niagara's lovely at this time of year. Excuse me,' he said making the cop step aside to let him pass.

'Ask for sixty . . . Betty's not a cheap date.'

'Who's Betty?'

'Ford.'

'Aye, very good.'

'It's my way of saying thank you.'

'North Pole, no T-shirt, Miss. Too fuckin' cool!'

Twenty-seven

Jay-Go rode the top deck of the number 41 night bus to Wester-house Road from Glasgow city centre with a noddy-dog drunk and an elderly couple who looked like it was way past their bed-time. It was the second bus he'd been on since leaving the hospital – a journey that had taken over an hour. Jay-Go liked the bus. If you avoided pub closing and school hours, they were a good way to get around and they were cheap. He didn't travel out of his area often, so the thought of blowing some of the money the Holy Man had given him on a cab hadn't even occurred to him.

The thick wad of cash was pressing against his thigh as he strutted his way up Grudie Street. The railing-topped wall of the community fire station was over to his right. A row of boarded-up terraced houses to his left: most of the occupants of which had either moved on or had flitted to the new houses further up the estate.

It was just after one o'clock in the morning.

The dark streets were deserted, the quiet disturbed by the distant sound of a heavy bass dub-beat banging away in some inconsiderate stoner's house. The air was filled with the incon-gruous smell of freshly cut grass wafting down from the square of green common at the top of the road.

Jay-Go was just about to turn right into his street when his mobile buzzed.

It was a message from Yogi Bearcat.

'Party was at your house? Heated Funny waiting out front. Picked up something else: not Funny. Be COT don't be caught.'

Yogi was a gang member with brains who lived on the estate. He monitored the police activity in the area with a selection of scanners he'd bought from the Internet. For a small subscription charge he would send text messages warning of any possible problems with, or sightings of, the cops. As Jay-Go was his dealer, he didn't have to pay. The enterprise was never going to earn Yogi enough money to buy a house, but the guy had enough successes to make it a popular service. He earned sufficient to keep him in dope and cigarettes.

The first part of the message was pretty straightforward. The police had raided his flat and were now waiting outside. 'Heated' meant they were armed. Jay-Go was pretty confident they wouldn't have found the heroin, but he'd left kit all over the table in the lounge. They wouldn't need to test it to know it was covered in residue.

The second sentence of the message was more worrying. Yogi had picked up something else on the scanner, but if it wasn't the police who was it?

'Be COT, don't be caught' was Yogi's sign-off – 'Be Careful Out There,' was a line from an old TV cop show.

Jay-Go thumbed a quick reply. 'Ta v much yogi. OUI'. If the message had come through two minutes later, Jay-Go would have walked straight into a set of cuffs.

Jay-Go's brain was frayed around the edges, making it difficult to hold on to a thought long enough to form any sort of plan. If the cops picked him up now, the 007 in his pocket would send him straight to jail, and if they'd raided his flat and found the Serb's heroin, he'd be looking at the big stretch –

anything up to life for possession and intent to supply a commercial quantity of class A.

And this haul was triple-A rated.

Jay-Go ran across the road and disappeared into the shadows shrouding the gable end of his apartment building. Partially obscured by the overgrown hedges that bordered the small gardens in front of each block, he sneaked a glance round the corner and saw a dark-coloured car containing four men parked in one of the bays at the end of his street.

Small wafts of smoke rose into the night sky through the car's open windows.

Jay-Go figured he had two options. Option one: drop the PPK in the bin, walk round the corner and front it out with the cops; stroll up to the car and bang on the windscreen: 'Hello officer. Is it me you're looking for?' Or option two: head up the back stairs of his apartment block and break in through the toilet window, retrieve the heroin, then climb through the roof space to the end of the building and make his exit through his neighbour's front door. They wouldn't be happy, but he'd done it before.

After that he'd go find somewhere else to stay until he could figure out his next move.

The biggest problem with option two being that the back door was usually bolted shut from the inside.

The harder Jay-Go tried to come up with an answer the more he realized he was reading the situation in Braille. A line of coke would sort him out.

Muttering 'This is shite' under his breath, he edged backwards along the side of the building – past a tall brick wall tacked on to the end of the gable – until he came to a set of metal gates used to secure the communal garden at the back of the apartment block known as 'dog-bog alley'.

He heaved himself up and over the metal gate, down on to the other side. The thin strip of overgrown grass ran the length of the block and was enclosed by high, wire-mesh fencing that reminded him of the exercise yard at Barlinnie.

The back door – shuttered with metal sheet – made a loud screech and several juddering creaks as he tried to force it open, but it wouldn't budge.

Jay-Go thumbed Yogi's number into his phone again.

'Need the cavalry, big man?'

'You could say. Ah need a diversion.'

'Get the Funnies away from the front of your house?'

'Bang on! They might be waiting inside too.'

'I'm in the zone, Jay-Go. I don't know how much good Ah'll be to ye. What's the deal?'

'Take a stroll over to my block, let them think you're me. Head up to the flat and put the light on or something, make it look like I'm home. You're bound to get huckled, so it's gonnae be an inconvenience, but there's fifty notes in it for you. I just need to get into my flat for two minutes. How stoned are you?'

'Three spliffs down. Nothing major. Why don't I just let you in the back door?'

'If I get lifted I'm in big trouble. Too risky.'

'Fifty notes, you say?'

'I'll meet you at the back gate and give you the money with the keys right now. And I'll throw in a wee wrap of something nice to go with, by way of a thank-you.'

'What's the catch?'

'I'll have to drop the gear by in the next few days, 'cause I don't have it on me.'

Yogi was weighing up the deal.

'I've never bounced on you yet, Yogi; you know I wouldn't be offering you that much if I didn't have it. You can tell the Funnies you're looking after my place while I'm away.'

'Where will Ah say you've gone?'

'Niagara.'

'It needs to be somewhere real.'

'Niagara is real, ya spanner.'

'What about Spain?'

'Who gives a fuck where it is? Make it up.'

'Ah'll do it for a hundred.'

'Fair enough. Ah can give you that right now if you want, it's just the gear I don't have.'

'Na! Bring it round the morra. If I get carted off to the station with that kind of dough on me I'd be answering questions for a week. See you in two minutes.'

*

DI John Mullin caught a movement in the wing mirror. He took a final draw on the single-skin roll-up and flicked it out of the window on to the road.

'Bandit at six o'clock,' he said to the three other officers in the car.

The men watched as a lone figure made his way down the east side of Grudie Street and crossed to the corner of Sielga Place.

'We'll let him get in. Give him a minute to get the kettle on. Word is, he likes to carry a shooter, so we'll go in hot, but no twitchy fingers unless he's actually got the gun in his hand. We're here to make an arrest, not funeral arrangements, all right? Neil and Seb come with me, Ross you wait at the bottom of the stairs. There's no point covering the rear of the premises unless he's going to jump from a second-floor window.'

Mullin turned to Neil and Seb in the back. 'If we have to use the ram, I'll do it and you two cover me, yeah?'

The two officers nodded.

'What's this clown up to?' asked Ross. 'Is it definitely our man?'

'Looks like it.'

*

With his hoodie pulled tight around his face, Yogi Bearcat strolled past the row of parked cars and round the side of Jay-Go's block of flats.

A hand suddenly reached out from a hole in the hedge and grabbed his arm.

'Fuck me, Jay-Go, you nearly gave me a heart attack.'

'What are they up to?'

'Just sittin' there. Where's the keys?'

'Here.' Jay-Go handed him a small set on a skull-and-cross-bones key ring. 'This is all yours,' he continued, fanning out a wad of ten-pound notes.

'Nice one.'

'Take it just now if you want.'

'Nah, tomorrow's fine.'

Yogi sidled round the side of the building and headed for the front entrance.

Once inside, he climbed to the second floor, then made his way along the narrow balcony overlooking the street below.

It took him a few minutes to work out which key fitted which lock on Jay-Go's heavily fortified front door, but eventually he turned the final deadlock and pushed through into the darkened hallway.

The air inside smelled stale and there was an undercurrent of dampness and food long past its sell-by date.

Yogi flicked the hall light switch, but nothing happened.

After feeling his way through the blackness he came to the entrance of the lounge and reached round the doorframe for the switch panel.

The lights were dead there, too.

Behind him was the door to the kitchen.

Yogi leant across and tried there as well.

Light from a single sixty-watt bulb, dangling from the kitchen ceiling, spread through into the lounge, casting long shadows across the coffee table littered with Jay-Go's gear and an untidy sofa scattered with clothes, empty DVD cases and ding-dinner containers.

Yogi headed for a lamp over by the window in the lounge. Jay-Go had told him to switch it on to let the cops know he was home, then take a seat and wait for something to happen.

As he picked his way through the rotting debris strewn across the floor, he was suddenly aware of a presence behind him.

Before he could turn he heard a familiar metallic click and felt the cold end of a gun barrel being pressed firmly into the back of his neck, forcing his face hard against the window.

'You have ten seconds to tell me where the heroin is,' came a voice.

'What heroin?'

'Nine.'

'You're supposed to shout a warning or something before you pull your weapon, fuckhead. I'll have you for misconduct,' cried Yogi.

'Eight.'

'I don't know anything about any heroin, ya fuck.'

'Seven.'

Yogi tried to push backwards off the window, but there was a hand pressing hard into the middle of his back, making it impossible to move.

'Six.'

If this guy was a cop he was coming on way too strong.

'I don't know anything about any fuckin' heroin, pal, all right? I don't live here. This isn't my flat.'

'Five.'

'Please. I'm doing a favour for a friend.'

'Four.'

Yogi struggled again, but it was no use, he couldn't move.

'Three.'

'Okay, okay . . . I'll tell you! Get the gun away from my head and I'll tell you.'

'Two.'

'It's in my car,' cried Yogi, stalling for time. 'It's in my car.'

'Where's your car?'

'Right outside the flat. If you switch the lamp on, I'll get the keys for you. They're in here somewhere, on the floor.'

'What make?'

'Eh?'

'What make is the car?'

'A Ford,' he answered quickly.

'How much of it is left?'

'Of what?'

The gun was forced harder into the back of Yogi's neck.

'The heroin.'

Yogi had no idea how much heroin there was, but he needed to keep the guy talking. 'All of it.'

'The whole two kilos?'

'Yeah, the whole lot. I haven't touched any of it. Two kilos.'

'One,' said the gunman, resuming the count.

*

John Mullin and his team were halfway across the road when the window in Jay-Go's flat exploded out, spraying the ground directly in front of him with shards of glass and tiny fragments of bone and tissue.

While the rest of his men scattered and took up defensive positions behind whatever cover they could find, Mullin dropped to his knees, shouted a warning that they were armed police officers and cracked off two shots up at the window. Then, shuffling forward along the ground, he made his way over to the hedge until it blocked him from the line of fire.

The four officers crouched or knelt, weapons drawn, waiting to see if there were any more shots coming.

Mullin signalled silently for Neil and Seb to cover so that he and Ross could break for the front door at the same time. It was a manoeuvre they'd practised many times in training. Presenting two moving targets instead of one gave the gunman more to shoot at, which made him more likely to rush the shot, reducing his accuracy.

Mullin mouthed the words 'After five', then held his left

hand splayed in front of him, folding each finger in turn as he counted backwards.

With no further communication the two officers were suddenly on their feet sprinting towards the front of the building, their weapons trained on the upstairs window.

*

Jay-Go had been watching from the corner of the building when the window exploded into the darkness. The loud crack of gunfire made him duck and press his back hard against the rough wall. Seconds later, just six metres or so from where he was hiding, he heard the rattle of the metal gate. A figure holding a gun climbed over and jumped to the ground.

Jay-Go's first thought was that it might be Yogi.

He was about to call to him when he realized he was wrong.

The guy's profile looked familiar, but it wasn't the Bearcat.

The shadows falling on his face made it difficult to make out his features, but he had definitely seen the guy before.

As the figure edged to the corner of the railings he glanced round and for a brief moment his face caught the spill from an overhead street lamp.

It was the guy who'd been eyeballing him in the Holy Man's pub: bawface Edi Leka.

Jay-Go fumbled for his gun, but Edi Leka was already halfway down the road. When he reached the corner of Grudie and Shandwick a car drew up and Leka jumped in.

Jay-Go wondered if the Holy Man had gone back on his word. Had he sent Leka to give him the bullet and retrieve the heroin?

If, on the other hand, Leka was still working for Abazi then the Holy Man needed to know the bawfaced little shit was not to be trusted.

He had no way of knowing for sure what had happened in his flat, but he could guess.

The plan to distract the cops and grab the caballo was off the rails: it was time to go.

Jay-Go broke from the shadows and, following Edi Leka's route, sprinted down to the corner of Grudie Street.

The only plan now was to keep running.

Twenty-eight

Marie Bain, Marie Leonard, Marie McGuire. The three names, in Bic-black ink, were scribbled on the last page of Sean McGuire's diary. For twenty years they had faced the faded airline ticket to Niagara sandwiched between the last page and the inside cover of the schoolbook-style jotter.

McGuire was a name from the past which for Keira brought with it 'the darkness'. Whoever Marie was, she must have taken it on at some point.

It didn't really matter what she called herself – she was one and the same person, with a story that Keira wanted to hear.

Keira had read the diary from cover to cover several times.

It was filled with random notes, brief descriptions of events, lost now in the intervening years. There were sums jotted in the margins: additions and subtractions – none of them in any particular order and all of them with the dollar sign beside them. There were references to poems, mainly Irish writers with a page number and line, but without the collection or poem titles it was impossible to unravel any meaning from them. Two initials, 'A' and 'H', appeared on several pages, usually alongside the figures. And as Jay-Go had already pointed out, it looked as though these figures were references to drug deals, with Sean McGuire receiving a small percentage for watching A and H's backs.

The first section of the notebook had simple dates and brief descriptions of events:

October 12th 1984. Arrived N.Y. 02.54am. Last connection to Birmingham Alab departed three hours ago. Nowhere to sleep.

Finally arrive Alabama. October 15th. Another five hours on the train till Tuscaloosa.

It wasn't until the last few pages, dated simply *Easter '92*, that the more revealing comments and descriptions came:

No point running to save your life, if your life isn't worth saving. Called Lep. Not sure it was the right move, but feel relieved. If they kill me at least I'm moving forward.

From that point on there were lots of references to Northern Ireland and to someone called 'M', whom Keira presumed to be Marie. One of the final entries referred to her uncle, Danny McGuire:

Danny is here! Lep must have passed on the message, but it has cost him his life.

There was a passage Keira had read over and over again trying to figure out the meaning:

The full tragedy unfolds. Held Danny for the first time in eight years. They've sent him here to kill me: my own brother! I am not the Thevshi.

Then the most chilling entry of all: one name scribbled in the margin and overwritten so many times it had almost made a hole through the paper. There was a large question mark in red ink beside it:

Owen O'Brien.

Seeing the name of the man she had killed made her want to throw up. Her face flushed in a sweat and her hands began to shake. It was several minutes before she regained her composure enough to close the jotter and place it on the bedside cabinet. She hadn't had a panic attack like this for several years now. When the nausea finally subsided, she lay back on the pillow and stared at the ceiling until eventually she drifted off to sleep.

Keira started to organize the entries into a timeline. She felt that if she could structure the diary by making it into some kind of narrative she would have control over it. It was a coping mechanism, a way of losing herself. She had drawn up a list of people and outlined areas that she wanted to explore further. It was no different from building a case or compiling evidence for the defence in a trial. She noted straight away that Sean McGuire had entered the United States on 12 October 1984, seven and a half months before she was born. So it was still possible that he had left Northern Ireland without knowing that her mother, Orlaith, was pregnant. For every question answered, another five presented themselves. Who was Lep? Who was A? Who was H? Who was Marie and who or what was the Thevshi?

There were supposed to be no secrets between them, but her grandmother had waited until she was dying to reveal the diary's whereabouts. She must have known of its existence for all these years. The diary represented an area of Keira's life that until now she had left undisturbed. For twenty years she had been Keira Lynch, not Niamh McGuire. Suddenly she wanted to know who her father was. She wanted to find out everything about him. Maybe this had been her grandmother's intention all along.

Although some of it made disturbing reading, the diary was a distraction from the vision that kept appearing in her head of Kaltrina Dervishi lying in a pool of blood on the floor of her flat. And there were plenty more images queuing up to take its place; David with half of his face missing, or the killer standing over her with his arms outstretched in the shape of the cross, taunting her, mimicking Keira in her most private moment.

How could he have possibly known, unless he had been watching from inside her flat?

Worse than all of these things put together, for Keira, was the fact that she had missed her grandmother's funeral.

She closed her eyes until the stinging sensation had passed.

The doctors had warned her that this would happen, the trauma of events over the last few days overwhelming her. But she wasn't ready to cry yet.

She wasn't ready to give in.

A rapping sound at the door broke her thoughts. 'Come in,' she said, placing her own set of scribbled notes on the bedside table alongside those of her father.

A nurse popped her head into the room. 'Bathtime! You ready for another big adventure?'

'I'd rather have a shower, Rachel, if that's okay.'

'If you're feeling strong enough.'

Keira nodded. 'I'm pretty sure I am.'

'There's only a bath in your en suite; d'you want me to see if the room across the hall's empty? It's got both.'

Keira nodded again. 'I never feel properly clean after a bath.'

'Back in a mo. I'm sure it'll be fine to use it, but I'll just check there's no one in there. Two seconds!'

Keira lifted her legs off the side of the bed and placed her feet on the floor. Even that simple movement left her feeling light-headed. She sat for a moment, then slowly stood up. She had been pushing to get discharged in the next day or so, but knew herself that she wasn't quite ready.

Rachel was back at the door. 'All fine! I'll help you across just now and get you in the shower, then Jacqui will bring your toiletries. She wants to change the sheets on your bed, too, so take your time over there. It's not your electricity bill; use as much hot water as you like.'

'I still get a bit dizzy when I stand up.'

'Blood pressure's a bit low, that's all it is. Nothing to worry about. You're well on the mend.'

'Still on course for getting out tomorrow?'

'What's your hurry? Sick of the sight of us?'

'No, sick of my own company! I need daylight and some fresh air.'

'Probably not tomorrow, but definitely in the next few days. Everything's just knitting together, so you'll still have to take it easy, but it's surprising how quickly some people recover. Another week and you'll be back at the gym.' The nurse took hold of Keira's right arm. 'You hold on to the drip stand with your other hand and let's get out of here. Maybe tomorrow we'll see if we can go up on the roof and catch some rays.'

'In Glasgow?'

'We'll take a brolly.'

Keira steadied herself by clutching on to the stainless-steel drip stand that held a bag of clear fluid, then the two women made their way slowly out of the room.

The armed officer stationed outside in the corridor – whose name she'd learned was Richard – held the door open for them as they shuffled past. 'Off somewhere nice?'

'Change of scenery,' replied Keira.

'Any slower, Miss Lynch, and I'll ticket you for holding up the traffic. It's the national speed limit in this corridor.'

'You should be a comedian, Richie. You've got the face for it.'

'Aye, touché, Miss Lynch, touché!'

Even though the thin jets of hot water stung as they hit the freshly exposed wounds and made her teeth set against each other, it felt good. Streaks of iodine from the area around her punctured skin poured over the toneless flesh of her stomach and down her bare legs before swirling around the shower tray and disappearing into the drain. Certain movements sent sharp reminders that the muscles damaged by the passage of the bullets through her body were still under repair, but Keira was aware that her strength was definitely returning. Her movements were still laboured, but they were getting easier by the day.

The door leading from the en suite through to the bedroom was open so that she could summon the nurse if she had any problems.

'I'll just nip over and see what's keeping Jacqui with your toiletries,' called Rachel. 'Will you be okay if I leave you for a second?'

Keira raised her voice over the sound of the spray. 'I'm fine.'

'If you've even the slightest worry, pull the cord.'

There was an orange nylon cord in the corner of the cubicle with a red triangular handle imprinted with the word ALARM.

She shook her head. 'I'm good, really!'

'Okay. Back soon.'

Rachel left the room, closing the door behind her.

*

Special firearms officer Richard Malloy clocked the suppressed nine-mil the guy was carrying too late to shoulder his own weapon and return fire. The first bullet hit side-on, just above the elbow, and knocked him off balance. The second grazed his temple close to his right eye and the third, which entered under his jawbone and exited through the top of his skull as he fell, was the one that killed him. It had taken less than two seconds to fire three bullets and the officer lay dead on the floor.

Engjell E Zeze pushed through the door the cop had been guarding to find the room empty.

It was obvious, however, that the bed had been recently occupied. Two notebooks sat on a pile of magazines on top of the bedside cabinet alongside a half-empty glass of orange juice.

The room was definitely in use, but where was its occupant?

Engjell picked one of the notebooks up. An airline ticket fell from the inside sleeve and fluttered to the floor, landing face up, the destination easily readable. A noise from the bathroom made him turn. A nurse was standing next to the bath holding a towel and a small toilet bag. The expression of surprise on her face had barely changed to one of confusion before she slumped backwards on to the floor clutching the entry wound to her chest.

Engjell watched her with a look of curiosity as she struggled to draw in enough air to scream. One more squeeze of the trigger delivered the kill-shot directly between her eyes.

Then there came another noise, this time from the corridor outside.

*

Nurse Rachel's first instinct on seeing the police officer slumped against the wall was to check his vital signs. It was only when she turned and saw the small, anaemic looking man with the gun standing in the corridor next to her that she remembered her first action should have been to press the emergency call button on her pager. It crossed her mind to shout a warning to Keira, but that would only confirm her whereabouts. Without saying anything, the man raised the gun and pointed it straight at her head.

'They've transferred her downstairs,' Nurse Rachel blurted out. 'She's out of intensive care ... getting better.' Then pleading, 'Please!'

The Watcher briefly considered what the nurse had said, before deciding that she was probably telling the truth. The gun discharged with a dull thud that sent her slamming backwards against the wall. A trail of dark red blood smudged the wall as she slid to the floor and lay beside the police officer, her breath coming in wheezing gasps. In the brief silence that followed Engjell became aware of the sound of running water. Momentarily distracted from taking the kill-shot the Watcher turned and, with the gun still pointing at the nurse, took a few steps further along the corridor. The sloshing sound suddenly stopped. Engjell stepped back along the corridor and stood listening at the closed door opposite Keira Lynch's room.

Someone was moving around inside.

A small puddle of water appeared from under the door.

Engjell raised the Beretta up to roughly chest-height, aiming at the door, then carefully placed a gloved hand on the door handle and started to twist.

*

Keira had been standing in the shower wondering whether her towel and toilet bag would ever arrive when she heard something in the corridor. The faint noise was almost drowned out by the water streaming from the shower head, but there was no mistaking the distinctive, percussive thump. She immediately turned the tap off and stood, dripping wet, hoping that she was wrong. Having nothing to dry herself with, she stepped out of the shower and quietly made her way through into the bedroom, where she pulled a sheet from the bed and wrapped it round her dripping body.

Something was wrong.

She strained to hear the sound again. The whirring hum of the extractor fan in the bathroom had just stopped. The entire hospital seemed to have fallen silent.

She edged towards the door leading to the corridor and leant forward to press her ear against its cold, veneered surface.

In the light from the corridor spilling under the door, two long shadows stretched out across the floor just to the side of where she had placed her bare feet.

Someone was standing on the other side of the door.

The handle started to turn.

*

Engjell suddenly became aware of a movement from behind. Spinning round, he saw the nurse's hand scrabbling at something clipped to her belt.

'You lied.'

He squeezed the trigger once more, but the final shot arrived too late. She had already pressed the emergency button on her pager.

Somewhere further along the corridor an alarm started to sound.

'Mutt!'

Turning back to the door, Engjell fired three more rounds that punched ragged, fist-sized holes through its hollow-core panels. It was amateurish, and unlikely to yield results, but there was no time for anything else.

The wailing noise of the alarm brought two male nurses running from the far end of the hallway.

Engjell E Zeze turned and headed calmly toward the exit, firing the remaining rounds blindly over his shoulder before unclipping the suppressor from the Beretta and pocketing both.

'There will be killing till the score is paid.'

Twenty-nine

Keira sat, eyes closed, tucked into the corner of the ambulance on a green high-backed chair. She was wearing a thin cotton hospital gown and white paddle slippers: there had been no time to dress properly.

Her forearms were clamped together between her legs: wrists pressed hard against each other making small circular movements.

The ambulance was speeding through the potholed city streets with the siren wailing loudly overhead.

It felt cramped and claustrophobic.

With no window to look out of, it was all she could do to stop herself from throwing up.

The hospital had erupted after the shootings, with police officers and medical staff running everywhere, no one allowed in or out and roads in the surrounding area closed to all but essential traffic: Glasgow was in lockdown. Keira had been held in the ward for a short while until Gary Hammond arrived on the scene, then she'd been led down the back stairwell to the ambulance bay. He'd told her not to look as they'd left the room, but she couldn't help it. Another image seared into her memory as if it had been put there using a branding-iron. The instant the door had opened to reveal the two bodies splayed across the floor Keira knew who was responsible. It was her fault these people were dead.

DSI Gary Hammond and another armed officer sat awkwardly

on the gurney in front of her with their feet dangling over the edge. Next to them, on the only other available seat, was a doctor.

Keira had Gary's jacket draped over her shoulders for warmth.

'How you feeling now?' asked the doctor.

Keira shook her head in response.

'Once the painkillers kick in you should start to feel a bit better.'

'It's like being inside the hull of a boat,' Gary remarked.

'In a storm,' cut in Keira quietly.

'You get used to it,' said the doctor. 'You're usually too busy with other people being sick to worry about heaving yourself.'

'Nice! How much longer?'

'Nearly there,' answered Gary. 'When we arrive, you stay inside the ambulance until the Doc checks you over and gives you the all-clear, then we'll get you inside the station and find you some clothes.'

'Then what?'

'Then we'll take you somewhere safe.'

*

An hour later Keira was in the back of an unmarked police car speeding along the A814 out of Glasgow. The road was bordered on both sides by a low hedge and surrounded by flat, arable land laid out in an irregular patchwork of fields. To her left, in the distance, across a paddock dotted with brown cattle that rested on the grass like huge boulders, she could see the calm grey waters of Gare Loch.

'I can't keep my eyes open.'

Gary Hammond glanced over his shoulder from the driver's

seat. 'You okay?'

'I barely remember getting into the car. What the hell was in that syringe?'

'Whisky.'

'Really?'

'Morphine.'

'I'm beginning to see the appeal,' said Keira, stifling a yawn. 'Just you and me?'

'There's an armed unit following in the van behind, and another couple of officers in the car in front.'

'What's going on, Gary?'

'Who knows. But, I think – now that someone's tried to kill you again – it's safe to assume they don't believe you're dead any more. We're throwing everything we've got into trying to find the shooter. We've got a name: Engjell E Zeze also known as the Watcher, but that's about all. It's as if the son-of-a-bitch is supernatural. He can just vanish into thin air. No sightings, no real leads, no nothing.'

'I thought Jay-Go was in the frame as well.'

'He is, but he's vanished too.'

Keira looked down at the clothes she was wearing: a light pink tracksuit top with matching bottoms and a pair of Nike trainers, none of which she remembered putting on or recognized as her own. 'What am I wearing?'

'One of the female officers nipped out to buy it. She's in the car in front; you can thank her when we get there.'

'She ever read *Vogue*?'

'You chose it . . . she brought a selection. It's just to get you to where we're going. We'll send someone to your flat later and get your own things, whatever you need.'

'Was I unconscious when I picked it?'

'It's fine.'

'Still has the label on.'

'Yeah, well, don't get it dirty; we'll take it back and get a refund.'

'When can I move back home?'

'I didn't think you'd want to.'

'I don't. I'm trying to get an idea of how long it stays a crime scene. It's not something I've ever really thought about.'

'You could move in just now if you wanted. The tech teams only take a couple of days to gather up their evidence, then you get the crime and trauma scene decontamination team to tidy everything up.'

'Who organizes that?'

'You do.'

'Who pays?'

'You do . . . or your insurance.'

'I don't have insurance.'

Gary shot her another glance.

'I've got nothing to steal . . . except a Bowie photograph . . . I'd rather have experiences than possessions.'

'Then it's down to you.'

'I didn't make the mess.'

'Send Abazi the bill.'

'What do these guys do?'

'The decon team?'

'Yeah.'

'They're like specialist cleaners. They return your property to its pre-crime state.'

'That must be a pretty shitty job.'

'Yeah, I suppose. Although I don't know anyone that doesn't think their job is shitty. That's why they're called jobs . . . short for jobbies.'

It didn't feel right to be smiling, but Keira couldn't help herself.

'Some of the council estates I've visited,' continued Hammond, 'it's difficult to tell what's the crime scene and what's their living room.'

'My belongings at the hospital . . .'

'What about them?'

'Can someone gather up the notebooks at the side of my bed? I don't want them to disappear.'

'Don't worry, they won't be touched. Nothing will be removed from the scene until I say it can go.'

'The *scene*? This time yesterday it was just a room in a hospital: now it's a scene.'

'Yeah, looks like you're starting a collection.'

Keira stared out at the passing countryside as though she was looking at it on the big screen: it didn't look real. She thought if she reached out and tried to touch it, there would be nothing there. Her senses were intact, but she felt emotionally disconnected.

'Where are we going?'

'A village called Rhu. Used to be called Row but, everyone mispronounced it so they changed it to Rhu. Just past the marina on the outskirts. Out of the way, but not too far from Glasgow if you need any medical attention. Your personal shopper's name is Rebecca Rey. Nice girl, easy going.'

'Why are you telling me?'

'She'll be staying with you.'

Keira didn't react. The morphine was still doing its job.

'How long for?'

'How long is a piece of string? This situation is off the Richter scale: seven bodies in the morgue and one on the subs' bench. It could take a while. Your mum's staying there too; just as a precaution.'

'Who's on the subs' bench?'

'You! We don't want the total to get to eight.'

'I thought I was number seven.'

'That's what I was going to tell you before you started on about your wardrobe. It looked for a minute like your friend the junkie was number seven. At least we thought it was him, but the prints don't match up. They haven't positively ID'd the body yet, but we think it's one of his hash-hombres: a guy called Yogi Bearcat from his estate.'

Keira was staring at the back of Gary's head, trying to focus her thoughts. 'Gary, I'm sitting here whacked out on brain bleach, barely able to speak, never mind think straight, wondering what the hell are you on about.'

'Jason Gormley, your pal: Jay-Go. Somebody tried to give him a facelift using a nine-mil. Small hole in the back of his head, big hole at the front. Only they got the wrong guy. We had a team right outside his house when it happened: reckoned this Yogi Bearcat was dead before his brain hit the floor, but we're struggling to come up with a scenario that fits. All we do know is that Jay-Go wasn't home at the time, so he wasn't the shooter. He's probably lying low somewhere.'

'Wait! How come seven bodies? I only count six.'

'We found out why Janica Ahmeti didn't show up.'

'Jesus!'

'Fished her corpse out of the River Forth near Stirling...

they're still looking for her head.'

Keira turned and stared out at the loch. Even with the morphine her wounds were suddenly throbbing and painful again.

Eventually, after a long silence, she said, 'I could have killed him.'

'Who?' Gary kept his focus on the road ahead.

'E Zeze, the Watcher or whatever the cocksucker calls himself . . . I had his gun in my hand, pointing straight at him, but I couldn't pull the trigger.'

'Yeah, well, don't be sitting there blaming yourself for acting like a normal human being. Ninety-nine per cent of us would have done the same. None of this is your fault, okay, so don't let that particular train of thought drop you off at the wrong station. Killing someone has the same emotional impact on these guys as you experience when you order a cappuccino . . . It means absolutely nothing to them. If you'd pulled the trigger . . .'

'The cop and the nurses . . .'

'. . . would still be alive?' said Gary. 'Is that what you were about to say? Okay . . . if Kaltrina Dervishi had booked a flight from Edinburgh airport instead of Glasgow, or Engjell E Zeze hadn't followed you into your flat with a gun in the first place, or the trained firearms officer had raised his weapon a split second earlier in the hospital or the nurses had called in sick that day or any thousand other variations on how this could have panned out . . . Too many if's, only one certainty . . . It's not your fault.' He paused briefly to let that one sink in then continued. 'We're not even a hundred per cent certain it was E Zeze in the hospital. The only people who got a look were a couple of male nurses, and all they can remember seeing was the gun.'

'I am. I'm certain . . . one hundred per cent.'

'You said you didn't see him.'

'I didn't see him.'

'So how do you know?'

'I smelled him. When I stood at the door listening, I could smell him on the other side. And on the way out: the smell of him in the corridor.'

'Like what?'

'Aftershave or cologne, but something not right: like it's reacted with his skin or doesn't suit his skin type, you know.'

She could see Gary didn't get it.

'When perfumers describe a scent they talk about the different notes, like it's a piece of music. With E Zeze the heart notes, top notes and bass notes are all playing a different melody. When it hits your nose the smell is off key; it's wrong.'

'I've smoked all my life: can't smell a thing.'

'Not even when you're in a restaurant, someone comes in wearing too much perfume and it ruins your dinner. You're sitting there gagging and they don't realize?'

'I've never had that.'

'You're lucky. My instinct is to say something, but I never do. I just sit there quietly, letting it spoil my meal: fantasizing about leaning across and saying, "I know you think you're giving off the modern, confident woman vibe, with an alluring and mysterious sense of hidden sensuality, but the tag line's 'splash it all over', not 'take a shower in the shit'." '

Keira caught Gary staring back at her in the rear-view mirror and stopped talking.

After a while she said, 'I'm bombed on Miss Emma.'

Gary shook his head. 'Did Jay-Go teach you that?'

'One of many! I think "Miss Emma" is morphine.'

'D'you have any idea what the aftershave is called?'

'No. But, I'll tell you one thing . . . E Zeze is so used to his own smell he probably doesn't realize how much he's putting on . . . and, it's not my dinner the son-of-a-bitch is ruining, it's my life.'

Thirty

Edwin Kade was changing the dressing on the back of his head when the doorbell rang. Even though the wound had scabbed over and was almost healed, it was still raised and sensitive to the touch. The shaved area around the branch-line scar left behind after the attack in the hotel room had short stubble starting to show through that made the sterile gauze difficult to stick down. Holding the dressing with one hand, Edwin sprayed some mouth-freshener in an attempt to disguise the smell of the large vodka he'd just downed, then headed out of the bathroom. He negotiated his way past the low coffee table taking up most of the floor area of the modern lounge-diner and flicked the noisy daytime television programme off as he continued towards the front door.

Through the peephole he could make out the distorted figures of two men standing casually in the hallway.

Edwin slipped the chain and opened the door.

'Jesus, you guys,' he said, standing aside to let them in. 'I'm going off my frickin head here. Literally! Did you ever imagine when all this shit started the three of us would be getting together in an apartment in Glasgow, Scotland: that's a diary entry you don't see too often. How's it hangin'? What's with the beards?'

Officer Tommy Aquino reached out and gave him a warm handshake as he passed on into the lounge. Officer Gregg Moran just nodded.

'What's up, Moran, that pencil you got stuck up your ass run out of lead?' said Kade, taking him on straight away.

'He's been like that since we left Fairfax County,' replied Aquino. 'I've never heard anyone complain so much in all my life about nothing that matters.'

Moran pulled a face. 'I've had four hours' sleep in the last twenty-four hours.'

'And you moaned for the other twenty,' cut in Aquino. "These potato chips are too salty; this beer is too malty; this seltzer is too fizzy . . ." We hitched a lift on a C130, you're lucky we got anything at all. It's been like travelling with my eighty-year-old mom!'

'Your mom's dead.'

'So she's got an excuse for being a cranky old bitch.'

'Where have you put yourselves up?' asked Kade.

'Technically, we're not here.'

'We're illegal immigrants,' chipped in Moran.

'We thought we'd stop over and offer you a lift. Get you out of this mess. See if we can make contact with Abazi before we have everyone breathing down our necks. We're just passing through, on our way to Germany, then doubling back on ourselves and entering the country legally on a commercial flight. That's why the beards. A precaution in case someone's watching.'

'Does this place have any security cameras? We don't want evidence of us having had any contact with you before we've made our presence known to the Brits.'

'There's an alarm, but no cameras.'

'The front door?'

'Video entry, but it doesn't record.'

'We thought about booking a room at the Radisson, but we

heard the room service gives you a headache.' Moran was looking round the apartment and refused to catch the pissy look Kade threw his way.

'Nice rental,' he said.

'Easier than staying in a hotel: cheaper too. You want a beer, Tommy?' asked Kade.

'Yeah, I'll have one if it's cold.'

'I'll have whatever you're on,' said Moran pointedly.

'I'm on vacation.' Kade let a little edge creep into his tone.

'Okay! I'll have a large vacation and orange.' Moran cracked a smile for the first time as he slumped back on to one of the sofas. 'And you're not on vacation, you're on sick leave,' he continued. 'We're still paying your salary, you son-of-a-bitch.'

Kade made his way behind a run of low-level cupboards that divided the rest of the lounge from the small kitchen area and opened the fridge door. He fixed a couple of screwdrivers, opened a bottle of St Mungo lager and handed the drinks out.

'Wait till you taste the beer: brewed locally,' he said, searching for some snacks to go with. 'It's been the highlight of my stay so far, I kid you not.'

Tommy Aquino drained most of the bottle in one go then let out a satisfied groan. 'Who the hell is St Mungo?' he said, holding the bottle at arm's length to study the label.

'Who gives a shit, if he makes beer this good.' Kade pulled open a large bag of potato chips he'd found in one of the cupboards and poured them into a bowl. 'It's good, yeah?'

Aquino nodded in agreement, 'Yeah it's good.'

'So what the hell is going on? You here to help me pack: carry my things to the airport?' Kade crossed the room with the bowl of potato chips and sat in one of the two armchairs facing the guys on the sofa. 'You know, I haven't heard a word from Abazi since the girl landed an overhand right on the back of my skull. You expect to get a sore head from a bottle of champagne, but not like this.'

'No contact with him at all?' asked Moran.

'The asshole doesn't pick up or return any messages. I'm totally out of the loop here. I haven't heard from you guys either. Been sitting here wondering what the hell is going down.'

'The local cops have been keeping an eye on you,' said Aquino. 'We thought it best to leave you alone in case this whole thing exploded . . . which unfortunately it has.'

'Yeah, it's all over the news here. Big story.' Kade took a large slug of his drink. 'It must have created quite a bang to get you two off your lazy asses and on to a plane.'

Aquino exchanged a look with Moran that Kade caught.

'What?'

'Are you well enough to travel?'

'Sure. I had to surrender my passport after the girl got whacked, though. They've only just made the connection that it was her in the hotel that night. I hadn't given the cops anything, but they made her on one of the hotel's security cameras. Might want to call me in to give evidence now. I think they may even have me down as a goddamn suspect. That's two headaches that bitch has given me.'

'Don't worry about your passport, we can sort that out later,' said Moran. 'Why did you travel on your own name?'

'I know! It was dumb. It was only meant to be a short trip.'

'What the fuck were you thinking? They know you're CIA.'

Kade sat shaking his head, 'What can I say? . . . It's a fuck-up. It was a routine trip and the girl screwed everything except me.

But I know what you're saying. I should have been more careful. Is there going to be a trial?'

'If they can find Abazi,' answered Aquino. 'We're here to make sure that doesn't happen.'

'We're closing him down,' cut in Moran as he finished off his screwdriver in one gulp. 'Son-of-a-bitch has laid us wide open.'

'If you can find him!' replied Kade. 'The guy is smarter than your average bear. He works all the angles. I wouldn't be surprised if he's already gone. With all the shit on the television and in the newspapers about the lawyer's murder, he'll know we're not going to be happy. He'll be expecting us to come after him. That's why he's not picking up. The guy's a fighter, but only when he knows he can win. If Abazi thinks he's in trouble he plays dead. I had a conversation with him at the dinner table – the night the girl went AWOL. All he talked about were the failings of the great dictators. He reckoned that the one thing they all had in common was they didn't know when to quit.'

'"The crisis point",' Aquino responded.

'That's right. He studies this shit looking for the patterns: where the regime went wrong, identifying the similarities and trying not to make the same mistakes. Paul Kagame – Rwanda, Ceauşescu – Romania, even obscure ones: Roman von Ungern-Sternberg from Mongolia, for Chrissake. This guy Roman was captured by his own troops and handed over to the Red Army. Abazi didn't like that. It's all about loyalty with him. He wanted to phone Bashar al-Assad in Syria and tell him he'd missed his moment. A couple of years ago Assad was offered a get-out clause. He could have gone anywhere: Paris, Berlin ... London, even. Taken his money and made a quick exit. But Abazi reckons Assad misread the cards. He tried to hold on and now he's got no out: the French won't touch him; the Germans won't touch him . . . he's screwed. Abazi asked me if I could get a number. Like the president of Syria is going to take his call. Abazi has a handle on all of this, that's why he's survived this long and also – if I can remind you – why we chose him. He knows when to fight and he knows when to run. I think he's chosen the exit door.'

'Where would he go? Back home?' Moran got to his feet and headed into the kitchen. 'You mind if I fix myself another. You were a bit light on the "vacation".'

'Sure, help yourself . . . I don't think he'd head home. He still has all the connections there, but things have moved on: different people in charge of the Clan. He'd be treading on rivals' toes, it'd be too much of a headache.'

'I thought all his money was tied up in property here?'

'They're all mortgaged to the max and sub-let or rented. His money is out already. The only people who would feel the pain would be the banks. He's free to go.'

'D'you want a refresher?' asked Moran from behind the counter.

Kade held up his glass, 'Yeah, sure,' then continued, 'I think he'll head over to France . . . Paris, most likely. He's been sending a lot of his money over there, possibly with a view to his retirement.'

Moran filled Kade's glass with vodka and orange and brought it over to him. 'Yeah, we want him to retire him too . . . to the big condo in the sky.'

'Thank you.' Kade took a sip and placed the glass on the coffee table. 'So, where we at? No one knows you're here?'

'Not yet,' answered Aquino. 'We thought we'd take a look around first without the cops or intelligence services following

248

our every move. If we can find Abazi and take care of him, we'll slip off and no one will be any the wiser.'

'Our biggest problem at the moment is the lawyer,' said Moran.

Kade looked confused. 'The lawyer? Whose lawyer?'

'The girl's.'

'How does she figure?'

'She's still alive.'

Kade's eyebrows were touching his hairline.

'We're still not sure how much she knows.'

'There was a survivor – holy shit! The girl's lawyer survived?'

'It was as much a shock to us too, believe me!' said Moran.

'This is a lot messier than I thought. You must have accessed her computer, read her notes. Is there nothing in there?'

'She writes everything longhand.'

Kade was staring back at Aquino. 'Are you shitting me? Longhand . . . I don't even know what that means. What about her assistant? There must be stuff on his hard drive.'

'The cops have that. They also have all her notes and note-books containing anything to do with the girl.'

'Put in a request to take a look. The cops must have some idea about what was said between the lawyer and the girl. Check out the lead investigator. Hell, if I'd known I could have done that from here on my Mac, instead of sitting scratching my ass for the last couple of weeks.'

'We start poking around too much, we'll alert them to our involvement. They'll wonder why we're so interested. And – right now, until we've fixed Abazi, we don't want that. The Brits have already sent an information request to Langley regarding your activities here.'

Edwin Kade looked uncomfortable. 'Yeah, well, like I already said, that was a screw-up, but so far I've been playing dumb. Told them I was on a stopover, which is – as near as damn it – the truth. What did you tell them?'

'Pretty much the same,' replied Aquino. 'We said that, as far as we're aware, we have no active operations on British soil.'

'But, it's piqued their interest,' followed Moran, 'and that's not good. The British security services have eyes on Abazi already.'

'Where are they hiding the lawyer?' asked Kade.

'She *was* in one of the local hospitals under armed guard . . . *Now*, we don't know. We'll hopefully find that out when we make an official appearance.'

Edwin Kade's brain was in overdrive: all the stuff he'd been watching on the news over the last few days suddenly clicking into place. 'The two nurses and the SWAT guy popped at the hospital, that's all connected?'

'Collateral damage.' Aquino shrugged. 'When Abazi found out the lawyer was still alive he tried to add her to the score sheet . . . again.'

'Unsuccessfully,' interrupted Moran, '. . . again.'

'Okay, so now I'm up to speed with what prompted your sudden appearance.' Kade took a large mouthful of his drink. 'Huddle up, what's the exit strategy?'

'How soon can you be ready to go?' asked Aquino.

'I've got an overnight bag. How does ten minutes sound?'

Moran nodded. 'Good. We've got a car waiting out back to take you up to Machrihanish. You can catch a military transport from there that will drop you in Mena.'

'Arkansas, you're shitting me! Jesus, it's a two day journey back to Fairfax from there.'

'If you'd rather stick it out here and take the twenty-year route via the pokey it's up to you. That's assuming you get time off for good behaviour.'

Moran was right. If the Abazi situation exploded in his face he could end up in a British jail for a long time.

'Don't, for Chrissake, call your wife to tell her you're coming in case someone's listening,' continued Moran.

'I screwed up one time, asshole.'

'We'll clean up in here, you go get sorted.' Aquino headed over to the kitchen area with his beer bottle and the half-empty bowl of potato chips.

Moran poured the rest of his drink down the sink and placed his glass in the clear plastic bag he'd just pulled from his jacket pocket while Aquino tipped the remainder of the potato chips into the sink and placed the bowl in the bag as well. 'Where's Kade's drink?'

'He took it with him.'

'Anything else?'

'Give the handle of the fridge door a wipe, and the vodka bottle,' replied Moran.

Aquino took a surface-cleansing tissue from a small packet he was carrying and used it to wipe down the handle of the fridge door and clean the vodka bottle, careful not to leave behind any other prints.

His phone made a short buzzing sound in his pocket.

He didn't have to look at it to know what it meant. 'That's the driver. We don't go now we're gonna miss the flight.'

Aquino stood for a second listening to the muffled sounds of Kade gathering his possessions together in the room next door, then whispered to Moran, 'What you thinking?'

'I'm thinking Kade's got a green neon above his head that reads, "Exit". We don't follow the sign, we gonna get caught in the blast.'

Reluctantly, Aquino nodded his head in agreement. 'Is he primed?'

Moran answered in a low voice, 'Yeah . . . it was in his drink.'

'How long?'

'Should be more or less instant. You go wait in the car. I'll go see where he's at.'

When Moran entered the room he found Kade sitting, slumped at the end of the bed. Kade slowly raised his head and stared up at him, drooling saliva from the side of his gaping mouth.

'What'd you do to me?'

His speech was slurred, his words almost incoherent.

'Just a little something to help you on your way,' replied Moran.

'Where am I going?'

'Vacation.'

Kade looked on helplessly as Moran pulled a handgun from the holster concealed under his jacket and started to screw on a suppressor.

Thirty-one

DSI Hammond was standing with a uniformed officer at the arrivals gate at Glasgow airport drinking a take-away coffee and eating a hot panini. He was only a few bites in when he spotted the two men passing through customs and heading toward him. Muttering 'Shit' under his breath, he folded the sandwich back into its wrapper and held out his hand as they approached. 'Welcome to Glasgow, gentlemen. Sorry it's not under better circumstances.'

'Don't wrap up your lunch on account of us,' said Tommy Aquino, extending his hand.

'It's breakfast.'

'Even more reason to eat up. DSI Hammond?'

'Yes, but call me Gary. I'm in charge of the investigation. This is Sergeant Iain Baird, he'll be our driver for the day. Take you wherever you want to go.'

'I'm Officer O'Donnell – but call me Joe – and this is my partner, Mitch Taylor.' Aquino indicated Gregg Moran with a flick of his finger. 'Call him whatever you like.'

The two agents flashed their fake ID cards, with their assumed names printed just above the barcode strip on the bottom left, then pocketed them, knowing that would probably be the only time they'd be used.

The four men set off in the direction of the car park.

'How was the flight?'

'Short,' replied Aquino. 'It was like, we'd only just taken off and they asked us to fasten our seatbelts for landing.'

'Are you guys based in Berlin?'

'Just passing through,' said Moran. 'We were just about to head back to the States when we got the call.'

'D'you want to check into your hotel first, drop off your things and freshen up?'

'Only carrying this hand luggage and I'm afraid this is as fresh as we get. If you don't mind, we'd rather get straight to it. We got a lot of ground to cover, and little or no time.'

'Sure.'

'Can we go direct to the crime scene: take a look around?' asked Moran.

'No problem,' replied Gary. 'Then we'll go to the morgue: get the formal ID out of the way.'

'Sure. When'd it happen?'

'The body was discovered yesterday evening, but we reckon he'd been lying there for a couple of days.'

'Any idea what went down?'

'A bit early to say. One thing we're fairly certain about, it was a professional hit. Two bullets fired – one to the head, one to the chest – either of which would have been lethal.'

'D'you think it's linked to Abazi and the hooker?'

'I don't know, possibly . . . I mean, at the moment that's the most likely scenario. I'm not sure how much you guys know.'

'A lot – but until we've spoken to your intelligence people, we can't say too much. I'm not trying to be an ass, I promise. We'll help you as much as we can, but we need to follow the rules.' Moran smiled at just how easily he was able to turn on the bullshit.

'I understand.'

'I will say this: Edwin Kade wasn't just a fellow agent, he was a friend. We have our own theories as to what has happened, but until we've got all the info, we don't want to disrespect the guy by blowing off too early.'

They had reached the car park.

Sergeant Baird stood next to a dark silver BMW 6 Series and pressed the immobilizer fob. He held open the back door to let Aquino in, then moved round the other side to do the same for Moran while Gary Hammond climbed into the front passenger seat.

Once inside the car, Baird made himself comfortable and started the engine. 'It's close to rush hour. We in a hurry, boss?' he asked.

'I don't want to be sitting in traffic.'

'Boo-Hoo and blue?'

Gary Hammond nodded.

'Fair enough.' Baird turned to look over his shoulder to the two CIA agents sitting in the back. 'Buckle up, gents!'

Two minutes later Gregg Moran indicated with a small lift of his eyebrows for Aquino to check the speedometer. The BMW was cutting through the late afternoon traffic on the M8 motorway at over one hundred miles an hour, Baird's attention focused solely on the road ahead as he weaved his way expertly between the cars.

Aquino had to raise his voice to be heard over the hi-lo wail and intermittent tri-tone of the siren.

'How's the lawyer doing, Keira Lynch?'

'Okay. It was touch and go at the start: lucky to make it. But she's making good progress now. Ninety-five per cent there.'

'Where's she at?'

'We moved her and her mother to a safe house just outside Glasgow. Still not sure why she's a target, but there still appears to be a legitimate threat.'

'She accepting visitors?'

'I'm sure we could sort something out.'

'I think we could throw some light on the subject: put her mind at rest.'

'Probably won't happen today.'

'Can we fix it up for first thing tomorrow morning?'

'Sure.'

*

Apart from the slight chill that comes with a house that's been left empty for a while and two guys in forensic whites moving around in the living area next door, Edwin Kade's apartment looked exactly the same as it had a few days earlier. Gregg Moran and Tommy Aquino were standing in the doorway of the bed-room surveying the blood-soaked sheets and stained carpet, Aquino shaking his head. 'Man this sucks! So, was he asleep or something? Doesn't look like there's much else out of place. No signs of a struggle.'

'That's the way it reads. Toxicology report says he'd been drinking. More likely he was passed out, then whoever was in the apartment with him did the business. The time of death is a guess, but they put it late morning/early afternoon rather than night time.'

'So there was someone in the apartment with him?'

'That's the assumption.'

'Have you lifted any other prints?'

'Not so far.'

'Was he on anything else . . . anything stronger than alcohol?'

'No.'

'So you think Kade knew his killer?'

'I think whoever shot him was in the apartment, or Kade let him in. No signs of forced entry, no break-in, nothing stolen. A straightforward hit – and yes, he probably knew the killer.'

'You mind if we have a look in his bags?' Moran moved over to Edwin Kade's holdall that was sitting on the far side of the bed. 'Looks like he was planning a trip.'

Before Gary Hammond could stop him he'd pulled it open and was delving inside.

'If you don't mind, Mitch, you really need to snap on some gloves before you start rummaging around.'

Moran looked up from the bag and made a convincing play of acting guilty. 'Holy shit, I'm sorry, I assumed this had all been tech'd, Jesus!'

'So far we've only removed the body, nothing else has been done.'

Moran made his way back to the doorway. 'I'm so sorry! Listen, I'll leave it up to you guys, but can you copy us in on all the forensic shit, let us know if anything comes up, even if it doesn't seem that interesting? We're working on a theory that Edwin Kade was involved in something he shouldn't have been. So far everything we've got supports that story, and to be honest the manner of his death has come as no big surprise. It just confirms our belief. We just need to back it up with concrete evidence. You know what it's like in this game: if it walks like a duck and talks like a duck, you can guarantee it's a fucking pig in disguise.'

'Sure,' replied Hammond.

'We kinda need everything,' added Aquino, 'no matter how trivial.'

'No problem.'

Hammond, Moran and Aquino moved back through to the lounge.

'Neighbours see or hear anything?' asked Moran.

'The block is mostly empty during the day. No one saw or heard anything out of the ordinary.'

'I thought you guys had him under surveillance?'

'We were keeping an eye on him, that's all. After he got smacked on the back of the head by the prostitute, we'd asked him to stick around in case he was going to be called to give evidence.'

'In her case or in the case against Abazi?'

'In her case, primarily. We were looking for any links there might have been to Abazi as well, although, as it stands, there is no case against him; not yet, anyway.'

'Okay, I think we've seen enough,' said Aquino nodding at Moran. 'Let's get Kade's ID out of the way.'

'What time d'you think we can go see Keira Lynch tomorrow?' asked Moran as they headed for the front door.

'If I pick you up at your hotel just after nine a.m. we could be there around ten-ish?'

'Sounds good.'

'We'll take care of MI5 tonight,' added Aquino. 'Let them in on what's been happening, then hopefully, in the morning, we can fill you in on what we think is going on here.'

Thirty-two

Officer Aquino was standing in the living room of the cottage staring out of the small rear window. 'Has she got a target in mind, or does she throw those things for a hobby?'

'She's trying to rehabilitate her shoulder: improve the co-ordination down the right side,' answered Keira's mother. 'Take a seat, and I'll let her know you're here.'

'Has she seen this morning's headlines?'

Orlaith stared back at him. 'Yes.'

'What's she make of them?'

'Why don't you ask her?' Orlaith left the cramped sitting room and headed through the kitchen to the back door.

'Are those things legal?' Moran asked Gary Hammond, his attention drawn to Keira's knife throwing again.

'Not if you're carrying them down the street, but if you're throwing them around your own home there's not much we can do.'

'Who's the other girl?'

'Rebecca Rey: close protection officer.'

'She armed?'

'Yes.'

'Any other cover?'

'We did have for the first few days, but not now: don't have the manpower. We were lucky to even get her. Local cops check in regularly and the whole house is fitted with panic alarms and cameras we can monitor remotely.'

Aquino watched the last two knives spin through the air and stick point first into an old railway sleeper propped against the drystone wall that bordered the small cottage garden. Keira Lynch turned when she saw her mother appear at the back door, then nodded to her and went to retrieve the knives, which were clustered together in a tight bunch near the top of the sleeper. Aquino exchanged a look with Moran and said quietly, 'Not bad!'

Moran nodded and replied, 'And the knife throwing is pretty hot too!'

Seconds later Keira was standing in the doorway of the living room holding the presentation box containing the knives.

'Surprising talent,' said Aquino as his opener.

'Why surprising?'

'I mean it's not something you see every day . . . you know . . . a woman throwing knives.'

'Unless you're in the circus, I suppose,' chipped in Moran.

'A woman?'

'A person! It's an unusual skill to have, is what I mean. You been doing it long?'

'It's sort of a family tradition.'

Gary Hammond made the introductions. 'Keira, these are Officers Joe O'Donnell and Mitch Taylor. Flew in from Berlin yesterday. They wanted to have a chat. Gentlemen: Keira Lynch.'

Moran made like he was about to shake her hand, but Keira didn't move. 'D'you guys have ID?'

Aquino raised his eyebrows. 'You're the first person to ask that.'

'You wanna see them?' said Moran.

'If you don't mind.'

Moran and Aquino fished out their identity cards and offered them over to her. After a cursory glance she handed them back. 'I've never seen one before so I don't know what they're supposed to look like.'

'So why ask?' replied Moran, already getting the sense that this was not going to be an easy ride.

'Why not?' Keira placed the box of knives on a drop-leaf table sitting in front of the lounge window. 'Let's sit outside. We don't usually have weather like this in Scotland, and I've been feeling a little claustrophobic of late.'

*

Rebecca Rey stood vigil at the far end of the neat little garden while Moran, Aquino, Hammond and Keira pulled up chairs and sat at a wooden table on the small patio area just outside the kitchen door. Orlaith followed them out with a tray of tea and coffee then disappeared back inside. The sun was still low in the morning sky, but it was already starting to get warm.

Aquino was still pursuing the knife-throwing line. 'I thought you might have a picture of Mister E Zeze pinned to your block of wood there,' he said, removing his jacket and hanging it on the back of his chair.

'I would if I could remember what he looked like,' Keira said matter-of-factly. 'My mind has blanked out everything, but his scent.'

'His scent?' Moran screwed up his face.

'He wears a weird cologne . . .'

'. . . that doesn't suit his skin type,' said Hammond, finishing off her sentence and earning himself a look from the two agents, like that was a new one to them.

'What type of cologne?'

Keira caught the exchange of looks between the three men. 'It doesn't matter.'

'Have you seen the stuff on the news and in the papers this morning?' Moran asked her.

'I've watched the news, but I haven't read anything yet.'

'It didn't come from us, Keira,' added Gary quickly. 'When I find out who's responsible I'll bloody crucify them.'

Breakfast News on the BBC had led with the story that traces of heroin had been found in Keira's flat, leading to speculation that the shootings had been drug related: it went on to say that police were investigating links between Keira and high-profile Glasgow crime lords.

'What d'you think is going on?' Moran probed.

'Should I have a lawyer present?'

'It's not a formal interview,' interjected Gary, 'just a chat.'

'I don't know what's going on,' she said after a brief pause. 'It looks like someone may be trying to discredit me.'

'Why?'

'I've no idea. "Blur the picture", perhaps, who knows? I feel like I'm part of a game, but no one has told me the rules yet . . . if there are any.'

'D'you know how the heroin got there?'

'No.'

'Okay, why don't you kick things off: tell us what you know and where you think it's at and we'll try our best to answer as many questions as you might possibly have?'

'Because I didn't ask to see you, you asked to see me, that's why. The onus isn't on me to tell you anything, the onus is on you to explain to me what the hell this is all about.'

Gary Hammond shifted uncomfortably in his seat.

'I appreciate that,' Aquino said gently. 'Unfortunately the glue we're using to stick all the bits together is strong enough to give us a headache, but not to hold anything in place. We were hoping you might know something that would help.'

Keira sat staring back at the two agents in silence.

'Anything you can think of to make it any easier for us to find out what happened to our colleague Ed—' started Aquino, but Keira interrupted him.

'It's not my job to make your life easier. I'm sitting here with a head full of memories I'd rather not have, and I suspect it's because of some shit that you or those like you are involved in. So don't come in here acting like Mister and Mister Nice Guy and expect me to start reliving it all so that you can have an easy life. *You* asked to see *me*, remember?' Keira's tone was controlled and measured as she continued. 'Either tell me what you feel I need to know or go away and leave me the hell alone.'

Aquino could see Moran preparing to take her on and jumped in. 'Woah, woah, let's just take a step back and come at this from a different angle. You're right, we should be giving you information, not the other way around. Our problem is we have a few gaps in our story that we were hoping you might be able to fill, make these events hang together a little better. But let's set that aside for the moment; that, as you have correctly stated, is our problem, not yours. We just wanted to come here and tell you what we think is going on, hopefully put your mind at rest as much as possible given the circumstances, then leave you in peace to get your life back on track.'

The expression on Keira's face was still difficult to read.

Aquino kept going. 'We've been keeping a close eye on Fisnik Abazi's activities for some time now in an effort to gain enough intelligence on him, not only to cut off his supply chain, but to close the son-of-a-bitch down entirely. The operation he has been running has a global reach, far beyond his capabilities, and we wanted to know why and how. We found out that he was using US military aircraft to smuggle his merchandise, not only into Scotland, but on from here, into the States. The only way that was possible was if someone from within the military was colluding. But every time it looked like we were closing in something would happen that would mess our game. That's when we started to have concerns that someone closer to home was also helping him.'

'Someone from within the CIA,' cut in Moran.

'We had no clues, no intel, nothing to point the finger at anyone from inside any of the operations we were running. Then bam! Edwin Kade gets brained by one of Abazi's hookers and suddenly the whole thing falls into place. We were on the edge of closing this whole game down when, not only does the girl get whacked, but Kade too. Leaving us floating on a sea of crap in a leaky life-raft.'

'Once again,' added Moran.

'What was in it for Kade?'

'What's in it for any of these guys? Money! Turns out he's got bank accounts all over the place full of cash. Deposits bags of cash every time, like he's a shopkeeper or something: in fact that was his cover story.'

'There was a small bag of heroin found at his flat too,' chipped in Gary Hammond. 'We just had it confirmed this morning that it was from the same batch that Abazi's putting out on the street. And matches the traces found in your apartment also. All from the same supply.'

'Why not close Abazi down sooner?'

'If we'd taken Abazi out, two minutes later someone else would have stepped in. We wanted to get a handle on the entire smuggling operation, then terminate the whole goddamn thing.'

'Was there any political pressure put on Patrick Sellar to release Kaltrina Dervishi?'

The question came from left field. Aquino wasn't expecting it. 'Who's Patrick Sellar?' He already knew the answer, but was buying himself time to think.

'The Advocate Depute. He released Kaltrina Dervishi on to the street. He was also in line to be the lead prosecutor in the Abazi case – were Abazi ever arrested.'

Aquino shrugged. 'Oh yeah, him. Well, he was under no pressure from our side. We wanted her alive. She was to be a key witness. We certainly let British Intelligence know we had an interest in her, but I wouldn't say that ran as far as influencing a member of your judiciary to make a decision that was – or wasn't – in the best interest of everyone concerned.'

'He mentioned to me that she would have no right to appeal if a deportation order was taken out against her, because she was considered a threat to this or some other country's national security. Would that other country have been yours?'

Aquino looked to Moran.

'Possibly,' conceded Moran.

Keira was slipping into lawyer mode. These guys came across as convincing, but all the best liars did.

'So in that sense, wouldn't you agree there was undue pressure placed, not only on my client, but on a representative of the law who is duty bound to remain impartial?'

'No, I wouldn't agree. The intention was to close down a major drug-smuggling ring – not to mention the side-effect that would have on the trafficking and prostitution that hangs off its back. The girl was the first breakthrough we'd had in bringing that about. In retrospect, using the whole deportation thing wasn't a smart way forward, but we were desperate. We were simply trying to find excuses to hold on to her as best we could without breaking any rules. But we're getting off the point. If this Patrick Sellar hadn't released her we'd all be in a much better position. We're still not sure why he did that.'

Keira let the conversation hang for a moment, then said, 'How does any of this help me get my life back on track?'

'The word from Langley is that Abazi has called in the removal van.'

'Who's Langley?'

She already knew the answer, but she'd learned from years of dealing with guys like this that it usually paid dividends to let them think they were smarter than her. The feeling of superiority they enjoyed meant they tended to underestimate her, which in most cases always proved to be an advantage.

'Sorry, Langley is the CIA headquarters in Virginia.'

'Okay.'

'Anyway, we think Abazi may have fled to Europe already, leaving behind a handful of his men to tidy up. If there are any positives to take, it's the fact that he's no longer in business. He knows we're coming after him. And without Edwin Kade guarding his ass, he knows we'll be successful this time.'

'And Engjell E Zeze?'

'He's nicknamed the Watcher. That's what they first called

fallen angels: Watchers. It's like he's supernatural or something. The literal translation of his name is Angel Black. We have no idea where he is. But, this is what I was going to say: we don't think you were ever intended to be a target. The problem, as we see it, is that you were the last contact the girl had. Abazi's probably figuring she's told you everything that's going on, so he might as well take you out as well. I would urge you still to be cautious, but Engjell E Zeze works for Abazi, and with Abazi gone I can't see why E Zeze would still want you dead. I think the risk to you has been considerably lessened.'

Moran's phone buzzed in his pocket.

'Sorry,' he said, pulling it out and checking the message. 'D'you mind if I quickly reply to this? I had an important meeting scheduled for tomorrow in the States, I just need to cancel it. Excuse me, it won't take a second.'

Moran stayed where he was and punched in a number.

'Hi, it's Officer Mitch Taylor here, just a quick message to say I won't make the meeting tomorrow, something has come up. I'll be back in the States at the start of next week, so I'll call you then to rearrange. Apologies for any inconvenience.' Moran hung up and slipped his phone back into his pocket. 'Sorry, but if I didn't do it now I'd have forgotten and caused all sorts of problems.'

Aquino hadn't taken his eyes off Keira the whole time. She still wasn't giving much away, but looked a lot more subdued. 'You figure you're in possession of any information that might keep Abazi coming after you, Miss Lynch?'

Keira returned his stare. 'No.'

The only information Keira was withholding now was about Kaltrina's son, Ermir, which as far as she was concerned was none of their business.

'You figure there's anything you want to tell us, might help seal Abazi's fate?'

She shook her head. 'No.'

'Then I guess we're all done,' said Moran as he pushed back his chair and stood up. 'If you think of anything that might be of use, we're staying at the Crowne Plaza, and this,' he handed her a scrap of paper, 'has our cell numbers while we're here. Abazi will be so busy looking over his shoulder for us, he won't have time to come looking for you.'

*

The atmosphere in the unmarked police car was tense as it sped along the road on its way back to Glasgow. Gary Hammond could tell the two Americans weren't happy.

'Does anyone else feel like they've been kicked in the balls?' said Aquino.

'You get the feeling she's not telling us everything?' Moran directed the question at Gary.

Gary was reluctant to give his opinion. 'I don't know. She's been through a lot in the last few weeks. I think maybe she's just had enough. She's under a lot of pressure.'

'You think maybe she is involved in handling the drugs?'

'No, I don't.'

'It wouldn't be the first time the lawyer turns out to be one of the main players.'

'Not in this case.'

'All I'm saying is, you might want to take a closer look.'

*

'We leaving tomorrow?' asked Moran.

'We've still got some work to do. We'll leave when we're done.'

The two officers were standing in the lobby of their hotel waiting for the lift to arrive. 'I'm gonna take a shower, try and freshen up a little. You wanna eat here or try to find somewhere in town?'

'Let's grab a few beers at the bar, then we can decide . . . You think she knows what's going on?'

'I think there's something she's not telling us, but that's as far as it goes. If she was on to us, we'd know about it by now.'

'You think it was subtle, making that call with the two of them sitting at the table?'

Moran looked round at him and smiled. 'Did you like that?'

'Not particularly.'

'What?' protested Moran. 'All they heard was me cancelling a meeting in the States . . . what's wrong with that?'

'And how did a bag of smack find its way into Kade's apartment?'

'No point being subtle about it. We gotta make this guy out to be badder than bad. We give these guys plenty of evidence that's all pointing in the same direction, there's only one conclusion they can come to – Edwin Kade, guilty as charged. You wanna know where they found the bag of heroin?'

'In his holdall?'

'Man, you're too good.'

'You can be such an asshole sometimes, you know that?' Aquino shook his head.

'Turns out our source was correct about it being placed in the lawyer's apartment, too. For whatever reason, it must have been removed – but not before some of it spilled on the kitchen table. I was reading through some of the scene-of-crime reports Hammond gave me and, bang, there it was: "Traces of controlled substance confirmed as heroin".

The lift arrived and the two men stepped in.

'Not enough to put her away for a long time, unfortunately,' continued Moran, 'but enough to grab a few headlines and fuck her over.'

Thirty-three

St Andrew's Cathedral sat on the north bank of the River Clyde near Glasgow's city centre. It was illuminated by large uplighters that made the building stand out against the dark, cloudless sky. The back two pews of the cathedral were taken up by Nick-Nick Carter, Big Paul and a handful of each of their respective gang members. They had gathered there at the Holy Man's request to 'pray for the departed and those on the metaphorical platform edge who were about to receive their one-way ticket to the afterlife in the form of a bullet'.

Even though there was obvious tension between the rival gang members, the rest of the congregation seemed oblivious to the stony-faced men.

'It's like visiting hours at the remand centre,' muttered Nick-Nick, shaking his head.

Big Paul leant across Edi Leka, who was sandwiched between him and the Holy Man, and whispered, 'We've found the little fuck.'

The Holy Man shot Big Paul a look. 'You're in the Big Man's house now, brother. Keep that sort of language for your own home, not in here.'

Big Paul didn't even blink. 'He's holed up in a bed and break-fast on the South Side. Wan eh Nick-Nick's guys saw him out at the off-licence buying some cheap cider and followed him.'

'What's it called?'

'Ah don't know: Magners?'

'The bed and breakfast,' the Holy Man said coolly.

'Ah'm just messin' with you. It's called the Ewington, in Queens Park. More a hotel really, but it's B-and-B rates. Nice set-up. Too good for that wee shite.'

'Are you sure it's him?'

'No mistake. Man, there's wanted dead or alive posters all over town. Even my ma knows what Jay-Go looks like.'

Edi Leka sat staring ahead, pretending he was listening to the priest. The rumour circulating after the incident at Jay-Go's flat was that Yogi Bearcat had tried to rob Jay-Go: that's why he got whacked. After shooting him in the head, Jay-Go had gone into hiding, taking the Holy Man's money and Abazi's kilo of heroin with him.

The story had worked in Edi's favour: everyone, including the police, was searching for the missing Jay-Go.

All Edi Leka had to do was make sure he got to him first, kill the son-of-a-bitch, recover the heroin and return it to Mister Abazi.

'There's nothing I can do tonight,' said the Holy Man. 'It'll have to wait. Can yer man keep an eye on him, let me know if the situation changes?'

'Ah'm sure he can.'

At the end of the Mass, as the rest of the congregation filtered out, the Holy Man passed the word around for everyone in his party to stay where they were, then walked down to meet the priest, who was already halfway along the aisle on his way to greet him.

'Everything all right?' asked Father David.

'No worries, Father . . . Could I have five minutes to address my gathering, then we'll be on our way?'

'Certainly, Mister McMaster, take your time.' As the priest turned heel and headed for the vestry, the Holy Man rejoined the group of men, most whom were now on their feet.

'Take a seat for a moment, gentlemen, this won't take long. A lot of you, I know, are wondering why this choice of venue and I'll come to that in a moment. The reason I wanted us to gather for Mass en masse was for everyone to get a good look at each other before Saturday night. In particular our new friend Mister Leka, without whom none of this would have been possible . . . Stand up, Edi.'

Edi Leka stood for a second, gave an awkward nod, then sat down again.

'It was Edi that gave us the information about the large shipment Mister Abazi will be receiving at the weekend and it is he who will make sure the gates are open and the alarm system disabled when we enter the premises. He is also the one responsible for fingering which building to target – a haulage warehouse on the Darnley estate. If and when the shooting starts, please make sure our friend Mister Leka is not in the firing line. The same applies to all of you. Take a good look around. Memorize as many of the faces that are unfamiliar to you as possible. I don't want there to be any casualties on our side caused by friendly fire. Mister Abazi is allegedly planning to retire, but not before he's sent us a "fuck-you-all" leaving present. He wants to flood the market with extremely cheap, extremely pure product in an attempt to kill off our business or kill off our clientele before he goes. Either way it's an act of sabotage. Which brings me nicely to the reason I've chosen St Andrew's as the venue for our wee get-together. When the cathedral was first being built, because of the prejudice against Catholics and the resistance to them having their own place of worship, all the work that was carried out during the day was dismantled in the middle of the night by saboteurs. Such was the level of interference, and the cost of repairing the damage done by the bastards, that it looked like the Church would run out of money and the project remain unfinished. Guards had to be placed outside to protect the construction works. However, congregations from other Christian denominations didn't like what was going on. They took collections, offered the money and worked to help the Catholic Church complete the building that we are sitting in now. This is why I brought you here. To show you what can be achieved with a little co-operation. Let us unite in a Holy Ecumenical Alliance Treaty . . . HEAT for short. For the ignorant amongst us, it means that we may not agree on a lot of things, but if we co-operate with one another, bury our differences for a short while and work for the common good, we can not only protect our business interests, but sort that wee bastard Abazi right out.'

When Holy Man had finished there was a brief pause, followed by an awkward smattering of applause.

*

Jay-Go sat on one of the two armchairs in the bay window of his room in the Ewington hotel. He was hunched over the round coffee table in front of the chairs rolling a joint. He'd scored some grass from a street-dealer in the park across the road from the hotel. The room was clean and comfortable with plenty of space to move around, but the colour scheme was doing his brain in – aquamarine coloured chairs, rose pink carpet, yellow walls and a floral patterned bedspread. As soon as the spliff was cooked he'd go for a walk in the park to get a break from the décor.

He pulled back the curtain.

The street lamps had just come on, but it would be another twenty minutes or so before it was dark enough to venture out. Over a week had passed since Yogi had copped it. In that time Jay-Go had managed to grow a short, stubbly beard. Using some of the money the Holy Man had given him, he'd also bought some new clothes. His hair was starting to grow back too, but he still didn't look different enough to feel confident going out in daylight hours. He had his own key to the front door of the hotel, so he could come and go as he pleased and avoid any unnecessary contact with the staff, but it was only a matter of time before someone clocked who he was and contacted the police.

Jay-Go's phone suddenly buzzed on the table. He stared at it, hesitating for a second, before picking it up and clicking on 'message'.

Ready or not, here I come, was all it said.

He put the spliff between his lips and lit up.

Taking a long, deep draw he sat motionless and continued to stare at the screen.

Eventually he started nodding his head, as though he'd come to a decision. He would have a couple of tokes to get him started, then finish the rest in the park. Ten minutes at most, just to get some fresh air.

Jay-Go placed the phone back on the table and stood up.

On the way to the door he lifted his PPK off the bed, tucked it behind his back and pulled on his jacket.

There was no need to check that the gun was loaded: in the

last few days that was all he'd done.

Jay-Go took a right out of the hotel and walked to the corner of Queen's Drive and Balvicar, then turned left, heading for the main gates of the park. Black metal railings ran at chest height around the perimeter, beyond which, through the trees and bushes, he could see the flat, well-tended square of a bowling green and its low club building lit from the ground by security lights.

The streets were quiet.

Somewhere behind him a car door clicked open. Jay-Go turned and saw a figure moving down Queen's Drive towards the corner, but the overhanging branches of a large sycamore tree obscured his view.

Jay-Go set off again, upping the pace this time.

Ahead, in a row of cars parked under the huge octagonal spire of the gothic-style Baptist Church, the doors of a white Ford Transit van swung open and two men jumped out.

One of them moved to block off his escape route down the side of the church while the other started across the road toward him.

Jay-Go turned, figuring he would head back to the hotel, but Edi Leka was waiting for him on the corner holding a handgun by his side.

Jay-Go whipped the PPK from behind his back and pointed it at the man crossing the street.

'Take another step and I'll fuckin' waste you, dickhead.'

The guy stopped in the middle of the road.

Edi Leka raised his gun.

Jay-Go was playing it cool. As he saw it, he was still holding all the aces. If they wanted to know where the heroin was hidden the last thing they'd do was shoot him dead.

It was still a risky call.

'Can I just say one thing, bawface, before this all kicks off?' Jay-Go said, addressing Leka. 'I could jump these railings and make a run for it and have youse chasing me all over Queens Park for half an hour shooting at me, and me shooting at you, but to be honest, I don't fancy my chances; I've never been a good runner. Add serial class A user into the mix and it's a blessing I can even walk. I had no idea the heroin belonged to Mister Abazi. If I'd known that at the time, I'd have left well alone, but we are where we are. If you promise to let me walk away, I promise to tell you where the heroin is, but it means going back to my hotel room to pick up a few thing in order to make that happen.'

'Why don't we just go for a ride in the back of our van and you take us to where we need to be? Or we just beat the shit out of you until you tell us, and we go get it ourselves.'

'You'd literally have to beat the shit out of me because I've swallowed the key.'

'We're in no hurry.'

'There's a combination too. And I don't know what that is. The only way I can find out is to phone somebody and say a code word, and the only way I can do that is if I have my phone, and that's back at the hotel. But if there is any pissing about I'll say the wrong code word: they'll hang up and you'll walk away with fuck all. Even if you go back and get the phone yourself and go through every number in my contacts until you get the right person: if they don't hear my voice they're not going say *niente*.'

Edi Leka kept his gun pointing at Jay-Go while he thought through what had been said. Eventually he nodded. 'Okay. But if I think there is problem even for one second . . . smack or no smack . . . I blow your fucking brains out.'

'Only fair.' Jay-Go lowered his gun and walked toward him.

*

Jay-Go and Edi Leka climbed the last few steps on to the landing then pushed through the heavy fire door into the hallway leading to Jay-Go's room. Edi had left his two companions at the bar downstairs, knowing he could easily handle the junkie on his own if there were any problems. His instructions were to recover the heroin, no matter what. If that meant waiting for the junkie to have a shit, so be it. Even if he had to shoot him in the head and cut him open, that was all right too. Edi figured he had a nose for this kind of situation. If Jay-Go was stringing him along he'd drop him right there in the room and go borrow a steak knife from the hotel kitchen.

Jay-Go turned the key in the lock and the two men entered.

His phone was sitting where he'd left it on the table.

Edi gestured with his gun for Jay-Go to pick it up, while he stepped to the side and checked there was no one hiding in the bathroom.

Just as Jay-Go reached the table there was a knock at the bedroom door.

'Who's that?' whispered Edi.

'How the fuck should I know?'

'Open up, Edi. I saw you walking in there with that wee fucker Gormley.'

'Don't open the door,' said Jay-Go, his voice rising in panic. 'It's the Holy Man . . . Don't open the door.'

Edi kept the gun pointing at Jay-Go and twisted the sneck.

'Wait, you need to hear me out...' started Jay-Go as the Holy Man entered the room followed by Big Paul, Nick-Nick and a heavy Jay-Go recognized as Happyslap from the Holy Man's bar.

Holy Man touched his forefinger to his lips and mouthed a silent 'shh'.

'I don't need to hear anything, horse-head, so keep your fucking mouth shut.'

All the guys except for the Holy Man were carrying.

'What are you doing here, Edi?' asked the Holy Man.

Edi was sharp, thinking on his feet: 'I hear you say you have no time to catch this shithead, so I think I do you a favour.'

'Good man. Showing initiative. I like it.'

'Bullshit,' cut in Jay-Go. 'He's here trying—'

The Holy Man raised his gun and pointed it at Jay-Go. 'Clamp it! Open that wee, skinny gob of yours again and I'll shoot you in the fucking mouth, d'you hear me, junkie?'

'But Holy Man—'

'Not another word.' The Holy Man was starting to lose his temper. 'There's nothing I like worse than somebody trying to do the dirty on me. You had your big chance, Gormley, and you blew it out yer arse. Now keep your mouth shut and let's go for a wee drive. On the way you can tell me where I can recover my merchandise. The game's a bogey, wee man.'

Edi Leka looked relieved as he stood to one side to let Jay-Go past. For whatever reason the Holy Man didn't seem too bothered that Edi had gone after Jay-Go: if anything, he had praised him for his efforts. All Edi had to do now was figure out a way of getting the heroin back from the Holy Man, which may not be so easy.

Happyslap led the way, followed by Jay-Go then Nick-Nick, who had his gun pressed hard into Jay-Go's back.

The Holy Man gave Jay-Go a wink.

'And the Oscar goes to . . .' said Jay-Go as he passed him.

'Aye, you did good, son.'

Big Paul handed the Holy Man his silenced Beretta.

'Not you, Edi,' said the Holy Man just as Edi made to push past him.

Edi Leka suddenly realized what was going on, but it was too late.

The first shot knocked his right leg out from under him; the second shattered the kneecap on his left. As he raised his arm to shoot back Big Paul stamped on it and kicked the gun from his hand with such force that it snapped his wrist.

The Holy Man was standing over him.

'There is something worse than someone doing the dirty on me, and that's someone doing the dirty on my friends. We know you were trying to get the heroin back from Jay-Go for Abazi and we know you've been doing the double shuffle on us. We are not going to show up on Saturday night and walk into the little trap Mister Abazi has waiting for us, d'you think we're fucking idiots?'

Edi Leka was writhing around the floor moaning in agony.

'We're going to show up on Friday night with an army and malky the fucking lot of you: you know why? 'Cause we are the Holy Ecumenical Alliance Treaty and that's the way we do things in Glasgow.'

Thirty-four

It was just after 8 p.m. when Patrick Sellar arrived home. He was talking on the phone as he pulled into the garage built on to the side of his house. Unclipping the mobile from its cradle, he grabbed his briefcase from the passenger seat, then squeezed out of the large Audi while the garage doors closed noisily behind him.

'The mechanism's buggered,' he said, explaining the intrusive metallic clunking sounds to James Mac Fadden on the other end of the phone.

The Honourable Lord Mac Fadden was a Senator for the College of Justice; a judge who sat in the High Court of Judiciary where the most serious crimes were dealt with. Sellar was looking to make Keira Lynch's life as difficult as possible and wanted Mac Fadden on side.

'There's something about her and this whole Abazi situation that's giving off a bad smell, James . . .'

Releasing the Dervishi girl had been a necessary but risky move that had almost blown up in his face. He'd made statements to the press about his conversations with Keira Lynch regarding the girl's release.

At the time, he'd believed Keira was dead and had overplayed his hand.

The fact that she had survived had come as a shock and made life very uncomfortable for him: people were starting to ask awkward questions.

The news that traces of heroin had been found in her apartment had let Sellar off the hook, but he needed to make the most of it, and quickly. It was the perfect way to discredit her if she started making noises and causing trouble for him. The quantity of drugs wasn't enough to have her prosecuted for dealing or trafficking, but the fact that they had been found at all was more than enough. The Honourable Lord Mac Fadden was an old friend and sympathetic ear who saw Keira Lynch as a troublemaker too, but it wasn't his professional advice Sellar was after. Mac Fadden also sat on the council for the Law Society of Scotland: the professional governing body for lawyers set up to oversee and regulate the profession. Even suspicion of involvement in drugs would mean automatic expulsion for any member.

In Scottish law there are three possible verdicts: guilty, not guilty and not proven. All Sellar needed was a verdict of not proven – 'we know you did it, but there isn't enough proof' – and Keira Lynch would no longer pose a threat.

Sellar nudged through a door in the side wall of the garage that led directly into the kitchen, and headed for the fridge in the far corner to pour himself a drink.

Suddenly he stopped and turned.

Something wasn't right.

'I'm sorry, James, d'you mind if I call you back in a minute, I've just arrived home and I need to get myself sorted . . . I'll call you back shortly.'

Sellar hung up, placed the phone on the kitchen table and made his way back toward the connecting door.

The lock had been tampered with.

The strike plate was hanging from the door jamb: sitting at

an awkward angle where it had been forced from the splintered wooden frame.

Sellar opened the door and peered back into the garage, listening.

The cooling fan on the car engine was still running.

Seconds later it clicked off and everything was silent.

Out of the corner of his eye he caught a movement that made him turn, but his reactions were too slow to protect his face from the blow. A fist slammed into his cheek and knocked him backward against the doorframe. Sellar started to scream.

'Please don't hurt me, please.'

Another blow caught him hard in the stomach, winding him, and another to the side of his head knocked him to the ground.

He was squealing now, 'Please just take what you want; please don't hurt me.'

As he cowered on the floor Sellar was struck in the side of the face by a savage kick that snapped his head backward against the wall where he slid, unconscious, to the floor.

*

Sellar's brain was grinding at the inside of his skull. He tried to push himself up from the floor, but had to stop as an attack of vertigo made his arms collapse from under him. Eventually he managed to manoeuvre himself into a sitting position, with his back resting against the wall.

The clock on the wall opposite read 8.35 p.m., which meant he'd been out for only a few minutes. It also meant his attackers could still be in the house. If they were after the safe they could be back at any moment demanding the combination. There was nothing of much value in the smaller of the two safes – a few hundred pounds cash, some insurance documents and a couple of fake Rolexes he'd bought on one of his frequent trips to Thailand. The larger safe, which was built into a cupboard in the upstairs hallway, contained some smaller works of priceless art – copies of which hung on the walls of the living room and the lounge. It had over thirty thousand in cash and most of his ex-wife's jewellery, which he'd managed to claw back from her as part of their separation agreement, but hadn't got round to selling. It also housed his 'dirt diaries': corroborated evidence of wrongdoing he'd gathered over the years, mostly against friends and work colleagues.

Some of it would never see the light of day, some of it already had. It was his nuclear option: back-up for when things weren't going his way. No one, not even his ex-wife, knew of the larger safe's existence.

If they wanted the code for that they'd have to torture him.

Sellar tried again and this time he managed to get to his feet. He staggered out into the hall and pressed the silent alarm on the small keypad by the front door, then suddenly feeling nauseous quickly made his way back into the kitchen and over to the sink.

He didn't make it in time. One step short of the basin he emptied the contents of his stomach all over the floor and across a pile of dishes sitting on the draining board.

He stood, bent double with one hand resting on the edge of the worktop and vomited again.

His brow was covered in beads of sweat, his face drained of colour.

He wiped the sleeve of his shirt across his mouth and saw that it was covered in fresh blood. He examined his reflection in the kitchen window to see where the blood was coming from, then rubbed his hand over his scalp and round the back of his head, feeling for cuts or grazes, but there was nothing there. He lifted his face to the ceiling and pinched his nose with his right hand to see if that was the source, but – again – there was nothing. Confused, Sellar stumbled over to the kitchen table and reached out for his phone. As he did so, something caught under the cuff of his left sleeve and sent a sharp, stabbing pain up the length of his arm. Sellar let out a yelp and dropped the phone to the floor. He stared down at his hand. It was dripping with blood.

He removed his jacket and dropped it on to the table.

The sleeve of his white shirt had a patch of red spreading slowly toward his elbow.

He carefully unbuttoned the cuff and rolled the sleeve back, then turned his hand.

He stared in disbelief.

A large surgical needle was protruding from one of the veins in his wrist.

The makeshift cannula was held in place by a piece of light blue electrical tape wrapped roughly round his wrist. There were still droplets of blood squeezing from its end: each small red bead swelling in rhythm with his heartbeat, then dripping on to his skin and trickling over the palm of his hand, down to his fingertips.

Sellar's head glanced off the corner of the table with a loud crack as he collapsed to the floor unconscious once more.

Thirty-five

Keira's mother pulled another bath towel from the washing line and dropped it and the pegs on top of the pile in the red lattice-work basket sitting on the grass by her feet. Grabbing hold of the moulded plastic handles, she carried the load indoors and tipped the contents on top of the kitchen table ready for sorting.

Orlaith suddenly stopped and looked up, convinced she'd caught a movement out in the hallway next to the front door. 'Keira? Is that you? I thought you were going for a walk . . . Keira?'

There was no reply.

She stood listening for any further signs of movement. Except for the gentle hum from the fridge in the corner, the house was silent.

She emptied another wet load from the washing machine and headed back out to the garden.

Just as she approached the threshold of the back door she saw him, standing in the same spot she had occupied just a few minutes earlier.

A small, stocky man wearing a black shirt, buttoned up to the neck. His hair was shaved close and his face – although not old – was haggard and tired looking, set in a permanent frown. Without speaking, he raised the gun he was holding and poin-ted it at her chest.

A noise from behind made her turn: another man was standing in the doorway leading through to the lounge. He too had a gun, this one dangling lazily by his side.

'Don't be scared, everything is be okay,' he said quietly in a foreign accent. 'Where is she?'

Orlaith's mind went blank, her thoughts whitewashed by the sudden surge of adrenaline. 'Not here,' she heard herself say.

'I think she's gone for walk?'

The man lifted his hand to his mouth and spoke something unintelligible into a small microphone concealed in the cuff of his jacket.

He turned back to her. 'Where?'

Orlaith opened her mouth to reply but the guy cut in, 'Where is she? Just to talk . . . We are not hurt her.'

His laid-back manner was strangely reassuring. There was a cool, dispassionate air about him that gave the impression he wasn't about to do anything rash. Orlaith figured if she screamed or tried to run he would probably kill her, but for the moment he seemed pretty relaxed. He touched his finger to his ear now, as though he was receiving a message, then started nodding: his attention not on Orlaith for a moment.

'Okay, we are leave you now,' he said. 'As you say, short and sweet. You stay quiet your daughter is safe. You call the police she will be dead. We are just to talk to her, so please, no police. You understand?'

Orlaith nodded.

With that he turned and walked calmly through the lounge, into the hallway and out through the front door.

Orlaith looked behind her into the garden, but the small stocky guy had disappeared too.

Polite! was her only other thought.

Two figures scrambled over the large mound of rocks that formed a breakwater on the western shore of Rhu marina. The women's outlines, silhouetted against the glistening water of Gare Loch, shimmered in the early evening haze.

On the far shore the low, distant hills behind Rosneath ran the length of the Garelochead peninsula in a dark flickering streak.

Moment's later officer Rebecca Rey crossed a small metal platform bridging the watery gap between the shore and four rows of pontoons that stretched into the man-made harbour in the shape of a giant pitchfork, each prong having twenty or so boats moored at right angles along its length.

'How you feeling?' she asked as she helped Keira across the unsteady platform.

'Better than yesterday, and yesterday was better than the day before. If I fall over, at least I'm still moving forward.'

'You're limping a bit. Are you still sore?'

'A pinch here and there, nothing serious. I still couldn't jog it. A brisk walk'll do for now. How far d'you think it is?'

'From here to the house?'

Keira nodded.

Rebecca looked back along the crescent shoreline to a small cluster of trees where the cottage was situated. 'I don't know . . . half a mile, maybe a bit less.'

'Half a mile! Shit! I feel like I've done a marathon.'

The two women stood for a while taking in the view across the Rhu Narrows, Rebecca aware that she was probably enjoying the moment more than Keira.

She'd been with Keira for nearly a week now and in all that

time had never seen her smile. Keira didn't watch television, or use a computer, preferring instead to read or review old case notes, boxes of which were piled high in her bedroom. Keira was polite and considerate, but she didn't engage. Her eyes remained dull, her expression flat; it was as though her mind had pulled the shutters down and turned off all the lights.

Today, however, she seemed different. Whereas before she'd hardly leave her room, it had been her idea to walk to the marina. Even at breakfast Rebecca could sense that something had changed: she'd turned a corner.

The boats were unusually still, barely moving as they floated silently side by side, creating little more than a ripple on the glossy surface of the harboured water. Even the birds were silent, lending an eerie undercurrent to the scene. The only sound to penetrate the quiet was the occasional rush of a car as it swept along the main road through Rhu on its way to Garelochead in one direction, or Glasgow in the other.

'I haven't shed a tear' said Keira eventually, as if trying not to break the spell, 'Not one. It's like my emotions are in lockdown: like I've forgotten how to be a human being.'

'You're being too hard on yourself. The fact that you're even thinking these thoughts contradicts what you've just said.'

Keira turned to look at her and continued, 'Not even when my grandmother died?'

'How honest d'you want me to be?'

'I raised the subject, so you can be as honest as you like.'

Rebecca thought for a second before continuing.

'I think you're just suffering from depression. Which, given the trauma you've been through, is hardly surprising. I say, *just* suffering, but I don't mean to belittle it. Depression can be a major pain in the arse. It has an impact on things like being able to cry. When my dad died it was nearly a year before the floodgates opened. Eva Cassidy singing "Songbird" started me off: d'you know it?'

Keira nodded, 'Yeah. Ironic.'

'I know! The opening line says there'll be "no crying". A week later, after I'd shrivelled up from dehydration, I finally stopped. It took a year for me to realize his death had actually happened. Maybe not realize, but accept that it had happened.'

Keira was staring at the ground. 'Yeah, someone else said that to me once.'

'When you're learning the most effective way to kill someone with a firearm you have to learn what makes them tick, so that hopefully – when the time comes – you don't have to pull the trigger. I don't speak French or German, but I'm fluent in "Body". It's the only other language I understand. The downside is you end up micro-analysing every gesture and facial expression of everyone you meet, wondering what lies beneath.'

'Have you been micro-analysing me?'

'You don't give much away, except for maybe the wrist thing. But you don't smile much, which makes you difficult to read.'

'My gran could always predict which boxer was going to lose the fight at the weigh-in. It was the one doing the smiling: you know that smug "I'm not scared of you" grin thing. Apparently it's a submissive action: smiling.'

'Is that why you don't do it much?'

Keira shook her head. 'No. I don't have much to smile about.'

'That's what makes me think you're going to be all right.'

'Because I don't smile?'

Rebecca nodded. 'It shows that you're stronger than most.

Don't worry, just because you haven't sprung a leak yet. When you do: I'm heading for one of those boats.'

The two women watched in silence as a long, narrow-beamed cigarette boat came into view around the point, motoring on idle across Rhu Bay. Eventually it pulled alongside one of the moorings at the far end of the pontoon, positioned nearest to the mouth of the harbour. The powerboat was just over twelve metres long and had a small open cockpit where the driver sat, its low, sleek lines complemented by a metallic blue colour scheme with contrasting go-faster stripes that ran the length of the hull. The metallic lettering on the side read *ХЕРОИН*.

The first thing that struck Keira was how different it looked from all the other boats in the marina.

While the driver negotiated the mooring, his companion, who had been standing beside him, jumped off and started along the pontoon toward the girls.

As he approached, Rebecca noticed that he was wearing a small black earpiece that had a wire extending toward his mouth.

The only way off the floating platform was to go past them, but Rebecca's training told her this was something different. The way the guy walked, the way he was staring at them, the self-assured manner all spelled danger. A noise from the boatyard behind them made her turn, just in time to see a figure duck behind one of the thick wooden stilts used to raise boats off the ground for maintenance. Over to her right another two shapes were moving along the shoreline, heading in their direction.

All their escape routes were blocked.

Rebecca let her hand drop slowly to her side and unclipped the safety-strap from her Glock service pistol.

Even Keira was aware that something wasn't right.

'I don't like this,' muttered Rebecca quietly. 'We're wide open here. We need to get off this jetty as quickly as possible.'

'There's someone behind us in the boatyard.'

'I've seen him. Let's move back across the bridge and see what happens. If it all kicks off, drop to the ground until I've dealt with him, then move as fast as you can up to the main road. Keira! Are you listening? KEIRA!'

But Keira wasn't listening: she was transfixed by the figure heading toward them along the pontoon.

Rebecca grabbed hold of her arm and tried again. 'KEIRA, WE HAVE TO MOVE!'

Keira was certain now: she recognized the approaching figure. 'It's him.'

The guy was less than ten yards away; too close for Rebecca. She drew her Glock from its holster and – aiming just above his head – shouted a warning. 'Armed police officer, stop right there. If you come any closer I will fire. STOP RIGHT THERE.'

The guy did as he was told, then, without prompting, held his hands out to the side and spun round in a circle to show he wasn't carrying a weapon.

Fisnik Abazi looked smaller in real life than Keira had imagined: dressed casually in jeans and a T-shirt and seemingly unfazed at having a gun pointed at him.

'I'm unarmed,' he said. 'But if you look behind me you'll see the man on the boat with a 50-calibre long-range sniper rifle. The gentleman behind you is carrying an AR15 semi-automatic and the guys walking along the beach have B&T MP9s.'

'Is this a sales pitch?' asked Keira.

Abazi stared back at her and made a face like he didn't get it.

'The guns; are you telling us their names in case we want to buy one?'

'I'm just letting the police officer know – in case she's weighing up her odds – what she's up against. Please, throw your weapon into the water, it's no good to you any more.'

Losing the Glock would leave them completely defenceless, but Rebecca knew she'd only be able to take down one target. With that sort of firepower pointing at them, if the shooting started there would be nothing left of her or Keira to bury.

'D'you mind if I drop it over the side here on to the rocks? If I clock off without my weapon I'll get a bollocking from my commanding officer. It's a disciplinary offence. This way it's out of reach, but at least I can retrieve it later.'

Abazi shrugged his shoulders. 'Go ahead.'

Rebecca held the Glock out over the edge of the pontoon and dropped it just to the right of the aluminium bridge. She watched it land in a crevice between two boulders close to the water's edge.

'I was told you'd packed your bags and left town,' continued Keira.

'The CIA's big problem is they think they're too smart to be outsmarted.'

'How d'you know it was the CIA that told me?'

'Because I don't think I'm smart, I know I am.'

'Is that why you've dropped by, to tell me how clever you are?'

'To tie up a few loose ends.'

'Am I a loose end?'

'Not at the moment.'

'What, then?'

'I want to hire you.'

Keira didn't raise an eyebrow. 'As what?'

'Ha!' smiled Abazi. 'You'd make a lot of money as one of my girls, but I'm thinking lawyer . . . for now.'

'I'm not practising at the moment,' replied Keira, letting a little ice slip into her tone. 'Got shot.'

'I have a cheque here as a down-payment, sort of like a retainer.'

'I can't accept money upfront, I'm afraid. It can be too easily misconstrued. I'd have to invoice you.'

'You've got the cop here as a witness. I'm paying for your services as a lawyer.'

'Why?'

'I've got a feeling I'm going to need representation soon; also, I have information you need to hear.'

'Go ahead. You can say what you like without me representing you.'

'No, I can't.'

'Why?'

'Because these are things I would say only to my lawyer. Lawyer–client privilege sort of shit.'

'Okay, I'm ready.'

'Not until we shake hands and you say it out loud, so we have a verbal agreement.'

'It's an oral agreement.'

'Who gives a shit! Just say the words, then we can shake hands and get down to business.'

Abazi suddenly touched his hand to the side of his head; listening to something in his earpiece. His focus shifted away from the two women to the boatyard behind.

A police car with blue-and-yellow Battenberg markings had just drawn up and a uniformed officer was making his way toward the metal bridge.

Abazi barked something in Serbian into the microphone.

The sniper on the boat eased himself lower and retrained his sights on to the approaching police officer.

Rebecca noticed that the figure standing by the stilts was nowhere to be seen: the guys on the beach had disappeared too.

'Tried you at the house, but no reply,' said the cop, addressing Keira from the landward side of the small bridge. 'Just checking everything's okay.'

'Was my mother not there?'

'No answer.'

'She's probably in the back garden, or taking a nap.'

'You two all right?' asked the cop again, addressing the question to Rebecca.

'We're good,' she replied. 'Just about to head back.'

'Grand,' added Keira. 'Out for a walk and drumming up some new business.'

'Aye, good luck with that round here,' said the cop, eyeing Abazi. 'Anything I can help you with, sir? You look a bit lost?'

The sniper slid his forefinger through the trigger guard and squeezed gently until he could feel the shot-break point. Abazi had one hand behind his back clenched into a fist: if he spread his fingers wide, that was the signal to open fire.

'I'm fine.'

The cop stared at him for a few seconds, but seemed satisfied.

The sniper followed him until he was back inside the squad car, then adjusted his grip back to a neutral firing position.

Abazi waited until the police car had driven off before moving to stand in front of Keira. 'I still haven't heard you say the words.'

'I agree to represent you,' she said flatly.

Abazi extended his hand towards her, but Keira didn't take him up on the offer.

'I don't have to shake your hand for it to be legally binding.'

Abazi stared back at her, wondering which way to take it. He admired her for having the balls to stand up to him, but on the other hand it could be seen as a challenge. He could take offence and smack her one, or just hand over the cheque and get down to business.

After a curt nod he held out the cheque.

Keira took hold of it and slipped it into her back pocket without even looking at it.

'So, what d'you want to tell me?'

'Not here. We go for a cruise. When I'm finished, I drop you off in time for dinner.'

'How do I know you won't just get us on board and kill us, then dump our bodies out at sea?'

'I just took you on as my lawyer, why would I want to kill you? And even if I did, what do I care where they find your body? Why give myself the hassle of taking you out to sea? I could just leave you here on the quayside.'

'Can I say no?'

'To what?'

'The boat trip.'

'Sure.'

'What happens then?'

'You don't learn the truth.'

'About what?'

'A lot of things.'

'Like?'

'Why Kaltrina Dervishi was really killed. Why that asshole

296

Sellar released her from jail. Why CIA officer Edwin Kade got hit . . . you want me to keep going?'

'I know most of the answers to those questions.'

'You think you do, but all you've got is the Hollywood version. Edwin Kade was not the name he gave to us. We knew him as Nicolas Kent. When we first heard that a CIA agent called Kade got busted we thought they were talking about someone else, before we realized.'

'So?'

'So, chances are the guys you're dealing with are not who they say they are either. I'm just throwing that into the mix as a little taster of what's to come.'

Keira stood for a moment weighing up the pros and cons. There was no doubt that Abazi's view on the situation would be worth hearing, but he was a dangerous man who just a few weeks earlier had tried to have her killed.

'You need more convincing?'

'Would you get on a boat with a heroin smuggler who trafficked girls for prostitution, and had previously tried to have you murdered?'

'I didn't order the hit on you, but I know who did.'

'Who?'

'Get on the boat.'

'Just me.'

'Has to be both of you.'

'As your lawyer, I would advise against taking a police officer hostage.'

'Don't get smart. I'm not in the fucking mood for smart. I'm going to give it one more shot then I'll have to terminate our contract . . . leave you here on the quay, like we just said.'

Keira wasn't sure if that was a death threat, but that's the way it came across.

'Okay, one more hors d'oeuvre. Let me ask you this,' continued Abazi. 'Did one of the CIA guys make a call when he was at your house?'

'What does that have to do with anything?'

'Yes or no?'

'One of them did make a call, yes . . . to cancel a meeting.'

'That's what it looked like to you, but what was he really doing?'

Keira shrugged. 'I don't know, is "cancel a meeting" a code for something?'

'His phone's menu has "Location services" switched on. There was no meeting. He's letting someone know where he is and – at the same time – where you are. Someone who has a contract to kill you and is probably on their way here right now.'

'You seemed to find me without too much difficulty. How do I know that someone isn't you?'

'If it was me, you'd already be dead.'

Thirty-six

As soon as they stepped on board, the two women were separated. Rebecca Rey was taken down into the small galley, out of sight, where her wrists and ankles were bound together and her mouth taped over, while Keira stayed topside with Abazi. She was sitting beside him on a padded leather bench that ran in a U-shape around the rear of the cockpit watching the water ripple along the side of the boat as it left the shelter of the harbour and started to pick up speed. The boat powered west across to Castle Bay, then swung left in a tight arc, hugging the craggy shoreline as it passed Culwatty Bay heading south toward the bottom end of the Gare Loch.

'Bit of a cliché,' said Keira, having to raise her voice to be heard over the noise of the engines. 'The boat.'

'Maybe, but it goes like the shit. Got two, staggered twelve-hundred-horsepower Mercury racing engines. Can outrun anything, except maybe a jet fighter. As far as I know, the cops over here don't fly that kind of kit yet. Used to be called a rum runner during Prohibition, now it's called a cigarette boat. Won't be long before they change it again to smack skiff, or dope dinghy, or some shit like that, 'cause that's all they're used for these days. That's what the boat's name means: it's *HEROIN* in Serbian.'

'Doesn't having the only boat in Scotland that looks like a Miami dope dealer's make it easier to spot?'

'This boat is virtually invisible to radar, unless the sea's flat

299

calm, but who says that's the way I want to play it. I drop you off, you phone it in; next thing the cops, the navy, the whole lot are out chasing this boat – it's easy enough to see with the naked eye. Maybe it's not so easy to catch, but that won't stop them trying to run it down. That's where you got to understand tactics. There's nothing in the rules of engagement says I still have to be on board when they do.'

'Why'd you try to plant a kilo of heroin in my apartment?'

Abazi gave her a stare, again deciding which way to take it. Eventually he asked her, 'Do you always come at things head on?'

'The very first time I cross-examined a witness in court the Sheriff advised me to ask simple questions. My first is always, "Why?" Also, if you want me to represent you, you have to trust me, and in order to do that you have to know what I'm thinking. Right now I'm thinking, "Why did you plant heroin in my flat?"'

'That was a black flag SAD operation.'

'Black flag?'

'I didn't plant it, but it was heroin taken from my stock. I wasn't too smart there, because when I found out, naturally I wanted it back. But that was the mistake I made. Straight away I've confirmed to everyone that it belongs to me and no matter how many times I deny putting it in your place, no one is going to believe me. The CIA played me: they knew if I tried to recover it I'd land myself in the shit. Is called a black flag operation: they do some sneaky shit and someone else gets the blame. No way you can trace it back to them. It's what this whole thing is about. Although catching me out wasn't their original intention. The original intention was to land you in the shit: make it look like you were involved in the drug scene. It's their insurance policy.

You go down, I get the blame, CIA aren't even on the rap sheet. Black flag.'

'What about the SAD? What's that stand for?'

'Special Activities Division. They operate within the CIA, but they're a law unto themselves, do what they like.'

'Why? Why would they want to take me down?'

'If the Dervishi girl told you everything that is going on, you're a threat . . . Did she tell you everything?'

Keira gave Abazi a look and said, 'I don't discuss my other clients' business with anyone.'

Abazi smiled. 'I like that. You're on the ball. Okay,' he continued, 'let's suppose she has, and you don't like what you're hearing, so you decide to do something about it. You got the CIA's balls in your mouth ready to bite, then suddenly you'll find you're not so hungry 'cause you've been neutralized by a bag of heroin. No matter what argument you come up with against them, no one's going to believe you, because in the eyes of the twelve good men and true, you're a drug dealer. Those two agents work for SAD. If they saw you and me talking right now they'd pull out their guns and shoot us both dead, wouldn't matter who saw them. I know everything they've been up to and they know I know. They're scared that if the girl has told you all there is to know as well, and I come along and back up the story, they are in the shit. Sneaky sons-of-bitches. Only thing that's true about them is they are all liars. They are like worst second-hand car salesman you ever met. They sell you a bright shiny Corvette with a little extra horsepower, and when you get outside you realize the extra horsepower is the fucking donkey that's standing behind the Corvette. And try getting your money back! They deny they ever saw you before, and if you make enough noise they sneak into your room at night and shoot you through a pillow. You and me, Miss Lynch, we're going to bring them down, and this is why we need to talk. They have already started on me: tipping off my business rivals to everything I'm doing. Your friend the Holy Man's been making moves against me because someone has been feeding him intel in an American accent. It's reached the point where the only way I can move is out, which in some ways is fine by me; I can go enjoy some of the riches I've acquired. I'm not anti-American, I'm anti getting fucked in the ass by Americans.' Abazi was smiling to himself as he continued. 'They're going to try to hang me for the Edwin Kade killing, too, I know it. What did they tell you I was doing?'

'They said you were smuggling heroin, with the help of someone in the US military and a rogue agent in the CIA.'

'Edwin Kade?'

'That's what they claim.'

'All of that's true, except there's more than one rogue agent involved. Joe O'Donnell and Mitch Taylor – which, I'll give you a hundred to one, are not their real names – are in it as well, but they set Kade up to take the fall.'

'Are they in it for the money too?'

Abazi screwed up his face. 'They tell you that's what Kade was doing it for?' He shook his head, then continued, 'They ain't in it for the money. They's fighting terrorism in Afghanistan, is the way they see it. They don't handle the drugs: they got no direct connection. They help with transport, supply of arms and a little protection every now and then: that's it. But they don't get involved in the messy stuff.'

'Indirect complicity.'

'In your speak, maybe; in mine they're back-stabbing, fucking car salesmen. Everything boils down to money in the end, though. The CIA support the Asian trade through Turkey and eastern Europe, make the supply chain secure and reliable so the producers can charge less to the dealers and the dealers charge less to the users and everyone's got the daytime-TV smile on – except for the Taliban and Mujahideen in Afghanistan, who are being undercut. No one is buying their drugs any more because it's too expensive, and there's a war on in their country so the supply is unreliable, and they've got no money coming in to support the struggle against the West. But how d'you think that scenario is going to play on prime-time in the USA? The CIA are smuggling heroin for the competition in their fight against terrorism . . . Not good! So rather than let that shit out, they order a hit on a twenty-year-old girl, take out one of their own and try to whack whoever else happens to get in the way.' Abazi stopped. 'Why are you looking at me like that?'

'A twenty-year-old girl who wouldn't have been involved in any of this if you hadn't brought her here. You've a long way to climb before you get anywhere near the moral high ground.'

'You think what I do is fucked up? The American government is spending all its money trying to protect something that doesn't exist: the American way of life. They got more people unemployed than the population of most other countries. They got people can't afford to get ill. They spend more money trying to protect all this shit than it would take to make everyone in the USA a millionaire. They give off all this crap about the war on drugs, but what kind of war you ever heard of where the main player is fighting on the same side as his enemy? They may not be getting drugs from Afghanistan because this week they're not

303

talking to the Taliban, but they're still getting drugs from central and south-east Asia. They're smuggling the goddamn stuff themselves. They're killing people to save lives – fucked up! They're smuggling heroin to stop terrorism – fucked up! They're telling people who are sick there's no money to make them better, because they're spending it all to keep them safe – fucked up! If you think I'm telling you all this to make me sound better, you're missing the point. I'm not trying to come across as the good guy. I'm telling you what you need to know so you can screw these assholes into the wall. The CIA asked me to provide the Watcher with whatever was needed to eliminate the girl, but I didn't order the executive action on her, or on you or on anyone else: that came from them.'

Keira was suddenly aware of the engine noise easing and the boat starting to slow.

The sun had now set behind the forested inclines of Benmore: a small hill that broke the horizon some way in front of them. Its black silhouette rose into the sky as it sloped away from the deep waters of Holy Loch, just west of their current position.

As they steered into Kilcreggan Bay the driver pulled back further on the throttle and let the boat glide through the twilight towards a large jetty protruding into the water like a long ghostly finger.

'Where are we going?' asked Keira.

'This is where you get off.'

'Are we done?'

'For the moment. I'm keeping a few things of interest back for later: can't throw everything at you all at once. When I get to where I'm going I'll be in touch, tell you some other things you need to know: dates, times – the specifics of how the operation works.'

'What happens if I don't feel like getting into a fight with the CIA?'

'You're already in a fight with the CIA. If you don't believe me, call them. Tell them you've met with me; see if you survive the next few days.'

The *XEPОИН* coasted to a stop alongside the jetty: the driver expertly manoeuvring it into position for Keira to step off.

She turned and looked at Abazi expectantly.

'The cop stays on board,' he said before she'd asked the question. 'My insurance. I give you my word I won't kill her. As long as we have no interference, she'll be released when we reach our destination. This boat is very fast, but it doesn't like too much ballast. If we do get chased, she will be shot and thrown overboard.'

Keira could tell from the expression on his face that he meant it.

Realizing she had no option but to leave Rebecca behind, she climbed on to the gunwale and stepped over on to the dry, wooden planks of the jetty.

'When you speak to the agents, they'll tell you to stay put till they get there. If that's the case, stay put, but do it somewhere else, 'cause someone's gonna come calling with a nine-mil tucked into their belt.'

The driver slid back the throttle levers and started to reverse away from the pier, pulling the boat round in a tight arc so that it was facing back out to sea.

Keira shouted over the boom of the engines, 'Wait! What's the deal with Sellar?'

Abazi lifted his fist to the side of his face with his thumb and pinky extended and mouthed, 'I'll call you.' The gesture looked odd, Abazi signalling to her like an old friend who had just met her for a coffee and had forgotten something as they parted.

There was no doubt that some of what he had told her was bullshit: lies to cover his own culpability. But that wasn't the point – enough of it was true.

Fifty metres to the right of where the jetty met the main road, Keira spotted a red telephone box. She checked her pockets for coins. An idea was coming together in her head: a course of action that might give her some control back over her life.

Her first move would be to make some calls: one to her mother to tell her to leave the safe house as quickly as possible, one to the Holy Man and one to the agents calling themselves O'Donnell and Taylor. It would set the play in motion and leave her with two possible outcomes. By the end of the evening she would be either in the back of a van on her way to jail, or in the back of an ambulance on the way to the morgue.

At that moment, Keira didn't much care which of the two outcomes prevailed; at least it would all be over.

She stood alone in the gloaming watching the white wake fan out and fade behind the narrow stern of the boat as it disappeared into the distance.

Closing her eyes, she concentrated on the sound of the water lapping against the upright pillars of the jetty. Every day for nearly twenty years she had performed the same ritual of self-crucifixion. Not for killing another human being, but for asking herself the same question, over and over again. A question she didn't dare answer for fear of what that answer might be.

Standing, alone, at the end of the jetty, the memory of

a feeling she'd once had flooded her mind: a certainty of purpose she hadn't felt since she was eight years old.

Keira opened her eyes and stared out to sea.

The question was 'Could she kill again?'

The answer was 'Yes.'

Thirty-seven

Tommy Aquino pressed the EXIT tab that was flashing red on his phone and placed the handset back on the table.

Moran was lying on the bed. 'Was that the lawyer?' he asked, looking up from the newspaper. The headline read, DRUG LAWYER COULD FACE CHARGES.

'Yeah!'

'These guys are really laying into her. You could pre-soak her in Tide for a year, you ain't gonna shift the stains from this lady. Got that asshole Patrick Sellar working her over, too: interview reads like he's a man on a seek-and-destroy mission. What's she want?'

'Abazi has made contact with her.'

'No shit,' said Moran, sitting up. 'When?'

'Just now. He wants to meet her tonight.'

'How'd he find her?'

'She didn't say.'

'Why'd she call us?'

'Says she tried the cop ... Hammond, but can't get a hold of him so she called us, figuring he might be here. She wants to know what to do.'

'What'd you say?'

'I told her she'd done the right thing and that I'd call her straight back.'

'So Hammond doesn't know?'

'That's correct.'

'We got to keep it that way. This could be the break we're looking for. Did she say where the meet with Abazi was supposed to take place?'

'An industrial estate on the South Side.'

Moran reached down and pulled a pouch marked 'Diplomatic' from his holdall at the side of the bed, thumbing the combination lock until it clicked and released the zip tabs.

The soft neoprene pouch was no more than four centimetres thick and barely the size of a laptop computer, but it contained two flat-black Sig P229 Daks with high-capacity magazines.

'Okay, so we've got to move fast.' He freed one of the guns from the foam padding and clipped in a magazine. 'Call her back and tell her to stay in the safe house and let us handle it – tell her we'll inform Hammond and take care of everything this end. Then get in touch with our friendly assassin and say it has to be tonight, warn him about what to expect at the lawyer's hideaway.'

'Like what?'

'Like cameras, alarms; the armed cop that's gonna have to be dealt with. No more fucking about now, Tommy. Let's get the lawyer out of the way and deal with Abazi at the same time.'

'You suggesting *we* hit him?' Aquino screwed up his face. 'Why not let the "friendly assassin" take care of Abazi? We've got the lawyer neutralized. She can say shit's brown, but no one's going to believe her. Let's leave her out of it for the moment.'

'We let it play out like that, it rumbles on and on. Who knows what the outcome's gonna be? If Abazi and the lawyer get together and start comparing notes, we're in the shit. Let's go sort Abazi out right now. That way we know it's done and we can catch a transport straight out of here. Did she give you the address where Abazi's at?'

'Welbeck Road, Darnley Industrial Estate: a distribution warehouse there.'

'Okay. You call her back while I look it up. In fact, tell her you've just spoken to Hammond and he says he'll be in touch when it's all sorted, or some crap like that. Anything that'll stop her from trying to contact him again.'

Tommy Aquino lifted his phone and pressed CALL BACK.

'Miss Lynch? It's Joe O'Donnell here. We've just spoken to Gary Hammond and he says to sit tight. He'll call you as soon as possible to let you know what's happening, but in the meantime you stay right where you are until we get this thing sorted.'

*

Welbeck Road was mostly deserted. A few abandoned cars and some litter were the only signs there had ever been any life in this bleak, industrial landscape.

The buildings that occupied most of the surrounding area varied in size from 750 square-metre industrial units up to large warehouses with loading bays capable of housing eighteen-wheelers. The tall metal gates leading to the car park of one of these large warehouses were wide open, the gatehouse deserted. On a small, cramped desk inside the abandoned cubicle, a newspaper lay open with a half-empty cup of coffee sitting beside it.

Three out of the ten bays were occupied by large articulated lorries, but there was no activity around any of them, even though the shutters leading into the warehouse were raised and the rear doors of the trailers were hanging open.

Aquino and Moran made their way silently across the dimly

lit car park and came to a stop at the rear end of one of the trailers. It was just after 8 p.m., a full hour before the meeting between Abazi and Keira Lynch was supposed to take place.

'You figure we're too early?' whispered Moran.

'I don't know what's going on, but my gut tells me this ain't right.'

'You figure we should split, or check the place out first?'

'We're here now. Let's stick our nose in a little further. If it still doesn't smell good, we go.'

Moran covered Aquino as he made his way up a set of stairs on to the loading platform and stood to the side of a large set of shutters. After checking there was no one in the loading bay area, Aquino signalled for Moran to join him.

The shutters opened on to a second platform that ran the length of the bays. From it, long roller-belts sloped away at right angles into the belly of the warehouse and disappeared amongst the rows of boxes and containers stacked from floor to ceiling. Aside from a few worker lamps at the far end casting a dim glow in the background, and the spill from the car park floodlights behind them, the warehouse was in total darkness.

Suddenly Aquino held up his hand.

'What's wrong?' whispered Moran.

'Listen.'

Moran stood in silence for a few moments, then nodded, 'I hear it!'

A low moaning sound was coming from somewhere over to their right, inside the warehouse.

Weapons drawn, the two men dropped silently on to the concrete floor, then – with Moran covering the rear – cautiously headed in the direction of the noise.

With each step the sound grew more distinct: a gurgling, chesty groan.

Moran tapped Aquino on the shoulder and made the shape of a gun with the fingers of his left hand. He pointed it at his chest then mimed the gun recoiling as it fired several times. Aquino got it straight away and nodded. It wasn't the first time either of them had heard the victim of a chest wound struggling to breathe. Aquino took a step forward and felt his right foot skid under him. He reached out to steady himself on Moran.

Peering down, the pair knew instantly that the black slick Aquino had stepped into was blood.

The gurgling sound was coming from somewhere close by.

Aquino eased himself against the metal uprights of a stack of shelves and sneaked a glance round the corner.

'Holy shit,' he gasped, recoiling involuntarily.

Moran held his Sig P229 straight in front of him as he stepped out from behind the shelving to take a look. 'Fuck!'

In a twenty-metre-square clearing, sandwiched between the high stacks of boxes, was a circle of chairs, sixteen in total, all of which faced into the centre. On each chair sat a man with his feet bound together and his hands either tied behind his back or hanging loosely by his side. Those victims whose arms hung freely appeared to have had their fingers removed, leaving behind gory stumps that dripped blood silently to the ground. Under their chairs smaller pools of blood had merged with one another to form a larger slick.

'This is some weird shit,' breathed Moran.

'They've been made to sit facing one another so that they see each other being executed.'

From what Aquino could make out it looked as though most

of them had been shot once in the chest and once in the head.

The guy in the chair closest to them was still alive. The right side of his face was missing and his right arm jerked slightly as if he was trying to raise it in a beckoning motion. Seemingly aware of their presence, he'd turned his head to face them.

'We gotta get out of here.'

'Wait! He's trying to say something.'

'I don't care if the asshole's trying to sing something! Let's get the fuck out of here.'

Aquino ignored him and eased closer.

Air gurgled and hissed from a gaping chest wound as the man tried to draw in air.

Aquino leant in with his ear close to the guy's mouth and asked, 'Who did this?'

Moran was getting jumpy. 'Who gives a shit? Let's get out of here.'

The guy mumbled incoherently, the words masked by the sound of blood burbling up in his throat. 'Thaynawdeh.'

'What?'

The guy tried again, 'Thaynawdeh.'

Suddenly Aquino and Moran turned as the roller shutters above all ten bays began to clatter shut in turn, starting from the far end and working noisily along until the only illumination left was the faint glow from the worker lamps on the far side of the warehouse.

Moran dropped to his knees and fired at a black shadow moving through the darkness along the loading platform. There was a burst of automatic gunfire in return that reverberated loudly around the warehouse, the glow from the muzzle flash momentarily illuminating several other figures lurking in the shadows.

Aquino ducked out from the stack of shelves and quickly fired two more rounds before stepping back.

Suddenly the air around him erupted as a hail of bullets ripped through the boxes and packaging by his head, sending him crashing to the floor. Another burst sprayed along the roller mechanism of the conveyor belt that Moran was sheltering behind, forcing him low to the ground. Seeing how exposed Moran was, Aquino signalled for him to come towards him. He rolled on his side and fired another burst, giving Moran an opportunity to scramble across the floor and tuck in behind him.

Moran's arms and legs were covered in blood.

'Jesus! Are you hit?'

'No! It's the blood from the bodies. What the fuck do we do now? That bitch has set us up.'

With their attention focused on the loading area neither of the officers noticed the five figures from the circle of dead bodies behind them slowly rising to their feet. In silence the resurrected drew their weapons from behind their backs and stood in the dark like ghostly statues, fingers on triggers, waiting for the signal to open fire.

A voice rang out from the platform, somewhere over by the shutters.

'CIA?'

'Yes. Hold your fire. We are CIA officers. Please step out with your weapons raised where we can see them.'

'Got a call earlier from my lawyer with a bit of information regarding some drug smugglers: needed a bit of advice. She happened to mention that you two gentlemen were interested in a meet with Mr Abazi. I suggested to her that you might want to drop by this evening and I could help set that up.'

The Holy Man stepped out from behind some racking.

'Who are you? What the fuck is going on here?'

'They're not dead.'

'Who are not dead? What the fuck are you talking about?' Moran raised his weapon and pointed it at the Holy Man.

'The guy in the chair behind you; that's what he's trying to tell you . . . they're not dead.'

As Moran and Aquino turned to look over their shoulders and saw the figures standing behind them, the Holy Man finished with, 'But you are.'

Thirty-eight

The voyage from Malin to German Bight had taken nearly three hours. Once they'd cleared the north-west coast of Scotland, Besnik Osmani had come to the cabin, ripped the tape from Rebecca's mouth and given her some water, but nothing to eat. The seas around Viking and South Utsire had been rough. Waves had slammed against the side of the boat without warning, knocking Rebecca to the floor. The cabin was dark and claustrophobic with an unpleasant plasticky smell. Even if they'd brought her food she wouldn't have been able to eat it; all she wanted to do was throw up. The thick black tape they'd used to bind her wrists burned where it had rubbed the skin raw. Her knees and elbows were grazed from trying to stay upright as the narrow hull of the *ХЕРОИН* pitched and tossed its way through the ragged North Sea waves.

In the past few minutes the engine noise had reduced to a low hum and the boat seemed to have come to a halt.

Outside she could hear the vague clank of metal, dull thumps and banging noises along with the muffled sounds of men shouting to one another.

Suddenly the cabin door flew open and the room filled with sea-spray and cold salt air mixed with a strong smell of diesel.

Abazi was silhouetted in the doorway, lit from behind by a spotlight mounted on the gunwale of a small fishing trawler that was tied up alongside. He had to shout to be heard above the noise of the wind.

'Hot or cold?'

Rebecca stared up at him. 'I don't understand the question.'

'Is straightforward; you want hot or cold?'

'Hot or cold what? If it's coffee, then hot, if it's beer – cold. I don't know what you're asking, so I don't know how to answer.'

Besnik Osmani appeared behind Abazi and squeezed past into the cabin. Without speaking he grabbed Rebecca by the arm and pulled her upright before dragging her out on to the wet, slippery deck of the cockpit.

The trawler was only a few metres longer than the cigarette boat, but stood much higher out of the water. They were surrounded by sea and darkness, with no land visible in any direction. The crest of each wave that broke between the bows of the boats was picked up by the wind and sprayed over the three figures in raw showery blasts.

Besnik pushed Rebecca on to the padded bench at the rear of the cockpit, where a cold puddle of seawater soaked through the seat of her trousers.

Even with the wind howling across the deck of the cigarette boat the diesel fumes seemed much more intense.

Suddenly Rebecca realized what Abazi's question meant.

They were planning to set the boat alight.

She could stay on board the *ХЕРОИН* and burn to death or be thrown overboard into the sea to drown. Hot or cold.

Abazi' s face was pressed right next to her ear, still barely audible even though he was shouting.

'We can't show up with an extra body: especially a cop. If you go for cold you might get lucky and die of a heart attack. The water out here never rises above minus five degrees, so it's possible. But drowning is not a pleasant way to go. You might stay afloat for a few minutes, but as soon as you start to sink, you'll want to catch your breath. You start taking in water. You can't help it; all the while your brain is screaming for air. It's slow. It's a struggle. Unpleasant. If I were you I'd stay aboard. Cremation goes back to the Stone Age. Fire was a miracle from the gods. It's noble, almost.'

Without warning Rebecca suddenly flicked round and caught Abazi on the chin with the side of her forehead. There was a satisfying crack as her head made contact. As he reeled back he swung his fist, but a wave slammed into the side of the boat, pitching him out of reach and sending Rebecca lurching forward along the deck until – unable to keep her balance – she toppled and struck her head and shoulder off the steering wheel. It was impossible to break her fall. She dropped heavily, catching her cheek and the side of her mouth on the corner of the dashboard. As she slumpd down on the deck she immediately twisted round and tried to sit upright, but another wave tipped her sideways and sent her sliding in a heap against the shallow wall of the cockpit. Blood spluttered from a large tear in her lip, her gums were aching and raw.

She lifted her head in time to see Besnick Osmani's foot swinging towards her, but too late to avoid the blow.

Her head exploded in a flash of white light.

She could feel Besnick kicking wildly at her, in a rage: first in the stomach, then stamping down heavily on her face.

Just when it seemed he would never stop, everything went silent.

When she next opened her eyes, Besnik and Abazi were already on board the trawler. Her vision was blurred and unfocused. It was difficult to tell for sure, but it looked like they were untying the lines.

Moments later the two boats started to drift apart.

Before long, all she could see was the dull glow from the trawler's masthead light bobbing around in the dark as it disappeared into the blackness. She wondered why they hadn't set light to the boat: maybe their intention all along had been just to scare her.

Rebecca braced her feet under the base of the driver's chair and used her stomach muscles to pull herself into a sitting position. Her eyes were stinging and there was an unpleasant taste in her mouth of chemicals mixed with blood and seawater. The smell of fumes was overpowering: far stronger than before. That's when she realized they had soaked her in fuel as well. It was in her hair, and on her skin: her clothes were saturated in it.

Her first thought was to get back inside the cabin and get out of her clothing, but when she tried the door it was locked. Rebecca lay on her back, raised her knees to her chest and – using both feet – rammed them against the door.

After several attempts there was a loud splintering crack as it finally gave way.

A dull thump cut through the howling wind and made her turn.

A flare streaked into the sky above, illuminating the sea around the cigarette boat with a dull red glow.

She could see the trawler again.

It struck her that it hadn't travelled as far as she'd first thought, then she realized that the fishing boat had turned and was heading back toward her.

Another flare shot through the darkness, this time skimming

the top of the waves, heading toward the *ХЕРОИН*. It landed just metres from the boat, fizzing and boiling the water as it sunk beneath the waves in a swirling plume of steam and smoke.

The next flare struck the bow and glanced harmlessly off into the sea.

They were going to set the boat alight after all.

The fourth smashed into the cockpit, fizzing around the deck in a blinding ball of red heat. Rebecca scrambled towards it and tried to flick it over the side using her feet, but the pitch and toss of the boat made it impossible. The flare slid away from her and tumbled down the short set of steps leading to the cabin. The air around her seemed to draw breath, then suddenly explode outwards with a loud, hollow bang. A ball of yellow flames mushroomed into the night sky.

Rebecca's hair was on fire. The intense heat melted her clothes and seared her flesh. The tape that bound her wrists and legs was gone. She would have screamed, but it was impossible to draw breath. Thick acrid smoke bellowed around her, choking her throat and clogging her lungs. She clambered to her feet – her entire body engulfed in flames – and plunged headlong over the side of the boat. The shock of cold as she entered the water paralysed her instantly, making it impossible even to tread water.

The flames from the burning boat illuminated the surrounding darkness. In her last few moments of consciousness, as her lungs filled with water and her body sank deeper and deeper beneath the waves, it looked to Rebecca like the sun had come out.

Thirty-nine

The silvery-grey taxi cruised silently through the dark, along the winding shore roads on its way back to Rhu. The car radio was playing modern country ballads: 'Next up, Patty Griffin singing "Ohio",' said the presenter, Ricky Ross, in a low, gravelly voice.

Keira's eyelids were weighed down by the music and gentle hum of road noise.

As she drifted off, her mind filled with a disconnected jumble of thoughts – the lyrics of the song taking on a different significance in her semi-conscious state. Patty sang dolefully about meeting on the other side. *I'm not ready for the other side*, thought Keira as she drifted off to sleep and her head dropped forward with a jolt.

If – as Abazi had predicted – the CIA's hired help was on his way, Keira would make sure she was ready for the son-of-a-bitch this time. She had missed her chance in the apartment with his gun in her hand: next time, she wouldn't hesitate. It was time to stop running from the past and turn to face it: it was time to change the game.

Suddenly a gruff voice interrupted her thoughts: someone asking a question.

She opened her eyes.

'That's us, darlin'. D'you want dropped here? Will this do?'

Keira looked around to get her bearings. The taxi had come to a stop on the corner of Manse Brae and Gareloch Road, just past the turn-off for her road, but it was only a short walk back along the side of the loch.

'This is fine.'

'Have you far to go?'

'No, it's just back there.'

'Aye, well watch out for the Highland Defenders. They're out in force this year. It's no wonder everyone in Scotland looks so peely-wally: they've had all their blood sucked out o' them by those wee bastards.'

Keira forced a smile and handed over some cash.

Once outside the cab, she filled her lungs with fresh air and took a moment to enjoy the reviving effects of the cool breeze on her clammy skin.

Two young guys leant against the wall of the Rhu Inn, just twenty metres along the road, puffing on cigarettes and mumbling to each other behind wisps of grey smoke.

As Keira approached, they stopped talking.

'Any chance I could borrow a cigarette?' she asked.

One of them reached into the pocket of his jeans and offered her over a soft pack of Marlboro.

'How long d'you want to borrow it for?'

'The rest of my life.'

The guy squinted at her.

'You're right, I don't mean borrow, I mean buy. She reached inside her pocket.

'Yer awright, darlin',' said the guy. 'Help yourself, you look like you need it.'

'Thanks.' She took a cigarette and handed him back the pack.

'Have you got a light?'

The guy pulled out a one-fifty throwaway and flicked the

spark-wheel. 'Want me to smoke it for you as well?' he asked, earning a grin from his pal.

Keira didn't know why, but she leant over and kissed him briefly on the lips. 'Thanks.'

She turned and set off along the road.

'What do I get if I give you the whole packet?' he shouted after her.

Keira ignored him and continued on past the post office, till eventually she disappeared into the darkness.

Across Church Road, at the far end of an open triangle of grass, just beyond a row of cherry trees, sat Rhu and Shandon Parish Church, its illuminated spire rising above the treetops into the night sky. The communal area of grass to the side of it had a drystone wall separating it from the church graveyard and sat adjacent to a sharp bend on the main road.

She made her way to the edge of the wall and leant against it.

At no point during her stay in hospital, or even the days spent in the safe house, had it crossed her mind to smoke, but tonight the old craving had returned. It was a sign that she was feeling better. The cigarette had burned halfway down, the point where she would normally flick it away, but tonight she decided to finish it.

Across the road a car drew up and parked alongside two grey stone pillars that marked the entrance of the drive leading up to the yacht club.

She watched from the shadows as a female got out and made her way round to the back of the car. The woman was small in stature, her hair cut in a neat bob. From where Keira was standing it was difficult to make out her features, but something in her manner, the way she stood – erect and stiff – was familiar.

And the car, a black Land Rover Evoque, reminded her of the one that had followed her down to Scaur.

After fumbling around in the back, the woman slammed the tailgate closed then stood staring down the single-track road, towards the safe house. The narrow stretch of road ran parallel with the yacht club's drive and was bordered on the near side by a tall hedge, and on its far side by the banks of Gare Loch.

Keira wet the tips of her fingers and pinched the end of the cigarette to kill its orange glow.

She eased back further into the shadows and watched as the woman glanced in her direction before moving to stand beside a clump of overgrown berberis and wild spindly trees that separated the thin stretch of road from the shore. The woman then vanished momentarily, her silhouette swallowed up by the melange of leaves and branches, only to reappear moments later as a dark shadow passing behind the overgrown vegetation. Keira's eyes strained against the darkness, but there was no mistaking where the figure was headed.

Keira made her way across the deserted main road and crouched down behind the Land Rover. From there she had a clear view along the entire length of the lane.

From seventy metres or so, to the left, there came a rustling in the bushes and the woman's silhouetted figure emerged, on the blind side of the house, where she stood for the next few minutes staring up at the darkened windows, turning occasionally to look back along the lane, but keeping her focus mostly on the house.

Keira winced as a sharp, cramping spasm from one of her wounds suddenly caught hold of her. Although she'd reduced her medication significantly, she still relied on it to keep her blood pressure stable and to take away the edge. It had been over seven hours since she'd last taken anything to dull the pain.

A car roared past, its headlamps momentarily blinding as they illuminated the lane like twin searchlights, before it disappeared round the sharp bend on the main road.

When she looked again, the woman was gone.

Keira quickly covered the ground between the back of the car and the bushes and was about to follow the woman's route through the narrow gap leading to the shore when she noticed a light come on in the upstairs window of the house . . . her bedroom.

It was unlikely that her mother had forgotten to set it before she'd left, so whoever this person was had somehow entered without triggering the alarm.

Keeping a watchful eye on the window, Keira made her way along the road and was soon standing outside the front gate.

A shadow passed in front of the bedroom window, then the light went out again.

Instinctively she ducked to the ground and shuffled her way to the end of the garden wall nearest to the shore.

A moment later the front door creaked open and the figure emerged into the darkness.

Keira scrambled over the rough, compacted soil and around the corner of the garden wall, where she crawled into a small gap between the barbed, arching branches of an overgrown berberis and the craggy drystone wall.

Footsteps sounded along the garden path followed by the rusty squeak of the gate as it swung open and closed.

She could hear the woman's shoes scuff along the surface of the road and come to a stop less than a metre from where she was hiding.

Close enough to reach out and touch.

Keira pressed herself hard against the drystone wall, careful not to make a sound. The woman was wearing a pair of flat shoes with bare legs and a skirt that fell just below the knee. Both arms hung casually by her side. In her left hand she carried something that was partially obscured by the folds in the fabric of her skirt: a metallic object that occasionally caught the light. In her right she held a phone.

As she shifted her weight the fabric fell away to reveal the outline of a handgun. She was muttering to herself in a foreign language.

Keira started to feel light-headed; suddenly she couldn't breathe. Her hands fumbled around on the dry earth by her legs, blindly searching for a rock or stone – something to use as a weapon. But there was nothing except the needle-like thorns of the berberis. One punctured her skin and made her draw her hand back sharply.

The woman punched a number into her phone then held it to her ear. 'Something is wrong,' she said, speaking quietly. 'She's not here ... the bodyguard, the mother, no one. The house is empty. I will wait only one half-hour, then I go.'

Keira heard the leaves in the trees rustling overhead and the bushes around her jostling against each other as a small gust of wind blew in across the loch. The push of air carried with it the hint of an odour: a whiff of scent.

She recognized it straight away.

A sudden surge of adrenaline made her feel sick to the stomach.

The stale body odour and clawing, musky aroma was unmistakable.

The Watcher was able to pass himself off as a woman.

Not aftershave, but perfume on a male's skin.

That was why it smelled so wrong. That's why he was able to 'disappear' so easily.

Engjell E Zeze turned too late to avoid the first blow.

Keira's fist caught him hard on the side of the face and tipped him momentarily off balance. A second blow glanced off the back of his head, with little effect, followed by a third, and a fourth. Engjell stepped back and lifted his arm to block another fist swinging toward him, then raised the gun and squeezed the trigger.

Keira instinctively kicked out, her foot catching E Zeze on the wrist just in time to send the bullet whistling off into the night sky. She grabbed for the gun, but E Zeze was too quick for her and snatched it out of reach.

As E Zeze spun back to face her, Keira lunged forward, cracking her forehead against the side of E Zeze's face with a sickening thud. Engjell E Zeze staggered backwards and dropped to his knees, momentarily dazed, but still with a firm grip on the handle of the gun. He cursed under his breath as he drew a hand across his mouth and felt warm blood stream from his nose. Quickly regaining his feet, Engjell stood staring up and down the empty stretch of road, but his attacker was nowhere to be seen.

*

Keira slammed the front door behind her, raced through the hall and into the lounge. The box of throwing knives was sitting on the table where she had left them.

Behind her she heard a loud splintering crack, followed by

another, then the sound of E Zeze kicking furiously at the front door.

She quickly flicked the catch then flipped the lid of the box open.

Keira stared around her in disbelief before looking back at the box. It was empty.

There was a loud crashing sound as the door gave way and E Zeze was inside.

The window casing to her left exploded, sending fragments of wood and glass flying through the air.

Keira ducked through into the kitchen, heading for the back door.

Another bullet smacked into the wall above her and another into the door just as she reached for the handle.

*

Engjell quickly followed Keira out into the back garden, but when he got there, the lawyer had vanished. He could feel a cry of frustration clawing at his throat, but stayed silent; his eyes filled with rage as he scanned the darkness for any signs of movement.

Then, in the gloom on the other side of the wall, beyond the bushes, he spotted a figure running along the shore, heading toward Rhu marina.

Engjell adopted the Weaver stance, drew the .38 to eye-level and started shooting.

*

The pebble-covered shore made progress difficult. Bullet after bullet fizzed past her. One hit the ground to her right and ricocheted with a fading whine out into the loch. Another bullet whizzed overhead, followed by a third that threw a small puff of smoke into the air where it struck the stones close to her feet.

Keira's lungs were on fire. She had already covered four hundred metres or so and wanted to get off the beach on to the road, but each time she tried E Zeze would open fire, forcing her closer to the water's edge.

Two hundred metres or so in front of her the large boulders of the marina's breakwater loomed out of the darkness.

Breathing heavily, she soon reached the foot of the boulders and started to scramble over their awkward, slippery surfaces. When she was halfway up she glanced over her shoulder, but there was no sign of E Zeze now.

The gap between the summit of the boulders and the edge of the marina's boatyard was less than a metre. But just as she stepped across her foot slipped from under her and she toppled over, landing heavily on her elbow and grazing her leg in a large strip from her knee down to her ankle. There was something wet running down the back of her neck. When she touched her fingers to the back of her skull she felt a warm, sticky patch of blood in a tangle of hair where her head had struck the boulder.

Keira crawled up the rough-stone slope into the boatyard and clambered to her feet.

Over to the west, on the far shore, the lights of Rosneath twinkled through the darkness, their reflection dancing and shimmering on the black surface of the loch. The village of Rhu stretched out along the eastern shore, its street lamps casting a dim, orange hue over the bay in front of her.

There was a movement in the shadows near a cluster of trees close to the marina after which a bright orange muzzle flash burst from the gloom and was followed almost immediately by a dull popping sound. The hull of a boat sitting on stilts behind her made a loud crack as the bullet slammed into it, ripping a hole the size of a tennis ball into the fibreglass. Keira turned quickly and headed for the metal bridge leading down on to the pontoons.

E Zeze was much closer than she'd thought.

Keira crossed the bridge and stopped. The shadow cast by the security lamps made it difficult to see the rocks below the pontoon. She paused for a moment, peering down into the darkness, then lowered herself over the edge.

*

Engjell scrambled across the large, slippery boulders and stood in the spot beside the boat that Keira had occupied just moments earlier. He looked down at the pontoons reaching out into the dark water, but there was no sign of Keira.

Engjell cocked his head to the side.

Something had triggered the security lights, so he was in no doubt that this was where the lawyer was hiding. He cautiously made his way along the edge of the boatyard, across the metal bridge and down on to the pontoons. Sail ropes snapped against their masts and buoys creaked as the boats swayed gently against their moorings. Engjell stood for a moment and listened. He thought he detected a faint splashing sound on the far side of one of the boats. Someone swimming.

Engjell moved cautiously along the nearest of the four pontoons, checking the water for any signs of the lawyer.

Suddenly a sensor at the furthermost end of the platform

triggered, illuminating a figure that shone out of the darkness like an apparition.

It was Keira Lynch, staring back at Engjell in silence, as though she had already accepted her fate. Standing there defiantly, with her hair clinging to the side of her face, dripping blood and seawater on to the dry boards of the jetty.

Engjell smiled. He never spoke to his victims, preferring their own screams or pleading cries to be the last thing they heard before they died rather than his voice. But for the lawyer he was going to make an exception: she had been a little more challenging than his usual prey: she deserved something better.

Engjell couldn't resist it.

'I've been watching you,' he said in a thin weedy voice.

He then slowly dropped his head forward and raised his arms out to the side in the shape of a cross.

The Watcher was enjoying the moment: the delicious feeling of power over another human being whose life he was about to extinguish. Engjell raised his eyes to savour the young woman's moment of torment, but the lawyer was holding something out in front of her, clasping it with both hands.

Engjell cocked his head to the side as the smile slowly disappeared from his face.

Rebecca Rey's police standard-issue Glock semi-automatic that Keira was holding made a loud cracking sound that echoed around the bay.

Engjell E Zeze felt the impact of the bullet as it slammed into his chest and sent him sprawling backwards on to the wooden decking.

When he next opened his eyes he saw the lawyer standing

over him, her finger through the trigger guard preparing to deliver the kill-shot.

He stared up at her in disbelief: his eyes full of fear.

But the shot never came.

Forty

The narrow La Galerie lounge in the George V hotel was buzzing with the low hum of early evening drinkers. Busy waiters strolled up and down the plush Savonnerie carpet delivering trays of cocktails and fine wines to the refined clientele of wealthy Parisians and overseas visitors enjoying the mood set by a musician playing lounge-jazz on the grand piano in the corner. Large vases filled with oversized blooms in contrasting lime-green and purple complemented the elaborate décor and added a more contemporary touch. Five crystal chandeliers hanging in a neat row overhead gave off a warm seductive glow that made spending money a painless experience.

The spray-tanned blonde sitting at a table for four near the piano laughed out loud at a joke that wasn't so funny. It was more about letting the Serbian guy who'd made the crack think she was having a great time. The laugh was the least false thing about her. Even the Manolo Blahnik kitten-heel pumps she was wearing were fakes. She looked a million dollars, but only cost a few thousand to construct. The Serb was paying nine hundred an hour and he'd booked her for an overnight, so right now he was the funniest guy on the planet.

'You got any friends want to party too?' he asked her in broken French, sitting there with his legs splayed open and his left arm draped casually over her shoulder.

'Sure, I got a friend,' replied Claudette, raising her eyebrow as far as her Botoxed forehead would allow. She gave him a look that made him shift his groin forward to stay comfortable and said, 'She loves to party,' like she was delivering a line in a cheap porno movie.

The Serb was in good shape – not bad looking in a rough sort of way, but his dress sense didn't fit with the five-star surroundings. The suit was off the peg rather than tailored and his black shirt was tucked into his trousers, which in her book was a no-no. Claudette's first thought when she'd noticed the loafers with no socks was, *Small time made good*. But what did she care: they were halfway through their first bottle of €14,000 wine and he had his hand in the air looking to order another. He could be as small as he liked as long as he remembered his PIN. The next question confirmed what she already knew: this guy had as much class as a double-shot can of ready-mixed pina colada.

'How much for her to swing by?'

'You want to know what she looks like or just how much she cost?' Claudette framed the question with a big smile so as not to piss him off.

'I'm more interested in what she does.'

Claudette took a sip of red wine and tipped her head over to the side to whisper in his ear. 'She's very pretty blonde, with long skinny legs and beautiful tits, who does whatever you want, but she likes to take control. If you think you can handle it, I will give Sophie a call?'

A waiter arrived at the table.

'Monsieur, you have a visitor in reception. Would you like me to bring her through?'

'No. I'd like another bottle of wine.'

'Oui, Monsieur. The 1995 Domaine de la Romanée-Conti,

Grand Cru?'

'Is that the one we just had?'

'Oui, Monsieur.'

'Yeah, that one, and will you tell those two guys to show the visitor up to my room? I'll be there in a minute.'

'Certainly,' said the waiter as he set off.

Claudette looked to the far end of the room where the Serbian had been pointing and saw two men dressed in dark suits sitting at the table nearest to the main lobby. They seemed more interested in who was entering and leaving La Galerie than in having any sort of conversation with one another.

'Friends of yours?'

'Bodyguards.'

Claudette made a face. 'You have a body needs guarding?'

She could tell from his big dumb grin that he liked that one.

'You tell me,' he replied, overplaying it.

'Why don't I get my friend round?' said Claudette, nuzzling into him. 'We can let you know.'

Abazi slid his hand across her thigh and down between her legs. 'I have to go take care of some business, won't take long. Call your friend, tell her to come by, then I take care of you both.'

*

'Pardonnez moi,' said the waiter as he approached the table where Besnik and Andrej were sitting, 'Monsieur has a guest in the lobby.' He indicated Fisnik Abazi with a slight gesture of his hand. 'He has asked if you could take the visitor to his room. He will join you shortly.'

Besnik was already on his feet. 'Andrej, go sit with the hooker,

335

keep her company until Mister Abazi gets back.'

Besnik left the table and headed out of La Galerie into the large marble-floored reception area. A woman was standing next to a statue of Marie Antoinette by the arched art-deco doors at the entrance.

The woman was of medium build, weighed less than a hundred and fifty pounds and had dark brown hair down to her shoulders. Besnik recognized her face, but couldn't remember where from.

'You are here for meeting?'

She nodded.

'Who with?'

'Mister Abazi.'

'Follow me.'

*

'You look different with your hair like that. It suits you.'

'Thanks.'

'You travelling in disguise?'

'Strathclyde police have put in a request to Interpol to have you put on the Red Notice list.'

'Is that good?'

'It's the closest thing they have to an international arrest warrant. Technically I'm breaking the law by not disclosing your whereabouts to them. It wouldn't be good for me to be seen with you.'

'You're my lawyer.'

'Doesn't make any difference.'

'Officially too; I notice you cashed my cheque.'

'I set up a trust fund for someone. It all went into that.'

Abazi looked surprised. 'All of it?'

'Yes.'

'Anyone I know?'

'No. A small boy whose mother and grandparents were murdered.'

'You're all heart.'

'I've changed my name too. It's Niamh McGuire now.'

'What happened to Keira Lynch?'

'She'd had enough. Niamh's in charge now. Any future cheques should be made out to her.'

'Who's Niamh McGuire?'

'Me . . . It's my real name.'

'Whatever you say.' Abazi flicked her a look, but wasn't interested enough to pursue the topic.

He handed her a sheaf of papers, 'Here.'

The headed notepaper read, *Médecin Généraliste*, with the name and address of a private clinic written below.

'What's this?'

'Copies of medical reports for safe keeping.'

'Why are you giving them to me?'

'It says there in black and white that I have longstanding medical issues, kidney and heart problems, that kinda shit; pneumonia, even.'

'You look fine to me.'

'Got the idea from Jacques Chirac, but he's not the only one. President Marcos, General Pinochet, Chris Kuruneri the finance minister for Zimbabwe, that's just a few: there's loads of them. They all got something in common – even a guy called Ladislaw Gura as far back as 1945, a member of the SS at Belsen – all of them, "too ill to stand trial". Goes without saying – you get busted, you're gonna be feeling fucking sick. Don't misunderstand me, I'm not intending to get caught, but if I am, then we've got this in our back pocket to let them know just how ill I feel. A bit of forward planning.'

'What d'you want me to do with them?'

'Keep them somewhere safe.' Abazi paused and gave her a tight little smirk before changing the subject. 'How d'you like my room?'

Abazi had taken the presidential suite for three nights. It had an office, a gymnasium and a lounge-dining area with its own separate kitchen. The lounge was floored in polished parquet and had thick panelled walls painted off-white. The room was filled with antiques and grand pieces of Louis Quatorze furniture upholstered in rich blue velvets and damasks, with contrasting details picked out in gold.

'A little too busy for my tastes.'

'I heard someone broke into Sellar's house and attacked him.'

'So I believe. I don't think they got away with anything. Sellar managed to fight them off.'

Abazi laughed. 'Is that the official story?'

'That's what he's telling everyone.'

'He really is an idiot. He screamed like a stuck pig for them not to hurt him, cried the whole time. They got exactly what they wanted.' Abazi pulled a small sample bottle from his pocket and threw it to her. 'For you.'

'What's this?'

'His blood.'

She placed the dark brown liquid gingerly on the coffee table in front of her.

'What do I want with Sellar's blood?'

'It has a story to whisper to you. You're holding his life in your hands now. Trust me: one day soon I'll text you the code. Then it will all fall into place. But like I told you; I don't give you everything at once. I'm still holding a few things back so you'll stay on-board.'

'Is that why you wanted to see me, to give me a bottle of blood?'

'Not only that.' He walked over and lifted a USB stick from the dining table. 'I have in here all the documents you'll need to fight the CIA. Flight plans, delivery dates, names and contacts throughout the supply chain working for the Americans. All the drug shipments they were involved in. Everything in here will back up your case.'

'Why not just courier it to me?'

'You think I'm going to trust all this shit to the post? This tiny little stick is an atom bomb. I don't want it falling into the wrong hands.'

Abazi brought the USB stick over and placed it in her hand. 'Did you hear what happened to the two CIA agents?'

'Not the full story: only rumours. The police are staying very tight lipped.'

'They walked bang into the centre of a party I'd laid on for the Holy Man and got themselves shot. But not before they'd taken out eleven of my soldiers.'

Abazi was watching for her reaction.

She gave a slight shrug and said, 'Shame!'

'Yeah. They must have been a pretty good shot to kill that many of my men all by themselves.'

She nodded. 'Must have.'

'I hear E Zeze is recovering well.'

'He's fine.'

'You should have killed him.'

'He's more useful alive. He's not being very communicative, but it's early days.'

'He's not going to say a goddamn thing. You should have put a bullet in his head when you had the chance. What happened, did you get scared?'

'No.'

'Then what?'

'Like I said, he's more useful alive.'

'You got something else you need to say?'

'What happened to Rebecca Rey?'

'Who she?'

'The police officer. No one has had any contact with her.'

'Who knows?'

'I think *you* do.'

'She hasn't come home?'

'No. You gave me your word you'd let her go.'

'I gave you my word I wouldn't kill her.'

'So what happened?'

'I kept my word.'

'D'you know where she is, then?'

'Like I said. *I* didn't kill her.'

'But, someone did?'

'Who knows?'

Abazi was heading towards the door. 'Well, lovely as it is to see you with your beautiful brown hair, Miss Lynch, I got some other business I need to take care of.'

'It's McGuire.'

340

'Huh?'

'It's McGuire now, not Lynch.'

'Yeah, sure . . . McGuire.'

'D'you mind if I quickly run to the toilet?' she asked, placing the USB stick and blood sample in her bag.

'Sure. That door at the end of the lobby, then first right.'

As she headed away from him Abazi shouted to Besnik, 'Call down to Andrej and tell him to bring the girls up. We're done here.' Besnik Osmani's huge frame appeared at the other end of the hallway. 'Sure thing, Mister Abazi.'

*

Claudette and Sophie were laughing as the lift door opened on the top floor. Andrej stood to one side as the pair of hookers stepped out then he held the door to let the elegant brunette in.

'What floor?' asked Andrej, with an unconvincing charm-school smile.

'Foyer, please.'

Andrej pressed the button marked 'F' and slipped out between the closing doors. He let the girls walk ahead of him so that he could watch their asses swaying from side to side as they sashayed down the corridor. 'When you finish with the boss, you come see me?'

'You couldn't afford my travel expenses, baby,' replied Claudette over her shoulder.

Although he had a key to Abazi's suite, Andrej still knocked before opening the door.

As he moved through into the small lobby he could tell that something felt wrong. Andrej had grown up with guns, served

341

time in the military: the faint, acrid smell of burnt metal was unmistakable. He drew his Glock from the holster concealed under his jacket and gestured with his left hand for the girls to stop.

'Wait here, don't fucking move,' he said, leaving them standing at the front door.

He leant forward slowly and peered round the corner into the hallway. The trail of blood started halfway along the corridor and led towards the bedroom, where Besnik Osmani's body lay motionless in the doorway.

Andrej was aware of a movement behind him and turned quickly, weapon raised, ready to fire.

Claudette froze when she saw the gun.

'Take your friend and go wait back in the bar,' he snapped at her.

Claudette didn't speak. The look on his face told her he wasn't messing around: the party was over. Claudette nodded and quietly did as she was told.

Andrej waited for the front door to click closed behind the girls before cautiously making his way into the lounge.

Fisnik Abazi was slumped to the side of one of the blue velvet sofas. He had been shot twice: once in the head and once in the chest. His hands were clasped round a stab wound in his throat; blood still seeping through his clenched fingers. It trickled down his wrist and dripped on to a glistening patch that was spreading slowly across his black cotton shirt.

Andrej took a few steps further into the lounge.

A noise in the hallway made him turn.

'I told you to go wait in the fucking bar.'

The brunette he'd held the lift for was standing there like a statue, with her arms down by her side, staring at him.

As he raised his gun, she suddenly flicked her hand out in front of her.

Andrej felt an intense, stabbing pain and reeled backwards, clutching at the knife embedded in his throat. As he sank to his knees, gasping for air, his Glock slipped from his grasp and clattered noisily to the floor.

Andrej watched helplessly as the brunette slowly made her way towards him and picked it up. In a last desperate attempt to save his life, he lunged at her and tried to grab the gun from her hand, but his clumsy effort failed and he fell heavily, face down on the floor.

As he drew his hands alongside his chest and tried once again to push himself upright he felt the tip of the gun barrel being pushed into the back of his neck.

Andrej screwed his eyes tight shut.

A handgun this close would be loud when it went off.

*

Niamh walked the wide, tree-lined stretch of the Champs Elysées until she came to the Place de la Concorde. With the illuminated Luxor Obelisk behind her she cut down towards the river heading for the Pont Royal, where she crossed the Seine and continued left along the Quai Voltaire towards Rue des Beaux-Arts.

The hotel, called L'Hôtel, had a restaurant, called Le Restaurant. Niamh booked a table for supper at reception and ordered two whisky sours to be sent up to her room.

Thirty minutes later, with one sour drained and the other almost finished, she stood naked in front of the bathroom mirror running her fingers gently over the raised mounds of skin left by the bullet wounds. The small, crater shaped scars had healed over completely now and were no longer sensitive to the touch.

She turned her hands – palms upward – and stared at the two thin lines, like red pencil marks, on each of her wrists. After a while she lifted her glass and downed the rest of the sour.

The empty glass clinked loudly as she placed it beside the auburn-brown wig on the marble topped bathroom cabinet. The sample bottle of Sellar's blood sat alongside. Using the tip of her metal nail file, she'd scratched a question mark into the white label wrapped around it.

Niamh closed her eyes then brought her wrists together and started rubbing them until the only sensation she was aware of was the warm contact of skin on skin and the slight, almost imperceptible bump as the scars crossed each other's path.

When she was finished, she let her head droop forward and slowly raised her arms out to the side in the shape of a cross.

Forty-one

Niamh McGuire and her mother Orlaith left the Bridge Bar in Newry, County Armagh, and crossed the busy road, turning left on to Upper Water Street. They both wore sober black suits, opaque black tights and black-veiled hats. They walked past a terraced row of shuttered shop fronts: each building in turn painted a pastel shade of blue, pink or yellow. At the Phoenix Bar they turned right into Margaret Street, then left at Margaret Square into Hill Street. Nothing had changed in the twenty years since they had last set foot in their hometown, but everything was different. The streets, the shops, the shoppers all looked exactly the same, but the Troubles were over, and the sense of danger that had been so much a part of life growing up there had disappeared.

Life had more or less returned to normal.

Niamh stopped when she saw the twin, grey-granite spires of St Patrick & St Colman Cathedral half a mile or so along the narrow one-way street. Her childhood had died just a few miles from here in the house where she had killed a man. She knew even then that her life would never be normal again. She had been taken to the cathedral immediately afterwards. It was there that they had washed the blood from her face and stripped and burned the clothes she was wearing in an attempt to destroy any evidence of the crime. She remembered the cold flagstone floor beneath her bare feet, where she had stood shivering under a blanket as Father Anthony handed her a change of clothes that smelled musty and damp. She remembered the murmur of whispered conversations when the doctor arrived and tended to her uncle Danny and her father, Sean. She remembered the hot tears streaming down her face and believing that they would never stop. The ghost of her childhood was waiting behind the doors of St Patrick & St Colman and the time had come to take it by the hand and set it free.

'Are you okay?' asked her mother.

Niamh gave a slight shrug. 'Better after that whiskey, but it feels like there's a flock of seagulls in my stomach planning a jail break.'

'Should have had a double,' said Orlaith, taking her hand.

'I did, but I could have drunk the bottle.'

Niamh looked at her mother's face. The worry lines were etched a little deeper and her skin was pale and tired, but she still looked beautiful. 'Are *you* okay, Ma? This can't be easy for you either.'

'Don't be worrying about me, darling, I'm grand.'

'When I was over seeing Father Anthony the last time, he gave me a diary that Sean had kept when he was in America. Gran told me about it. She didn't want me to tell you, I don't know why. I think she thought it might upset you to know that she'd had it all those years, I'm not sure. At some point, can we sit down and talk about what happened? I want to know who he was. I want to know what you went through. I need to find out who I am. I've never asked before because I always thought of it as your story; it didn't belong to me. But I want it to be our story now, Ma. I don't want there to be any secrets between us.'

Orlaith pulled Niamh towards her in a tight embrace and

whispered quietly in her ear. 'I've never told you, because you never asked. But, you're right: it is time to let go. Let's get today over with, then I'll tell you everything you need to know.'

As they approached the steps leading up to the entrance of the cathedral they saw Father Anthony waiting for them.

'I was getting worried you wouldn't come.' He reached out to greet them both with a warm handshake.

'Sorry if we're a wee bit late, we stopped in the Bridge for a steadier.'

'You look a lot better than you did the last time I saw you. You had us all worried there for a moment.'

'A few gunshot wounds, Father. Nothing serious.'

'I admire your attitude. It's good to see you looking so well. And Orlaith – you look younger than ever. If I didn't know any better I'd say the two of you were sisters.'

'It's the tears I've cried: keeps my skin well moisturized.'

'Aye, I don't doubt it, I don't doubt it! Now we've a difficult day ahead of us, but together we'll get through it.' He led the two women up the steps. 'Before we go in, I should just warn you that word of the service spread around. You know what it's like here. If you burp on the streets of Newry the whole of Armagh turns to beg your pardon. So there are a few more people than you might have expected.'

Niamh gave her mum an anxious glance.

'How many are we talking?'

The priest held open the large mahogany door that led from the entrance lobby into the cathedral and ushered them through.

'It's more or less full.'

*

The mosaic-tiled floor of the central aisle, with its brown and white Celtic banding pattern, stretched out in front of Niamh and Orlaith towards the altar. A sea of nearly one thousand heads filled the light oak pews on either side. Small garlands of white lilies hung from the end of every pew and the area in front of the altar had two large arrangements in tall fluted vases.

The two women bowed their heads and let Father Anthony lead them down the central aisle. As they passed each row in turn, the congregation rose to their feet like a gentle wave rolling silently to shore. Someone near the back started to clap, followed by another, then another, growing louder and more intense with each person that joined in. By the time Orlaith and Niamh had reached their seats on the front row every person in the cathedral was standing and clapping in a spontaneous show of support.

Father Anthony made his way to the altar, where he waited quietly for the applause to die down.

It rumbled on for nearly five minutes before it started to fade, then the priest raised his hands for silence and gestured for everyone to be seated.

'We are gathered here today, not only to commemorate and celebrate the life of Kathleen McGuire, but to remember all the victims of the conflict that has blighted our country for so many years. Every single person in here has suffered a loss and I think it says something, not only about how far we have come, but about what sort of person Kathleen McGuire was, that as I look out at the congregation, I see members of both sides of our community – both faiths, whether they be Catholic or Protestant –

standing side by side, united by their own personal grief, united by a collective sense of loss and drawn together to give thanks for this remarkable woman's life. Some of you already know that Kathleen herself lost both her sons to the Troubles. She also lost her husband early on and struggled to bring those boys up as a single parent. Twenty years ago she had to flee, along with her daughter-in-law and her granddaughter, and start a new life elsewhere. But these trials and tribulations are not what set her apart from everyone else. When she lived here, Kathleen McGuire ran an open-house policy. I see many faces I recognize who have benefited from her kindness and compassion. She was always on hand to help. If she had money she would lend it, if she had food you would not go hungry, when she ran out of time, it was as if she could wind the clock back and make more. She carried the stresses and strains of these troubles with dignity and pride. A humble woman, who took nothing for herself and gave everything of herself: and *that* is what made her remarkable. I was lucky enough to know her, not only as a parishioner, but as a friend. Now, many of you have asked to give eulogies today so, for the moment, I will say only this: I spoke to Kathleen just before she died and also to her granddaughter Niamh – of whom she was very proud. Niamh told me that her grandmother's final wish was to be cremated and her ashes scattered over the graves of her sons Sean and Danny. Kathleen herself told me that she would like a piper to play at her funeral, although, as she put it, "Not one of those fecking eejits in a tartan skirt. It's the uillean, or nothing."'

There was a peal of laughter from the crowd of mourners.

'Kathleen also asked that I should choose a piece of music and I can think of no better piece than "Róisín Dubh": the

Dark Rose. "The Erne shall rise in rude torrents, hills shall be rent, The sea shall roll in red waves, and blood be poured out, Every mountain glen in Ireland, and the bogs shall quake Some day ere shall perish my Little Dark Rose!'"

A piper emerged from a door to the left of the altar and slow marched his way to stand facing the congregation at the head of the aisle. The characteristic cry and drone of the Irish pipes reverberated round the cathedral as he played the lament.

Father Anthony looked down at the two women sitting in the front row and felt a burning at the back of his eyes.

*

Niamh stared straight ahead with her hands clasped between her legs, the scars on her wrists pressed firmly together. Orlaith stretched her arm around her shoulder with a gentle squeeze and watched as the tears streamed down her daughter's pale cheeks.

Forty-two

The man sitting outside Café Piazza, opposite the entrance to the cathedral, finished his coffee, peeled a twenty from a bundle of notes and slipped it under the saucer. He cleaned his thick-rimmed reading glasses with a napkin and carefully placed them back in their case. He tugged thoughtfully at his beard as he watched the two women and the priest disappear behind the cathedral's large oak doors. Pulling his Birmingham Barons baseball-cap down to hide his face, he left the table and walked across the road. The black and gold wrought-iron gates to the left of the cathedral's front entrance were open, allowing access down the side of the main hall.

He made his way past two tall granite gateposts until he came to one of the smaller oak side doors, where he stood and listened.

When the pipes started playing 'Róisín Dubh' he crossed himself, then turned and slowly headed back out on to Hill Street.

The sky had just clouded over and the first smattering of rain started peppering the pavement in small, dark grey dots.

The man smiled to himself and raised his hand to hail a cab.

'Where ye headed mister?'

'Airport please: Belfast International.'

'Ye off home?'

'This *is* home,' replied the man.

Acknowledgements

I would like to thank the following people for their help and influence – whether directly or indirectly – in the writing of *Blood Whispers*.

My brother-in-law John McGovern for his patience and for introducing me to Gerry Sweeney on what turned out to be a very informative afternoon (albeit a brief one). Both John and Gerry are busy lawyers working at the coalface of crime in Scotland. As I sat in Gerry's office and listened to them chatting with one another, I realised two things: first, that their depth of knowledge and expertise on matters legal was quite overwhelming, and second, that mine wasn't. Any legal references contained in this book may have been inspired by their conversation, but the accuracy and application of the references is entirely the fault of the author.

A Slovakian friend of mine told me once that 'history, literature, philosophy and the Arts illuminate the human condition, but it is teachers who are the torchbearers'. With this in mind I would like to thank June Mitchel and Isobel McNaughton who, at the time, were enduring the trials of teaching English at Victoria Drive Secondary School in the suburbs of Glasgow. Between them they helped foster an appreciation of the arts in myself and some of my fellow classmates, treated us like adults and steered us through the madness that is adolescence. Without their influence I would not have experienced many of the highlights in my life and for that I will be eternally grateful. This is just to reassure them both that some of us were listening.

Thanks also to Hannah Griffiths and my editor Katherine Armstrong (who can magically transform incomprehensible ramblings into readable prose) at Faber & Faber, to my agent Robert Caskie at Peters Fraser & Dunlop and to the great god Google for giving me access to the world from a hut at the bottom of my garden.

Thank you Noam Chomsky, Richard Dawkins, Hermann Hesse, Mick Rock and Hector Berlioz (you may have guessed that these names fall into the indirect category).

And finally one huge singular thank to my wife Shauna for her forbearance and for making a convincing show of looking interested whenever I attempted to unravel the complexities of a particular plot point by talking it through with her. The expression on her face (for my benefit) was of one intrigued, but I suspect she was secretly thinking 'chocolate'.

Seventy Times Seven

**What happens when the man you have to kill is the only
man who has the answers you seek?**

A hit man trying to find answers to his brother's murder.
An informer trying to flee his past.
A family under threat.

Rural Northern Ireland and small-town Alabama: Two places
connected by a deadly act – an act that draws two men, and
those closest to them, into a spiral of lies, violence and murder
as they try to lay their ghosts to rest.

But can you ever be forgiven for the sins of your past?

'One of the finest debuts of the decade.' Ken Bruen

'A brutal, extremely addictive and vivid portrayal of the sins of men finally catching up with
them. This is a very strong debut tinged with sadness that will stay with you long after the final
page.' Crimesquad.com

'An impressive debut . . . Fast and bloody, though with some moving touches, and Sinclair
scores top marks for the exceptionally vivid dialogue.' *The Times*